In the Defense of Liberty

In the Defense of Liberty

Keith Maillard

Freehand Books acknowledges the financial support for its publishing program provided by the Canada Council for the Arts and the Alberta Media Fund, and by the Government of Canada through the Canada Book Fund.

 Canada Council Conseil des Arts
for the Arts du Canada
 Alberta Government Canada

Freehand Books
515 – 815 1st Street SW   Calgary, Alberta   T2P 1N3
www.freehand-books.com

Book orders: UTP Distribution
5201 Dufferin Street   Toronto, Ontario   M3H 5T8
Telephone: 1-800-565-9523   Fax: 1-800-221-9985
utpbooks@utpress.utoronto.ca   utpdistribution.com

Library and Archives Canada Cataloguing in Publication
Title: In the defense of liberty / Keith Maillard.
Names: Maillard, Keith, 1942– author.
Identifiers: Canadiana (print) 20230152643 | Canadiana (ebook) 20230152651 | ISBN 9781990601415 (softcover) | ISBN 9781990601439 (PDF) | ISBN 9781990601422 (EPUB)
Classification: LCC PS8576.A49 I5 2023 | DDC C813/.54—dc23

Edited by Lee Shedden
Cover photo © mahziar ebi/Shutterstock.com
Author photo by Mary Maillard
Printed on FSC® recycled paper and bound in Canada by Imprimerie Gauvin

For Alice

"A lot of things have happened to me ;
—and in me ; a hell of a lot of things.
and I am not sorry for any of them —"

I would remind you that extremism in the defense of liberty is no vice.

BARRY GOLDWATER, 1964, in his acceptance speech as the Republican candidate for the presidency of the United States.

June

1.

"When I first seen you, I thought you was a girl."

Mason had been hearing shit like that for a while and he knew what he should say but he couldn't get the words to come out. He wasn't thinking right. The pain in his side was real ugly. He was sitting in the cab of a truck rolling north and Mom and Irene were probably still waiting for him to come back. The old man would have passed out by now. Surely to God he would have passed out.

The trucker wasn't going to let it go. "Closed all the barber shops, have they?"

"Yeah. Every one. They're on strike."

The trucker deserved better than that. When people were nice enough to pick you up, they deserved a little pleasant conversation. Mason had a shit-kicker hillbilly accent he put on for truckers and he used it. "You seen the Beatles on Ed Sullivan?"

The trucker was chuckling. "The Beatles, huh? What's with them? The girls like you with all that hair?"

"Yeah, some girls."

Beautiful goddamned Ohio Country, all that green and golden light. Mason could see sun motes floating in it but they seemed a million miles away. Why the middle of afternoon? Used to be the old man would wait for nightfall. Used to be you could count on that.

"Bet you got a lot of girlfriends, huh? Good looking boy like you?"

Mason had heard that line so many times he knew it was a pass. "Yeah, I got a few." That was his standard answer.

He hadn't paid much attention to the trucker before but now he looked at him. Late thirties maybe. Sweaty from the sun. Good head of hair on him, but thinning in the front. Bit of a beer gut. You don't stay in shape driving truck. Why were they never cute, the guys who made passes at him?

The trucker was staring straight ahead through the windshield, telling him some long pointless story. Mason was losing a lot of it to the rumble of the road but he didn't have to say much except "oh, yeah" and "right." The trucker was saying that he liked picking up hitch-hikers because you got to meet all kinds. He was open-minded. There was this boy he picked up once. About your age. A real card. They stopped at a motel and had a shower together. It was lots of fun. Yeah. He was a real little monkey. "Right," Mason said and laughed.

A shower, huh? Like that old joke, I dropped the soap in the shower. Mason considered it for a minute. He wouldn't have to see the trucker, he'd be behind him. But no. Mason knew exactly what the trucker meant by "a real little monkey" and Mason could not possibly do that. "Yeah," he said, "it takes all kinds."

The trucker dropped Mason at the Junction. The highway ran between Cincinnati and Detroit so there was always somebody on it, but the fifteen mile stretch to Merida was another matter. Mason could have stood there all night but he was lucky and got picked up by a mom and pop and their two kids coming back from a church picnic. Nobody said anything about his hair, but they all stared at it, especially the kids. Being good Christians, they drove him all the way to his door. There was no sign of Eilum's beat-to-shit Buick so Mason had the place to himself.

He let himself into their basement apartment, but it was all too fucking depressing, so he came back outside, walked around the house and up to the front porch, threw himself down on the glider and fired up a smoke. He wasn't supposed to be on the porch, it went with the house upstairs, but the girl grads were gone for the summer. The best places never made it to the university housing list, just got passed from friend to friend, so if you wanted to keep your place from one school year to the next, you had to pay for the summer even if you weren't going to be there. Mason had planned on being there, working on his honors thesis. He'd only gone home for his birthday. For a while they'd fooled him into thinking that everything was going to be all right. He'd had enough presence of mind to grab his birthday card before he took off. There was a crisp new hundred-dollar bill in it, the most money he'd ever seen at one time in his life.

Down in the basement the phone was ringing. It rang twenty-six times. Most likely that was Mom calling to say that Dad was sorry. The son of a bitch was always sorry. Mason supposed he should take some of the responsibility for the fuck-up, the old man had been well into the sauce so Mason should have known to keep his mouth shut. He couldn't remember much of what the old man had been saying or what he'd been saying back to him but it had started out general, Goldwater vs. LBJ and shit like that, and then they'd moved on to the Commies and Vietnam, and somehow those topics had revealed all the terrible things wrong with Mason until finally the old man had got around to his hair. Mason didn't remember what unforgivable thing he'd said after that but his father had slapped him for it, and pushed him hard, and he'd stumbled over something and ended up sprawled out on the floor, and then his father had kicked him in the side, and fuck, he was almost out of smokes.

In Eilum's room, in one of his jackets, Mason found a crumpled pack of Luckies with four left in it so that made things a little bit better. Then he saw on Eilum's dresser a fifth of George Dickel not even opened yet and that made things a lot better. Mason unscrewed the cap, took a good slug, and felt it burn all the way down. He hadn't had a thing to eat since Mom's big breakfast and that had been a million years ago. He stood there a minute letting the whiskey settle in on him. He went back outside and took the fifth with him.

It was night now on the girls' porch, or damned near to it, that mysterious gray-blue summer twilight that he would have loved if he'd been in his right mind. He drank to it, and to himself. It was his birthday. On this day, the fourteenth day of June in the Year of Our Lord Nineteen-hundred-and-sixty-four, Edward Mason Macquarie had turned twenty-one years of age. That meant that in his society he was considered a man. Well, fuck that shit.

He sat there drinking till he heard the chimes in the McKinley Tower bong ten times. Then, buzzed good on the George Dickel, he walked carefully down the front steps and around the house and into his apartment and continued on into his little ratty bedroom. That bottle of sleeping pills from the university doctor was in the top drawer of his dresser. When insomnia got him, he couldn't sleep at all, not a wink, nothing, nada, and if he had an eight-thirty the next day, that was fairly horrible, but the pills left him with a dark thick sludgy hangover, worse than if he'd got pissed on port, so he'd only taken them twice. There'd been fifteen in the bottle, so with two down, that left thirteen. Two at a time, that was six gulps of whiskey. He was dizzy and burning from it. With a seventh gulp he washed the last pill down.

Later Mason wouldn't be able to remember how long it was before he hit the bathroom but it couldn't have been too long because after the first heave, he could see whole undigested sleeping pills in his vomit. If he'd been able to think, he might have counted them but what he did automatic was flush the toilet. There were a few more pills in the second heave, and in the third, bits of his breakfast that must have been hanging around all day without digesting.

He heard the phone ringing out in the kitchen. It seemed to ring forever. He hoped to God he was done throwing up but he wasn't. Spasm after spasm hit him, his whole body knotted in on itself, contracted around the burning pain in his guts. His vomit stunk of whiskey and that made him sicker. He kept throwing up more bits of food, then some disgusting brown lumps, then a mucousy liquid, then nothing. The fucking phone was ringing again and he had the dry heaves.

Then he must have been unconscious for a while. Unconscious, hell, he'd been out like a brained catfish. Woke up facedown on the bathroom floor. The pain woke him, in his head. Never felt pain like it. Phenomenal. Like somebody banging his brains with a jackhammer. He needed water, tried to force himself to his knees, and discovered that he'd shit himself.

He pulled his boots off, stripped his jeans and underwear off, and shoved his bare ass over the toilet seat. Liquid squirted out of him. It smelled so foul that he contracted, dry heaving again. His shirt was soaked with sweat. It was like his body was trying to get rid of every bit of moisture in it. Through the bathroom door, out in the kitchen, it was as black as pitch. Scrabbling on his knees, he got ahold of the toothbrush glass, filled it with water from the sink, and drank. Within seconds he was heaving again. The water came up streaked with blood.

"It's not that uncommon," the doctor said. "Irritation of the mucous membrane of your stomach lining."

"Scared the hell out of me," Mason said. That was putting it mildly.

"What were you drinking?"

"Some of that fine George Dickel Tennessee sipping whiskey."

"How much?"

"The best part of a fifth, I guess."

"How fast?"

"I tossed her right down."

"Is it possible that you might have learned something from this experience, Mason?"

"Yes, sir, it is definitely possible."

Mason was playing dumbass hillbilly for all it was worth, and the doctor seemed to be buying it. He'd got the old one today, good old Doc What's-his-name, and Mason was glad of that because it was the young one who'd prescribed the sleeping pills, and he didn't want anybody thinking about sleeping pills because if they did, they'd lock him up. He'd tried to kill himself early Sunday night, and this was Tuesday morning, that's how long it had taken him to get here. He'd been able to keep water down for a while but he still hadn't tried to eat anything. He felt like shit.

This was his second failed suicide attempt. He'd had a pretty good shot at the first one but an improbable combination of things had conspired to keep him alive. The only reason a semi would be on campus was to deliver something, and that particular semi had already delivered it, so was running with an empty trailer. The brakes had recently been replaced and were operating at close to a hundred percent. The trucker was a young guy with excellent eyesight and lightning reflexes. Even with all that going for him, Mason had been knocked flat but the worst he'd got out of it had been abrasions on his knees and elbows and a sprained left wrist. That had been the winter of his freshman year and now he couldn't remember exactly what had been going through his mind. When the cops showed up, he'd pretended to be piss-ass drunk because he didn't want them to think it was a suicide attempt.

"Okay, let's look at your side." The doctor poked and prodded him, asked what hurt and what didn't, and concluded that Mason did not have a broken rib, but it might be cracked. "How'd you do that?"

"Fell down."

"You must have fallen on something kind of hard?"

"I guess so."

"Take it easy and it'll heal itself in about a month. I should give you pain killers, but I can't because of your stomach."

"Doctor? Can I ask you something? A couple weeks ago I came in and asked to see a shrink and they put me on the waiting list. I got an appointment in September. I was just thinking it might not be a bad idea if I saw somebody sooner than that."

The doctor looked into Mason's eyes and Mason looked back with what he hoped was a sincere and earnest expression. "You know, son, I think you're absolutely right."

When Mason walked out of Student Services, he had an appointment to see a shrink the next day so at least he'd accomplished something. Although it made him edgy, he didn't know how much he could tell a shrink. It had been a fuck of a long time since he'd had anything to eat and his stomach was reminding him of that dismal fact. The best place to go was the Golden Buckeye. Everybody just called it "the Buckeye" but there really was a big golden one made out of wood hanging over the door, lost most of its gold though, looked like it had been hanging there a hundred years. Mason had enough change in his jeans to buy a pack of Camels from the machine, asked the waitress about soup, and she said, "You

17

can get any kind you want, it's just Campbell's out of a can," so he ordered beef consommé, that's what the doctor had told him to start with, and the first sip was heaven. He fired up a Camel, sipped the consommé, and contemplated the dining room.

The campus sure emptied out in the summer, it was lunch time but only a few people scattered about, and there, sitting by himself, eating what looked like a BLT, was Queer Walter. The suicide attempt had done something weird to Mason's mind, everything was exactly the same but different somehow, sharper. He could have walked into the Buckeye a million times and not noticed the old wood golden buckeye. He could have not noticed Queer Walter.

Merida's one and only hardware store was owned by Walter Pfefferman and if you went in there to buy thumbtacks or some damned thing, there he'd be looking just like he was today on his lunch hour, in clean chinos and a plaid shirt, and he knew everything there was to know about hardware, and if you had some project you were doing, he'd be glad to tell you in detail how to do it. Then, in the evening, Walter would reappear, and he would be fucking immaculate, in a nice suit, his shoes shined, his hair combed, smelling of Old Spice, and he would spend the evening hanging around with Merida U boys, buying them beer if they were old enough to drink, laughing at their dumbass jokes. Mason liked Walter, most people did, everybody said he was harmless. Once when Mason had run through his money before the end of the month, Walter had bought him a burger. Walter was a nice looking fellow in his forties who'd never married and lived with his mother.

So what was Mason doing contemplating Queer Walter in the Buckeye? Well, for one thing, he was glad he wasn't gay because that was a fucking hard row to hoe, but then again, when he looked down deep inside himself, he knew he was just as queer in his own weird way. It took him awhile to come to his next conclusion. If people had roles in life, kind of like getting a role in a play, then Queer

18

Walter definitely had a role and everybody knew what it was, but if Mason had a role, nobody knew what it was, and he sure didn't either. Well, hell, maybe he was just as gay as Walter Pfefferman.

When everything has gone to shit, the only thing to do is clean up, that's what Mason's mom always said, and she meant it for Irene, but Mason was the one who took it to heart. He went to the bank and broke the crisp new hundred into tens so he could spend some of it, ran his foul clothes through the laundromat, bought fresh milk and six cans of soup. Now that his draft card said he was twenty-one he could buy liquor, so he bought a fifth of George Dickel to replace Eilum's. He cleaned out the ice box, swept all the floors, even in Eilum's room, washed the dirty dishes that had been piling up in the sink. He was so blown out and weak that all that effort exhausted him and he had to lay down. The basement apartment had little slit windows high up where you could see people's feet walking by sometimes. When the sun was at the right angle, it came through and lit the place up, and then it wasn't half bad down there. The phone had been ringing off and on but he wasn't ready to talk to his mom yet.

Mason didn't wake up till evening and he thought he might live. He took a shower, put on clean jeans, and ate a whole can of mushroom soup with crackers crumbled up in it. Nothing in the entire history of the world had ever tasted as good as that Campbell's mushroom soup. The phone rang three times and then stopped and then started up again, and that was a code signal from his sister telling him she was calling from a phone booth. "Hey, Reenie. Hi."

"Oh, Eddie, thank God." The minute she'd heard his voice she'd started to cry. "Where the hell have you been? We've been so worried about you."

"Sorry. I didn't feel like talking to anybody. Don't call me Eddie, okay? I just, you know—"

She was yelling at him and crying so hard he couldn't make out much of what she was saying, probably all the things she'd stored up the last couple days when she hadn't been able to reach him. If he pulled the phone back a few inches from his ear, her voice sounded like it'd been squeezed down to something ridiculous, a tiny little squawking voice from a Donald Duck cartoon. He let her run for a while and then started yelling back at her. "Reenie, Reenie, Reenie, hey. Come on. Reenie."

"Eddie. I can't believe you'd do that— Have you been there the whole time? Not answering the phone?"

"Well, not exactly. Yeah, I have been here, but—"

"And you didn't answer the damn phone? That's so mean. How could you do that to us?"

She was as mad as a hornet. She always cried when she was mad. Yeah, he had probably scared the bejesus out of her. Shit, he'd scared the bejesus out of himself. Poor Irene. He'd never once thought about her when he was trying to kill himself. "Reenie, he kicked me."

"You were egging him on. Why on earth didn't you get a haircut?"

"Fuck that shit."

"Don't talk to me like that."

"I'm not talking to you like anything."

"We thought you'd just walk around the block a couple times. He was sorry. Right after, he was sorry. He kept saying, 'When's Eddie gonna come back—?' It was kind of pathetic—"

"Pathetic, my fucking ass. He's always sorry. Jesus, Reenie, he's slapped me around before, you know that, but he never kicked me. That was a first. He knocked me down *and kicked me*."

"He says he didn't mean it. He says you stumbled and fell over something."

"Oh, for Christ's sake."

"If you'd just talk to him—"

"Not a chance."

"At least talk to Mom."

"No, thanks."

"Eddie—"

"Don't call me Eddie. When'd she start drinking with him?"

"She didn't have that much to drink."

"Fuck, Irene, she was pissed out of her gourd."

"Look. Eddie. You can't, you know— You can't just walk out of our lives— If you'd just talk—"

"I'm not gonna walk out of *your* life. Talk? Jesus. And stop calling me Eddie. I've told you and told you and told you. You call me Eddie one more time, I'm going to hang up on you."

He listened to her cry for a while. He never knew what to say to her when she was like this. "You can tell Mom I'll call her when I can. Okay? I just don't want to talk to her right now. You tell her I'll talk to her soon, okay? I'll call her when I can."

"Yeah? Shoot. Yeah. Mason? You'll break her heart."

"For fuck's sake. Her heart was broke years ago, and I didn't break it. Aw, fuck. Listen. Irene. You promised me."

"Now's not the time to get into that."

"Jesus, you sound just like her. You've got to get out of there. Anytime you want, I told you—"

"Stop it."

"Why are you still living there?"

"Stop it, stop it, stop it, stop it, stop it."

"Jesus, it'd be so easy. You type what? A hundred and ten words a minute? And take shorthand. Do double entry bookkeeping. I told you, you'd get a job at the university in two seconds flat. There's all these girl grad students who need roommates—"

"And *I* told *you* I don't want to talk about it."

"Hell. Reenie. There's a whole hell of a lot of things you don't want to talk about."

Mason did what he always did when the whole world was coming down around his ears, jumped on his bike and took off. He loved that bike. It was one of the few things he owned that he felt truly attached to, a girl's bike, an English three-speed, a Norman, night-time blue. When he'd bought it, used, it had needed a new chain, so he'd taken it completely apart, cleaned it, oiled it, replaced the chain, and put it back together again. Before that, he hadn't known a damn thing about bikes, but now he did, and that was how he liked learning things. He was shooting off into the late evening against a darkening sky, not sure where he was going, headed out toward the edge of campus, just wanting to move it, move it.

Summer and only a few classes going, mostly remedial shit, so all his friends had left town, although he didn't have any friends that weren't Eilum's friends first, that crew of crazy engineers that came around because they thought Eilum was a fucking riot, which he was if you didn't scare easy. Anyhow it was great to be moving again, kicking his feather-light little bike into third gear on this slight down stretch and feeling the wind whipping back his hair that everybody wanted him to cut, well, fuck them, and without planning it, he was shooting through the twilight toward Henry Algren's house. Seemed like an odd place to be going because he kind of doubted that the TAs were really friends of his, history grads working on their PhDs. He'd been to a number of their parties because they'd invited him and they seemed to like him okay but he didn't know what they'd think about him turning up out of nowhere.

Mason rang the bell and Henry's wife Lorianne appeared on the other side of the screen door. "Oh, my goodness, Mason Mac-quarie," and her face lit up. Maybe she liked him as much as he liked her. Wouldn't that be nice?

"I was just, you know, out for a ride on my bike, and I seen your lights . . . saw your lights—"

"Come in," she said. "Yeah, come on. Come in. We're just listening to some jazz."

Lorianne had to be four or five years older than he was, she was a wife and a mom, but she always looked young. Her hair was a sandy brown, not quite blond, hung down damn near to her waist, and she brushed it straight back and held it with a band. From the moment he'd first heard her voice he'd known her for a fellow hoopie, could be his cousin, had that pale-eyed backwoods look that sometimes didn't sit well on a girl, but it sat well on her. She painted her short nails baby pink, wore lots of eye makeup but nothing else, not even a touch of lipstick, so her eyes looked huge like some animal's you startled in the woods. She had on white flats tonight and a plain blue dress with a full skirt like a little girl might wear, and Mason liked everything about her. "Let me get you something to drink," she said and called out, "Look who's here."

Mason followed her toward the kitchen, stepping over rag dolls and stuffed animals, signs of Lorianne's little daughter now most likely and thank God in bed, passing the archway to the living room, heard Carl yell, "For Christ's sake, it's The Kid," and Henry chimed in, "Get him a beer."

"Sorry," he said to Lorianne, why was he sorry? "Can't drink tonight. My stomach's kind of messed up."

The last time he'd been here for a party, the big blow-out at the end of the school year, he and Lorianne had wandered outside to get away from the noise and the smoke, had accidentally met under a tree and talked for a good hour, so he knew a lot about her. Because the out-of-state tuition at Merida was slightly higher than the national debt, most of the students were Ohio residents, but a lot of them had started out somewhere else like Mason and Lorianne, both from the great sovereign state of West Virginia. Lorianne was from someplace down in the coalfields where Mason had never been, her favorite aunt was a school teacher so she'd got a lot of encouragement for being smart, and then after the mine shut down, her dad got a good job at the Goodyear plant up in Akron and they moved up there. Lorianne aced the Boards, won herself a full scholarship to Merida, shot through her BA with straight As, had been working on her master's when she met Henry and got married and had Tammy, and she loved her kid but felt real bad about not finishing her degree. Maybe after Henry got his PhD, she'd go back. The way she'd said it, Mason knew she'd never do it.

"Ginger ale?" she was asking him now. "Coke? Wow, Mason. Your hair's getting real long. You letting it grow out for some reason?"

"No. Just, you know, the Beatles kind of thing. Ginger ale's fine, thanks."

"Thought maybe you were in a play or something." She was looking at him so hard he felt peeled. "I like it," she said, "it looks good on you."

Mason carried his glass of ginger ale into the living room and saw that the men were looking at him curious, yeah, what are you doing here, little boy? He hadn't had either of them as TAs since his freshman year, and they'd been okay, not the best and not the worst. Henry Algren was a short kind of sweaty redhead and not the good-looking kind, a dull muddy red, thinning out bad, showing lots of shiny dome. His skin was damn near as red as his hair, blotchy, didn't look a bit healthy, and he had small wet blue eyes. A garden gnome would have looked nicer to Mason than Henry Algren and he could never figure out how Henry could have got himself a wife as pretty as Lorianne. "What are you listening to?" Mason asked him. Henry collected jazz records.

"Miles Davis." Henry handed Mason the record jacket. It was in French. Where the hell did Henry get his records?

"This is all improvised," Henry said. "Fucking incredible, huh?"

Mason knew zip about jazz but the sounds of it in Henry's

living room always haunted him later and he kept wishing he'd ask Henry to write down some titles for him but he always forgot. The jazz tonight was super-haunting, fit right into Mason's bike-riding twilight mood. "Listen to the bass player," Henry said. "Miles is so out there we forget about the bass, but listen to what he's laying down."

"Yeah," Carl said, "what a groove."

They listened for a while. "Frenchman," Henry said. "They just picked him up."

"Jesus, is he ever good," Carl said. "Without him, Miles wouldn't have any place to stand."

Henry and Carl were best friends and you hardly ever saw one without the other. A real Mutt and Jeff team, Henry the short squat one, Carl the tall gangly one, a raw-boned goofy guy with Buddy Holly glasses. Henry was the nice guy and Carl the prick. As a TA, Carl had been so vicious that most of his students had been afraid to say a peep back to him, but not Mason, and they'd duked it out on a number of occasions. The TAs had graded that class, and after trashing Mason for the entire semester, Carl had given him an A.

But what was Mason doing here with his old TAs? There'd always been a party going on when he'd been here before, lots of other undergrads, but this was an intimate little gathering. The big fat tabby cat had gone to sleep on Henry's lap and the guys were working on a quart of Stroh's Bohemian, and then, in case anybody wanted to kick it up a notch, there was a silver tray with some shot glasses on it and a fifth of that good old Evil Williams. Mason's stomach turned over just looking at it. "So, Kid," Carl said, "that's quite a head of hair you've got on you."

Mason didn't know what to say, and Henry said, "He's exploring his cultural heritage."

Fuck, Mason thought. "Yeah," he said, drawing the word out into two syllables and leaning on it so it could mean anything.

"Ye-ah?" Carl said, making fun of Mason's accent. "So? Kid? How's your hammer hanging?"

"Straight down," Mason answered instantly, "just the way it should," and got a laugh out of them. He was lucky with his nickname, "The Kid" wasn't so bad. Carl nicknamed everybody. Henry was "Hopeless" because he'd been working on his PhD longer than any of them and was nowhere near done with it. Lorianne was "Doll Normal" and it had taken Mason a long time to get that joke because in his dialect of English *doll* and *dull* were pronounced exactly the same.

Now Mason heard women's voices out in the kitchen, so there was another woman here besides Lorianne, must have been putting Tammy to bed because he heard her say, "—didn't make it through the second story, what a little sweetheart," and Mason knew that voice but couldn't place it, and then there she was stepping through the archway and Mason felt something like an electrical jolt because it was Jessie Collier. Another TA. He hadn't had her way back as a freshman, he'd had her just last fall and he had a crush on her about the size of a football stadium. "Mason," she said, surprised to see him.

"Jessie," he said back. That's what she'd told her students to call her. She was looking into his eyes too long and he didn't know what to make of that. She'd TAed for Dr. Braithwaite's upper level course on Reconstruction. You don't expect a single university course to rearrange your whole damn mind for you so it's amazing when one does. Mason had started out with the soppy romantic southern sympathies he'd been carrying around since high school but by the end of the semester Jessie had kicked all that crap out of him and he'd ended up just as pissed off about Jim Crow as she was. That seminar with her had totally changed the way Mason thought about history. She was brilliant, knew her subject inside and out, definitely gave a shit, and was the best TA he'd ever had.

Jessie and Lorianne and Mason had withdrawn to the far end of the room because Jessie hated cigarette smoke and Carl and Henry were huddled around the hi-fi, deep into the jazz, getting loaded and chain smoking. Mason could have used a smoke himself but was holding off because he wanted to be with the women. They were talking about Tammy, how cute she was but what a handful, oh my goodness, and Mason was just sitting there. Lorianne seemed to be hitting the sauce pretty good, but Jessie wasn't.

In seminars you've got a lot of time to notice things and Mason had spent a lot of time noticing Jessie Collier. She had her own carrel up on Level Five of the library where the history collection was, even had her name on it, and whenever he was in the stacks and she was in her carrel, of course he noticed her, he never would have dared to go talk to her, but here she was now so close that he was noticing how straight and white her teeth were, maybe braces as a kid and that meant well-off people, and how big and broad her hands were, how she gestured with them, how short she clipped her nails. She must have been noticing him too, the bump on a log. "How have you been, Mason? Congratulations on the Freddy T."

He'd won the Frederick T. Armstrong Scholarship in American History. It was a big fucking deal and she must know all about it because she was one of the people who'd recommended him for it. "I'm okay. Thanks. Yeah, I'm real glad about the Freddy T."

"So what's your honors thesis going to be on?"

He never could identify her accent. It was a kind of a neutral accent, a little rough though, nothing soft or country about it. "Haven't figured that out yet," he said. "No. Well. Not really. Just, you know, some American history." Brilliant, Mason, you hoopie moron, and he had to keep going. "That's what I'm going to do this summer, you know, sit in the library and try to figure it out. Nineteenth century, I guess."

He hadn't given her a whole lot to work with and he could see her searching for her next try but then Lorianne jumped in. "Don't you just love Mason's hair?"

Oh fuck, he thought.

Nobody said anything. Lorianne had just created one of those horrible embarrassing moments that freeze everybody up. Both women were looking at him and Jessie couldn't very well say, "Yeah, it's pretty," or "Yeah, it's cute," and he saw her eyes send him a message but he didn't know what it meant.

Getting out of the hole she'd just dug, Lorianne quick as a wink changed the subject. "Hey," she said to Jessie, "have you heard from Sarah?"

"Oh, yeah. She called when she got there, but I haven't heard from her since. They're probably keeping them pretty busy."

"Jessie's roommate's over at Western," Lorianne told Mason, "getting orientated. She's in the Freedom Summer Project. You know, going to Mississippi to help organize the Negro voters."

"Good for her," Mason said.

"Are you scared for her?" Lorianne was asking Jessie.

"You're goddamned right I am. Scared out of my mind," and then she and Lorianne went off on their own, talking about how danger-ous it was in the South with all the redneck assholes down there, Birmingham and Bull Connor and the KKK and all that other dire stuff, talking about Martin Luther King and the Freedom Riders. Alabama had been bad enough but Mississippi was even worse, the absolute pits, and roommate Sarah was so courageous to go down there, risking her life. They seemed to be intentionally leaving Mason out of the conversation and that was okay. He liked sitting there with his mouth shut, watching Jessie, how animated she was.

Collier, what kind of name was that? Some ordinary English name, yet she had a dark complexion like a Greek or Italian, black hair and the kind of eyes that get called "flashing," never wore a speck of makeup, nothing, ever. Hair cut short in a pixie, shorter than Mason's. Women students at Merida had a strict dress code, so Mason had never seen her in pants before, wearing black capris tonight, and she looked terrific in them. Barefoot.

When she'd been TAing, Jessie had never tried to look like a lady professor, no, she'd dressed in kilts and knee socks like a coed. She was long-legged and Mason loved her in kilts and knee socks, and she was lean but not skinny, and tall, a lot taller than everyone else in the room except for Carl. For someone who expressed such strong opinions in such a strong way, she could've had a big deep voice, but she didn't, hers was a light voice, clear and bright as a girl's.

He sensed somehow that Jessie was just as aware of him as he was aware of her, and when he looked into her eyes, she was already looking at him, and damn his soul, he had to say something. "How's your PhD going? Um, you know, *your* thesis?"

"I'm going to finish the son of a bitch this summer." She sounded like she wanted to kill it.

"Are you?" Lorianne said. "Really? You're kidding. Really." Lorianne was well into the sauce by now, slurring a bit, and she sounded like she was ten years old.

"Really," Jessie said. "Ev said he'd read it in August. Incredible, nobody does a goddamned thing in August, but he said he would."

Ev? Mason couldn't believe that anybody would call Dr. Everett Braithwaite that but Jessie had just done it. "So if there's not much wrong with it," she was saying, "it could go to the committee in September and I could be done before Christmas."

"Sweet Jesus, be praised." Lorianne, laughing, stood right up, wobbling, walked over to the tray with the whiskey on it, poured two good shots, brought them back, and handed one to Jessie. "Honey, you do it. You finish up that son of a bitch."

Jessie stood up. "I will."

The women toasted each other. Lorianne downed her whiskey in three tentative ladylike gulps but Jessie knocked hers back like sinking the eight ball.

"You hear that, Henry? Jess is going to finish her thesis this summer."

"Yeah, yeah, we're all going to finish this summer."

"Ha, ha," Carl said.

"Henry's coming up on his five years," Lorianne whispered to Jessie. "I'm worried sick."

Some polite part of Mason told him that he shouldn't be sitting down while the women were standing up so he stood up too. Now the women were looking at him again, and the men across the room were looking at him, and he was right there on the hook. He said the first thing that came into his mind. "What's your thesis on, Henry?"

That seemed to be the biggest joke anybody had ever heard. The men were laughing and Lorianne was giggling and even Jessie was having a chuckle. "Go on, Hopeless," Carl said, "tell him."

Henry stared at the ceiling with a God-help-me look, cleared his throat. "Who Serves His Country Best: Rutherford B. Hayes and the Compromise of 1876." That got another round of laughs. Then Henry said to Carl, "Okay, your turn, you prick."

"My thesis. Um, yes. 'In Pleasant Conversation: James Monroe and the decline of the Federalist Party, 1815–1820.'"

Now they were killing themselves laughing. Mason couldn't understand why they thought their thesis topics were so funny. "Okay, Sappho," Carl yelled at Jessie, "over to you."

Jessie didn't think her thesis topic was the least bit funny. She said it in a flat voice. "To Call No Man Master: Lucy Stone and the Fight for Women's Rights, 1836–1893."

Mason hadn't stuck around for much longer than that. They'd all done their best to be nice to him but he'd never stopped feeling like the odd man out and he shouldn't have dropped in like that. After a while it got boring watching people get pissed when you're sober as a hoot owl. "Party on Saturday night, come back," Henry had told him. Would he? Maybe.

He felt tired and sick, probably from trying to kill himself and then not eating much of anything since then, drifted along on his bike through the night campus, listening to the wheels click, didn't feel bad about going home to his empty apartment, needed to sleep and knew he would. The thing about his two suicide attempts was that he hadn't planned either one of them. Neither time had he been thinking, well, gee, I think I'll kill myself now, but one thing they both had in common was a kind of mental blur, a shitty unfocused anxious feeling, thoughts coming and going and not adding up to anything, and both times he hadn't known he was going to do it up until he'd done it. That scared him.

2.

"The doctor will see you now." The *doctor?* Holy fucking hell, she must have got into medical school when she was twelve. She was offering her hand. "I'm Dr. Fairfield. Come in, Mason." Yeah, the sign on the door said Dr. Elspeth Fairfield MD.

She had a big desk in her office, didn't sit behind it, settled into one easy chair, expected him to sit in the other one, facing her, and he did. Was that supposed to make things feel friendly and nice? She had a clipboard with some paper on it, was reading it. All stuff about him? How much did she know about him? Fucked up stomach and cracked rib? His whole damn university transcript? She was writing something on it. "What brings you here today, Mason?"

Well, Jesus, tried to kill myself last Sunday, nope, couldn't start there, so what? Whatever he said would end up in his university file. Or maybe not. He didn't know. Coming here was definitely a mistake. He'd been expecting the shrink to be some old bald guy radiating wisdom but Dr. Elspeth Fairfield MD didn't look much older than thirty. It wasn't fair.

"Well," he said, "I don't know. Exactly. Kind of, you know, feeling kind of anxious, I guess. It's kind of, you know, sometimes it's hard to see the point to being alive."

"Oh? And this is a recent development?"

"Sorry, I don't quite get you."

"You used to see the point to being alive?"

"Yeah, I guess I did. Or maybe not. I don't know."

Burgundy suit, straight skirt, not too tight, matching heels, not too high, makeup, not too much, beautifully manicured nails. It was like she'd read some instruction manual on how young professional ladies are supposed to look and she'd done every single thing it said. How the hell was he supposed to talk to her?

"'Kind of anxious,' you said. Does that interfere with your normal activities?"

"Yeah. Well, sort of. I guess. Well, I'm not real sure what my normal activities are. I'm not sure I *have* any normal activities."

Now they were just sitting there in their two chairs looking at each other. "Do you mean that the things you're doing don't feel normal?"

"Yeah, I guess that's what I mean." He hadn't meant anything at all, it had just been a smartass thing to say, but she was right, a lot of things lately didn't feel exactly what he'd call normal. He thought about it. "I seem to be spending a lot of time looking at myself in the mirror."

"Oh? How much time?"

"A couple hours maybe."

"Doesn't that strike you as excessive?"

"Well, *of course* it strikes me as excessive. Everything I'm doing strikes me as excessive. Look, I went home for my birthday and I got in a fight with my old man and he slapped me around and then I come back . . . came back . . . and drank too much and messed up my stomach and ended up having to see the doctor about it. I've been sick as a dog."

"Do you want to tell me about the fight with your father?"

"No, I don't."

Once again they were sitting there looking at each other like two cats. She was very good at not showing what she was thinking. She had big blue eyes, a little bit lighter than China blue. She used a touch of black mascara and hardly any eye liner at all. "Okay, Mason, but can I get some background information? You don't mind telling me that, do you?"

"Nope. Go ahead."

He answered her questions automatic like he was filling out a form. History major, going into his fourth year, good grades, won a big scholarship so he's doing an honors thesis. After he graduated he was supposed to go straight into the Master's program but he wasn't sure he wanted to do that, although he probably should because if he didn't, he'd get drafted. He was from a big family, well, it had started out that way. Originally from Mason's Landing down the river on the West Virginia side, no, not exactly a town, his grandparents had a farm down there. His dad was in the war, didn't come home till Mason was nearly five, and then, later on, when Mason was in high school, the old man got a job in Raysburg and moved the family up there, so they were down to just Mason and his mom and dad and sister. Then in a couple years the old man got another job in Cincinnati and they moved again.

"Did you find those moves disruptive?"

"Damn straight they were. I liked Mason's Landing, didn't want to move. And then just about the time I was getting used to Raysburg, we had to move again. I hated Cincinnati."

She was looking at him, probably waiting for him to tell her more about it. His senior year had been the worst year of his life, the absolute pits. All of a sudden he was in a new school where he didn't know a goddamn soul and nobody gave a shit. Yeah, and there was that mean little prick named Skip who'd choked him out in the school yard. That was the most frightening thing that had ever happened to him and he should probably be telling a psychiatrist about it but he could not possibly tell it to Dr. Elspeth Fairfield MD.

"Well, the thing was . . ." he said. The thing was what? "The reason we kept moving . . . You see, the old man's got a drinking problem and when he's on the wagon, he's not half bad, he's a salesman, did I tell you that? Always on the road, and it's way too easy for him to . . . you know, stop somewhere and have himself a quick one. And when he falls off the wagon, that's a whole other story. But he's always sorry after. He's always talking about starting over, making a whole new life. That's why we kept moving."

"Do you want to tell me about your fight now?"

"Okay. Sure. It was about my hair."

"It is quite long."

"Yeah, I guess so. Did you see the Beatles on the Ed Sullivan show? I just thought that's something I'd like to try out, you know. Before that, I was doing a kind of Elvis Presley."

"I saw the Ed Sullivan show too, Mason, and your hair is much longer than the Beatles'."

"Yeah, I guess it is."

"How do people react to it?"

"People? I don't know, you mean my old man? He just hates it. He wants to kill me. Or do you mean people in general? Yeah, people are looking at me funny now."

"How do you feel about that?"

"Well, it depends on who they are. People keep telling me I look like a girl."

"How does that make you feel?"

"I don't mind it."

"You don't mind looking like a girl?"

"No."

This was strange, this wasn't what he'd expected at all, but maybe Dr. Elspeth Fairfield MD might be exactly the right person to be talking to. Wouldn't that be a joke? "I like looking like a girl," he said.

She had nothing showing on her face except a very careful expression he'd call "interested." She wrote something on her paper. She'd been writing on it the whole time. "You *like* looking like a girl. I see. And how would you characterize your relationships with girls?"

"Relationships?"

"Are you dating anyone?"

"Well, no, not exactly." What the hell did *exactly* mean? The correct answer was no, he was not dating anyone. "I had a girlfriend in Raysburg." Well, she wasn't *exactly* his girlfriend.

"Were you close?"

Cindy Ewing. The only reason he went out with her was that she was Luke Ewing's little sister. Mason never knew what Cindy was thinking because she didn't talk much. "I wouldn't say we were close, no, but I missed her after I left Raysburg." That was true enough.

"And that's the last time you were dating anyone?"

"Right."

"So you haven't dated anyone since high school?"

Now he was getting truly pissed off. "That's correct."

"Is there anyone in your life you feel particularly attached to? Anyone? A male friend? A relative? Your mother?"

"My mother?" He couldn't believe she'd said that, the whole idea was ridiculous. "We were close when I was little, but lately? No, I'd say we were kind of distant lately. We don't really talk to each other. My sister, the same. Irene and I should be close but we're not. Yeah. We're not a great family for talking to each other. But particularly attached to? I like my roommate but I've never been able to figure out if he's a friend of mine or not. And then there's this bunch of history TAs but I guess they're not really friends of mine either. I guess there's really nobody right now. Jesus— Excuse my language but that's a hard thing to realize. I mean there's nobody. There's my thesis advisor, Dr. Braithwaite, but I only see him for maybe ten minutes once a month and he's this old guy, this old professor, and I like him and all, but *attached?* That isn't what you meant. Jesus, I guess I'm— Back in Raysburg— I had friends in high school."

"And sometimes it's hard to see the point to being alive?"

"Yeah. You got it. Listen, Doctor, I get real— It's hard to put into words. It's like I'm anxious, like everything seems kind of, you know, pointless, shitty, just flat and stupid and miserable, and I'm anxious and edgy. Twitchy. Restless. Can't sit still. I don't know. Driven. I'll take off and ride my bike around or, I don't know, ride my bike around, or maybe drink too much, and sometimes I don't know what I'm going to do. I've just got to move or do something, and sometimes I don't know what I'm going to do until I do it."

"Do you feel as though you're not in control of yourself?"

"Yeah, that's it exactly. Yeah, I'd say you got that exactly right."

"You must find that frightening."

"Yes, I do. It's real frightening."

"I'll give you something that will help you with that." She swiveled her chair around, picked up her prescription pad from her desk, and wrote something on it. "Is this a good time for you? Ask Rachel to schedule you for two weeks."

"Doctor? What do you think? You know, about me, about anything I said?"

She looked at him for a few seconds before she answered. It was that same nothing-on-her-face look. "I can see that you're troubled, Mason. I'll try to help you. You're very well defended."

Shit, he thought, *well defended.* Was that a good thing or a bad thing?

The McKinley Tower was the tallest structure on the Merida campus and it sat on top of the oldest surviving building, the Old Main Library. The tower had been added half a century later, but they'd matched the original architecture so well that it was hard to imagine Old Main without the tower on it. If you jumped off the McKinley Tower, you'd fall past the three floors of the tower and then five more floors of the library so you'd be going at a pretty good clip when you hit the concrete steps at the back of the building. An old-fashioned wrought iron railing was the only thing separating Mason from that fall. He stepped up so he was tight against it and looked down. Fear whooshed through him like a big wind and he jerked back, sucking air. Animal instinct, he thought. You can't argue with that.

The quickest way to get onto the roof of the McKinley Tower was to sneak onto the old creaking staff-only elevator that would take you up to Level Seven, the Offices of the University Librarian. There, if nobody saw you, you could zip through a door that also said STAFF ONLY and you'd find yourself in a long hallway that would lead you to a steel door that said NO ENTRY. If you said fuck it and went through that one too, you'd be on the stairs going up to Level Eight which had nothing on it but the motor that cranked the elevator up and down, the mechanism of the ancient clock in the tower, and a lot of empty space. If you kept on going through three more doors you shouldn't be going through, you'd end up on the roof and everybody knew that. You weren't a real Merida student unless you'd gone sneaking up there at least once. Legend had it that some sad sorry undergrad long ago had jumped, but if they had, the university must have covered it up good because Mason had never found a record of it, and if the university didn't want people jumping off the McKinley Tower, it would be real easy to stop them. If there had been a single lock on any one of those five doors, Mason wouldn't be here. They're all fucking idiots, he thought.

He walked away from the railing, sat down with his back against the brick cube that sheltered the stairway, and stared up at the evening sky. He liked the long days in June, how late it would get before the light faded away, streaky blue-grey cirrus clouds now. He was glad to be alive, suddenly glad, and Dr. Elspeth Fairfield MD could go fuck herself. She must have missed out on that special school where doctors go to learn to write inscrutable code because her handwriting was neat and clear and it said "Mellaril." He'd biked over to the medical library and looked it up in the Physicians' Desk Reference. It was a brand name for thioridazine, an antipsychotic drug used to treat schizophrenia. So that's what you gave crazy people, not just people you thought were confused or sad or a little bit anxious, but people you thought were foamed right out of their skulls. Not only that, but she'd given him double the standard dose. The prescription was still folded up in his shirt pocket with his cigarettes. He took it out, crumpled it into a ball, threw it across the roof, and watched the evening breeze take it.

All Mason knew about himself was that he was hopelessly fucked up, sick, weird, and crazy in a disgusting horrible way he couldn't talk to anybody about, and he'd known that for a long time. An honest-to-God psychiatrist with MD after her name obviously agreed with him because she wanted to give him twice the dose you'd give your ordinary bug-eyed screaming maniac. He'd thought maybe a shrink could help him figure out how he'd got so fucked up and maybe help him do something about it, but no, all she'd wanted to do was drug him. He'd got his hopes up, maybe that was the reason he felt so hurt. Maybe he was crazy in a way that even psychiatrists couldn't figure out. *Well defended?* What the fuck did that mean? It took a huge amount of effort to pretend to be normal and any psychiatrist ought to know that.

All of a sudden the clock in the tower started to chime, wow, incredible. Sitting where he was, directly above it, he felt that huge metallic sound ringing right through his whole damn body. He counted nine bongs and that meant that the library was closing but that was okay, he'd been locked in before and knew a way out through a staff-only door down on ground level. So what was he doing sitting on the McKinley Tower after closing hours? Was this suicide attempt number three? Well, it wouldn't just be an attempt, it would definitely get the job done, but Mason's desire to jump was a little less than zero. That was because he was in his right mind at the moment and could think about things in a rational way, but what would happen if he wasn't? One of these days that same sudden out-of-nowhere impulse that had shot him in front of a semi and dumped him full of whiskey and sleeping pills might flip him off the Tower. He stood up, walked back to the railing, pressed up against it, took a deep breath, and looked down.

Fear again, whoosh. Holy fuck, that was a long way down. Just feel it, he told himself, and he felt it. His body would blow completely apart on the concrete steps. What would it be like to be falling and think, shit, I don't want to be doing this? He forced himself to stand there and look down until he could breathe normal, until something in him flattened out and said, yeah, I could do it. If I had to.

He walked back to the brick cube and sat down again. Whether or not you wanted to kill yourself depended on what you thought about death. If you thought there was some kind of happy afterlife, then you were more likely to do it, but Mason figured the odds were pretty good that death was lights out, and if it was, then there could be no good reason for killing yourself unless you were in such horrible pain you couldn't stand it. Yeah, that was right so far, because something is always better than nothing, but that was rational thinking and what happened if you weren't rational?

Mason sat there watching the sky go from blue gray to night, watching the stars come out. He wasn't trying to think through anything, he was just sitting there. Then he had that same feeling he'd got earlier on, so fucking glad to be alive, glad to be able to sit there and see the stars. Okay, he thought, I'm rational at the moment so

41

what am I going to do with it? Okay, so if you were really ready to kill yourself, you were kind of invulnerable in a weird way because you'd passed over the fuck-it line and you could do anything, even weird shit, and anything you did was bound to be more interesting than being dead.

3.

Mason slept late and was amazed when he woke up because it had been the best night's sleep since he'd tried to kill himself. His rib didn't hurt too much and his stomach just felt empty. He tried cream of asparagus soup with a slice of toast broken up in it and it wasn't half bad. He went into his bedroom, stripped his clothes off, and studied himself in the full-length mirror. Yeah, it did strike him as excessive how much time he spent looking in the mirror. There was his body the same as always, some things he liked about it, some things he didn't. He'd lost a little weight from not eating for a few days and that had its upside and its downside. When he sucked his stomach in, it was nice and concave and his hipbones stood out, he liked that, but if he wanted to look more like a girl, he should be a little bit heavier so he should start eating normal again. He'd never liked the hair on his legs and he sure didn't like it now. Well, he was over the fuck-it line, wasn't he?

He locked himself in the bathroom, drew a hot bath, sat in it and shaved his legs. He'd only done it once before, when he'd been eleven, when he'd dressed up like Irene and walked down to the Landing. He went slow and careful so he wouldn't cut himself. His legs felt a bit raw afterwards so he rubbed them with hand lotion and ducked back into his bedroom to look at himself. Hell, yeah, that was better, exactly how he wanted his legs to look. But there was a downside to that too. Hot weather was coming and he wouldn't be able to wear shorts.

Ride it out, fuck. Merida's campus was supposed to be one of the prettiest in the state, a broad pleasant walkway running through the center of the quad where Mason was riding hard at the moment, standing up on the pedals, whishing by on either side of those buildings that always looked to him like *Saturday Evening Post* illustrations for the golden college years. That horrible feeling he'd tried to describe to Dr. Elspeth Fairfield MD was coming back again full tilt. He got to the ROTC building, made a loop and started back, kicking it so hard he broke out in a sweat. So much for thinking when he'd woke up in the morning that everything was getting better. He was afraid of the McKinley Tower now but he was headed straight for it because that goddamn tower was on top of the library and the library was his home.

By West Virginia standards the land around Merida could be considered flat but it wasn't really, had a kind of rolling undulation to it, and Old Main had been built on a hill. If you entered from the back, you'd be walking directly into Level One where the staff processed books, but if you entered from the front as Mason was doing today, you'd be on Level Two and in the summer you'd be assaulted by the rattle of the fans. For years the university had been promising to install central air conditioning but they still hadn't got around to it, most of their budget going into the gleaming new Science and Tech Library over on the eastern side of the campus.

There was nobody to be seen on Level Two except for the ancient library lady drowsing at the check-out. Mason pushed through the turnstile and into the big reading room with its long tables and battered old wooden cabinets that held the library catalog. No matter how shitty a mood he was in, it always gave his heart a lift to walk in here. When they'd been designing libraries in the old days, they must have wanted everything to be solid and eternal, so the stacks were massive, built of good old hardwood, stained and varnished, and they could never be replaced by modern movable shelving because they were load bearing. The next thing on the agenda must have been light, so Levels Two, Three, and Four didn't have ceilings in their centers and you could look up through all that soaring beautifully empty space to the distant vaulted ceiling and feel how it really was like a cathedral, yeah, a temple dedicated to books. Laid out on an east-west axis, Old Main had great ancient leaded windows set on both the eastern and western walls. When the sun was up on a cloudless day, it was always shining in, shining down the aisles between the stacks, making everything glow as bright as heaven itself and in the summer ramming the temperature up into the 90s.

Feeling like he was walking into an oven, wishing he could wear shorts, Mason kept on going up the big broad staircase. The levels followed the Dewey Decimal System so history was on the very top, Level Five, where Jessie Collier had her carrel near the eastern wall. He always looked for her. She wasn't there today and he felt a kind of loss. He never bothered with the catalog anymore, he'd memorized the 900s. He walked through the stacks, touching the books as he went.

He already knew a lot about Henry's thesis topic, the Compromise of 1876, but there was always more to know. Carl's topic was another matter, all he could remember about President Monroe's administration was the Monroe Doctrine, of course, and that Federalism had been squashed, so he had a lot of reading to do on that one. The main topic on his mind was Jessie's. He'd never heard of Lucy Stone. He found a big book on the women's suffrage movement that had her in the index, added that to the other books, checked them out, clipped his bag onto his bike, and took off.

Mason made a couple loops of the campus and then thought, shit, maybe I'm just hungry, so he drifted over to the Buckeye. He got there just about dinnertime so the restaurant side had a good number of people in it and one of them was Queer Walter sitting alone in a booth. For some reason Mason felt like talking to him. "Hey, Walter, mind if I join you?"

"Mason. Glad to see you," big grin and offered his hand. "Yeah, join me. Sitdown sitdown. Howya been? Here all summer?"

"Yeah, all summer. Got an honors thesis to write," and there they were, pumping out the old bullshit like a couple buddies from way back, and the funny thing was, Mason was glad to see Walter. "You having the special?"

"Yeah. The fried chicken. Not half bad."

Mason didn't think he could face the fried chicken so he ordered a cheeseburger. Walter was staring over into the bar side where they'd set up a portable TV between the bottles. Barry Goldwater's grim face was flickering on the screen and Walter said, "He's on a roll. Nobody can stop him now."

Fuck, Mason thought, he's a Goldwater supporter. "Maybe not," he said. "Rockefeller and Scranton and those people are trying—"

"Right. The Eastern elite liberal establishment—"

"Oh, for Christ's sake, liberal *establishment?* That's just the left wing of the GOP."

"Yeah? Well maybe the GOP shouldn't have a left wing. Rockefeller and Scranton? They might as well be Democrats. Anyhow, they can't stop him now. He's got it nailed."

Barry Goldwater scared the absolute screaming dog-fuck out of Mason. "There's still some people in the Republican Party with common sense," he said, "and they're afraid of him. They think he's an extremist."

"Extremist? Hell no. He's just offering the American people a real choice for a change, a choice, not an echo. A lot of Republicans want to get back to basics, do what's right for America. Personal responsibility, respect for the small businessman—"

"Not an extremist? Scrap Social Security, get out of the UN, blockade Cuba, use nuclear weapons in Vietnam? Jesus, he's not far off the Birchers. Better to die on your feet than live on your knees. *Not an extremist?* Come on, Walter, he sounds like Dr. Strangelove."

Then they were talking politics for Christ's sake, but they were still smiling at each other. Walter described himself as "like most Americans" and he was frankly sick of the US getting kicked around by any two-bit country that was inclined to do it, and what was this containment shit anyway? Didn't they know who they were dealing with? You could trust the commies all right, trust the commies to be commies. No, you couldn't contain them, got to stop them, roll them back, shut the bastards down. It was a matter of the free individual God-fearing American standing up to godless collectivism, nobody said it was going to be easy, took courage and conviction, and then Walter was proceeding to ring the big bells, LIBERTY DEMOCRACY FREEMARKET, and Mason was contemplating Walter.

Strong jaw on him, big Roman nose, not a man you'd call handsome but a nice looking fellow. Somewhere in his forties, going soft in the belly but not too bad. Fancy wrist watch, big gold ring on his right hand, crest on it like some kind of grad ring or service ring, broad flat fingernails. Hair the color of brown that most people had when they had brown hair, not losing any yet, that neat once-every-two-weeks trim. Eyes with the sympathetic look of somebody who'd help you out, the good old small-town salesman who'd stand behind his product. Yeah, Walter was a decent guy and still Mason wasn't attracted to him. Was Mason not attracted to men or just not to men as old as Walter? Men were sure attracted to him.

Vietnam was where they'd got to by now. "We've got no business there," Mason said. "They've been fighting a colonial war forever, and we've just inherited it from the French. Left to their own devices they'd just turn into a neutral kind of benign little communist country sort of like Yugoslavia, no threat to American interests whatsoever. The best thing for us is to get the fuck out of there as quick as we can do it."

Instead of getting mad that he was being disagreed with, Walter grinned and chuckled. "What's your major, Mason?"

"History."

"You're a bright kid."

Mason shrugged. Now he was listening to the standard Goldwater shit about small government and lowering taxes. "Walter," he said, "not once in the history of the United States of America has lowering taxes ever improved the economy. And you may recall that Herbert Hoover had a pretty good shot at it."

Walter chuckled again. "Hell, kid, you weren't even born yet. Let me ask you something. Do you trust Lyndon Johnson?"

Mason had to think about it. "No," he said.

Walter offered his hand and they shook on it. "See," he said, "there's something we agree on."

"Walter," Mason said, "can I tell you something personal?"

"Sure. Shoot."

"I'm worried I might be gay." Mason hadn't planned to say that. What the fuck was he doing?

Walter looked off at the TV in the bar for so long Mason was afraid he wasn't going to say a word. Then he looked back and said, "What makes you think that?"

"Well, I kissed a boy once." Mason felt his stomach tighten up. Maybe he shouldn't have ordered a cheeseburger.

"Yeah? Do you want to talk about it?"

Bobby Springer. He was fourteen and Mason fifteen. They used to wander around in the woods up back of Mason's Landing, catching crayfish in the crick, both quiet boys. Mason had thought about

48

it a lot and he'd never been able to figure out just who kissed who. They were fooling around and Mason pretended to kiss Bobby, a big joke, just fooling around the way boys do, the next minute they should have been wrestling or chasing each other or some damn thing, but instead they were kissing each other.

Something about how sinful it was made it hot. Forbidden. Absolutely they should not be doing that. Shouldn't even cross their minds. Mason was thinking, oh, fuck, I'm kissing a boy. That made it real hot. And it wasn't like a little peck. "We pressed into each other like automatic, you know, our legs like—you know."

Mason figured that Walter did know. Walter was giving him a sympathetic look. Mason had been trying to eat his goddamn cheeseburger but he wasn't having much luck.

"He was a quiet little kid and so was I. We were these two— The other boys teased us. Not too bad though. The kids at the Landing were nicer than— Hell, I don't know whether that's true or not, whether they're nicer than anybody else or not, but we didn't get teased too bad. He was like me. I was like him. Anyhow, I said, 'We probably shouldn't be doing this,' or something like that, and we jumped apart, and we walked home without saying a word to each other, and we were never friends again after that."

"Sad."

"Yeah, it is. It *is* sad. A million times I kicked myself for it. Kept asking myself, why did I say that? I made him feel bad. I didn't want to do that, but that's what I did."

"Sounds like you feel worse about hurting his feelings than about kissing him."

"You know, that's probably true."

"You think about boys a lot? When you're thinking about sex?"

"No. Not really. Every once in a while I do, but mainly I think about girls."

"So that's it, huh? You kissed this boy once? And you're worried you might be gay?" Walter was grinning at him. "You ever read the Kinsey report?"

Mason shook his head.

"Guys fool around with each other a lot more than they'd ever admit. If every guy who ever fooled around with another guy was gay, then half the men in America would be gay. Hell, maybe even most of them."

"Maybe so," Mason said. "I don't know anything about it. It's just that—" Just that what? He didn't have a fucking clue.

"You know, Mason, I think you're probably worrying too much."

Yeah, Mason thought, sitting here with my legs shaved, I'm probably worrying too much.

"You want a beer?" Walter was asking him.

"Naw. Thanks. I've been sick. My stomach's kind of fucked up and I can't drink right now."

The waitress appeared with their bill and Walter snatched it.

"Thanks, Walter. You didn't have to do that."

"Aw, hell, you kids never have any money."

They looked at each other across the table. I like him, Mason thought, Goldwater supporter or not. He's a good guy. "Fuck, I don't know," he said. "I'm not attracted to men, but men are sure attracted to me. They keep coming on to me. Starting in high school. Most of them old fuckers."

"That doesn't mean you're gay, Mason. That just means you're cute. You can't help that." He gave Mason a look that had a lot more to it than any of the words he'd been saying.

Jesus H. fucking Christ, Mason was riding. Aimed west. *Off into the sunset,* he thought, and that was funny. This part of Ohio was beautiful in its own way but not the way the world ought to look. Steep hills should be wrapping around you and you should be able to ride up to the top of one of them and look down. Sweating and out of breath, he stopped, turned his bike around to face the way he'd come, and stood there trying to have some clear thoughts about anything.

Back east the light was all full of motes and bugs, shimmering and golden, and the campus was a hazy little toy box of buildings, like a mirage, with the straight line of the McKinley Tower sticking up like a smudge. It would be dark by the time he got back. Shit. He must have wanted to see if he was attracted enough to Walter to go to bed with him. That was based on the premise that Walter went to bed with boys, but maybe he didn't, maybe all he did was hang out with them. But anyhow Mason had concluded that he did not want to go to bed with Walter, although he could do it for the experience, but why did he want the experience? A couple years ago he'd said to himself that the first cute guy who make a pass at him, he was going to do it, but so far that cute guy had not appeared.

The minute him and Bobby Springer had started kissing each other, Mason had slid one of his legs between Bobby's. That meant that one of Bobby's legs was between his. Mason could feel that Bobby was like a rock down there and that meant that Bobby could feel that Mason was like a rock down there. That hadn't stopped either one of them. If they had kept on going, they would probably both have come in their pants, and Walter Pfefferman could say all he wanted to about the Kinsey Report, but that felt pretty goddamn gay to Mason.

4.

Mason was trapped in the bathroom mirror again. He still had his long sideburns from his Elvis days. They were the last thing holding him to boy. He estimated where a girl's hair growth would stop and shaved off the sideburns up to there, shaved the rest of his face, fooled around with his hair, brushed it around his face the way a girl would.

All last summer he'd been stuck at home, and Jesus, had that ever been one long hot boring summer, working at Shillito's for a buck an hour, laying around the house at night, watching Johnny Carson. "Look," Irene said to him, "if I take you to the drugstore and buy you anything you want, will you just leave my damn stuff alone?" What she'd bought him he kept in a cigar box under his dresser alongside the big Sears and Roebuck catalogue he used to jerk off to. He pulled the cigar box out and took it into the bathroom. Remembering how Lorianne did it, how Dr. Elspeth Fairfield MD did it, he ringed his eyes with black liner. Then he wiped a lot of it off until nothing was left but a soft smudgy line.

His eyelashes were a light sandy brown like his hair, but when he brushed them with black mascara, you could sure see how long they were. That really changed his face, made him look like a different person. Maybe he could wear makeup in a way so nobody would notice, or not notice much. Back in his bedroom he sat naked in front of the mirror. He'd spent hours riding, trying to stop thinking about all this shit, but he hadn't been able to stop thinking about it. Girls' bodies were so much more beautiful than boys' bodies with all that stupid stuff hanging down, what a ridiculous way to design an animal.

He had a pair of Irene's stretch panties he kept hid in plain sight with his underwear, and he put them on. He liked how they smoothed him out. Maybe his old twenty-eight-inch jeans would fit him, and they did. Last winter he'd bought himself a pair of sand-colored cowgirl boots from the country-and-western store in Cincinnati, "a present for my sister." They were cut delicate, had a low heel and a squared-off toe, were in that sneaky area between boy and girl, and that's what he'd wanted. He put on a clean white dress shirt, did a military tuck so it fit tight to his stomach, one of the few useful things he'd learned from the old man. Last summer he'd asked Irene for some of her perfume and she'd poured a little bit into an Aspirin bottle for him, F# by Fabergé. He dabbed it behind his ears, onto his throat and wrists. What the fuck was he doing? He hadn't been planning anything, one thing just happened after another.

Mason forgot sometimes how far away Henry's house was. On a bike, if you liked to kick it down and move, not far at all, and his cracked rib wasn't hurting all that much, maybe it was healing faster than the doctor had said it would. The last of the sun was shining red-gold low through the fields back of Henry's house when he got there, rows and rows of corn, way out of town in real country Ohio. In a couple weeks the first of that corn would be ready, and Mason liked sweet corn okay but he liked horse corn better, late in the season, when it was chewy and dark.

He slid to a stop in front of Henry's porch, swung off with the ease and advantage of a girl's bike. Usually Henry's parties were loud and spilling outside, people everywhere, on the front porch, on the back porch, in the yard, out under the tree where he'd talked to Lorianne, but even though it was summer, nobody was outside yet. You didn't have to ring the bell when there was a party on but Mason hadn't been raised that way so he rang it. He waited so long he didn't think anybody had heard him, but then there was Lorianne herself, looking at him through the screen door. "Oh. Mason. Macquarie," she said and stepped out onto the porch with him. Now she wasn't just looking at him, she was staring at him.

Fuck, was she shocked? Was he that shocking? "Lorianne," he said. What the fuck was he doing? Maybe he should turn around and go home.

Then she smiled the same warm I-like-you smile from the last time. "Oh, my goodness," she said, "you've done your eyes so pretty. I hope you don't mind me saying that, I'm not teasing you, I mean it as a compliment, the boys are going to give you shit, but to hell with them, they don't— You don't mind if I tell you how pretty you look, do you? If you do, just say so. I'm so glad you came, it's not— We're having a good party, Jessie's here, she'll be so glad to see you—"

If she was shocked, so was he. He'd just been doing one thing after another, and this is where he'd got to. Christ, man, he thought, you're fucking nuts. Lorianne was talking so fast he couldn't follow her. Had he embarrassed her, or was she trying to cover up something else, fill in some mysterious blank revealed here on the porch? "The minute I met you," she was saying, "I knew we were birds of a feather, two weird outsider hillbilly kids stuck here in this goddamn terra incognita in the middle of goddamn Uh-hi-uh—"

Blue must be her color, another one of her little-girl dresses with a big circle skirt, sky blue with white trim, a summer dress, lovely for evening, and matching blue heels. He was remembering again how much he liked her, he even liked her mistakes, and she was still talking "—tell you about *my* thesis, it was just a master's

55

but I could of gone on and done a PhD, everybody said so, but no, had Tammy instead, no, no, no, but nobody— Nobody ever asks about *my* thesis, oh, you'll probably think I'm stuck on myself—"

The sun was behind the house, they were standing in the big shadow it threw, twilight on the porch but the last of the hot red blaze hazy in the distance. Then she did something strange, took both of his hands in hers. She'd never touched him before. "Come on," she said, "Come in." Her fingers felt warm and alive.

Pungent smell, sort of like burnt flowers, somebody must be burning incense, and the house was full of people, nowhere near as many as if school had been going but enough so they had to stand and mill around, history students mostly, some he knew and some he didn't. Jazz playing, well of course it was, and from his chair by the hi-fi, Henry waving, "Hey, it's The Kid," and then both Henry and Carl were staring at him, oh fuck. Where was Jessie? There, over in a corner, talking to a girl grad, and he saw Jessie see him but she didn't send him any kind of signal, just looked, her dark eyes flashing. Lorianne was still holding onto one of his hands. "You want to smoke some tea?" she whispered to him.

"I don't know. Sure."

Now Lorianne was leading him somewhere, back toward the front door, then up the stairs. She opened the door to a bedroom, led him in and shut the door behind them. That burnt flower smell was overwhelming. She picked up a hand-rolled cigarette from a big ashtray on the bed table.

She lit the cigarette, gave him a playful kind of wicked grin, and then inhaled, and inhaled, and inhaled the deepest possible inhale, and held it. Forever. Eventually the smoke trickled out and she giggled, passed it to him. Mason felt like a hoopie idiot. It was marijuana, of course it was. He'd always wanted to try it, so here was his chance. Smoking Camels had toughened his lungs up, so he could drag it in just as deep as she had.

Then he was sitting on the edge of the bed with Lorianne, patting the tabby cat. It was a good ole cat. They smoked the whole marijuana cigarette all the way down till there was nothing left of it. Mason kept trying to feel something but he wasn't feeling anything so maybe he wasn't doing it right or maybe the marijuana wasn't that strong. He could really hear the jazz downstairs in the living room, even through the closed door he could hear it, super clear, and he'd never understood before how interesting it was, the bass, that big slapping sound, he was following it and every note was a revelation, he'd have to ask Henry who was playing, a fucking genius playing, and Lorianne took his hand and squeezed, like she could read his mind, her eyes filled with sparkle. People couldn't read each other's minds, could they?

In some inexplicable way Mason was now back downstairs in the living room, feeling the heart of the bass, drawn to the hi-fi and that stupendous fall of notes, thinking too many things at once. He couldn't seem to follow any of his thoughts to any kind of conclusion. He wasn't even sure if he could remember where they started. "Jesus, Mason," Carl was saying, "what have you done to yourself? You look like a pederast's wet dream."

Shit, Mason thought. What the fuck was he doing here? He was wearing makeup and girl's boots out in public. He'd never dressed up and gone out in public since that time when he'd been eleven and all the old ladies had thought he was Irene. But this was different, this was dangerous, he didn't really know these people, they might turn on him, do something terrible to him, squash him out like a bug. He had to—had to, had to— He attacked back with the first thing that came to mind. "Yeah. Okay. So what about the Era of Good Feelings? Good feelings, hell. A big fucking publicity stunt. President Monroe traveling around the county dressed up like a Revolutionary War soldier, squashing the Federalists. For what? One party rule?"

"What do you know?" Carl said, pretending to be amazed. "The pretty boy has a thought in his head."

"He won the Freddy T.," Lorianne said.

"Hark," Carl said, "Doll Normal has spoken."

Mason had lost track of her but she must have followed him into the living room. She took his hand again. Wasn't that a bizarre thing to do right there in front of her husband? This was getting too weird too fast and Mason wanted clear of it. Way too weird. Way too fast. "Who's that?" he asked Henry, pointing at the hi-fi with his free hand.

"Mingus. The great Charles Mingus. Cookin', huh?"

People milling around. Some of them he'd never seen before, like those two girls staring at him, they looked real young, looked like undergrads straight from small-town Ohio, hadn't figured out yet that bright red lipstick wasn't cool any more. "Monroe was the right man at the right time," Carl was saying. "The key was Jackson. New Orleans."

Looking at him. The girls. Giggling. Mason was afraid. He felt fear like a cold marble column shoved down his throat and into his stomach. Shit, he thought, there's no way out of it. "Yeah, that destroyed the Federalists, sure, but for what? That's not important."

"Oh, yeah, you know, huh? Okay, Kid, what's important?"

"The Tallmadge Amendment. We could have ended slavery in 1819, or started to anyway—"

"Not without ripping the country apart. The Georgia— What's his name— The representative from Georgia. 'Seas of blood,' he said."

"Yeah? So what? Why wait for 1860? 'Let it come,' Tallmadge said."

"That was just a stupid sideshow. Both those guys were idiots. Nobody was going to war. Nobody with a brain in his head."

"Fuck, man," Mason said, hanging on hard, "a whole series of compromises. The constitutional compromise of 1787—"

"That's what democracy is. Compromise."

"You can't compromise with something that's fundamentally wrong. It's the same fucking set of arguments today. Goldwater's still spouting the same old crap. Um—states' rights—"

—set of arguments. A whole set of arguments— Jesus, in his mind he'd had a whole set of arguments just a few seconds ago. It was finding the words, that was the— It was finding the words— Oh, he remembered. "Exactly the same crap. Yeah, states' rights. Back then it was an excuse for slavery, now it's an excuse for segregation. But even at the time—" At the time, at the time—at the time— "Jefferson," he said.

"Jefferson?" Henry said. "Jesus. What a hypocrite. A fucking slave holder—"

"High flying idealism," Carl said, talking right along with him, "but you've got to deal with real shit—"

The TAs. The boys. They sounded like they were in stereo. Spooky. Mason wondered if the red-lipstick girls could hear it too. He smiled at them and their eyes darted away. That hurt him. Was he that weird? Was he some kind of leper? "Economic realities," Henry said. "Trade. New York and New England—"

"Yes," Carl said, "exactly. That was the problem with the war with England. Not any high lofty—"

The voices were mixing up with the great Charles Mingus, like he'd composed the whole works, then another voice, higher up, a relief, came sailing in at the top. *Jessie.* "All *men* are created equal. Why don't you just stop right there?"

She was wearing jeans tonight, and Mason simply could not believe how great she looked in them, how much he felt for her, this tall cool girl he hardly knew, his TA from last fall, it felt like falling in love. No, he was just being an asshole.

"For God's sake, Sappho," Carl said, "you've got a song with one note."

"Yeah? Maybe I do. And I'm going to keep singing it." So tall and straight, beautiful, angry-eyed, gray blouse tucked into her jeans, wearing what looked exactly like boy's dress shoes. Blasting words at them: "Fundamentally wrong—social position—bedrock—women—"

Henry and Carl blasting words back at her, Lorianne's hand warm and moving in his, squeezing, and she was looking at him, sparkle-eyed. He had the strong sense that he and Lorianne were in it together, the girls against the boys, exactly the way he used to feel with Irene when he was little. "*Women,*" Jessie said, "if you don't start there, you're not going anywhere. You can't create a slave class until you've subjugated women."

"Watch out for Sappho," Carl told Mason, whispering as though he was letting him in on a big secret, "she's further to the left than Vladimir Lenin."

"Lorianne," Henry said, "you've got to stop smoking that shit. It's making you silly." She let go of Mason's hand.

Somebody years ago had painted the kitchen daffodil yellow. It was a great color for a kitchen, but it needed a new coat of paint. "I'm hungry all of a sudden," Mason said. He didn't know why anybody should care, but he said it anyway. "My stomach . . . I fucked it up good, so I couldn't eat there for a while. It's still kind of, I don't know . . . queasy. Or something— Yeah— But I'm so, God, I could eat— I don't know."

"Sugar," Jessie said.

"What?"

"I bet you want sugar." She really was much taller than he was.

"Yeah, oh yeah," he said. "Yeah. Sugar."

She was looking directly down at him but somehow not into his eyes, how could that be? Oh, she was looking *at his makeup,* and then, with a minute shift in her gaze, she made eye contact and there he was, the deer in the headlights. She looked away.

60

Fuck, he thought, weird, he thought, I want to be invisible. People were piling up on the other side of the kitchen, waiting to get into the downstairs can, kids he should know but didn't, history students. They were getting beers out of the case on the table. Too many voices. Boys' voices, girls' voices. "I hate it when Carl calls me Doll Normal. It's so insulting. I'm smarter than he is."

"You're smarter than both of them put together."

"Jess, you're so sweet. I might be a doll but I'm sure as hell not *normal*. Jesus. They don't even know what a doll *is*. I bet you do, don't you, Mason? I bet you played with dolls."

"Yeah, I did," he said, embarrassed. "With my sister."

"See, I knew you did. A doll is magical. If you're a little kid, if you're—"

"Do you like the taste of beer?" Jessie was asking him.

"Oh yeah. I love the taste of beer."

Just as though she was in her own kitchen, Jessie popped open the freezer, took out a carton of vanilla ice cream, scooped two big scoops into a beer mug, poured beer over it, shoved a spoon into it, and handed it to Mason.

Who would have thought of it? "Oh, Jesus, this is good!" It went down easy. He was slurping it right down.

"Nobody ever asks me about *my* thesis. It's like I don't count. I could be working on my PhD too, you know. If I hadn't had Tammy. Oh, I don't know, sometimes— I wasn't in history like you guys," she said to Mason. "I was in English."

"She was writing on Djuna Barnes," Jessie told him.

"Who?"

"See. Nobody knows her. Everybody should know her. All those damn courses where they teach *The Wasteland*, they should be teaching *Nightwood*— Jess, you never drink anything. It's not fair. You're so goddamn sober." Lorianne darted away, vanished through the archway into the living room.

61

"She's blotto," Jessie said. "She should go to bed. If Tammy wakes up, guess who's going to have to take care of her?"

"Um," Mason said.

"I quit smoking that shit a long time ago," Jessie said. "It just made me paranoid."

Lorianne was back, carrying two shot glasses full of whiskey. "I don't want this," Jessie said.

"If you don't drink yours, I'll have to drink them both."

Mason felt Jessie's anger like a spark that built, snapped, and sizzled. "Don't *do that* to me, Lorianne." She took the two shot glasses, first one and then the other, from Lorianne's hands and set them down on the kitchen counter, each with a click. Lorianne stood there passively and let her do it. Then she said, "Hold me. Oh, Jess, Jess, just hold me," and fell forward into Jessie's arms, clinging to her.

Jessie took all of the smaller girl's weight, supporting her, and stroked her head. "You're a disaster," Jessie said softly. "Come on, we're going for a walk." She looked directly at Mason. He felt the enormous pressure behind her eyes. "Come on," she said, "you too."

"I'm Ruth amid the alien corn," Lorianne told them and sounded quite happy about it. They had walked all the way to the edge of the farmer's field. Jessie and Mason had stopped, but Lorianne had kept right on going until she was standing between the corn plants. Behind them, the house was a dark bleak rectangle with yellow light pouring out of the windows. They were so far away that Mason couldn't hear the jazz but he could hear the windows.

"The sad heart of Ruth," Lorianne said, "when, sick for home, she stood in tears amid the alien corn. Do you know that? That's Keats."

"I'm not up on my Keats, to tell you the truth," Jessie said.

"My heart aches, and a drowsy numbness pains my sense, as though of hemlock I had drunk—"

"Right. A little too much hemlock—"

"'*Tender* is the night.' That's where that comes from, did you know that? Oh, Ruth, wonderful Ruth, 'Intreat me not to leave thee, or to return from following after thee.' Two girls. People forget that. That story we like to tell about perfect love is about *two girls*. Oh, Mason, are you ever sick for home? I know I am. Wake up sometimes in the night and think I'm back there, think I can hear the crick running, but it's just the rain, and I think why, why, why? Jess, honey, I know you're trying to keep me out of trouble, and I'm trying to be good, really I am. Mason, do you have a smoke?"

Jessie offered a hand, Lorianne took it and allowed herself to be led out of the corn and aimed back toward the house. She'd been talking non-stop ever since they'd come outside, and Mason wasn't following anything she was saying, but it was clear to him now that she had been an English major, carrying all that shit around in her head. He lit two Camels, one for her and one for himself.

She took hers, dragged and coughed. "Whew, what is this? You smoke straights. I'm going to be okay, Jess, I really am. It's just that sometimes things seem, you know, really— Oh, Mason, you're so pretty, you're like a boy in an old book, I can see that book clear in my mind, can see the picture, an etching maybe, something like that, *impaled*, that's the word that Djuna uses, you know, for what happened to us with the old books— Oh. Damn. I wish I'd finished my thesis."

"You still can."

"Yeah. Maybe. It's so sweet you believe in me, Jess, lots of times I don't believe in me. Sometimes I wake up in the night, and I think why, why, why? 'I was doing well enough until you kicked my stone over, and out I came, all moss and eyes—' That's Djuna, genius Djuna. She got it. Nobody else got it. None of the moderns.

Not Eliot, not Pound, nobody but her. Mason, you absolutely *have* to read *Nightwood*. It'll change your life. Oh, my goodness. Jess, you go on in the house, I want to talk to Mason."

"Are you kidding me?"

"You know how Henry doesn't like us to be together? You go on in. What if Tammy wakes up? Not that she's going to. She can sleep through anything. Once she's asleep. But what if she does? No, Henry shouldn't think we're out here together. Five minutes. Please? I'm okay. It's wearing off. I'm really okay. I want to tell Mason something."

"**Djuna says,** 'A man is another person. But a woman is yourself, caught as you turn in panic.' Only Djuna could write that line, *caught as you turn in panic*. That's what makes her a genius. Okay, but who's caught? The *you*. That's what I first thought. The internal speaker. Then I thought, no it's *the woman* who's caught. Or maybe it's *both of you*."

Mason was alone with Lorianne. Even though he was hanging on her every word, he didn't have the remotest idea what she was talking about. She'd never looked more like something out of the forest, run or bite. "What if it's *the moment* that's caught? What if *the turning* is the key? A woman is yourself, caught as you turn in panic."

There was only a couple feet between them. She stepped forward, canceling the distance. Because she was wearing heels, they were the same height. "A woman is yourself," she said, "caught as you turn in panic. On her mouth you kiss your own." She kissed him.

He thought for a minute she was kissing him to prove the point of her story, but no, she was kissing him to be kissing him. *On my mouth?* he thought.

He wanted them to be equal because neither of them was the boy. He wanted to kiss her the way a girl kissed. Was this how they did it? Giving up everything? "You smell like a girl," she whispered.

64

He was going to tell her that it was Reenie's perfume, but then he thought, no, that wasn't right. He'd always wanted to touch her, and now that he could, he stroked the back of her neck behind the flow of her hair, stroked the fine shape of her collarbone. He was hot but in the peculiar way he got hot. He wanted to melt for her, giving up everything. "Mason," she said, "you're like something preserved in amber."

"Lorianne. Are you out here?" Henry's hard angry voice, coming from the direction of the house. Mason felt it like a physical assault, an ice-cold sting delivered to his chest and then ratcheting throughout his entire body. "Yeah, honey," she called back, "just taking in the night."

Mason and Lorianne were hidden behind the thick dark tree. Time had drifted away, and he couldn't estimate how long they'd been standing there kissing each other. Nobody could see them from the house, could they? What if Henry decided to walk out here and found them? "You stay here," Lorianne whispered to him. "Wait a few minutes and then come back through *the front door*," and she was gone, leaving a puzzling blank like the key words left out of a paragraph.

Mason heard her voice, and Henry's. They weren't much farther away than the other side of the tree. He couldn't hear what they were saying but he could hear their feelings, low-banked, angry, and suppressed. He heard them walking back toward the house, heard it when Lorianne stepped from the softness of the lawn onto concrete, the skritch of her heels. Mason was supposed to go back into the house through *the front door*? Absolutely not. Lorianne was Henry's wife, and what Mason had to do was get the fuck out of there. But he couldn't make himself move.

He leaned back against the tree, pressed the palms of his hands against it, could feel how old it was by the roughness of the cracked bark. The night was so fucking clear. Looking up, to his left, he could see the Big Dipper. He followed the pointers to the North Star, the way toward Toledo and Detroit, but locations had left him, and there was no Toledo and no Detroit, nothing to connect him to anything.

His bike was at the front of the house, his *girl's* bike. What if it was gone, but no, there it was. "Mason? What are you *doing?*"

Mason and Jessie had arrived at his bike at the same moment. He could see her clearly. Black hair, brilliant eyes, moonlight cold. She'd asked him a question. He should be able to answer it but he didn't have the answer. "Going home" would have been easy but it would have been a lie.

"Oh, Mason," she said, "you're so stoned."

"No," he said. "I don't feel anything. It must not work on me."

She laughed. "For Christ's sake, man, you're higher than a Sputnik."

When he didn't say anything, she said, "I'll drive you home."

Mason did not completely trust anybody. Not even his sister, certainly not his mother, not his crazy roommate, not any of his high school friends, not sugar-coated Lorianne, but he trusted Jessie Collier. Why should that be?

The fuzzy purr of the unwinding campus, Jessie's boxy little station wagon absolutely still, and the streets moving by, quiet clear night in Merida, Ohio, had he been asleep? She'd just said something. What was it? "Just stay on Jefferson," he told her, that's what had been fuzzed away in his brain, waiting for him to say it. "I'll tell you where to turn."

God, what an exquisite profile she had. "Mason," she said, "what's with the makeup?"

"I don't know."

"Don't give me that hillbilly bullshit. Of course you know. You won the Freddy T."

He couldn't find a word.

"What do you think?" she said, staring straight ahead through the windshield. "We're a bunch of sophisticated Bohemians and you can do anything? Well, this ain't Paris, buddy."

"Yeah, I know that."

"Do you? I want to tell you something. This is small-town America, the *heart* of small-town America, and you're headed for trouble. I was talking to Sandra, one of our grad students, and . . . Okay, when you came in, she said, 'Oh, my goodness, is that a boy or a girl?' It really was hard . . . From all the way across the room it really *was* hard to tell. Unless somebody knew you. I don't know what kind of game . . . or what you're trying to prove . . . I don't know, Mason, there's places in New York where they would appreciate that stuff, but not here, for Christ's sake. Watch yourself. If you keep going around like that, some asshole's going to beat the crap out of you. Are you listening to me or am I just talking to myself?"

"No, you're not just talking to yourself. Yeah, I am listening to you. To tell you the truth, I've had kind of similar thoughts—"

"And another thing. Lorianne. She's married, married, married. She may not want to be, but she is. *Married.* Got that? Don't fool around with her. Not only is she married, but the situation's messy. I mean dangerous. I mean it. *Dangerous.* Did you hear me?"

"Yeah, I hear you." He hadn't needed Jessie to tell him that Lorianne was dangerous.

He showed her where to turn off, down the alley behind his building, and he'd never felt more like an ignorant hoopie. He didn't understand a fucking thing. Jessie pulled over by the fence, jumped out of her little station wagon, flicked his bike out of the back, easy, like it was a toy. He took it from her, stood there holding the handle bars. He loved that bike. "I heard everything you said," he told her. She must have been waiting for something, waiting for him to go inside. "Jessie," he said. "Jessie, I have such a terrible crush on you."

"Oh, for Christ's sake," she said, laughing. She bent and kissed him lightly on the forehead. "I think you're cute too but that's neither here nor there. Okay, Mason, listen to me. At the risk of sounding like your mother, I'm going to sound like your mother. I'm going to tell you exactly what to do and you're going to do it. Agreed?"

"Yeah. Sure. Agreed."

"Go inside and get in bed and stay there."

5.

The day was half over. Mason was glad the girl grads were gone so he could sit on their porch, drinking coffee and smoking cigarettes like some dismal loser in a country tune. At least he was getting some reading done. He should be over at the library getting more books but just couldn't make himself get up off the glider and go there. Jesus, that marijuana shit was like being on another planet, Jessie had been right, he'd been higher than a kite the night before and he hadn't even known it. Then he saw Eilum's Buick drift by on the street right there in front of his nose, slow and easy as molasses. Eilum didn't look at him but shoved one big hand out the car window and gave him the finger. Mason couldn't remember when he'd ever been so happy to see somebody.

He jumped up and ran around to the back of the house to where Eilum had parked in the alley. "Jesus Christ, man," Eilum yelled at him, "what the fuck's going on around here anyway? Could it be another beautiful summer afternoon in this cosmopolitan center of feverish intellectual activity located in the heart of the great state of Ohio where nothing the fuck ever happens?"

"I think you got it, buddy."

Eilum was in full crank, banged open the door to the passenger's side. "Yeah, well shit. Don't just stand there, fuckface, give me

69

a hand." Cookie tins, paper bags, bowls with waxed paper floating on the top. "Country ham, potato salad, coleslaw, fresh tomatoes, the works, yeah, from my grandma, even half an apple pie, you'll love it. What the fuck's with your hair, man, it's longer than my sister's."

"Exploring my cultural heritage."

"Yeah? Was there many feeble minded in your family? Hey, buddy, look what I got here." Eilum was waving a metal can at him.

"What's that?"

"That's for me to know and you to find out. You'll love it."

T. Davis Eilum. Six foot two and built like a linebacker. Dark brown hair a scraggly mess, got it cut when he remembered, and brushed it never. Bulbous nose, thick lips, insinuating grin like he knew all about some shady plot and you were in on it too. Large shiny blue eyes that seemed to have something wrong with them, eventually you figured out that the thing that was wrong with them was that Eilum never made eye contact. It wasn't that he didn't do it much like people who are shy, it was that he *never* did it, when he was talking to you, he was always addressing somebody much taller than you were, somebody standing a few feet off to your right. They met in the men's dorm their first winter at Merida, not a good time for Mason, he'd just jumped out in front of the semi.

It was sometime after four in the morning. Mason had an eight-thirty the next day but couldn't sleep, not a hope in hell, had been laying there in bed listening to his roommates snore, feeling the ugly sore burn on his knees and elbows, the throb in his wrist where it had been sprained, the doctor had put a splint on it and it itched. He'd been trying to come up with some plan to improve his life but he couldn't think of a thing except for changing his name. *Eddie* Macquarie was the useless little fucked up candy-ass who'd made the jump, but the guy who'd survived it had to be *Mason* Macquarie. Lots of reasons. It was his middle name, and his mother's maiden name, and it had a good ring to it, lots of good associations. He'd grown up at *Mason's* Landing, and then there was *Mason* County in West Virginia, and the *Mason*-Dixon line, and moonshiners were supposed to sell their products in *Mason* jars, and there was that secret society called the *Masons*, and they'd put that weird-ass eye in the pyramid on the one dollar bill, and he'd always admired them for that, and then there was Grandpa *Mason* who'd said, "Hell, when I was a kid, lots of little boys wore dresses till they went to school and nobody thought a thing of it."

He got up, quiet, pulled on jeans and boots and his heavy winter coat, and stepped out into the hall. You could see from one end of the hall to the other the whole length of the building, at night it was like something out of an Alfred Hitchcock movie, and standing down at the far end of the hall was another boy, just standing there. When he saw Mason, he started walking toward him, and Eddie would have gone back in his room, but Mason thought what the fuck. They met halfway down the hall, and the boy, good Lord he was huge, stuck out his hand, stared off somewhere over Mason's right shoulder, and said, "Name's Eilum."

"Mason," Mason said. It was the first time he'd used that name. They went outside together and walked around on the cold deserted slushy streets of the campus and smoked cigarettes. Mason couldn't remember what they'd talked about but he did remember that neither of them asked the other what he'd been doing up at four in the morning. Next year the two weirdos got a room together, and the year after that they were juniors so they could live off campus and they got this dirt-cheap basement apartment. Eilum never talked about his family just the way that Mason never talked about his. They both lived in Cincinnati and they'd hitch-hiked there and back several times together but they'd never visited each other's homes and, without either of them having to say it, it was understood that they never would. Mason knew Eilum pretty well by now, well enough to know that there were things about him he'd never know.

Holy Lord Jesus in sweet shiny heaven, the whole world was turning weird-ass yellow. Eilum's voice was boomy like he was talking from the inside of a huge stone something-or-other, fuck. They were passing back and forth that metal can and a hunk of old rag, toweling it was, yeah, like a wash rag. Holding that up to their noses and breathing deep, whew. Mason didn't have a clue where Eilum might have got that can of chloroform.

"Am I going to vote?" Eilum was saying. Mason had asked him that awhile back, something on the order of a hundred and forty-seven light years ago. It had seemed like a sensible question at the time.

"*Am I going to vote?* Okay, Mase, let me tell you something. In 1908 on a fine summer's evening the entire population of Scottsburg, Ohio, looked up and saw a girl on a bicycle, one of those old-fashioned kind with the big front wheel, ride right across the sky in between the clouds. Some mirage or some fucking thing but nobody's ever been able to explain it. The whole fucking town saw her. You got that? That's just for starters. We're not even getting to the rains of sardines yet, coming down on towns hundreds of miles from the ocean. Or the frogs. Rains of frogs. Or various flying objects. Lights like headlights or saucer-shaped things. Lots of saucer-shaped things. Phosphorescent owls. Hoop snakes, fireballs, things that ain't supposed to be. Everybody's lying to us all the time, Mason, trying to tell us not to worry, they got it all covered. Well, hell, man, they got nothing covered. We got a whole fuckload of shit to worry about."

Mason passed the can back. Eilum took it, poured more chloroform onto the wash rag, held it to his nose and mouth. He pushed the can back to Mason.

"Now let's move on to the US Air Force," Eilum said. "Hundreds of sightings, I swear to God, hundreds. Are they reporting them to the American people? Are you kidding? Might create a panic. Yeah, right. Knowing that we're in contact with intelligences far superior to ours, that we have been in contact with them for fucking *years.* Sure as hell don't want the American people to know that, do we?"

Mason automatically poured more chloroform onto the rag and breathed it in. The world was getting spinny, kind of. "The most important event since man first crawled out of the slime," Eilum was saying, boomy, "the most important event in the entire history of the human race, but some real powerful people, the shadow boys, they don't want the American people to know dickshit. Okay, JFK was right on the edge of blowing the whole fucking mess wide open, so they had to eliminate him, right? Yeah, got to shut that fucker up. And they want me to vote for president? They want *me to vote for president?* Well, fuck them, fuck every one of them. Barry Goldwater can go fuck himself. Lyndon Johnson can go fuck himself. The entire government in Washington, DC, can go fuck itself. And so can you, fuckface."

"Eilum, I'm gonna pass."

"Shit, man. Don't pass. I told you. Stop. Just before you're gonna pass. Take it right to the fucking edge and stop."

"City morgue," Eilum yelled into the telephone. He'd grabbed it up before Mason had a chance to say, "Don't answer it."

"Ha, ha, yeah, Mrs. Macquarie, yeah, you've got the right number. Yeah, it's me, Eilum. Just having us a little fun. Yeah, he's right here." Eilum shoved the phone at Mason. "It's your mother."

Oh Jesus goddamn. The shape and texture of the phone felt weird in Mason's hand. "Mom?"

"Eddie? *Eddie!* Your dad was sure you'd call him today. He's been waiting around all day. It's Father's Day, did you forget? It's not fair. Are you going to call him? He's so sad. It's just *not fair* what you're doing."

"What? What? What?" Doing? Whacked out of his fucking gourd, that's what he was doing, poisonous sun through the slit windows, everything too fucking *yellow*, teary sing-song in his ear, he could understand the words but couldn't attach them to anything. Hadn't called, hadn't called, *hadn't called*, not once. Not even once. Even on Father's Day. How did he think his dad felt? It was cruel. Poor old guy, he works so hard. And Irene. Your poor sister. She's so worried about you.

Eilum had piled up the table with all that food, was slicing off huge hunks of ham, gobbling them down with heaping forkfuls of potato salad, smacking his lips, cutting off more ham, staring off into the corner of the room, sweat running down his forehead. Mason was never going to eat anything ever again in his entire life. "Mom! He knocked me down and kicked me." Did he give a shit if Eilum heard that? No, he did not give a shit.

"Eddie? What are you talking about? He didn't do anything like that."

"*What?* Yeah, he did. You saw it. You were right there."

"Why do you make up these stories? You keep making up stories like that, you're gonna lose all your friends. Nobody's ever gonna believe you. Eddie? Nobody likes a liar."

"Mom? I went to the goddamn doctor, okay? He examined me. I had a cracked rib."

"Don't swear. Are you going around telling people that foolishness? Is that what you're telling people now? Up there at the college, living the life of Riley and us paying for it. Do you expect us to keep paying—"

"*Mom!* Carrying eighteen hours, getting straight As, and picking up any kind of crappy work I can get. That's the life of Riley? And I get a scholarship every damned year."

"How much does that pay for? Your tuition, that's about it."

"That's not true."

"And you think you can just take the summer off and lay around—"

"Hey! This is the first summer I haven't had a job since I was sixteen. You and Irene were egging me on. Work on your thesis, you said. Get your education. That's what you've been telling me my whole life. Your education's the most important—"

"Oh Lord, Eddie, don't be so selfish. We never minded helping you, but how do you think we feel when you're going around telling lies about us?"

Fuck, Mason thought. Could he live on the Freddy T? It was one of the big undergrad scholarships but was it big enough to live on? His rent was paid through August so that was taken care of, but how much was left from the hundred? Jesus. Could he make it to September? "I don't need your money," he said.

"Don't be like that. If you'd just call your dad and wish him a happy Father's Day and apologize . . ."

"*Apologize?* Holy Jesus, Mom, he knocked me down and kicked me."

"No, he didn't. You just stop that. You just stop that right now, Eddie Macquarie. I don't want to hear any more of that foolishness. You know how your dad is, all you had to do was come home with a haircut. Was that too much to ask? After everything he's done for you?"

"Hey. Mom. Somebody's knocking on my door. Gotta go, call you later."

Outside the sun was enormous, falling out of the sky, where had the day gone? Mason didn't want to think about his goddamn parents, maybe if he didn't think about them, they would cease to exist. Both he and Eilum had passed. Eilum had simply rolled off the kitchen chair and onto the floor, snoring like a buzz saw. Mason at least had made it to bed, on his feet now, head stuffed with ripped-up cardboard, mouth sucking an ant hill. Maybe he should try to eat something.

"I love the summer," Eilum was proclaiming, grinning at it, "days so fucking long." They seemed to be walking toward Eilum's car. That was fine with Mason, anywhere that was not their rattrap apartment was fine with Mason.

Summer but Eilum still wearing his slide rule, yeah, because it was his badge. Eilum wore that slide rule on his belt so everybody would know at a glance that he was an engineer and therefore dangerous. He attracted other engineers because they thought he was wonderfully nuts. They drank hard in the grand old engineer tradition and wandered around the campus singing their grand old song that had been around since Genesis:

We are, we are, we are, we are, we are the engineers.
We can, we can, we can, we can, demolish forty beers.
Drink up, drink up, drink up, drink up and come along with us.
Cause we don't give a damn for any old man who don't give a
damn for us.

Any course that had math in it, Eilum got an A in it, any course that didn't, he didn't, and that meant it would take him a year longer to get his engineering degree than it took most guys. In addition to his uncanny aptitude for math, God had given Eilum hands that all he had to do was close them into fists and they became objects perfectly designed for punching human heads. Eilum's old man had sent him to the gym to work out with the pro, hoping it would calm

IN THE DEFENSE OF LIBERTY

Eilum down some. It didn't, but it gave Eilum a fast sneaky left and a thunderous right that could deck anything short of a buffalo. Eilum was the king of the sucker punch, and three times Mason had seen fraternity boys go down in mid-laugh. Maybe because he was so a hundred percent dumbass all-American male, Eilum was of the it-takes-all-kinds persuasion, well, except for fraternity boys, he hated those fuckers, but he never seemed to mind the peculiarities of his considerably less than a hundred percent male roommate.

Eilum always said that if he didn't make it as an engineer, he was going to become a Holiness preacher, claimed that when he was a little kid, he used to go to meeting with the Jesus Jumpers, "and you better believe I jumped with the best of them." Eilum could do a hillbilly act more extreme than anything Mason ever tried. If somebody was making a movie about moonshiners and revenuers with phony characters right out of *Li'l Abner*, Eilum would get cast for it in two seconds flat. Where exactly Eilum was supposed to come from was kind of vague, but somewhere down where the Hatfields and the McCoys had fought it out, down where Sid Hatfield had blown away the Baldwin-Felts detectives in the mine wars. Eilum even let it drop that he might be distantly related to old Two-gun Sid. But that didn't seem to go with the two, or was it *three*, fancy-ass boy's schools that Eilum claimed to have been expelled from. It had taken Mason a while to understand that Eilum's shifty stories weren't meant to be history. Not exactly lies either, they were more like legends, and that meant that there was no need for them to sit still and behave themselves.

"Marahoogie, huh?" Eilum was saying. "Yeah, heard there was some of that shit coming onto campus. Having never tried it myself, I cannot attest to its effects. But there's one thing I can attest to, that cute little wife of Henry's is hot to trot. From the sound of it the lady checked you out, and you rang her bell but good. Yep, that sounds like it."

After his good long snooze on chloroform, Eilum was doing just fine but Mason sure as hell wasn't. They were drifting along in Eilum's Buick, oozing forward on idle, Eilum not steering at all, reclining back in the seat, having himself a smoke and working on a quart of Bavarian. Mason was sucking down a graham cracker milkshake they'd picked up at the soda fountain at Heike Lewis. It was the only thing he could imagine putting in his stomach.

"Yeah, Mase, the marahoogie probably helped it along but there's a certain kind of girl that prefers the artistic type."

"Artistic? I'm a history major, for fuck's sake."

"Yeah, but you look artistic, all that hair, Jesus, and you act artistic. You take a girl that likes the artistic type, she wouldn't look at a colossal dickhead like me for half a second, wouldn't even waste my time on a girl like that, get me nowhere fast, so that's where you enter the picture. You see, Mase, we're in the realm of female psychology here, and believe me, buddy, that's mysterious, then you throw in the marahoogie, it gets even more mysterious, but there's one thing here clear as a bell, buddy, and that's old Henry must not be sticking it to her regular. These young moms, you know, get accustomed to it regular, and then if they don't get it, they start humping chair legs."

Given that nobody was steering it, the Buick had drifted across a sidewalk and was on its way onto somebody's lawn. "Jesus Christ, Eilum."

"Aw, hell, man." He passed the quart to Mason, grabbed the wheel, slammed her down into first, dug out of there raw and fast, ramming her up into second, throwing up dirt and grass, on the street in third and stomped her good, over sixty and still digging for it. "Sweet Jesus," he exclaimed as though staggered by these recent events, "how the world goes by."

They were burning across campus at ninety now, luckily not another car to be seen. Without any warning Eilum pulled a hard left and slid them sideways onto the foot of Fraternity Row. "Ha!" He killed the engine, rolled out of the car, grinned at the sky and stretched. "Hey, man, what do you say we have us a little stroll on this fine summer's evening?"

Mason got out. He didn't know what else to do. He couldn't just sit there, could he? The sun was still high enough to pour huge hot light down the hill, making all those fancy-ass fraternity houses glow like they were in a set for a Technicolor movie. He could see a cluster of boys in the distance emerging from the Sigma-something-or-other house. Walking down the hill now, four of them, young, undergrads, oh so clean, crisp summer shirts, loafers and pressed chinos, sheared hair, oh man, trouble. Eilum was headed up the hill straight for them. Sucking up the last of his milkshake, Mason trailed along behind.

For a moment it looked like Eilum was just going to let them go by, but no. As soon as they came abreast of him, he sank into an orangutan crouch and hollered at the nearest one, "Hey! Buddy! It's in your ear!"

The fraternity boys froze, dumbfounded. "Fuck you, man" one of them yelled and Eilum launched a lightning right in his direction. Even though the punch was strictly for fun, landed on the empty air a good foot short of the target, the boy flinched and jumped back. Eilum hocked out a good big laugh and fell into a boxer's stance like Cassius Clay warming up, bouncing on the balls of his feet, throwing blurs of punches. The boys darted away sideways, off the sidewalk, took off down the hill.

Eilum straightened up, let his hands fall to his sides. "Well shit," he said, "I invited them nicely but they don't want to go. Can't say as I blame them. Too nice an evening to be duking it out with some ridiculous asshole. Come on, Mase, let's see what we can see."

He strolled on up the hill, Mason following.

Not another boy on Fraternity Row, deserted just the way it should be in the summer, thank God. Maybe the fun and games were over for the night, wouldn't that be a treat?

"Sheriff and high police coming after me," Eilum was singing to himself, "coming after me, Lord, coming after me. Ah, what's this?" A shiny new looking frog-green Triumph with the top down. "Hey, check her out, buddy. An honest-to-God British fucking sports car."

Eilum ran his fingers over the beautifully waxed hood. "New York plates," he said. "Now what can we deduce from that, Mase? Okay, there's this asshole living in the fair state of New York and when he reaches in his jeans, what's he find? Gold, that's what. Then one day as the loveliness of summer advances on him, he thinks, well, shit, I'm feeling like having a run in my beautifully engineered li'l green machine, yeah so maybe I'll motivate on out into the great fucking state of Ohio."

Eilum opened the door to the driver's side, checked the ignition, felt around on the floor. "Okay. Well, he may be a fool but he's not an utter fool. If he'd left us the keys, we woulda had us a little ride."

Wearing a smug and greasy grin, addressing an invisible man seven feet tall standing well off to Mason's right, he said, "What do you think, buddy? Should I hot-wire the son of a bitch?"

Mason didn't reply. "Naw," Eilum said, "too much trouble." He unzipped his fly and hauled out his dick. Like everything else about him, it was huge but it was also oddly particolored like a piebald horse. He let loose a powerful stream of piss into the Triumph. Mason knew from long experience that it was pointless to say a word.

Eilum thoroughly soaked the driver's seat then redirected the flow to make sure the passenger's side got its fair share. Holy Jesus, he must have a bladder the size of a basketball. Eventually he got done, shook his dick a couple times, folded it back inside his pants and zipped himself up. There was so much piss in the car it was dribbling out the open door and onto the road. Eilum gently shut the door. "Ah," he said, "the pause that refreshes."

"**Everybody knows** that a married woman's got the inalienable right to get dicked, and if her husband ain't banging her, well then she's got to get it somewhere, right? Only stands to reason." Wobbling across both lanes, Eilum was blazing the Buick down the road at over a hundred. Mason was braced in the seat, hanging on for dear life. The only destination that he knew of on this particular road was Henry's house. "Eilum? Jesus. Where the fuck you going?"

"Old Henry's probably a hand-job artist, don't you think? Sure he is. Got that shifty sweaty look to him, don't he? Pulling his pud like your average loony-bin cretin. So what's his juicy little wife supposed to do? Well, she's out reciting poetry to artsy boys behind trees. You see my logic here, Mase?"

"Eilum! Fuck you, man. What are you doing?"

Eilum was aimed straight for Henry's house. Stomped the brake down hard and sudden, slammed Mason forward in the seat, screamed them to a dead stop just a few feet short of Henry's front steps. "Jesus fuck, man! What the fuck—"

"Got to check things out, don't you think? Get us a little of that empirical evidence—"

"Fuck you, man, this is not funny."

"No, no, no, man. No sweat. Just gonna see what's what."

"Come on, Eilum. Please. Just— I got the joke, okay? I really got it. Now can we please just get the fuck out of here?"

"Ah, buddy, maybe you got the joke but you still ain't got the full picture." Eilum pointed. Lorianne was bounding down the steps to see what on earth had been making all that goddamn racket in her front yard.

"Let me tell you something, Mase," Eilum said, "and this is the straight scoop. In this sorry life, filled as it is with sorrows, uncertainties, and countless unpredictable woes, there's only one thing that's certain, and that's that you should never pass up a fuck. You know why? Because every time you pass up a fuck, then you're one fuck behind."

Lorianne was looking in the car window. "Mason Macquarie," she said.

He got out of the car, slammed the door hard. "Hey. Lorianne. I'm sorry. Jesus. I'm really sorry. It's just my crazy roommate—"

What the fuck was Eilum doing now? He was digging out of there, laying rubber. He was blazing down the road to the west. Then he screamed through a tight U-turn so he was aimed back toward campus. Digging for his top end, he blasted past them trailing a high-pitched cackle like a Doppler effect. "You son of a bitch!" Mason yelled after him.

Lorianne was laughing like this was the funniest thing she'd ever seen. "Mason, Mason, Mason, oh my goodness."

No, she didn't always wear blue, tonight, red and white gingham, big bold checks. Her hair usually so neat, brushed shiny and held back with a band, tonight hanging loose and tangly, some of it down her back, some of it over her shoulders, Jesus, she had a lot of hair. Barefoot. She painted her toenails pink too. She didn't look right, he couldn't say how, it was more than just her hair. He didn't know what to think. He couldn't think straight. "I didn't mean to be here—" What the hell could he possibly mean by that? "My roommate—"

"Shhhh."

What? He was prepared to walk away, start that whole long walk back, but she took both of his hands in hers, smiling her sweet smile, but he could smell the whiskey on her, he didn't like that, and

82

something in her eyes, a pale hard look he'd seen somewhere else. "Come on," she said. "Come in."

He knew it wasn't right but he allowed himself to be led up the stairs. "Look who's here!"

"Hey," from Carl, "if it ain't the pretty boy." Fuck, was that his new nickname now?

Jessie, plumb-bob straight, standing near the open front doorway, arms folded like she was watching over everything, and Mason wasn't ready for how hard it hit him, seeing her. "Your timing's impeccable," she said. He felt her anger like something physical, like ice water thrown over him. I'm sorry, he thought, sorry sorry sorry.

Lorianne led him into the living room and then let go of his hand like she was just depositing him there. Henry was sprawled in his usual spot in front of the hi-fi. "Thanks a whole bunch, Lorianne." His voice didn't sound right.

"Oh, you think I just made him appear? Waved my magic wand? Poof? No, he just dropped in 'cause he likes us."

Henry's place was always so neat but tonight utter chaos, couple of open cases of Stroh's, empty bottles all over the damn place, piled up ashtrays, the air reeking with smoke, blue with it, dirty dishes everywhere, shot glasses, they must have killed that fifth of Evil Williams, it was laying on its side, and there was a new fifth of Four Roses, cracked open and going. Jesus, and it wasn't even full dark yet.

"So honey," Lorianne was addressing Henry, "aren't we running an intellectual salon here? People can just drop in, right? To test out their brilliant ideas? We're just delighted to see Mason, aren't we?"

Henry was staring at her but he didn't answer. Jazz going, that kind called be-bop? Flurry of notes from somebody's trumpet. "The best minds of our generation, right?" she was saying, "the cutting edge artists, the avant garde. Gonna piss off the bourgeoisie, aren't we, dear, with our outrageous ways? Just like Paris between the wars. Hemingway's gonna drop in any minute now."

Something wrong with Henry, his eyes shooting some secret message to Lorianne, not a nice message, then he looked away at nothing, his face scrunched up. He was just packed into his big chair, tense, not moving, his jaw working.

Carl slid on up to his feet, popped the cap off a beer, and offered it. Mason didn't want it but he knew he had to take it. "Thanks. Who's playing? That's a great sound."

"The Diz," Carl said.

"With the two Sonnys," Henry said.

Mason nodded like those names meant something to him.

"Have something to eat," Carl said. "There's plenty."

Yeah, there sure was. Eilum should have stuck around, he would have loved this spread. Two card tables set up in the living room, the cheap kind with the cardboard tops, and both of them just heaped. Hoagie buns, lots of them, and ham, turkey, salami, pepper loaf, pepperoni, cheddar cheese and Swiss, canned corned beef, a couple of cans of sardines, one of them dribbling oil all over the table, hard-boiled eggs, chopped up lettuce and tomato, diced onions, green olives and black ones, ketchup, hot German mustard, Miracle Whip, Cheez Whiz, sweet pickles and dills, good Christ enough food for a dozen more people, and nobody had put a lid back on a damned thing, all of it just sitting out there in the heat, drawing flies. "Thanks," Mason said, "yeah." He pretended to be studying the food.

"Okay, honey," Lorianne said, "so maybe it's goose and gander time. You had your sweet little coeds here to visit, right? And I was the perfect little hostess, wasn't I? Aren't I always the perfect little hostess? Okay, so now it's my turn. What if I want to sleep with Mason?"

Henry's head jerked up. "Jesus, Lorianne, that's not funny. I've just about had it with your shit."

"Yeah? Well, the feeling's mutual."

"Stop it. You're just going to embarrass yourself. Yeah, you're going to hate yourself tomorrow. Clean up your act. Lay off the sauce. Make some coffee. Put some shoes on, for Christ's sake."

"*Shoes?* Oh, dear Lord in heaven, that's the first thing that pops into your little pea brain?" She exaggerated her accent. "Aw, come on, sweetheart, you know I didn't own a pair of shoes till I was out of hah school. Us ignorant hoopies are like that. Hard yaller callous on our feet an inch thick."

The jazz on the hi-fi had taken control of the room now, nobody talking. Mason had frozen solid as a brickbat. Fuck these people.

Suddenly Carl was attempting to sing. "The first time I seen little Maggie, she was standing by the still house door . . ."

Thank God for Carl trying to be funny. "Shoes and stockings in her hand," he was singing, "little bare feet on the floor."

"Yeah?" Lorianne fired right back at him, "and the *last* time you seen her, she was setting on the banks of the sea."

Carl gave her a good laugh, that's the way he liked things to go, you deciphered his stupid in-jokes instantly and you came right back at him instantly and flipped him one better. Even Henry had to smile at that. Maybe it was all going to be okay. "Hoopie girl speaks," Carl said.

"You're goddamn right, hoopie girl speaks. Yeah, us hoopies, living in our shacks built out of road signs way somewhere out back of the ridge, plunking on our banjos, speaking Chaucer's English, drinking white moon, dodging revenuers, shooting strangers, screwing our relatives, sleeping with a passel of coonhounds, living on pan-fried squirrel and dandelion greens, maybe a possum thrown in every once in a while just for the sake of variety."

She'd got both Henry and Carl laughing with that one. Maybe Mason was the only one who could see how icy cold furious she was.

"Fuck you guys," she said then, her voice different, "from the great metropolis. New York, London, Rome, Paris, none of them can live up to Canton, Ohio, right? Well, you guys can just go fuck yourselves," and she spun around directly toward Henry. "Who do you think you are to think you're better than me? I'm sick of you treating me like dirt. Bringing your little coeds in here. Slapping me around every time you feel like it."

"Jesus," Henry said, shocked, addressing all of them, "I never touched her."

"Oh? Really? You never touched me so it would show."

Jessie all of a sudden was across the room. She pushed Mason hard. "Get the fuck out of here."

6.

Through the door like a shot, hitting it on down the road, Mason didn't stop running till he got a stitch in his side. Who the fuck were these people? What the fuck was he doing with them? He bent over, hands on his knees, trying to catch his breath, straightened up, turned to look back west. The sun had dropped out of the picture and all that was left was a slice of blood-red light. Then another dire thought came sailing up out of nowhere, holy fucking Christ on his birthday he'd tried to kill himself. That was just a week ago. What was he trying to do, forget it ever happened?

Maybe he should go see Dr. Elspeth Fairfield MD and tell her the whole goddamn story. No, he couldn't do that, she'd put him in the university hospital. She'd asked him if there was anyone he felt particularly attached to and he'd sat there in her office thinking about it and then what? He'd just walked out of there and forgot all about it? That was damned near the way he lived his whole damned life, just walking out of places and forgetting all about it. Well defended? That was a fucking joke. *What if I want to sleep with Mason?* What was he supposed to do with that, forget all about it? *Get the fuck out of here.* Yeah, asshole, you do that. And then just keep on moving.

He was walking on the left side of the road like he'd been taught, because you want oncoming traffic to be aimed at you, not coming from behind you, and he was so used to riding out here he'd forgot how far it was, going to take him forever. No street lights but there was a big fat moon, not quite full yet but getting there, so it wasn't too dark. He couldn't tell if the stitch in his side was from running or from his rib, but it was still hurting even after he got his breath back, so it was probably his rib. Something else he hadn't seen clear before now, just how desperate he'd been to drop in on his old TAs like that, how pitiful that was. What was he doing, going from pillar to post trying to find somebody who'd talk to him? Used to be there was people he was particularly attached to. He'd been so happy to see Eilum and look where that had got him. Shit, he felt alone.

He heard a car coming from behind him. Something told him to get out of sight so he jumped behind some bushes and crouched down. Here was Henry's old rusting out gray Dodge coming at a pretty good clip. Went by, and Mason saw that Henry had his trunk crammed full of boxes, the lid tied down with a piece of rope, and right behind him was Carl in his ridiculous '50s Chevy with the fins. They were headed toward campus. Did Mason give a shit? He did not give a shit. He kept on walking.

Just when he was coming on to streetlights, he heard another car behind him. He didn't figure it was anybody he knew, didn't bother to look, was surprised when Jessie's boxy little Studebaker pulled up next to him. "Get in," she said.

Staring straight through the windshield, holding the wheel tight with both hands, she was so pissed off at him he could feel it like an electrical charge coming off her. Was this what fate had planned for him now, to keep riding around with Jessie in her car while she was pissed off at him? "It wasn't my idea to go out there," he said. "My roommate just dumped me out there. It was a joke."

"Some joke."

"I wasn't even gonna come in the house except that Lorianne came out and saw me. She dragged me in there."

Still she didn't say anything. "I didn't want to be there," he said. "I just wanted to get the hell out of there."

Maybe she was giving him the silent treatment. Maybe she was going to drive him home, and then he was going to get out, and then she was going to drive away, and that would be the end of that, his TA from last fall, the best TA he'd ever had. It felt so hopeless he could sink down into it and drown.

"Mason? I was one of the people who recommended you for the Freddy T."

"Yeah? I figured you were. Thanks."

"There were other candidates who were just as good as you."

"Yeah? I figured there were."

"I made a big pitch for you, so I feel responsible . . . well, partially responsible. You've got a great academic career ahead of you if you want it. But . . . Look, what's going on between Henry and Lorianne is none of your business. They've split up. *Maybe* they have. He's left her. *Maybe* he has. This isn't the first time they've gone through this little charade. Who knows what they're doing, but whatever it is, it's really none of your goddamned business. Am I getting through to you?"

"Oh, yeah, you're definitely getting through."

"Even if they've split up, that doesn't mean that Lorianne's fair game now."

"I don't think she's fair game."

"What she said about wanting to sleep with you? She just said that to get Henry's goat and she got it. It was not an invitation."

"I didn't think it was an invitation."

"She'd had a couple of drinks but she was nowhere near as drunk as she was playing it. If she was really plastered, I wouldn't have left her there alone with Tammy."

"I don't know, if it's a . . . To tell you the truth, she scared me half to death. I'm not going out there again. Swear to God."

"I'm delighted to hear that."

She pulled up across the street from his place. Eilum's Buick wasn't there so that meant he was off somewhere doing more crazy-ass shit. Mason was glad he wasn't there. Now he had to keep Jessie talking to him. He was desperate to keep her talking to him. What the hell could he possibly use to do that?

"Jessie," he said, "I get your point, I really do. Yeah, it really is none of my business, and that's exactly . . . I mean I get it, okay? But can I . . . ? You know, change the subject? Seeing as you're here, can I ask you something? About, you know, Lucy Stone? Okay? How could she spend her whole life defending the rights of women and then get married? She'd . . . what? Vowed? That she'd call no man master? And then she got married. Why'd she do that?"

Jessie had spun around to look at him but it was dark in the car and he couldn't read her face. Her voice came out sharp and hard. "Maybe because for the first time in her life she wanted to feel normal."

She turned back to the windshield. "Boy, you sure took me by surprise with that one. Where the hell did Lucy Stone come from? But that's a smartass answer I just gave you. It's really difficult . . . Even with tons of primary source material, it's impossible to see all the way into people's hearts. There's always something . . . some core of them you're not going to get. I don't know why she married. Not really. She and Blackwell were trying to redefine marriage so it would be a contract between equals. For two years they wrote letters back and forth about that stuff and it looks like he talked her into it. Maybe she wanted to have a kid. And she had one. That's the normal thing women are supposed to want."

"What about the big fight in the women's movement?"

"For Christ's sake, Mason, do you read *everything*?"

"I wanted to know what your thesis was about."

He knew he'd got her hooked now. "Do you mind if I smoke?" he said.

"Yes, I do mind. I'm allergic to cigarette smoke."

She got out of the car. He didn't know what she was doing but he got out too, and then he figured it out, she'd got out so he could smoke. That was gracious of her. He fired up a Camel.

Looking at her baggy blouse not tucked in and her ballerina flats so old they still had round toes, somebody might think Jessie Collier didn't give a shit how she looked, but they'd be wrong. If you don't give a shit, you don't dress all in black and your blouse isn't perfectly pressed and you sure don't wear your capris just about as tight as you can them get on. "You know what the fight was about, right?" she said.

"Yeah. The Fifteenth Amendment."

"Yes, that was the flash point." She began to pace back and forth just the way she did when she was teaching. "There's always two kinds of people. There's the ones who stand on principle, who absolutely cannot compromise that principle. And then there's the practical types, you know, the ones who tell you that politics is the art of the possible. Well, Susan B. Anthony and Elizabeth Cady Stanton stood on principle. *Everybody* should be enfranchised, so how could you even think about enfranchising Negro men and not enfranchising women? But Lucy was one of the practical types. It's a terrible mistake to separate the two issues, she said, but we've got to support the amendment. Let's get the Negro men enfranchised and then we'll move on to women."

"Yeah, I read about it, the big fight about it. Was she right?"

"Right? Hell, Mason, we're talking about events a hundred years ago."

She stopped pacing, stood there looking at him. "Yes, of course she was right."

"Jessie?" he said, "do you have time to sit and chat awhile?"

A breeze was stirring, nice, enough to ruffle his hair like the air was alive. He'd be sad when he couldn't sit on the girls' porch any more, looking out at the night through the frame made by the branches of that white oak, exactly the kind of old tree you wanted in front of your house, looked like it had been there forever, its roots cracking the sidewalk. The porch had everything a porch ought to have, a glider and a few wicker chairs and a weather-beat table where you could put your coffee, right now it had Jessie's feet on it, bare, she'd kicked off her flats. She had big substantial feet with high arches, looked like feet built to do the job, but she probably had trouble buying shoes.

She was telling him about her roommate Sarah who was working with the civil rights people down in Mississippi, telling him because he'd asked her. "She loves how cooperative every-thing is. She loves how they call the police *the POlices* . . . 'Don't worry about me,' she kept saying, 'nobody's as safe as a white woman in the South,' but *in the very same conversation* she told me that the girls shouldn't wear hoop earrings because the cops could stick their fingers through the hoops and rip them out. That's safe?"

She was lit from the side by the street light. Whoever had styled her hair had given her exactly Audrey Hepburn's pixie, parted on one side like a boy's but little feathery bangs over her forehead. She talked with hands, very expressive, and she didn't need makeup, she had lots of natural color. "If I was a few years younger, I'd be down there too."

"How old *are* you?" The minute he'd said it, he wished he hadn't.

She didn't answer right away and he thought he'd pissed her off. Then she said, "I'm twenty-eight. How old did you think I was?"

Mason knew women well enough to know that even coming from Jessie Collier that was a trick question. "I thought you were younger than that," he said, which was a lie. He'd thought she was thirty or close to it. When he imagined honest-to-God adults, he imagined them thirty.

He couldn't tell if his answer pleased her or not. She wasn't saying anything. A long time ago Mason had learned that if you straight out asked people questions, a lot of the time they'd straight out answer you. "How'd you get interested in history?"

She thought about it. "It was kind of inevitable. My dad's a historian. University of Chicago. Joseph Minotti—"

She let that one hang, looked over at Mason. Then she said, "Collier's my married name. I'm married and divorced but I'd prefer it if people didn't know that."

She was still looking at him like she expected him to say something but he didn't know what to say. He was shocked that she'd been married. He hadn't guessed that about her.

"The dean of Grad Studies wanted to list me as Mrs. Collier but I talked him out of it. It's just . . . you know, nobody's business. Anyhow Dad's written four books but the one everyone remembers is *Hun or Home: Allied Propaganda in the First World War*. Maybe you've read it?"

"Nope. I haven't made it that far into the twentieth century yet."

He'd got a laugh out of her. "Mason, you are funny. You are genuinely funny. You should read it. It's a landmark study. How did *you* get interested in history?"

She'd just turned the tables on him. He wanted to say something else she'd think was funny. "Hell, if I was in my bedroom fighting the Battle of Chancellorsville, I didn't have to be in the kitchen fighting the battle of the Macquaries."

Mason hadn't been planning on bitching about the old man but that's what he was doing and he couldn't make it funny anymore. Telling her all kinds of shit he probably shouldn't be telling her, the old man's short temper, his comings and goings, selling door to door, encyclopedias, dish sets, aluminum siding, any damn thing. He had the gift of the gab, a top notch salesman when he was sober, well liked by people who didn't have to live with him, and all the time Mason was telling Jessie this stuff, he was worrying about Lorianne. Henry slapping her around every time he felt like it. Jesus, he couldn't imagine how anybody could hit Lorianne. The very thought of it hurt him. But lots of guys slapped their wives around and if anybody ought to know that, Mason should.

"Mom always said, 'You know how he is, don't aggravate him,' so I'd grab a book and take off." He started out on Nancy Drew because that's what his sister read and he read them too, until he ran out, and then he found the Civil War and you could never run out of that. "You know, Jessie, you could name damned near any battle and I could sit here right now and talk you all the way through it."

"So your father? He was in the war?"

If they were gonna talk about wars, Mason wanted it to be the Civil War but she was going somewhere else and wasn't about to be sidetracked. "Oh, yeah," he told her. "Army. Fought in Europe. Or did something in Europe. Where exactly, I don't know. He never would talk about it. Took him longer to get home than it did other guys. Some people said he'd been in the VA Hospital but nobody in the family would talk about that either. Maybe he got injured, or had battle fatigue or some damn thing, but he sure as hell had one short fuse."

"A lot of men came back with battle fatigue, a lot more than most people realize. I have an uncle like that. Was he violent?"

Jesus, she was like a dog that can smell a bone buried somewhere. "Violent?" Mason said. "Yeah, you could use that word. Yeah, you could apply that word to him."

Shit, where was this all going? "He kept moving us. It was *his* family, by God, and he was going to take charge of it."

Mason laughed, bitter, remembering some of the places they'd tried to live. "That dingy place above the feed store down at the Landing and then there was an old falling down house in the middle of nowhere halfway to Factor, and Mom didn't even have a car. But eventually he'd go on a bender and pull some bizarre shit and then he'd be gone, whoosh, just vanished. And we'd pack up and move back to the farm. Grandpa hated him. He'd say, 'Your father's never been right since the war. It ain't his fault, but he shouldn't be taking it out on you and your mom. You stay here with us. You're just fine here with us.' Well, I sure wanted to stay on the farm but Mom always believed in new beginnings. 'You should have known him before he went overseas.' She must have said that a million times. 'The nicest man you'd ever want to know.' Then, when I turned fifteen, we made the big move, the one we couldn't get out of, up to Raysburg, to a cheap little hole down on the south end of the Island near the racetrack. 'Lots of riff-raff down here,' Mom used to say."

Mason was in his sophomore year at Raysburg High and Irene in her first year at Raysburg College, and Mason came home from school one day and found Mom laying on the floor. He did what he'd seen them do in the movies, threw water on her, and that brought her around but she couldn't get up. Irene came home and they helped her onto the couch. Her mouth was all swolled up and she had a ringing in her ears and her head hurt terrible but she couldn't see a doctor, they had nothing to pay him with. They kept the household money in a Crisco can in the cupboard and the old man had taken it all, he hadn't even left the change. They had some things in the house, flour and canned goods, but not much else. Mom had been working as a waitress at a little diner down near Raysburg Steel, she couldn't work, Irene took some of her shifts, early morning shifts, and then went on out to the college on the bus. She was just beat to shit all the time, falling asleep on her feet. Mason got on as a stock boy at Kennaghan's Hardware, working after school, getting paid under the table eighty-five cents an hour. There was no sign of the old man, nary tail nor whisker.

Irene dropped out of college, said she'd go back later but never did, got on at Carleton Glass as a file clerk, bought an old Packard on the installment plan. Mason could drive it when she didn't need it. Mason made it through his sophomore year and got a summer job washing tractor trailers for Allied Trucking. Eventually Mom got so she could go back to waitressing. So things weren't so bad. They were getting by. Then guess who turns up?

Life's really gonna change this time, by God, a whole new start, he's joined AA, he's found Jesus, and Mason's thinking, seems to me I've heard that song before. But no, the old man's got a real job this time, in the menswear department at Greene & Harris, and that lasted for a while, and just about the time they'd got fooled into thinking that things were going to be okay, he went on a wild-ass bender, a real screamer, and got his sorry ass fired. Oh ho, so there's that whole new start all over again, and this time they're moving to Cincinnati, you know, that golden city of infinite opportunity. Mason had to do his senior year at a new school where he didn't know a soul, he never made a single friend, he thought to hell with you, studied his ass off, nailed the Boards, applied to a bunch of places but Merida offered him a full scholarship, so here he was. "I want to say thank you again for recommending me for the Freddy T," he told her, "and thank you for believing in me. I'm not gonna let you down."

She nodded but didn't say anything. They sat there looking at each other and he didn't know what she was thinking and then the bell in the McKinley Tower started up. Mason counted eleven bongs. The university didn't really need to do that, did they? Keep reminding you what time it was.

"It shouldn't be so goddamned hard for working people to get an education," she said, sudden and angry. "It makes me sick. Hell, it shouldn't be so goddamned hard for working people to *live!* Jesus, you've had a hard life, Mason. I'm sorry. Look, if there's anything . . . Your thesis. If you want to bounce some ideas off of me, or, talk about parts of it, or . . . If you want me to read a draft . . . You know where my carrel is or if I'm not there, call me."

"Thanks, Jessie. I really appreciate that."

She swung her feet off the table, stood straight up and stretched, and he was struck by the full force of it, what a big strong girl she was. She shoved her feet into her ballerina flats and smiled at him and he felt that smile go all the way through him like she'd cut him in half with something warm. Oh God, Jessie, he thought, I could fall in love with you so easy. "How did it get so late?" she said.

What question was he going to ask her next to keep her there? "Fathers?" he said like he was kicking off a topic sentence. "It's ah . . . kind of weird, about . . . you know, *fathers.* They're supposed to be this great thing, I don't know, this great guiding force that helps to shape you, but for a lot of us, they're kind of . . . I don't know, just a washout, or the mysterious vanishing man or . . . you know, just shit. Slapping their kids around and like that."

God, he wasn't doing too well but he had to keep going. "I've met guys who liked their fathers . . . and some who, you know, who seem to think their dad's second only to Jesus, but . . . So . . . all right, there's . . . Seems like you liked your father. That's kind of . . . Did you learn a lot of history from your father?"

Her face changed. He wished he could read her better. "The patriarchy," she said. "That's what you're talking about. Yes, I did learn a lot from my father."

She let herself fall back into the wicker chair. "Dad's an old-time lefty and he always treated me more like a son than a daughter.

I always knew I was supposed to be his heir. It was a kind of a burden, to be honest."

Then she did something he'd never seen her do before, pinched the bridge of her nose and held it, kept her hand there, her eyes shut. After a while she dropped her hand and opened her eyes and looked at him. "I didn't plan to be a historian," she said. "I fought it the whole way."

The Red Scare in academia started in 1949 when the University of Washington fired three professors. That seemed to Mason a peculiar place for Jessie to go when she'd just been talking about herself, but that's where she went. The Association of American Universities said that if you were a member of the Communist Party, that extinguished your right to a university position. Well, back in the '30s everybody had been in the party, everybody in the intelligentsia, and of course that included her dad. But after the Stalin–Hitler pact in '39, he broke with the party, said that anybody who stayed in after that was either badly deluded or a hopeless dunderhead, and he'd said so in print. He'd flirted with Trotskyist positions for a while and then he'd become a democratic socialist. He was known for his vigorous criticism of the Soviet Union. He didn't have anything to worry about, did he?

Jessie's teenage years were miserable. She'd inherited her father's coloring and her mother's height, and she thought that was a terrible combination. She kept getting taller and taller and *taller*. She was an awkward obnoxious girl, too tall, who always got As in everything, always had opinions about everything, and was so used to hanging around with adults that she couldn't relate to kids her own age. It took her forever to make friends but eventually she did. "Four of us. The smart girls. We created a little clique that the other kids recognized and even kind of respected. And mirabile dictu, a couple of boys even started asking me out. Then my father took the Fifth."

"That was what? The height of the Red Scare? McCarthy?"

"Yes. Although it wasn't just McCarthy. There was a whole crew of commie hunters all over the United States, a whole network of them, some of them officials of various kinds, some of them just amateurs, and they'd been going long before McCarthy jumped onto the band wagon. It was like a religion to them. And the biggest commie hunter was the director of the FBI, J. Edgar Hoover, that rotten prick. Now they weren't just going after people who were members of the party, they were looking for people who *used to be* members of the party and if you got called to testify, you were supposed to name names, say who else had been in the party with you. If you didn't name names, that meant you weren't truly repentant. The only way to get out of it was to take the Fifth. You know what that means, don't you?'

Mason laughed. "Where are we? Back in your classroom? Of course I know. The Fifth Amendment prevents you from having to testify against yourself."

"Right you are. Well, my father got called up in front of HUAC and he was not about to rat on his friends so he took the Fifth. It wasn't as though people didn't know what he thought. Any time Dad ever has a thought he writes an article about it. But that didn't matter, if you took the Fifth, everybody assumed you were guilty."

Professors all over the country were falling like leaves. If they were tenured, they had a chance of keeping their jobs, but if they weren't, they were gone. Jessie's dad was tenured, his students loved him, he had a great publication record, and all that saved him, but a lot of people were out to get him. Some idiot from the American Legion wrote a nasty critique of *Hun or Home*, claiming it was un-American. The commie hunters circulated that damned piece everywhere and it definitely put a damper on her dad's career.

Jessie wasn't looking at Mason now, she was staring out between the branches of the big white oak. "I lost all my friends," she said. "I got shunned. One of the girls came right out and told me she was sorry but she simply couldn't be seen with me. The other girls didn't bother, didn't say a word, just turned away or crossed the street to avoid me. The boys who'd been asking me out all of a sudden vanished. That was the end of my senior year in high school. I won every academic award they had to give and I kept walking up onto the stage to get all those awards and nobody in my class would clap for me.

"It affected all of us. Dad used to have people over all the time, visiting scholars, other people from the history department, and they'd have these big jolly debates in the living room, hashing over history and politics, and I used to love those nights. I'd sit there and listen, and then later on when I got older, I'd offer my own opinions and Dad was always so proud of me. Well, those nights were over, and a few people did drop in, a few of his colleagues and old friends from the party, but I wasn't welcome in the living room anymore. They'd sit in a corner talking in these low voices, almost whispering, and it just—"

Mason waited for her to go on but she didn't. He was listening so hard he could hear the crickets and katydids that had been just a low background hum before. He wondered if he should say something to try to get her talking again, but then he thought, no, she'll talk when she's ready.

"My mom was a high school history teacher," she said, "and her principal called her in and suggested that if she took early retirement, it might not be necessary to have the internal investigation the school board was suggesting. She wasn't even fifty. And she'd loved teaching! And my big brother, Joe Junior, must've decided right around that time that if he was living under capitalism, he damned well better be good at it, and he is. He's a wealthy man today but . . . I don't know how to put it, he's lost some important part of himself along the way. My little brother was still in high school and he decided that the one thing that would save him was football. He got injured a half dozen times but he won a big trophy, best all-round something-or-other, and went on to play college ball. Now he's a high school football coach in Fort Wayne, Indiana. God, it all sounds so strange when I tell you about it, and somehow all so mundane and predictable.

"My dad wanted me to go to some prestigious place like Vassar or Bryn Mawr but I wouldn't hear of it. If I went to one of those places, I'd be the girl whose father took the Fifth. I decided that I was going to become anonymous, more than anonymous, that I was going to become Betty Coed, the most all-American girl in all of America, so I went through the university catalogs and picked what I thought was the most Betty Coed place I could find, and that was Penn State. I knew Dad was disappointed in me but he didn't say anything. He'd always let me make my own decisions.

"I can't begin to tell you what it felt like, the atmosphere of that time, it was just this sick feeling of dread all the time. They executed the Rosenbergs the summer after I graduated, and that just—"

She shifted her weight in the chair and looked back at him again, searching his face. He didn't know what she wanted. "It was hell," she said. "It was as though we had become the enemy. I slouched around the house all summer wearing nothing but the same old pair of baggy Bermudas day in, day out. I was scared. I went to sleep scared and I woke up scared. The main thing I can remember from that time is being scared."

Penn State was everything Jessie wanted it to be. Sports was the most important thing on campus and nobody had a serious opinion about anything, certainly not politics. "Betty Coed was supposed to pledge a sorority so I came within a half an inch of doing it, but then I heard a voice inside me, the one that saves me from myself from time to time, and it said, 'Jessie, who the hell are you kidding?'

"I'd decided that I was going to be an English major because that's what nice girls did, but I took the intro course and the New Criticism was all the rage. We were doing close readings and it turned out that I was Joe Minotti's daughter after all. Oh, I thought, I see what this is for! If you restrict yourself to looking at nothing but the text as though it's a document you found in a bottle, you strip away all political context and then you can make up any clever bullshit you want and it won't matter a damn. I thought okay, go with your own grain, major in history. Of course I aced everything. I knew more than most of my professors. But I'd learned by then that I should never let on that I knew more than my professors.

"I was in the student lounge in the history department one day and one of the professors said to me, 'Ah? Miss Minotti? Are you by any chance related to the historian, Joseph Minotti?' Somehow I produced a little laugh and I said, "Oh, that's funny. You're not the first person to ask me that. No, there's no relation. It's a common Italian name.'

"Wherever I was supposed to go that afternoon, I didn't go there. I just walked around campus, around and around and around. I kept thinking, okay, Jessie, now you've sunk just about as low as you can go."

By the time she got there, the huge wave of vets pouring into Penn State on the G.I. Bill had started to abate, although there were still the trailers and the little buildings all over campus that had been brought in to accommodate them, and the guys who'd stuck around for advanced degrees were still there. That's how she met Rick Collier. He was finishing up his PhD and he was her TA, an honorable man because he didn't ask her out until the grades were in. He was six-two, had been a high-school basketball star and his old friends still called him "Dunk." She could wear heels and he was still taller than she was and everybody saw them as the perfect couple. He got his PhD and she got her BA and they got married.

"Okay," she said, "if you were going into American history, you had to pick a safe area. You had to avoid the twentieth century because if you weren't careful, you could say something un-American. It was best to stay well back in the nineteenth century. Rick's PhD was on the Copperhead Movement in Ohio, the Clement Vallandigham affair in particular, and not only did nobody know anything about that but nobody gave a shit, and so it was a perfect thesis topic, and he was a decorated war veteran and that made him even more perfect, and he got hired as an assistant professor at Ohio State, the perfect place for him, and we moved to Columbus. His best friend in the history department was another young professor, Greg. He was working on James Madison and that was even better than safe. If you were working on a Founding Father, that was like yay, America!

"We probably should have waited until Rick got tenure, but everybody was absolutely certain that he'd get it easily, so we took out a mortgage on a little house made of ticky-tacky directly across the street from Greg and Barbara's place. She and I were supposed to be sweet little faculty wives. I tried my best, damn it, and we'd have joint dinner parties in their house or our house. We'd invite other professors from the history department and Barb and I were supposed to sit there with the other faculty wives and smile sweetly and listen to the boys argue but guess who couldn't keep her mouth shut?

"Eventually it became obvious that Rick and I had no business whatsoever being married and once we both understood that, we had a surprisingly amiable split-up. I didn't expect him to support me for the rest of my life and I didn't want any of the furniture or the household goods. All I wanted was the money that my dad had put into our house and he borrowed it and gave it to me. Then he did one of the nicest things anyone has ever done for me. One day, just talking to the sky, I'd said that I wished I had a little station wagon so I could put everything I owned into it and be free to roam. Rick and his friends found that little green Lark for me and did a lot of work on it so it was just like new. Everything I wanted fit into it and I drove back to Chicago and sat down with my dad and said, 'Okay, what do I do now?'

"Dad, being my dad, said, 'Go and get your own damned PhD.'"

"'Where?' I said and he gave me Ev's book on American foreign policy. He'd known Ev for years. They'd been comrades in the party. Ev had read the handwriting on the wall a lot sooner than anybody else had. All the way back in the '40s when dreary little Merida University had been advertising for someone to head their history department, they were astonished and delighted to discover that someone of the caliber of Dr. Everett Braithwaite had applied for the position. So before the anti-commie brigade could get to him, Ev vanished into this backwater—"

"Hiding out in plain sight?"

"That's it exactly. I was looking for a backwater too at that point in my life and Merida seemed like a perfect place for me to go if I wanted peace and quiet and that's exactly what I wanted. Ev seemed like the perfect person for me to study under. He was a brilliant scholar, a revisionist historian like Dad, definitely a lefty, and very very smart. Dad asked me if he should give Ev a call and I said, 'Absolutely not, if I'm going anywhere, I'm going on my own.' With the kind of transcript I had, of course they admitted me to the graduate program. As soon as I arrived on campus, I walked into Ev's office and said, 'I'm deeply honored to meet you, Dr. Braithwaite. I'm Joe Minotti's daughter.' Whether that redeemed me or not, I don't know, but it sure felt good."

Mason waited for her to continue with her story but that seemed to be the end of it. He didn't know what to say. He had to say something. "Thanks for telling me all that," he said. "I really appreciate you telling me all that. I didn't know a lot of that stuff about . . . you know, about the professors, how bad it got."

She didn't say anything. All she was doing was looking at him while they sat there and listened to the crickets and katydids. Then the damn university clock went off again. Neither of them had to count the bongs to know it was midnight and that must have been her cue, or maybe she just took it that way. She stood right up. "Oh, my goodness, I've talked your ear off."

Mason stood up too. He was going to follow her down to her car, that would be polite. "Mason?" she said, "I just wanted to say . . . Okay, when you're signing up for courses this fall, don't take any that I'm the TA for, okay? Do you understand why? You don't grade your friends."

July

7.

High summer in Ohio, not even noon yet and already pushing ninety. Out in the world not a breath of air and in the library? Holy fuck. The fans were cranked up to full tilt, thrashing out lots of noise but not much of a breeze, and it was hotter than the hinges of hell. It was gonna take forever before Mason's legs looked like he'd never shaved them so he was stuck in jeans and his sweat glands were working just fine. The heat was rising and so was he, plodding up three staircases just like he did every damn day because he had to see if Jessie was up there. By the time he got to Level Five he felt like a pot roast.

Walking along the balustrade, he let his hand ride along the old wooden railing worn glossy by generations of students, looked down to Level Two where the reading desks with their banker's lamps were so far away they might as well have been toys in a doll house, looked up to the high vaulted emptiness of the ceiling where the light, scorching and brilliant, poured through the leaded windows, felt what he always did, an awe that was damn near religious. Jessie hadn't been in the library once since the heat had got so bad and she certainly wouldn't be here today, but holy fucking hell, there she was, in her carrel, a dark silhouette with the light blazing behind her.

Wham, his heart slammed into his throat. He'd had crushes on girls before but he'd never felt about anybody the way he felt about Jessie Collier. Even if she was nothing more than a flicker in the distance, he always got that same sweet-painful kick when he first saw her. Now, walking closer, he could feel it through his whole body, making him quivery. Why the fuck did it always take him by surprise?

She did a lot of communicating with her eyes and he wished he was better at figuring out exactly what it was that she was communicating. "Mason," she said, "let me give you some scholarly advice . . . and this is ex cathedra. When you're writing a paper and you're on a roll, do *not* say to yourself, okay, I'll put the footnotes in later."

"Yeah. Right. I'll make a *note* of it."

He'd got a smile out of her. She was so sweaty she looked like she'd just stepped out of a hot bath, her face shiny, her dark hair curled tight to her head, beads of sweat rolling down her face, circles of sweat staining the armpits of her plain white blouse. Her ancient leather book bag sat where it always did, on the far left side her desk. Stacks of books all around her. A ring binder open in front of her. She always brought her lunch in a brown paper bag. She picked it up. "Let's get the fuck out of here."

Since she'd switched from TA to friend, she'd stopped watching her mouth and it still shocked him every time she said fuck. Where he came from, girls didn't talk like that.

He watched her stand up and walk around the desk. The university dress code required that women wear skirts on campus and she was wearing one, a bit on the long side, unbleached linen hanging down droopy from the humidity, the pleats coming out. Her plain brown leather sandals looked exactly like something somebody would have worn in ancient times. "I love your sandals."

"Oh, thanks. They're really comfortable. Had them handmade for me in Provincetown."

Was he supposed to know where that was? "Doesn't the strap between your toes bother you?"

"It did at first but I got used to it. They're just great. The leather moulds to your feet. I could walk in them forever." They made a distinctive click on the old hardwood of the staircase. "How's your rib?"

"The pain's gone, mostly, just a little twinge now and then."

They stepped through the big doors and out into the world. Still wasn't much of a breeze but it was a relief to get out of Old Main. He'd been to visit her at her carrel so often they'd settled into a routine. They walked along University Avenue with its endless rows of maples, sat on the shadiest bench under the largest maple. She took a bottle of Coke out of her bag, popped the cap off with the opener she always remembered to bring with her, took out her sandwich neatly wrapped in wax paper, offered him half. "I can't keep eating your lunches," he said.

"You haven't eaten one lately. Besides, it's too fucking hot to eat."

Peanut butter and jelly, moist and soggy. He took a bite and washed it down with warm Coke. This was the high point of his life these days, sitting there with her, eating halves of her sandwiches. He was glad it wasn't cheese today. She really didn't give a fuck about food, just ate something to have something to eat, her mind on her thesis. All her cheese sandwiches had on them was a slice of cheddar and a smear of mustard. They were right smack in the middle of farm country but you'd think she'd never heard of tomatoes or lettuce.

"Talked to her twice," she was telling him. He always asked her about Sarah, her roommate down in Mississippi. "She sure isn't complaining about not being allowed to go out in the field *now*. She's scared shitless like everybody else."

She was staring off into space, methodically chewing on her half sandwich. "Fucking J. Edgar Hoover," she said, "that miserable prick. 'We will not wet-nurse troublemakers.' But then if white guys go missing, that's a different story. Of course they're dead. Everybody knows it. They were dead the night they vanished."

The three missing civil rights workers. They'd been in the news so much that their names had got drilled into Mason's head, the two white guys, Goodman and Schwerner, the Negro, James Chaney. Nearly a month ago, exactly on the night when Mason and Jessie had been sitting on the girls' porch swapping stories of their lives, the three had been released from jail in Philadelphia, Mississippi, had driven away in a car that everybody knew belonged to CORE and had vanished without a trace. The next day the car was found burned out in a swamp. "This goddamn country's racist to its bone marrow," Jessie said.

They'd brought in the Navy to search for them. They hadn't found them yet but they'd been hauling black bodies out of the Mississippi River where the KKK had been dumping them. LBJ had invited the parents of the two white guys to the White House but of course not the parents of the black one. The FBI was finally doing something although it wasn't clear what. Hoover kept on saying that the FBI wasn't down there to protect civil rights workers.

"Did you see the editorial in the *Merida Monitor?*" Mason asked her. "A whole rant against the kids going to Mississippi. Didn't quite say that they brought it on themselves but came close. Okay, you've got your civil rights bill now, just be nice and don't piss people off."

"Right. Classic."

"The *Monitor*'s solid for Goldwater."

"Of course it is."

"Does he have a chance?"

"Of getting nominated? Of course he will."

"No. I mean for president."

She thought about it. "Oh hell, Mason, it's not very likely. Lyndon Johnson is one of the cleverest politicians ever to occupy the White House and he's riding on a dead man's coattails, but . . .

Okay, Goldwater. He has lots of support, some of it obvious, some of it not so obvious, hidden in little pockets all over the country. He's saying what a lot of people have been thinking, putting it into words for them, making it respectable. He could take the whole fucking South. Everybody says they'd never vote Republican down there but that's simply not true. The key issue down there is *race* and Goldwater voted against the Civil Rights Act.

"So if he could take the whole damn South and then . . . He doesn't really need the Negro vote. In the north . . . if he could get the same damn bunch of yahoos that loved Joe McCarthy, the wacko anti-communists. And then if he could get the white backlash vote . . . Look how well Wallace did in the north. Makes you wonder about the American proletariat, doesn't it? Agency of change? That's a joke. Yes, if the stars were aligned exactly right, we could have a Goldwater presidency. And then God help us."

He watched her while she talked. Sometimes he thought he'd memorized her but when she was right there in front of him, she was always brand new. She had full lips. If she ever wore lipstick, it'd be too much. Long straight nose. Lean face, curving in under her jaws. Didn't pluck her eyebrows much, shaped them a little, they were thicker than most girls', helped to show off her eyes, yeah, her eyes were what got to him, what stayed with him. It was only at night they were so dark they looked all pupil, now in sunlight they were a luminous dark brown. He'd put some thought into it, decided that the right name for that color was burnt umber, but he'd never found the right words to describe the honest way she looked out at the world, straight and steady.

Yeah, he'd been thinking about Jessie Collier a lot, and that was putting it mildly. She wasn't just a big tall strong girl, she was a big tall strong girl who looked like a boy. It was kind of obvious, something that must have hit him right away, and then he must

113

have jumped away from it. Wearing one of her plain blouses today that could be a boy's shirt, so baggy it made her look like she didn't have any breasts at all. Her pixie cut, curled up tight to her head from the humidity, could be a boy's haircut, her big hands with the nails clipped short, the shape of her narrow hips under that droopy linen skirt. He couldn't avoid thinking about it. If he was falling in love with a girl who looked like a boy, that was kind of hopeless, wasn't it? Maybe that just meant he was gay.

"I'm getting through your reading list," he told her. He wanted her to know that. "What were you thinking when you made it? Okay, now I'm going to give Mason the most depressing shit I can possibly find?"

She laughed. "What did you want? The home of the free and the land of the brave?"

"No, it's good, it's good. Stuff I didn't know about."

"Anything that feels like your thesis topic?"

"Maybe. A few things." Okay, here was his chance to tell her what he'd found out when he'd taken off on his own, researching the Masons, but he wasn't ready to talk about that yet. Using his own family for his thesis didn't feel right somehow. "Still sort of thinking about Ohio settlement," he said. "It's where we are."

"Oh, aren't we ever! I hate this goddamned place. It's as white as a sheet . . . and . . . Hey, that's the perfect metaphor, isn't it? But I bet there wasn't much Klan activity around here. They didn't need it. Any black person who showed up, they ran them right out of town."

"Really? Did they do that?"

"Sure as hell they did. Don't let the sun set on you, *boy*. Lots of these little Ohio towns did that. And now the university's bragging about how it's integrated. Bullshit. What, all six of them? Everybody knows they've got a quota and they've got to be *our kind of Negro*. Maybe I should have gone to Wisconsin. The only thing good here is Ev."

"That's sure true. All I had to do was take one course with him and that turned me into a history major and then— Jessie, I never did tell you how important your course was to me, you know, the one I took with you and Dr. Braithwaite last fall."

"Was it?" She was pleased. He could hear it in her voice.

"Yeah. I've been planning to tell you this. It wasn't just the best history course I ever took, it was . . . between you and Dr. Braith-waite, it was like a bomb going off in my brain."

She laughed. "It was fairly explosive for me too. Oh, boy, were you ever a handful! You're so obviously bright and you loved to argue and you were such a goddamned Confederate. I thought what on earth am I going to do with him?"

"Yeah, well, I had all those battles in my head. I'd been reading that shit for years. The South had the best generals."

"The South had the most *interesting* generals. They lost the war."

"Yeah, they did, but . . . You can't beat Lee in the Valley, digging in. He set the standard for every army up until the airplane. And then taking on Hooker? And Stonewall's flank attack? You can't beat that stuff. And the crazy ones, John Hunt Morgan, Nathan Bedford Forrest—"

"Forrest? Jesus! The first Grand Wizard of the fucking Klan."

"Was he?"

"Mason, you should know that, for Christ's sake."

"Yeah, I should. But while I was reading about all those battles, not once did I think about slavery. Not once. Until your class. Especially your seminar. Yeah, I do like to argue, and wow, did we ever go at it and you damn well destroyed me. I'd go out of there just shattered and I'd think, okay I've got to think this through and get back at her, and I'd read my ass off and get a whole new set of arguments and I'd come back and you'd destroy me again. *Get the facts right, Mason. Primary sources, primary sources.*

"And then it started to sink in, holy Jesus, *slavery*. All that stuff we read. I thought, hey, it was wrong, it was fucking evil. Those Southerners thought they could *own people*. How the hell did that come about? You made it all clear and . . . You just completely turned my mind around. Completely. And I thought, Jesus, she's more than smart, she's been working on this stuff and she knows it inside and out and she gives a shit. And then I thought, hey, that's what a historian is and that's what I want to be. You taught me that, so thank you."

He hadn't been planning to open his heart like that, he'd just slid into it. He'd been looking away at the sky, now he looked back at her and saw that he'd thrown her for a loop. It took her awhile to find any words. "Oh, my goodness, Mason. That's one of the nicest things anybody's ever said to me."

As he was floating along home, Mason was still brooding about Jessie. When he'd been working at Allied Trucking, there had been a hand-written sign in the office that said, "ENGAGE BRAIN BEFORE OPERATING MOUTH," and that was advice he should definitely be taking. He hadn't been trying to snow her, every word he'd said was true, but he'd probably embarrassed her again. "You don't grade your friends" she'd said but he couldn't figure out what being a friend meant to her.

She must have been embarrassed by how much she'd told him that night sitting on the girls' porch because he hadn't heard anything more about her life since then. She always seemed glad to see him, almost like she *expected* to see him, and she shared her lunches with him, let herself say fuck in front of him, but now she never said anything personal. And she was still acting like his TA, making reading lists for him, delivering neat little lectures like the one she'd given him on Goldwater. No, it wasn't like having a friend, it was more like having a friendly teacher you saw every day or two. No, he shouldn't have said any of that stuff. Now he was embarrassed.

He turned onto Jefferson. It was slightly downhill and he was letting the bike do the work for him. He looked up and what the fuck, there was goddamn Eilum with no shirt on standing on the roof of their house. With his big hairy arms crossed over his big hairy chest, Eilum was regarding the world below him like he owned the whole goddamn planet.

Mason rode around to the back. A three-quarter-ton pickup truck was parked in the alley and those two other engineers, Dave and Mick, were unloading shit from it. Coils of wire, metal tubing, an honest-to-God arc welder. They'd already got an old wooden ladder leaned up against the back of the house. All that was going where? Onto the roof, obviously. "The friggin' antenna," Eilum yelled down at Mason.

Right. The antenna. For weeks Eilum had been working on his radio kit, a real space-age number that was supposed to receive every radio signal known to man. He'd finally got it done and now it had to have a gargantuan antenna so it could haul in faint distant transmissions like the aliens chatting with each other or Russian cosmonauts sadly dying in outer space. "You talked to the landlord?" Mason yelled up to him.

"Fuck him. It's just gonna look like a TV antenna. Besides which, you know how he is. When's the last time you saw him around here?"

Upper level engineering students were required to take some ball-breaker course crammed full of math. Eilum had got an A in it but Dave and Mick had most definitely not so that's why they were here in the summer. Mason was delighted that Eilum had run into them. Sometimes the other engineers could keep Eilum reined in a notch while Mason by himself had never had much luck in that department.

Okay, so there they were, engineers working on an engineering project, not girls who looked like boys but honest-to-God real
boys. Yeah, boys being boys, shirts off, baggy shorts, old basketball
shoes, yeah, half-naked boys in the steamy hot sun, laughing, yelling
bullshit at each other. If Mason was supposed to be gay, shouldn't
he be getting hot just looking at them? He already knew from long
familiarity that his sexual attraction to T. Davis Eilum was a little
less than zero but how about the other guys?

Dave, sometimes known as "Dopey," had his hair buzzed off
like a lot of the engineers, a thick meaty boy with a bit of a beer
gut, on his way to becoming a sloppy-ass man, and Mason found
him fairly repellant. Michael, known as "Mick," was another story.
Slender as a teenager, Mick had a nice flat stomach and big chocolate-brown eyes. Lots of boys were growing their hair out now,
going for that Beatle look, and Mick had a lovely head of hair on
him. Could Mick be the cute boy that Mason had said yes to years
ago but who hadn't shown up yet?

Well, no, that was not possible. If Mason went to bed with Mick,
all the engineers would know it and then everybody on campus
would know it and then Mason's life at Merida University would
be over, and besides which, Mick was an engineer so he was most
likely straight as a plumb bob. Okay, Mason thought, let's just take
reality out of the picture. He imagined some fantasy world where
boys went to bed with each other on a regular basis and it was all
perfectly normal. Was Mick cute enough?

If you kissed a boy who'd been out working in the sun, would
he taste salty? Mason tried to imagine kissing Mick the way he'd
kissed Bobby Springer but he couldn't do it. Well, not unless Mason
imagined himself dressed up like a hot little tart in a *Playboy* spread
but then any connection to reality had long ago departed and all he
was doing was standing there in the full light of day telling himself
another jerk-off fantasy. Jesus, he thought, if you're gay, shouldn't

you get hot just by looking at these guys, thinking, wow, goddamn, great stuff, *boys*! You shouldn't have to try to talk yourself into it, should you?

Hitting it on down the road, Mason was already a couple of miles beyond the campus, the sun on his back like a nuclear blast. Out of breath and sweating buckets, he settled down on the seat and let the bike roll on under its own volition. Where the hell did he think he was going? Indiana? Yeah, right. They were still calling it *The Land of Indians* even though they'd killed or driven out every one of them. Used to be nothing but forest here. The Iroquois used to hunt here, the Huron, the Chippewa, the Delaware, the Wyandot, the Miami, the Shawnee, probably a lot more that Mason couldn't remember or had never heard of. Now every inch of it owned by some fucking white man.

Down in Mississippi they were pulling black bodies out of the river. They didn't even know who some of them were. If you were black down there and you said the wrong thing at the wrong time, you could just vanish, and that had been going on forever, *the southern way of life* they called it. All this summer more shit going on, people getting arrested, beat up, jailed, churches getting burnt, fire bombed, those three civil rights workers getting lynched. Yeah, everybody knew they were dead. Okay, so how, in the very same world, could you have Barry Goldwater running for president and T. Davis Eilum building a huge fucking antenna on the roof *to listen to aliens*? And Mason was worrying about whether or not he was gay?

He felt like shit, as empty as a paper bag. All he had in his stomach was a half of Jessie's peanut butter and jelly sandwich and some of her warm Coke. Fuck me, he thought, it's all hopeless. He turned his bike around and headed back for campus. Maybe he could get something at the Buckeye, or maybe not, he didn't want to spend the money, and he saw that he was coming up on

Worthington, the ancient building that housed the history department. Maybe Dr. Braithwaite was in. On a day like today? Not too likely. But it wouldn't hurt to check.

The history department was on the second floor so it shouldn't be getting cooler walking up there, but it was. Then Mason saw that all the classrooms on the west side had their doors shut to keep the sun out and two huge fans were going, one at each end of the long hallway, one blowing air in from a big open window, the other blowing it out. Intelligent design was being demonstrated all right, and it was working, it was like walking into an oasis. The secretary must have been at her desk earlier, she'd left papers scattered around like clues. Even with the fans it was quiet, unnatural somehow, and Mason stopped stock still, soaking in that peculiar quiet, sensing a change in the day or maybe in himself. Well, hell, he'd come for the water cooler as much as for anything else. Without hardly pausing to breathe he knocked back two full cups. The door to the Head's office was standing wide open. "Dr. Braithwaite?"

A familiar rumble, kind of belligerent. "Yes?"

Dr. Braithwaite wasn't at his desk, he was lounging back in an easy chair by the window, his feet up on a hassock, and what the fuck, he was such a sight that Mason was tempted to laugh but knew he damn well better not.

A tall man, Dr. Braithwaite looked like he'd been a powerhouse once but was slowing down some, how old? Probably pushing seventy. Hair white on top, streaked gray on the sides, a bit long but not so long that it would bother anybody. Bushy eyebrows, stray hairs poking out at odd angles. Wrinkles around his eyes that crinkled up when he smiled, deep gouges from the sides of his nose down to a mouth set firm as a clamp. A down-to-earth jaw. His eyes seemed like little more than thin slits but if you stared back at him through his old-fashioned wire-frame glasses, you'd see that he was checking you out good. Not a friendly face, lots of students were afraid of him, though when you got to know him, he was friendly enough, even kindly as Mason had found out on more than one occasion. Hard to see him as a person, damned near an institution, the model of the distinguished professor, usually in a tweed jacket and a striped tie, Dr. Everett Rutledge Braithwaite, the Head of the Department of History, and here he was in his office wearing wrinkled old Bermuda shorts, a gaudy Hawaiian shirt with palm trees on it, and no shoes or socks. "Oh. Mason. I'm afraid you've caught me somewhat dishabille," and he started reaching over to the floor to pick up his socks.

"Excuse me, sir, with all due respect, I don't really care one way or the other if you've got shoes on."

Dr. Braithwaite's eyes were on Mason's hair. "No, I don't suppose you do," with the quick edge of a grin. "Sit down, Mason. What can I do for you?"

Well, for starters you can tell me what the hell I'm doing studying American history, but nope, he couldn't say that. There was another big chair in the office and Mason sank into it. He'd been sweating so much that his shirt felt wet against his back. "Uh, my honors thesis. I was trying to get, you know, a head start on it."

"Good for you. Tell me what you've been working on."

"Working? I don't know. Ohio Country settlement." That was the same vague answer he'd given Jessie but he had a lot more on his mind than that. If he was going to go anywhere with it, he needed some help. Okay, if you couldn't talk to your thesis advisor, who the hell could you talk to? "I've been kind of looking into my own family. I guess that's not what you're supposed to do, right?"

"Why not?"

"You can do that?"

"Tell me what you've been doing."

"Okay, I've been researching this . . . You see, I grew up on the Ohio River. In a place called Mason's Landing. It goes back to two brothers, Elias and Thomas Mason. They claimed land on the Virginia side back in the 1700s. I'm descended from one of them. Not sure which one. Never got that clear in my mind. I'd have to call my grandmother and ask her." Jesus, he was sounding like an absolute hoopie moron.

"Okay, there's this family story. Just one of those old stories you hear your whole life and . . . When you're a little kid, it's just a . . . I don't know, like a piece of furniture that's already there in the house. So here's the story the way I remember it. The two brothers went off hunting one day and they'd left their family behind. Well, some Indians crossed the river in their canoes and killed the family. When the Mason brothers got home, they were mad as hell, as you can imagine. They weren't supposed to cross the Ohio, but they did it anyways, chased down those Indians, caught up to them, and killed every one of them. And I guess the point I got when I was a little kid was . . .You know how little kids are, always trying to get the point? Well, there were two points. One was that times were tough for the early settlers and the second point, the *main point*, was . . . you don't mess with the Masons."

Dr. Braithwaite was looking at him with a kind of steady regard so Mason figured he should just keep on going. "Well, it finally occurred to me that if it really happened, it probably made it into somebody's account, and yeah, it did. It's in a few accounts. It was in the spring of 1791. I kept tracing the accounts back . . . Our library's real good for this stuff . . . And the farthest back I can trace it is to a book published in Raysburg, Virginia, in 1826. *Notes on the Settlement and Indian Wars in Ohio Country and the Western Parts of Virginia and Pennsylvania* by some guy named Hiram M. Teeter. All the later accounts seem to be referring to him but he just tells the story and doesn't bother to say where he got it from."

"No, those old boys were not great for citing their sources."

"Anyhow, Teeter's story is completely different from the one I heard growing up."

The way Teeter told it, only one Mason brother was off hunting and that was the younger one, Tom, and he had his eldest son with him. Left back at the cabin were Tom's wife and his two younger sons, one of them in his teens and the other a little boy of six. The Indians were Wyandots, a small raiding party. The older boy was cutting timber and the Indians tried to ambush him but he must have heard them coming, got off a shot and most likely wounded one of them before they tomahawked him and took his scalp. The ruckus alerted Mom. She told the little boy to run to his Uncle Elias' cabin and she took off in the opposite direction. Well, the Indians ran her down and tomahawked her. Then they grabbed up some goods from the cabin, jumped into their canoes, and shot back across the river.

It was Tom Mason who'd lost his wife and one of his sons but it was his older brother Elias who was hot for revenge. They were supposed to be living at peace with the Indians at the moment but some of the Indians were still making these little raids across the river. The new president, Washington, had issued an edict that forbade the settlers from crossing the Ohio and the settlers thought that wasn't fair. If the Indians crossed over to commit depredations, the settlers thought that they should be able to chase them back over to the other side and that's exactly what Elias Mason wanted to do. He rounded up some men from around there and formed a party of about thirty, including an old scout named Reuben Dunbar who knew the Ohio Country.

It took Elias a couple of days to get his party together so by the time they crossed the river, the trail was cold. They guessed which way the Wyandots might have gone and went that way but there was no sign of them. They kept on going deeper into Ohio Country. Reuben Dunbar was scouting out ahead of the party and he came across a small Indian encampment. He reported back that they seemed to be a peaceful bunch minding their own business and they weren't Wyandots, looked like Miamis to him. Elias Mason said he'd come out there to kill some Indians, and by God, he was gonna kill some.

Reuben didn't like that. "They're not the right Indians," he said.

"An Indian is an Indian," Elias said.

"It's not right," Reuben told him. "I want no part of it." About half the party agreed with him and they rode away. The Mason party waited till just before dawn and then they rode into that Indian encampment, took them by surprise, and killed and scalped every single one of them, including the women and children.

"Reading that story," Mason said, "did not exactly fill me with delight."

"No," Dr. Braithwaite said, "I don't imagine it did."

"Okay, so now I want to get to the truth of the matter. Maybe it got written up in some newspapers from the time or maybe it's referred to in some family papers and . . . I don't know how to find that stuff. Are there indexes or . . . something?"

"Yes, there are indexes, but . . . Look, Mason, this is an under-graduate paper. Save that level of research for next year when you're doing your Master's. You've already got your paper. Go back and interview whoever told you the family story."

"My grandparents."

"Right. Don't ask them any leading questions. Just take down whatever they say verbatim. Sometimes what people forget is more interesting than what they remember."

"Hey, that's true. I never thought of that . . . But you mean that's all I have to do?"

"For an undergrad thesis? Absolutely. Just write up what you've told me. Write it up in a scholarly way, of course, and *you* cite *your* sources. That would make a dandy little paper."

Well, hell, that was easy enough, Mason should feel relieved but he didn't. He still had a lot on his mind. Dr. Braithwaite was just sitting there, his bare feet up on the hassock, looking like he had all the time in the world. He picked up his pipe and fired it up. He had one of those special pipe lighters that was shaped like a circle, fit right around the pipe bowl. He blended his own tobacco, had jars of it sitting on a shelf in between his books. Mason always liked seeing that tobacco leaf there in those glass jars. He enjoyed the smell of that pipe smoke. It had something sweet in it. "Jessie gave me a reading list," he said.

"Mrs. Collier. Yes."

"Lot of things on it, I wouldn't have . . . Journal articles I never would have found on my own. There's all these things I'd known about but not in any great detail. A lot about the slave trade. It was a really big part of the economy in the early days."

"Yes, it was."

"A lot of the Founding Fathers were slave holders. Washington, Jefferson, Madison . . . Washington was a rich man. He started out as a land surveyor and he was always a land speculator. Our first congress was a whole bunch of land speculators, couldn't wait to get out here into Ohio Country, make a few bucks. The Indians were warlike folks, you sure didn't want to get yourself captured, but in their way the settlers were worse. All the Indians wanted was to be left alone, it was their land, but the settlers? Nobody ever had any intention of honoring any of those treaties. The Treaty of Paris? 1783? Nobody invited the Indians to that one. Washington just wanted them gone. He had a whole big plan for getting rid of them and it worked.

"The War of Independence? All we wanted was to be able to do what the British did. As soon as we got them off our necks, we started building us an empire of our own. The American character built on the frontier? Yeah, that's right. You screw things up, you say, 'Fuck it, I'm moving west.' Oops, sorry about the language—"

"In this case your language is absolutely apt."

"You need the frontier to keep the economy ticking along. You run out of frontier, what do you do? You start fooling around in the affairs of other countries. You've got to have some place to sell your surplus, right? So you've got to make things safe for American business. Well, you know all about that, Dr. Braithwaite, you wrote a whole book about it. All those South American countries. Mexico. Cuba. And the Philippines. Anyhow, we're still at it and it doesn't look like we're gonna stop any time soon. Vietnam."

Dr. Braithwaite drew in some of that sweet smoke and blew out again in a slow cloud. He was studying Mason.

"We can't kill Indians now," Mason said, "so we're gonna kill Vietnamese peasants. I can't go back and change what the Masons did but I can try to change what's going on right now."

"Yes, you can."

"Those, uh . . . You know, those kids down in Mississippi? I keep thinking I should have gone down there. Maybe that's the kind of thing I should be doing. It's . . . It's *real*. Isn't just sitting around reading books. I don't know. Jessie keeps talking to me like I'm going for a PhD."

"Well, are you?"

"It's a lot of work. It's a lot of years."

"What would you be doing if you weren't in school?"

"Good question. You mean if I wasn't drafted?"

Mason considered the jobs he could list on his resume. Stock boy, bus boy, washer of tractor trailers, washer of dishes. "I really don't know."

"What interests you? What are you passionate about?"

"American history." They both laughed.

"Mason, let me tell you something. Everybody's got his own work to do and nobody else can do it for you. Some people should be down in Mississippi. Other people should be writing books."

Mason sat there and thought about it and it finally dawned on him that the big question he'd wanted answered when he'd first walked in, Dr. Braithwaite had already answered it a long time ago. "I've had three classes with you," Mason told him, "and you always say the same thing in the first class."

"Oh?" Again that sharp quick grin. "And what is it that I say?"

"You won't know where you're going if you don't know where you've been."

Talking to Dr. Braithwaite always made Mason feel calm, like everything was worth it, but today that feeling didn't last long. As soon as he stepped outside, the sun slammed him again. Like he always did, he checked the big ashtray outside the main doors. When school was on, he could sometimes find a dozen good long butts sticking out of the sand. Because it was summer he only found three, put two in his pocket and fired up the other one. While he was standing there smoking, the McKinley Tower bonged four times. Shit. The worst time of day.

So where was he going now? Some place downhill for Christ's sake, so he settled onto his bike like a dead man and let himself be carried down the slight incline that was Adams Street, rolled past the post office, through the seedy part of town with its rat-trap hotel and cheap-ass pissy beer joints, and on down into the warehouse district. He was headed for the only thing that could pass for a body of water anywhere around there, back home it'd be a crick but here they called it Woods Run, in July not much more than a trickle.

He drifted past the old abandoned Merida Lumber building that nobody would admit to owning, every window smashed, its big doors splintered and hanging open, and then he hit bottom so he had to pedal. On past warehouses for God knows what, past a big one for tomatoes, arriving in huge crates in trucks, departing neatly packed into boxes. He'd never before thought about how tomatoes made it from harvest to supermarket. Jesus, they picked them green. No wonder they tasted like shit.

Enough of this, he should head back to campus, so he turned up a street where he'd never been before, read the sign that told him it was Pioneer. Of course Merida would have a Pioneer Street and he was having to work. He was dying for water and something to eat. Well, okay, the cheapest thing at the Buckeye was a grilled cheese sandwich for thirty-five cents and water was free. Pioneer was taking him past a bunch of crappy old rundown houses, out of nowhere a girl's voice was yelling, shrill, "Hey, that's a boy!"

Oh fuck, a bunch of Merida townies, teenagers, half a dozen of them sprawled out on their front steps, smoking and drinking pop. His quick glance showed him big sweaty boys in jeans, leggy girls in shorts. One of the girls was yelling, "Hey, sweetie-poo, I *love* your hair."

"Faggot," one of the boys yelled with a laugh. Mason peddled harder.

"Hey, he's got a *girl's* bike!"

They were all yelling now, "Faggot, faggot, faggot." Mason stood up on the pedals.

In the bleaching light of late afternoon the big old buckeye hanging over the door looked even more dejected than usual, most of its gold paint long gone, wood showing through, dried out and cracking. Pathetic, Mason thought, or maybe it's just me. He'd ridden like a maniac to get away from those rotten townies but he could still hear their voices in his head.

Hesitating as his eyes adjusted to the flat shade of the restaurant side, he crept into the Buckeye like it was a church. There was Walter sending him a jaunty salute and a politician's grin. Most of the campus might be emptied out but still Walter had found himself a couple of cute undergrad boys to feed hamburgers to.

Walter would welcome him to his table if he wanted to go there, but Mason knew that Walter wouldn't really want him to go there, so he returned Walter's salute and kept on walking.

The bar side was even dimmer, downright murky with all the cigarette smoke, and there was Eilum with the engineers, sprawled out around a far table, yukking it up and guzzling down a pitcher. "Got your antenna done?" he yelled at them.

Dave yelled back, "Fuckin' A doobie John rights," but before Mason could get to their table, somebody else yelled, "Mason Macquarie!" Carl, shit.

The way Carl was turned, facing the door, facing the sun, his big Buddy Holly glasses took the light like matched flares. "Yeah, you, ace, get your sorry ass over here."

For some reason Mason didn't think he had any choice, sat down with Carl, and there was Henry Algren and the red-lipstick girls Mason remembered from Henry's party. Nobody in their right mind could have thought those girls were anywhere near twenty-one, but maybe it was just the way things went in the summer, maybe nobody gave a fuck, what were they doing with Carl and Henry?

"So what's with you, pretty boy, trying to slough off the old slouches?" That was just Carl jerking him around as usual but Mason couldn't find a single good word. The last time he'd seen Carl had been at that horror show out at Henry's house. What was he supposed to do? Pretend it never happened? "This gentleman here," Carl was saying, addressing the girls, "is the deserving winner of the prestigious Frederick T. Armstrong Scholarship in American History."

The girls didn't say a word. "Mason," Carl was telling them, "is an expert in the demanding field of Tautological Studies. You have heard of that, haven't you?"

The girls nodded, big-eyed. "Yes," Carl said, "a very demanding field indeed. You are required to examine all of the insights of the great historians and then reproduce them in a way that sounds as though you had thought of them yourself."

The girls had nothing to say to that either. They were scared, Mason could see it, nailed to the edges of their chairs like two spikes. They knew they shouldn't be on the bar side, four glasses on the table but theirs untouched. Mason tended to think that all girls were pretty, and these two were even prettier than that, but whatever tiny town they came from must be stuck way back in time. Their cute off-the-shoulder sundresses were like something from the '50s and they wore their hair in that short neat style like Irene used to, the only way to keep it like that was to spend half your life in curlers. Mason felt a wave of sympathy for them. Poor kids, they should stay away from assholes like Carl and Henry.

Yeah, Henry. He didn't seem to be part of anything going on, looked sweaty and vacant, his red hair sliding away from his bald scalp, his eyes focused on a puddle of beer on the table in front of him. Mason wasn't bouncing back with the wit the way he was supposed to, so Carl had run out of words and the silence was twisting out a little too far, and in that silence Henry looked up directly into Mason's eyes and said in a low mean voice, "What the fuck are you laughing at?"

Mason hadn't been laughing, he hadn't even been smiling. Nobody at the table had been laughing. Eilum and the engineers were laughing but they were all the way over on the other side of the room. Dave had launched into song, "The answer, my friend, is blowing out your end," and Mick and Eilum had joined him on the chorus, "The answer is blowing out your end!"

"What?" Henry said to Mason. "You think this is funny?"

The girls were appalled, both staring down at their pretty sandals. They had to be just dying to get the hell out of there but couldn't think of a polite way to do it. Even Carl looked clueless, his mouth hanging open and his eyes flashing glass.

Henry was examining Mason so hard he might as well have been looking for head lice. Then he sat back in his chair, shrugged, sighed, pushed one of the girls' glasses of beer across the table to Mason. "You just don't get it, do you?" he said.

8.

Buzzed on that one fucking glass of beer Henry had shoved at him, Mason was riding hard to try to get clear of some monstrous thing, he didn't know what. He was most of the way to Henry's house before it dawned on him that's where he was going. When he'd told Jessie that he didn't intend to see Lorianne again, he'd meant it. Yeah, it had felt like a promise, even more than that, it had felt like a *vow*, so what the fuck was he doing? He felt exhausted and sick. I'm not in my right mind, he thought, I should go home. But he kept right on going.

Henry's house looked different in the daylight. In his memory it had turned into something out of the *Twilight Zone* but it was just an old country house like the other ones around there, beat up and weathered, needed a coat of paint, but looked friendly and lived-in, some of Tammy's toys laying around on the grass, bright splotches of color. He walked up the front steps and found the front door standing open and the screen door not even hooked. "Hey," he called out, "anybody home?"

Lorianne answered him from somewhere in the distance. "We're out here. Come on back."

He hesitated a minute. Where was *here*? Was he supposed to walk through the house? He didn't see any reason not to, so he did, past the living room, through the kitchen, to the back door. Jesus, the place was immaculate. Lorianne must be spending all of her time cleaning. He pushed through the screen door and there she was, on the porch, winding the clothes line in and taking down her laundry. "Oh, my goodness, Mason Macquarie." Maybe he'd ridden all the way out here just to see her smile at him like that.

"It's so nice of you to come out and visit me." She was wearing her hair in pigtails. It was kind of startling. "It's hard being way out here without a car. You just missed Jessie."

Fuck, he thought.

"She's a real friend. Comes out every day to check on me, brings me milk and things. How are you, Mason? My goodness, it's hot, isn't it?" She flipped the end of one of her pigtails. "Just had to get the hair off my neck, it was driving me in*sane*. Henry just loathes me in pigtails. Says they make me look like a hillbilly girl. Told me if I ever wore them again, he was gonna cut them off. Well, hell, I *am* a hillbilly girl and he's not here, is he?"

"I think you look great."

"Well, thank you, sir." She made a little dip like a shorthand curtsy.

He'd never seen her before when she wasn't wearing a dress but she was in camp shorts today, beige and very short. She must have been tanning, using oil or something, her smooth legs gleamed in the sun. A plain sleeveless blouse, ivory colored or maybe that color they called ecru, and white sneakers, not too pointed, clean and snow-white like they'd been through her wash. "Here you've caught me taking my unmentionables down," she said.

"I won't look."

"Oh, I don't care. You've got a sister, don't you?"

Nevertheless he turned away from her and walked over to the porch railing. Tammy, down below on the walk, was riding her tricycle from one end to the other, making sounds like rummm, rummm, rummm. "She thinks she's a tricycle motor," Lorianne said. "She's advanced for her age. That's what Jessie says anyway. Most kids her age can't ride around like that."

The back yard in daylight wasn't spooky at all. That big tree where he'd first talked to Lorianne, where she'd kissed him, where he'd hid from Henry, wasn't some bizarre sinister shadowy entity, it was just a grand old sycamore. At night he hadn't seen the clothes lines and the poles. Some lines way out in the yard had sheets on them and a little breeze was finally coming up, the sheets moving with it. A dirt road in the distance separated Lorianne's yard from the farmer's field grown July-high with corn.

"Henry would just hate seeing me like this. Keeps telling me I should dress like a faculty wife. I say, 'Okay, sweetheart, you become a member of faculty somewhere and I'll be more than happy to dress like your little faculty wife.'"

Henry? Nothing made the least bit of sense. Why had Mason ridden out here like something was chasing him? Henry had set that off somehow and here he was at Henry's house talking to Henry's wife. Lorianne might as well be a different girl from the one he remembered, and it wasn't just the shorts and pigtails. He felt like he'd arrived in some weirdly unreliable world, but the trick with this one was that everything was supposed to seem perfectly normal. Okay, then he should say something about Henry. "Um, how's he, a . . . So, Henry . . . ? Is he working hard on his thesis over the summer?"

"His thesis? His *thesis?* He's just about out of . . . It'll be five years next spring and then he's out of a job. You want to know how much he's got done?"

She grabbed up an empty basket and walked down the steps and into the yard. Christ, was she ever angry. She'd been hiding it pretty good before. He followed her. She started yanking clothes pins out of one of the sheets and firing them into the basket. "He hasn't got much done?" he asked her.

She didn't answer.

"Let me help you," he said. "It goes faster with two people."

She flipped the sheet over the line and he caught it. She located the two corners on her side and he did on his. They walked away from each other, pulling the sheet taut, and then walked toward each other, letting it fold in the middle. "You must have folded lots of sheets," she said.

"Yeah. With my sister. A million."

"I love it when they're dried in the sun. On a day like this they dry stiff as a board in no time flat and they smell so sweet . . . smell like sun."

"Yeah. Like the sun."

She laid the folded sheet into the basket "Okay," she said, "here's the crux of the matter. Henry is not a historian, he's a collector. Started off when he was a little boy collecting stamps. He's still got his stamp albums, his pride and joy. Then he moved on to World War II souvenirs, you know, the stuff the GIs brought back. He specializes in German stuff. He's got two big boxes of it."

"German stuff?"

"Yeah, posters and flags and medals, all kinds of stuff. And you know he collects jazz records. Well, now he's collecting anything to do with Rutherford B. Hayes. He's been over to that Hayes collection in Fremont a million times. Any time he gets bored, he jumps in his car and drives over there."

She wasn't folding the next sheet. "He comes back and he's got more notes. Any book that's ever been written that's even remotely related to Rutherford B. Hayes, he owns it. The books are all marked up and stuffed full of pieces of paper. The pieces of paper all have numbers on them and the numbers correspond to note cards. He's got five boxes of note cards in alphabetical order. Any time Rutherford B. Hayes ever took a piss, Henry has got it noted down on a note card. He's got a master list, all typed out, that tells him what note cards go with what books. He's got to keep typing it out over and over again. And then those numbers correspond to entries he's made in the notebooks. There's different notebooks for a whole bunch of different topics. In order to make entries in the notebooks, Henry has to have everything just right. Can't be too early in the morning or too late. Around eleven, that's the perfect time. New pot of coffee. He's got to have six pencils, no five won't do, *six* pencils, HB, sharpened to fine points. Then maybe, if everything's just perfect, if I go out with Tammy in the stroller and take a really long walk, maybe he can make a few more notes. Everybody says, oh, poor Henry, he can't finish his thesis. *Finish?* He can't even get started."

Turning up at that time of day, Mason should have known he'd be invited to dinner and he couldn't say no, could he? He was getting used to being there, thinking that everything might turn out to be all right after all, and it had been a hell of a long time since he'd enjoyed eating anything as much as Lorianne's potato pancakes. She knew exactly how hot the skillet ought to be, how long to keep them sizzling in the butter before flipping them so they wouldn't break apart, so they'd come out golden brown on both sides. "Terrific," he told her, "as good as my grandma makes."

"They should be. I learned from *my* grandma."

She was feeding a pancake to Tammy in her high chair. "Tay? Toe?" Tammy said.

"That's right. Po-ta-toe."

"My grandma puts chipped beef in them too," he told her.

"Yeah? Well, I sneak a little bit in. She's a picky eater. Turns up her nose at meat. But she'll sure eat Mom's potato pancakes, won't you, honey?"

"Tay! Toe!"

Lorianne was playing a game to keep Tammy eating, making her fork into something flying around in the air, maybe a bee. "Here comes another bite, buzz buzz buzz," and to Mason, "Are you close to your grandma?"

"I guess. I grew up on the farm . . . Well, off and on."

"The *farm*? What kind of farm was it?"

"Just a . . . I forget how many acres it is. But lots. Used to be a big operation back when the river was a main mode of transportation. So big they had hired men for the harvest. Grandma and the girls would spend whole days baking pies for them. But that time's long gone. Just Grandma and Grandpa Mason now and it's down to, you know, just a family farm. They don't keep cows anymore. Or hogs. They still grow their own vegetables though, still keep chickens."

"Chickens? My grandma lives on a chicken farm."

"You're kidding."

"No, I'm not. It was never a big operation. Always just a little chicken farm."

"Ah . . ." He was having an odd thought. "When you were growing up . . . ? Did you become acquainted with chickens?"

She had to laugh at that. "Oh yeah I did. Of course I did."

"The dumbest animals in the world."

"That's absolutely right. The dumbest. I used to think a carrot has more brains than a chicken."

"Chick. In?" Tammy said.

"That's right, honey, we're talking about chickens. Tell me she's not smart. She knows them from her picture book."

Something had been twitching at his mind and then it took him by surprise, it was the memory of the first time he ever saw a chicken slaughtered. Heard the bang of the ax coming down on the block, saw the chicken running with no head, blood streaming behind it, that was clear and sudden, but he couldn't remember who'd killed it. Grandpa Mason? That hired man John who came around sometimes? "Do you remember seeing chickens killed?" he asked Lorianne. "You know, getting their heads chopped off? The way they run?"

"Ooo, yeah! I hated that. It scared the daylights out of me when I was a little girl."

"Yeah, me too! It's like they're thinking, holy shit, something terrible's just happened! I've got to get out of here! . . . Yeah, you just lost your head, you dumbass."

"That's right," she said but her attention wasn't on him any longer.

That awful memory of the chicken running with no head came accompanied with the feeling of wind on his bare legs. He'd still been wearing Irene's dresses then. How old could he have been? Four? Five? Thinking about it was making him sick.

"Who's my little darling?" Lorianne was asking her daughter.

"Me, me, me!" Tammy yelled, waving her chubby little hands in the air. It was eerie how much she looked like Henry.

Lorianne was getting lots of pancake into Tammy and it occurred to Mason that this was the first time he'd seen Lorianne when she hadn't been drinking. She'd been pissed out of her mind and high on marijuana when she'd kissed him behind the sycamore. Maybe she didn't remember it. Maybe she didn't want to remember it.

"I can't believe we both have grandmothers living on chicken farms," she said. "That's just too . . . Where your people from? Originally?"

"Pennsylvania. That's all anybody ever said, not a city or anything, nowhere in the British Isles, just Pennsylvania."

"That's funny. Mine too. Pennsylvania. You know, Mason, there's this strange feeling I've had about you ever since I met you. That we're . . . I don't know how to put it . . . that we're two halves of the same penny."

"That's right. That's exactly right. I've had the same thought. We might even be related. We look kind of alike, don't we? What's your maiden name?"

"Blesdoe. Used to be Bledsoe but that was back when nobody was literate and some official wrote it down wrong so we've been Blesdoe ever since. Mama's name was Harris."

"What's your grandmother's maiden name? The one on the chicken farm."

"Lorinda Archer."

"No connection yet. How about your other grandmother?"

"She's passed on. Mary Ann Ferguson."

"Nope. Do you know any of the old names in your family?"

"Oh, you want me to go backwards and sideways? Let's see. Akins. Erwin. Venn."

"*Venn?* I'm pretty sure one of my Mason ancestors married a Venn."

"Yeah? And I'll bet her mother's name was McPhee."

"Hey, that sounds right! How on earth did you know that?"

"The Venns and the McPhees were very fond of each other, married each other over and over again. That's the family story anyway."

"My God, that was our family story too. The Venns and the McPhees—"

She offered him her right hand. He took it and they shook like boys. "Hi there," she said, "cousin."

Lorianne took the picture book out of Tammy's hands and laid it on the bed table. Tammy was out like a light. "Now isn't she the sweetest little thing?"

"Yeah, she sure is."

He probably should have left any time after dinner but he hadn't. He'd stayed while Lorianne had changed Tammy and given her a bath and put her to bed. He'd finally figured out this weird world where everything was supposed to seem normal, he knew it from his mom. When everything's gone to shit, you clean up. That's what she used to tell Irene. He wasn't sure Irene ever got it but he sure got it. Maybe the old man would have vanished for just for a day or two, or maybe for months, you'd never know, but what you're defending against is the absolute screaming chaos he left behind. It isn't just that there's all kinds of crap everywhere all over your home, it's what he's left in your mind. Nothing makes any sense. Nothing's true. You've got to put your own order on it. Make it make sense. Make some pattern you can live with. Make some things true. That's what you're doing when you're washing your floors, doing your laundry, putting everything away where it ought to go.

Tammy slept with her arms wrapped around the big ole tabby cat who didn't seem to mind, who was giving them one of those inscrutable looks cats give people, her pupils gone huge and round in the dim light. "Orville knows it's her job," Lorianne told him. "She puts Tammy to bed every night."

"Orville?"

"Funny, huh? Carl named her. One of his silly jokes. Orvie came with the house, just turned up one day and never left. Carl was living here with Henry, but after we got married, I moved in and Carl moved out. He's never forgiven me."

He followed her into the kitchen. "Excuse me, Mason. I've got to clean up now."

Right, he thought. Of course you do.

"You just sit down and relax," she told him.

"No, let me help you."

"Oh no, you're the guest."

"It'll go faster with two people."

She looked at him for a moment, summing something up in her mind. "Okay," she said, "I'll wash and you dry. Now you get to see how vain I am." She took a pair of pink rubber gloves out from under the sink and pulled them on. "I will *not* have rough red hands."

She ran the sink full of soapy water. "Henry will not boil an egg or wash a plate. He didn't want to marry me but the minute he did, he decided he owned me . . . Yeah, just set that against the wall." She meant the high chair. "Thanks."

He stacked the plates and cutlery and brought them to her. "Yes, indeed," she said, "I was supposed to be his perfect little wife. Aw, Mason, this place was turning into an absolute pigsty. It's summer, so the boys want to sit around every night and get loaded and listen to cool jazz and I'm supposed to wait on them hand and foot? Okay, boys, so maybe I'll join you. I can sit around too and not do a goddamn thing. I can get shit-faced too, let's see how you like that. Well, they didn't like it one little bit."

He'd thought that maybe she'd stopped being angry awhile back but no, it was still burning in her like a low banked fire. "Ever since he left, Henry's been coming out here to pay me these little visits. Not every night but lots of nights. He'll get a good snoot full and decide he wants to have a chat. Sometimes things can get a little wild so I called up the locksmith and that sweet man drove all the way out here and changed the locks for me. So then Henry came out around midnight, banging on the doors, yelling, 'Let me in, Lorianne, let me in!' He was mad as a hornet. I told him, 'Henry, you come back in the afternoon sober and I'll talk to you just as long as you want.'"

Far in the distance the McKinley Tower begin to chime. They both stopped and counted eight. *"All the clocks in the city began to whirr and chime,"* she said in a quoting voice. *"O let not Time deceive you, you cannot conquer Time.* Do you know that poem? That's W.H. Auden."

"No, afraid not. With me, poetry just goes in one ear and out the other."

"That's too bad. It's the poets that tell us the truth. Here's some more of it. *O plunge your hands in water, plunge them up to the wrist; stare, stare in the basin and wonder what you've missed . . .*"

"That's pretty bleak."

"Well, life's pretty bleak. You want to know how Henry and I came to get married? I probably shouldn't tell you this, but I will anyway. Promise you won't repeat any of it."

"I promise."

"Okay, Henry and Carl can be very amusing, like a two-man comedy team, and they were fun to hang around with. They'd buy me sandwiches and beer and . . . you know, I never had to pay for anything. And one night they start feeding me these vodka drinks, sorta like screwdrivers but with lots of 7 Up in them. I didn't have much experience with that sort of thing. They just tasted like soda pop to me. And so, of course, I ended up completely blotto, and Henry says, 'Don't worry, honey, I'll take you home,' and he pours me into his car, but he doesn't take me home. The next morning I wake up in Henry's bed wondering how the hell I got there. The minute I go to the bathroom . . . You probably don't want to hear all this but . . . Okay, I knew things weren't right down there. I didn't know what to think. Henry's being very nice, drives me home, and then later in the day . . . I'm thinking, hey, he wouldn't have done *that*, would he?

"Guess what happened next? I missed my period. I couldn't believe it. Who the hell would screw a passed out girl? That's just one step up from necrophilia. So I go to see Henry, and he says, 'Oh that's a cryin' shame, Lorianne, how do I know it's mine?' And I said, 'Because you're the only man that's been anywhere near me, that's why.'

"Well, it wasn't really his problem he said, so I pointed out to him that I had two brothers in the service and they did come home on leave from time to time and they might very well pay him a little visit. Okay, so the next thing I know Henry's arranged for me take a drive with him to Covington to see some fine doctor there, a real specialist in these sorts of problems. I said, 'Henry, do you honestly expect me to go see some quack in Kentucky and let him poke around in me with a coat hanger?' So the next thing I did is I went to visit your Professor Braithwaite. I called up his secretary and made an appointment just the way you're supposed to do it and I went into his office and told him the whole damn story. And that's how I came to marry Henry."

They had moved outside to sit on the front steps. It had cooled down some and the sun had just set, leaving behind a smear the color of raspberry jam. She badly needed to talk, he knew that, and his job was to keep her talking. "So your grandma," he asked her, "she's still living out at the farm all by herself?"

"Sure is. Everybody wants her to sell the place and move down to Solid where they can look after her, but she won't do it. She's lived there her whole married life and she's going to die there, that's what she says. 'I don't believe in running to doctors,' she says. Whatever she believes in, it's working. She's pushing eighty and you'd never know it. She gets around that farm like . . . I try to keep up with her and I just can't do it. She just exhausts me. But everybody's worried about her anyways. Uncle Arch and Aunt Nell go out there and bring her groceries and check up on her and then Aunt Nell calls up Mom and tells her all about it and then Mom calls me up and tells *me* all about it. My mother just hates Henry. She'd love it if I left Henry."

"You thinking of leaving him?"

"Mason, you know . . . when you've got a sinking ship, shouldn't you get off before it's totally sunk? Can I smoke one of your cigarettes?"

"Sure." He had one with a filter on it but he didn't think she'd want to smoke something he'd picked out of the ashtray outside Worthington. "They're straights."

"Yeah, I know. Let me smoke one anyways."

He lit one for her and one for himself. "Grandma just adores Tammy," she said. "If I was to go back down there with Tammy and move in with her, everybody would love me to pieces and when she goes, she'd probably leave me the place. That's what everybody says. That's all I need, a chicken farm. Yeah, that's what I've always wanted my whole damn life, a chicken farm up in the hills back of Solid, West Virginia."

He'd thought she was mainly talking to herself but now she was looking straight into his eyes like she wanted something from him. "Yeah," he said with a laugh, "a chicken farm."

"But I could do it, you know. I've got a BA and it wouldn't take much to get me accredited so I could teach school in Solid. I'd be home. But I'd be giving up on myself. Do you know what I mean?"

"I know exactly what you mean."

She stood up all of a sudden and walked into the house. He didn't know what she was doing until she came back with an ashtray, that big green glass one that usually sat by Henry's chair. Mason had never seen it when it hadn't been piled high with butts but now it was washed clean. She put it down on the step just below them. "I wouldn't be the first girl from down around Solid to come home with a baby and no husband, not by a long shot, but I'd be Mrs. Algren and that would make all the difference."

"Yeah," he said, "I know what you mean. It's the same way at the Landing."

She butted her smoke out in the ashtray. She hadn't smoked all that much of it. He dragged on his and listened to the birds doing whatever they did at twilight, their sign-off call or whatever it was. "I'd be a respectable woman," Lorianne said. "Yeah, that's *Mrs.* Algren, she teaches in the hah school."

He'd had enough of the Camel. He butted it out. Turned to look at her and she was somehow close. She moved easy through that little distance and kissed him. It was a real kiss but light and gentle, their tongues didn't even touch. "You better get out of here, honey," she said. "You don't want to be here if Henry shows up."

9.

Rain. A goddamn steady downpour. Well no shit, it had to rain sometime, couldn't go the whole summer with no rain. The farmers would love it, Mason usually would love it, the sound of it, the look of it, but today he didn't. He couldn't ride in it.

He'd been awake for a long time but he couldn't find any reason to get up. It had turned downright chilly. He'd wrapped himself up in a blanket but he still wasn't warm enough. He could feel the spray on his face from the little slit window above his bed but he couldn't be bothered to close it. If he was awake enough to count the bongs from the McKinley Tower, then he figured he could describe himself as *wide awake*. The first set he'd counted had been six bongs. Now he'd just counted eight bongs, fuck. That meant he'd been laying there wide awake for two hours.

Jessie had got right to the point the way she always did. "You told me you weren't going to see her again."

Mason had stood there in front of her carrel like a hoopie moron with not one good word to say. Finally he'd said the only thing he could think of, "I just wanted to see how she was doing."

"Oh, did you? And how did you assess the situation?"

"She was . . . I don't know. She was doing better."

147

"Oh, was she?"

The library was hotter than hell as usual, the fans cranking away as usual, Jessie sweating as usual, but she was sitting there staring at him, leaving him standing in front of her desk like a nasty little boy in the principal's office.

"I gather that you've heard the whole damned story now. Are you satisfied? Just what the hell did you think you were doing? Encouraging her to go back to West Virginia?"

"Wait a minute," he said, "I never encouraged her—"

"That's the last thing in the world she needs. Of course she's got to get Henry out of her life. Henry's a fucking pig. But teaching school in some piss-ass little town back in the hills?"

What the fuck was he supposed to say? Was she expecting him to argue with her? "She needed somebody to talk to. I never told her—"

"What on earth were you *thinking*?"

Christ, she was so pissed off at him he couldn't believe it. Now she was giving him another one of her lectures, this one about the patriarchy, telling how this was a perfect example of what happened to girls all the time. "Do you have any idea how hard it is being a woman academic? How many women professors have you had since you've been in university? None? Right?"

"Um, yeah. None. Right."

"And then when somebody comes along with a genuine spark of genius—"

"Wait a minute, Jessie. I think you're—"

She wasn't about to wait a minute. It was the first time she'd looked honest-to-God Italian to him, talking a mile a minute, her dark eyes flashing fire, waving her hands in the air. "When Lorianne got pregnant and married Henry, the whole English department mourned. Dr. Dyson said he'd never seen anything quite like her. Startling and unique . . . and the depth of her scholarship was just . . . He was shocked at how good she was. And now they're saying to each other, 'Well. See. Don't waste your time and energy on a girl. That's what happens with girls. Every goddamn time.'"

Sweet Jesus, he thought, this isn't fair. "Look, Jessie, all I did was . . . She wanted to talk—"

Now she was yelling at him. "Yes, it *matters* to me."

It was like she was running on her own train track and didn't give a shit about his. "I've been trying and trying and *trying* with her, I've offered suggestion after suggestion. She could leave Tammy with her mother in Akron and go to see her on the weekends. It's not that far of a drive. She could even finish her master's in Akron. They have a university there. It's not much of a university but it's better than none at all, and if she wanted to transfer, I'd do the paperwork for her. Oh, I can understand why she doesn't want to be parted from Tammy. If she was mine, I wouldn't want to be parted from her either, but dammit, Mason, people with Lorianne's talents don't come along that often . . ."

This was absolutely hopeless. This was the third time he'd really pissed her off and it was starting to feel like three strikes and you're out.

"—and here you are barging in not knowing a goddamn thing about it, a bull in the china shop. God knows what you're doing. Were you trying to hit on her? After what she said about wanting to sleep with you? She didn't mean it like that . . . Well, Christ, yes, of course she's a very attractive young woman and she knows it, and yes, she does use it. She's very good at manipulating the patriarchy. Do you want to know why? *Because she has to.* The last thing in the world she needs right now is some cute smartass guy coming onto her, encouraging her to go off in—"

Mason couldn't take any more of this shit. He turned and walked away, quick, headed for the stairs down and the way out. He heard her yelling after him, "Mason? Mason!"

Two hours laying there, his thoughts scattered all over the place, he couldn't focus on a goddamn thing. He could have been reading any of those books stacked up by his bed but they were mostly from Jessie's list so there wasn't any point to reading them. He wouldn't be seeing her again.

He should get up, *do something*, but he still couldn't find any reason to do something. I'm laying low, he thought, not the first time he'd thought it. Where had that come from? Some line from some old western he must have read, *Don't worry about me, boys, I'm just laying low.* Okay, he told himself, if you get up, you can have a cup of coffee and a smoke. Well, in order to have a cup of coffee he would have to put a spoonful of instant into a cup, fill the kettle with water, wait till it boiled, pour the boiling water into the cup, and add a little milk and sugar, and that was all just too fucking much.

Living with Eilum was like living with a big clumsy animal, he made lots of bangs and thumps. Mason couldn't hear a bang or a thump or even the distant nasty static of Eilum's radio, so he figured Eilum was where he usually was every morning, laying around in the Buckeye, chowing down a full stack of hots with link sausages, drinking a gallon of black coffee, reading the *Merida Monitor*, shooting the shit with anybody who walked in the door. So Mason was alone in the apartment. Even if he wanted to go join Eilum, he couldn't do it, didn't have near enough gold to last him until the Freddy T kicked in. If it hadn't been raining, he would have forced himself to get up and go for a long ride and that probably would've helped, if you could call convincing yourself that life was worth living a help.

Jesus fucking Christ, he seemed to be setting a record for how long he could lay in bed. He could make it into a funny story someday even though it wasn't the least bit funny. Well, the terrible sickening heat was gone, that should be making him feel better but it didn't. He didn't feel much of anything. He felt tired. *I'm just laying low, boys.* Okay, he told himself, to hell with the cup of coffee, if you get out of bed you can have a smoke.

Before he could change his mind he jumped out of bed, pulled on his underpants and jeans, shoved his feet into his sneakers, dug his old gray raincoat out of the hall closet, and walked quick around the house and onto the girls' porch. The rain was blowing on him sideways, blowing hard, but he fired up a Camel and stood there anyways, looking out through the frame of the trees and into the street. If you're a regular smoker, cigarettes stop making you dizzy, but this one was making him dizzy. Ridiculous how much time it took up, the stupid things you did every day like laying in bed or getting out of bed or smoking or drinking coffee or taking a shit or eating. The rain blurred everything.

Back in bed, he couldn't get Lorianne out of his mind. He'd checked *Nightwood* out of the library, it was right there on his bed table, but it had turned out to be incomprehensible and kind of repellant and he didn't want to read any more of it. That book didn't have anything to do with how he felt about Lorianne, how much he liked and admired her. She was so brave. Look how far she'd come from that dumb little town down in the coal fields. People in the English department had been calling her a genius, and maybe she was, who knows, but anyhow she'd been doing just fine until Henry had fucked her up, literally. She'd cleaned up her whole goddamned place. She'd been sober as a stone. Mason had felt peaceful with her. He'd loved her hoopie girl pigtails.

He got up, pulled the big Sears Roebuck catalogue out from under his dresser, slid back into bed, and started flipping through the pages, looking to see if he could match Lorianne's clothes. Yeah, there was a plain sleeveless blouse the right color, they even called it ecru, and he stuck a piece of paper in to mark the spot. Then he found beige camp shorts like hers, just as short, and plain white sneakers with that old-fashioned look, not too pointed. They were cheap too. Lorianne must have told Jessie about his visit and he wished he knew exactly what she'd said. He knew that Lorianne liked him, she wouldn't have told him all that personal shit unless she liked him, she wouldn't have kissed him, but he didn't know what that kiss meant. He was kind of afraid of her now, afraid that she'd expect him to be just like any other guy.

Eilum was home. He was banging on Mason's door. "What?"

"Hey, ole buddy, come here a second. I want you to check out something for me."

Shit. He got up and followed Eilum into his pigsty room. "Caught me a real strange fish this time," but all Mason could hear coming from Eilum's fancy-ass radio was nasty off-the-wall static. Eilum was grinning at him, well, he was grinning at that tall guy off to Mason's right, and then Mason could make out a voice inside the static. "Hear that fucker, Mase? Just what language is he speaking?"

Eilum bent close to the speaker so Mason did too. When Eilum had banged on his door, Mason had thought maybe it'd be good for him to talk to somebody, maybe give him some kind of relief, but having to stand there and listen to the voice in the static was giving him no relief. He felt some dark sinister thing about it, something hidden in the words he couldn't understand. "Fuck," Mason said, "I don't know what language that is."

"What did you take in school? Spanish?"

"Yeah, Spanish."

"Well, that ain't Spanish."

"No, it's not."

"You get used to the sound of some language, you know, from hearing it in a movie. Like Italian, *Ciao, Marcello*, right? So we've seen, what? Italian movies? French movies? German, how about that? You know what German sounds like? Could that be German?"

"No," Mason said, "I don't think it's German." Some strange-sounding language full of snaps and hisses, could be any language, could be saying anything, made him think of that rotten son of a bitch who'd called him a Nancy boy, he'd never heard that before, it was like something from a foreign language.

"Sure as hell not Chinese, right? Could it be Russian or Polish or one those whatever the fuck they are, Eastern European languages?"

"I don't know, Eilum. Could be. Maybe Slovak." Whoever it was inside that static was talking up a storm. Mason couldn't hear a single word that sounded like anything he knew. All that shit he couldn't understand. Jesus, he didn't want to think any more about it.

"I'll tell you what, ole buddy, either I've got some European station by some weird-ass meteorological fluke or else it's one of those stations that does, you know, an hour for some folks that live in their town. Polish. Slovak. Whoever they are. And then it's just some American station and then it's no big deal. But if that's the case, then they're gonna have to give their call letters in English, and I've been listening for it, and I ain't heard it yet."

"Okay. Eilum. Maybe it's Europe. Yeah, maybe you got Europe. You just keep listening."

Was he going to spend the whole goddamn day in bed? No use trying to jerk off, every time he tried, he was as limp as a noodle and nothing he was thinking was making him the least bit hot. He could keep on going, think of some really extreme stuff, but he always hated himself afterward, thinking how sick it was, depraved. He hated that word, depraved. Nancy boy was the worst thing anybody had ever called him. It was so unexpected. Nobody had ever called him that, he'd never heard that before. He'd never been choked out before either. All he knew by now was that he wasn't in his right mind and he had to get out of that goddamn basement.

How could the post office look so strange? It was just the same post office it always had been, little brick building with the flagpole next to it, there, innocent in the rain. The thing about being choked out is that you can't breathe. When he came to, he was laying on the ground in the school yard. The last thing he could remember, he'd thought he was gonna die. The boys must have all taken off, the one they called Skip, the one who'd choked him out, but there were kids walking by and they just looked away, pretended they didn't see, and some teachers must have seen it through the windows, they could have stopped it, but it was a rough neighborhood and they figured what happened outside of school was none of their business. Nobody helped him, nobody came to help him. He couldn't breathe. He couldn't hold it in his mind for too long, only for a few seconds. He'd thought he was gonna die.

Used to be forest all around here, but thousands of people had died so they could log it all off, grow corn and tomatoes, put in towns with streets and houses, so that little post office could sit there, the stars and stripes hanging down miserable in the rain. The Battle of Fallen Timbers. The Treaty of Greenville. "My heart is a stone," Tecumseh said, "heavy with sadness." No treaty was going to keep the whites out of Ohio Country. Jesus. Americans were good at slaughtering people. Yeah, he thought, that's what we're good at. Weren't you supposed to take the flag down when it was raining? Wasn't it against the law to fly the flag in the rain?

Riding slow, he headed back toward campus. Why the fuck had he just sent a money order for $10.75 to the Sears and Roebuck Company when it was the middle of July and all he had now was $52.25 to last him until September? Well, the old man had paid his rent the whole summer and no matter how much he hated Mason, he couldn't take it back.

But wait a minute, let's just get to the truth of the matter. That's why he'd gone into history, not just because he'd liked reading about the Civil War but because he wanted to get to the truth of the matter, so what *was* the truth? The old man may have written his name on the check but the money had come from Mom and Irene just like that crisp new one hundred dollar bill on his birthday had come from Mom and Irene. If the old man was working, Mason had yet to hear about it. The last he'd heard, the old man was busy managing his investments, whatever the fuck that meant. Mom and Irene had stopped calling him so they must have written him off and that meant he didn't have a home anymore, although he couldn't really call that dump of an apartment in Cincinnati a home, all last summer he'd wanted to get the fuck out of there, but it was like a focal point on the map where he could aim himself if he had to, and now that focal point was gone. Where was he supposed to go now?

Riding his girl's bike in the rain, getting just as soaked as he'd thought he would, wearing a men's ugly gray raincoat, thinking about it. Who the hell wanted to be a man, *his investments*, Jesus. Girl's raincoats at least kept you dry, men's raincoats didn't have hoods, you're supposed to wear a hat, and he was, a cowboy hat he'd bought at the country store where he'd bought his cowgirl boots, he probably looked ridiculous, and he heard the McKinley Tower bong twelve times. Jesus, if it was noon, you sure couldn't tell it.

Remembering when he was alone in the house with a fever, eleven years old, when he still had hope. That was back when he was Eddie, thinking maybe it ain't just that I look like Irene, maybe I *am* Irene, and he shaved his legs and dressed up like Irene, put on her raincoat yellow as a lemon, and old Lula Krieger come by in her ancient black straight-eight Buick and picked him up. He had to buy something at Cochran's so he bought a bag of flour. Maybe that never happened. Maybe it was all a fever dream. But it was so clear in his mind, he was out there walking with a fever, getting soaked and chilled, his teeth chattering in a hard cold bitter rain, blowing hard, blowing sideways up from the river.

The rain was slowing down some, turning misty. It hazed over everything. He left his bike in the rack at the front of Old Main and he was exploring an idea so simple he hadn't seen it before. He walked up through the main entrance and on past the reading room and up the broad stairs to the truly beautiful part of the building that was like a cathedral. The sound of the fans and the sound of the rain falling on the library, the sound coming from all over the library, made a music that comforted him strangely, and he looked up through all that lovely empty space, all the way up to Level Five where Jessie had her carrel, and the light coming through the enormous windows was soft and hazy like the rain.

This was his library, his home, he saw now how it could cradle him and comfort him, and he felt a surge of joy so sweet, so intense, that his eyes filled up. He could sense that Jessie wasn't there today but he walked slowly up to Level Five anyway and all the way back to the eastern wall and stopped in front of her carrel and he'd been right, she wasn't there, and that was exactly the way it should be.

He'd never understood before how simple it was. When he looked out over the campus, that hard cold knife-edge clarity would be gone, everything would be softened by the haze of the rain that was *his* rain, that was made for him today. He could take off this men's ugly raincoat for good and the rain would comfort him and hold him. It was as sweet as could be, and comforting, so close to him now, just up the freight elevator and then quick as a wink through those five doors that were never locked, then he'd be high above the campus where nobody could hurt him ever again. He'd be a girl forever, the blood splashing from him like rose petals fallen in the rain, and he'd be washed clean, broken and beautiful in the rain.

He'd been staring off at nothing but now he looked down. He wasn't quite seeing things. He looked down and read the words on the official card in its wooden slot.

J. COLLIER

DEPARTMENT OF HISTORY

FACULTY OF GRADUATE STUDIES

TEACHING ASSISTANT

Holy sweet Jesus fuck, he needed something real. He grabbed the wooden railing with both hands and squeezed until he saw his knuckles turn white, until he could feel the wood hurt him. You're not rational, he told himself. You're not thinking straight. You won't get to see how beautiful you look broken on the concrete steps. You'll be fucking dead and you won't know a goddamn thing.

10.

Jessie lived just a few blocks off campus in the west end of town where the rents were too high for Mason. He'd ridden by there a few times just to look at it, one of those old houses they divided up for students, nothing special about it. A mailbox by the front steps told him that the first floor apartment on the right belonged to FEINGOLD – COLLIER. The rain was still coming down like crazy, but at the moment, thank God, it wasn't coming down on him. He took off his ridiculous cowboy hat and shook the water off it. You don't arrive at somebody's door with a hat on your head. He rang the doorbell.

"Oh, for Christ's sake." Barefoot, in cotton pajamas, vertical red and white stripes that made her look tall and lean and like she had no figure at all. Music was playing inside. "You really are the king of bad timing. You must have a sixth sense for it."

That sounded like a fuck-off to him but then she said, "Well, I suppose you'd better come in. Distract me."

He couldn't read her expression. Her eyes were swollen and red. She took his hat, tossed it onto an old wooden coat rack. "What on earth have you been doing? Deep sea diving? You look like a drowned rat."

He unbuttoned his raincoat, peeled it off, started to shake off the water, but she took that away from him too and hung it up.

"So here you are, huh? Out of nowhere. Just like that. How'd you know where I live?"

She was gone, moving fast. Then she was back, throwing a towel at him. "I thought you were avoiding me," she said.

"Yeah, I guess I was."

The towel was big and fat, white, it felt like a brand new towel. He dried his hair with it. "I thought you were really pissed off at me," he said.

"I *was* really pissed off at you. You can be pissed off at your friends but they're still your friends."

He followed her into the living room. Two easy chairs with hassocks, each with its own side table and stand-up lamp. On the floor around one of the chairs were thousands of Kleenex, all balled up. "Yes, I've been crying and it's none of your fucking business."

She pointed at the chair with no Kleenex around it and he sank into it.

"My tongue's too sharp. I've been told that my whole life. That's an apology if you want it. But I still think you're an asshole. Okay, so what's going on with you? You look utterly miserable."

"Yeah, I guess."

She was looking at him hard. "You want some tea?"

"Sure."

"You like Earl Grey?"

"I don't know what that is."

"Well, you're about to find out."

She made a quick pass around her chair, picking up Kleenex and flinging them into a big green metal wastebasket. She didn't get them all. Then she headed toward a door on her left, most likely into her bedroom, stopped there. For a moment they were staring at each other, eyes locked. Then she said, "My mother told me never to entertain a gentleman in your pajamas," and disappeared through the door.

He'd thought that he knew who she was but now he wasn't so sure. From where he was sitting he could see right on through her whole apartment, just one big long room with bedrooms off to the sides, every available wall lined with bookshelves, it'd be like living in a library. Only one piece of art on the walls, a framed print, he guessed it was one of those French guys, everything blue and fuzzy with some orange lights shining, water, a bridge, some boats. The living room area had the two easy chairs, a coffee table, the hi-fi sitting on a cabinet with the records underneath. Then came the dining area with a little turquoise drop-leaf table, beyond that the kitchen sink smack up against the back windows, the stove and ice box off to the left. He had to hand it to whoever designed the place, it was neat how they'd crammed everything in.

The music playing was a girl folk singer, a high soprano, unaccompanied. He'd heard her before but he couldn't remember her name. She'd just been a background noise but now he listened to the words she was singing. "She wore no jewels, nor no costly diamonds, of silken stockings she had none at all . . ."

With no warning his eyes flooded with tears. He took a deep breath and held it to stop himself from crying. It was a sign, he didn't have to think about it, he knew it, he could be dead, and he looked outside himself and saw that he'd been there before, even though he'd never set foot in the goddamn place, the rain blowing hard against the windows.

Jessie had just come back. Still barefoot, she'd changed into an old ragged sweat suit, dark blue cotton, the sweatshirt said Penn State Athletics. She threw herself down in the other easy chair, looked like she could be sitting on the bench at a track meet, waiting for her event. She saw his eyes on her, said, "I was something of a jock back in my day."

Nothing surprised him now, everything was too weird to surprise him. She was more than his good old trusty TA from last fall.

He had imagined being in love with her but he hadn't imagined it right. "Who's that?" he said, pointing to the hi-fi.

"Carolyn Hester." She paused to listen, they both paused to listen. "Twas early early, all in the morning, I hit the road for old Donegal—" then she hit the button to make the tone arm lift. "I've had just about enough of her for one day."

If you were living in that folksong world, you could hit the road for old Donegal and it would always be early early in the morning and you could always come back for the girl later, but Mason knew that song wasn't for him. Those songs were never for him.

"So what's wrong?" she said.

He had no answer to that.

"Okay, just sit there and be miserable."

He had to say something, even if it was stupid, even if it didn't come close. "I don't know, Jessie." Then he told her what he'd told Walter, "I'm worried I might be gay."

"So what if you are? What's wrong with that? I am too. That's what you're doing here, isn't it?"

That tea called Earl Grey had a flavor to it so peculiar Mason couldn't say whether he liked it or not but he knew that for the rest of his life whenever he drank it, he'd think of Jessie Collier.

"Some ridiculous pretext," she was saying. "Show me how you'd kiss your boyfriend or some damned thing. She must have known how ridiculous it was the same as I did. We were in the seventh grade. I didn't even know . . . Well, I did and I didn't. I knew it intellectually, but when it came to physical changes in my body? I wasn't ready for that, wasn't even close to being ready for that. And then it haunts you for years."

"Yeah, it does." *Physical changes?* That was a funny way to put it, delicate.

"Do you know what happened to him?"

"Bobby Springer? No. Lost track of him. How about your girl-friend?"

"We stopped . . . I made an effort to keep track of her. For a while. We stopped being friends that year. She went to college somewhere, Northwestern, I think. Met some guy and married him. Hell, I did the same thing. I used to tell myself that it didn't mean anything, that all adolescent girls play around like that. Mason?"

"Yeah?"

"Look, this has to be strictly between you and me, okay? If you repeated any of this to anybody, it could really hurt me. Do you understand that?"

"Oh, yeah. I understand that. I'd never say a word to nobody . . . anybody."

"I didn't think you would but I had to say it, okay? I'm, ah . . . The boys are about to award me a PhD. I had to work twice as hard as any man to get it and . . . But the slightest . . . Okay, and then I've got to get a job somewhere and hang onto it until I get tenure. And if there's the slightest hint . . . *of anything*. Caesar's wife. Do you know about her?"

"Oh, yeah. Caesar's wife must be above suspicion."

"That's right. That's dead right. Well, okay, Sarah and I weren't just roommates."

The Dear Jessie letter had arrived on Saturday, twelve goddamn pages of it. Jessie's first reaction was to be absolutely furious. "She could have waited until she came back to tell me. She could have called me up and we could have talked about it. But no. *Twelve fucking pages*. She pulled out all the stops. She even quoted the Port Huron Statement at me, the bitch."

Jessie should have seen it coming. The honeymoon had definitely been over for a while but she wasn't quite ready for those goddamn twelve pages. "She's dropping out of grad school, devoting herself to the civil rights movement full time, the most important political movement of our age. She'll pay her half of the rent until the first of September, that's only fair. As though I give a fuck about the money! She'll get her stuff out the last week in August. Oh, yeah, and our little fling . . . or whatever-it-was . . . is over. I've got my head in the sand, hopelessly stuck in the nineteenth century. I'd heard that before, but not that . . . What we were doing was *petit bourgeois self-indulgence*. Sorry, Jess, she says. It's been swell. She'll have good memories and she hopes I will too. Nowhere in the twelve pages does she mention what's fairly obvious, that she's got herself a boyfriend down there."

Jessie jumped up and began pacing back and forth. "Amazing how our emotional life depends on the weather. You get a rainy day, not just a drizzle but really coming down steady, all gray and overcast, goddamn depressing, and it all catches up to you."

"Yeah, the rain got to me too."

"You find the right music to break your fucking heart and you play it over and over again. Jesus Christ, I'm just wallowing in it."

"Yeah, I know what you mean. Everything seems kind of, you know, hopeless."

But Jessie didn't want to compare notes on how depressed they'd been. She was off on her own train now, talking fast. "I loved her family. I thought they were just great. I thought of them as my in-laws."

Sarah was Jewish, from New York, her family well off, in the schmatta trade, "that means clothes," upscale women's wear. "She gets all these free clothes. When she gets dressed up, she looks like a goddamned fashion plate. Jesus, the first time I saw her . . . We had one of our parties, in the department, where we could meet the new history grads. She was wearing a little blue suit and heels, everything about her . . . and I thought, Jesus, I'll never be friends with that prissy little thing. And then, before the term's over, we're in bed."

Sarah took Jessie home to New York with her over Christmas break. Of course the Feingolds didn't know that Jessie was Sarah's girlfriend, they just thought she was her goyishe roommate. But she had a gay uncle, "Doesn't everybody have a gay uncle?" He took them to some of the clubs, the ones where you have to know somebody to get in the door.

"I can't tell you how moving it is, to meet other people like you. But lesbians are very suspicious. Well, they've got every right to be. But Sarah's uncle gave a kind of . . . He authenticated us. One night . . . It was the first time in my life a girl made a pass at me. I was absolutely delighted. And the gay boys . . . whoo! Amazing. Did you ever see a drag show?"

"Aw, come on, Jessie, where on earth would I have seen a drag show? The biggest city I've ever been to is Cincinnati."

"You'd love drag, Mason. Some of the young queens . . . my God, they're just gorgeous, like Hollywood starlets. And funny? Jesus! You've got to go to New York, Mason, really. I can give you some names of people to call."

Chicago was a fine town, that toddlin' town, but New York was the center of the universe, easy to get around on the subway, you could go anywhere, do anything. They had a fabulous time. They had dinner on the lower East Side where everything was kosher. One night, strictly by accident, they wandered into a meeting of a society dedicated to the preservation of Yiddish literature. They saw Lightnin' Hopkins at the Ethical Culture Society. "He was drunk but not too drunk to play. Just drunk enough. He said, 'You know what I'm gonna be singing to you about? I'm gonna be singing about *sex*.' And he did too." They even went into a sex shop. "If there'd been a man working in there, we would have come back out in a flash, but there was a girl . . . She got our number the minute we walked in the door. She sold us the cutest little toy . . . well, not *little*. I got to act out my fantasies of being a boy. It was really fun."

They saw Carolyn Hester at Folk City in the Village and fell madly in love with her. "I was as close to her as I am to you. Ah, fuck, Mason, you get a miserable rainy day and then you make it worse. You read those twelve pages over again, and over and over. You play the same fucking song over and over again."

Jessie pointed at the record lying there innocent on the turntable not playing anything. "Once I had a sweetheart and now I have none . . ." She wasn't trying to sing the words, it was more like she was chanting them. "She's gone and leave me, gone and leave me . . . Gone. And. Leave me. In sorrow to mourn. *Petit bourgeois self-indulgence?* I thought we loved each other."

He thought for a moment that she was only doing what the song had told her to do, that she was mourning in sorrow, but no, it was more desperate than that, it was like some terrible force had moved through her and cracked her violently from the inside out. She fell down into that easy chair like she'd been discarded, arched back and howled.

Just like when Irene cried, he didn't know what to do for her but it felt mean to just sit there and watch her cry. He knelt by the side of her chair and took her hand. She let him take it. She squeezed his hand hard.

Just like with Irene, all he could do was wait for it to be over. When she could get words to come out, she said, "You're a good person, Mason."

She lay there panting. Then, abruptly, she let go of him, jumped stiffly up, and with a few steps was at the cupboard above the stove. She took down a fifth of whiskey, poured herself a shot glass full of it, and knocked it back in one quick go. It was like something out of a late-night movie where something terrible happens and the hero needs a drink, a detective movie, maybe. Mason didn't like it. "I've got to smoke," he said.

She pointed at the back door. "There's an ashtray out there."

Jessie's apartment shared the back porch with the apartment next door, a few old wooden chairs lined up on both sides, and beyond that the sorriest excuse for a back yard Mason had ever seen. Early in the summer somebody had cut the grass short, hadn't bothered to water it, and it had all been burned to a lifeless brown. Then, of all pathetic things, there was an old cracked concrete bird bath right smack in the middle. It had been there so long it had settled into the ground crooked. A scraggly hedge separated the yard from the back alley where Jessie had her Studebaker Lark parked and then you were looking at the back wall of a big brick building that was one of those dismal off-campus rooming houses. If he hadn't teamed up with Eilum, he'd probably be in a place like that. He couldn't imagine anything worse.

He dragged in smoke. It was making him dizzy. He hadn't smoked for hours. He looked at his right hand holding the Camel, thought about how eventually that hand would be just so much meat with nothing left for it to do but rot. Yeah, right, along with the rest of him, and what happened to your thoughts? Energy cannot be created or destroyed, did that apply to *you?* Maybe not. He'd always known that fear, it was like a mean old dog that kept coming back. The best thing to do was think about something else.

Okay, Jessie's shot of whiskey. With lots of people one shot leads to another shot, leads to a lot more shots, and he couldn't imagine her pissed out of her mind but maybe that's where she was headed. He didn't want to have to deal with her if she was pissed out of her mind, even now, sober, she was scary. He'd thought that he knew her but he didn't really. He'd seen her as some sort of infinitely superior person, above it all, not bogged down in messy human emotions. Well, no, it turns out that she could cry just like anybody else. Had he known she liked girls? Well, sort of. It hadn't come as a surprise anyway. Fuck this shit, he thought, I could be dead. The rain was still coming down pretty steady. He'd smoked the Camel down so short it was burning his fingers. He butted it out in the old ceramic ashtray. No, death wasn't a sad story you were telling yourself.

Back inside he picked up the big green wastebasket and started going around on the floor for the Kleenex she'd missed. She'd plunked herself back into her easy chair and sat there watching him. All that crying must have exhausted her, she looked beat to shit. "You don't have to do that."

Yes, he absolutely had to do that. "It's okay," he said. "You had anything to eat lately?"

She just laughed.

"I'll make something," he said. "Okay?"

"There's nothing here."

What was she talking about? He'd already seen all the canned goods on her shelves. "You mind if I look?"

Well, okay, dinner so far seemed to be a big hit. They were sitting at the little turquoise table just like normal people, and Jessie was eating like she hadn't seen food in a while. She'd got some of her energy back, was talking to him the way she had on that night when they'd sat together on the girls' porch, telling him stories about her life, and he was delighted by that. There had been no second shot of whiskey.

"This is truly amazing, Mason. Thank you. The perfect dinner for a rainy day. I never would have thought of any of this."

"I'm good at making something out of nothing. I've had lots of practice."

He'd just used what he'd found. A head of lettuce, a few eggs, and some bacon had led to a wilted lettuce salad. A couple pounds of hamburger, not too old, some stale bread, a few onions and potatoes, a bottle of Heinz ketchup and a can of mushroom soup had led to meatloaf with mashed potatoes and gravy.

"How'd you learn to cook?"

"Mainly from my grandma. She kept trying to show Irene but I was the one who learned it. I was determined to be the girl."

"Well, good for you. I'm a terrible cook. I can follow a recipe but that's about it. I've been told that I have no sympathy with the ingredients and that's probably true."

"So anyhow . . . you were telling me about President Eisenhower. He signed some kind of a . . ."

"Oh, right. An executive order that banned gay people from working for the federal government. *Sexual perverts*, that's the term that was used . . . I mean it was used in the official documents and the goddamned *New York Times* . . . and sexual perverts were supposed to be a security risk, easy to blackmail . . . somehow naturally attracted to communism. J. Edgar Hoover went after them big time, the miserable prick. Thousands of people were fired."

So that terrible summer after Jessie graduated from high school, it wasn't just that her father had taken the Fifth, there was a lot more to it than that. She was laying around the house, sick with dread, wearing nothing but her one old pair of Bermuda shorts, reading *The Well of Loneliness*. "If you're a lesbian, or if you think you might be one, it's the most depressing book ever written."

That fall when she went off to Penn State, she was determined that she was absolutely *not* going to be a sexual pervert, that she was going to be the most normal girl the world had ever seen. It was damned hard work. "As a girl, I was an utter washout. I felt like an imposter. Dear God, my slip showed, my seams were crooked, my stockings had runs in them and were always falling down. And heels? A couple of times I damned near broke my ankle. Straight skirts? Did you ever wear a straight skirt?"

Mason was embarrassed. "No. When I . . . It was just when I was little, I wore Irene's dresses. They were just, you know, little kid dresses."

"You ought to try it sometime. I mean the old '50s straight

169

skirts. God, they were damned near as bad as Edwardian hobble skirts . . . Why did you start wearing your sister's dresses? Did your mother put you in dresses?"

"I don't know. It's . . . kind of lost in the mists of antiquity." He'd wanted her to smile at that, and she did. "I don't remember back that far. And Mom won't talk about it. Any time I ask her, she just changes the subject."

"That's not very useful . . . Well, anyhow, I had a beautiful tweed suit with one of those insane skirts. Everybody told me how great I looked in it. *I* even thought I looked great in it. But walking any-where? Jesus! Rick loved me in that suit."

Barb and Greg, their best friends, lived right across the street and that's how the snake got into the garden. Barb was the perfect '50s housewife. She knew all the cute little tricks from the ladies' magazines. Her slip did not show, her seams were never crooked, she took over Jessie as a personal project, shared recipes with her, picked out clothes for her. The boys were at the university all day so Jessie and Barb spent a lot of time together. One afternoon they were talking about how difficult adolescence was for girls and one thing led to another.

By then Jessie had realized that she did not like sex with men, did not enjoy having a penis shoved inside her, but it was some-thing she had to put up with because it was part of the marriage deal. "My natural sexuality . . . I'm naturally very aggressive and I arouse really fast and Rick . . . Six-foot-two ex-basketball star and decorated war veteran . . . He was afraid of me! Yes, really. He even suggested that I have my testosterone level checked. Jesus fucking Christ! No, I was not going to have my testosterone level checked, my testosterone level was just fine, thank you. Okay, I thought, you want me to lie there and do nothing, that's exactly what you're going to get. But then when Barb and I became lovers . . . *She* wasn't telling me I was too aggressive."

For the first time in her life, Jessie was having great sex. Yes, she thought, I really am a lesbian and we're not hurting anybody and there's nothing wrong with anything. Then Greg came home sick with a cold one afternoon and caught them. "It was like a scene out of a French farce. He walked right in on us. We couldn't deny it. He'd caught us *in flagrante*. Barb sold me out, the bitch. 'Oh, it's all Jessie's fault! The nasty girl seduced me.' Greg's reaction to sexual perverts was absolutely visceral, sheer disgust, he hates me to this day, but Rick had a more enlightened opinion. He thought it was a matter of *mental illness*. He felt sorry for me. That's one of the reasons our divorce was so amiable."

Jessie stopped talking, looked down at her empty plate. He reached for it, but she picked it up first. "Here I am just sitting here letting you wait on me."

She picked up his plate too, carried both plates to the sink. "Ah, Mason, the next girl I meet who says . . . and Barb and Sarah both said it, or words to that effect . . . The next supposedly straight girl I meet who says, 'I'm not queer, I'm only queer for you,' I'm going to run as fast as I can in the opposite direction."

They were back in the living room, drinking more of that Earl Grey tea, and they'd been talking for hours. They'd reached that magical point where they could say anything to each other, say whatever came into their heads. Mason had told her about his thesis, how simple Dr. Braithwaite had made it seem. He'd told her what he could remember about growing up, about walking down to the Landing in his sister's clothes and getting picked up by old Mrs. Krieger and not knowing if it was real memory or a fever dream. Now he was telling her about the worst year of his life, a kind of a match for hers. Both of their senior years in high school had been the absolute pits and he felt that connected them somehow. "They just left me there, lying laying there on the school grounds right in front of the fucking windows. People must have seen it. Teachers must have seen it."

"Jesus, Mason, that's utterly horrible."

"I looked it up. It was a choke hold. Sometimes they call it a rear arm bar—"

"You *looked it up?*"

"Sure. In a wrestling book. That's how you learn things . . . you look them up." If anybody ought to know that, she should. "It's real dangerous. You're shutting off the blood supply to the brain. It happens real fast. That's why it's illegal in high-school wrestling. You can kill somebody with it."

She was the first person he'd ever told about this shit. "It was a rough neighborhood. It was cheap, that's why we were there. Lots of hillbilly kids, hoopie kids and kids from Kentucky, and it's kind of a . . . Hoopie kids, at least where I grew up, were nice kids, they were . . . neighborly. But you take them out of West Virginia and stick them somewhere else . . . God, they get mean. I don't know why that should be."

His only friends were *Merriam-Webster's Collegiate Dictionary* and *Roget's Thesaurus.* He was working his fucking ass off. It was the only way out of that Cincinnati slime pit. He wanted a scholarship somewhere and Merida offered him one. So he got exactly what he wanted and the next year there he was taking ROTC because it was a land grant institution, taking men's PE where everybody made fun of him, stuck in the men's dorm with a bunch of animals who didn't give a shit. He considered telling her about the first time he'd tried to kill himself but decided not to. He didn't want her think he was suicidal.

"Jessie. I'm still thinking about those little bastards . . . back in Cincinnati. Skip and those other little pricks. Why'd they decide I was gay? Is there . . . ? Do I have some kind of sign on me?"

"No. It was probably . . . You were the new kid on the block.

You're a small guy and you're fair and you've got a pretty face. At seventeen . . . Is that what you were? You probably looked a lot younger."

"Yeah, I did."

"And it's too easy for boys to call each other queer. They do that all the time. I know because I've got two brothers."

"Yeah, you're right."

"Now it's your hair."

"Aw fuck, back then I was wearing a crew cut."

Another one of those uneasy moments settled down over them when they were just sitting there looking at each other. "Why did you decide to let your hair grow?" she asked him.

"It wasn't something I decided. I walked up to Campus Barbers . . . I was gonna go home for Christmas and I needed a haircut. And I walked up to the door and I just couldn't go through it. I had a feeling."

"A *feeling?* What the hell does that mean?"

"Just . . . you know. Something inside. Some feelings you can't argue with."

"Really? I argue with my feelings all the time."

Mason had thought that they were winding things up but there still seemed to be more to say. He had his coat on and his hat in his hands but they'd got stopped in the hallway just inside the front door. "You do own a suit, don't you?" she was asking him.

"Oh, yeah, sure I do."

"Okay, so wear it sometimes. Get a haircut. Save the makeup for your private life. You're a good scholar. Play it right and you'll get absorbed right into the patriarchy. Academia is . . . There's lots of room for eccentricity. Just walk around campus when school's on, you see professors . . . some of them are so strange. You look at them and you think, well, it's a good thing that the university exists

173

because otherwise there wouldn't be a place for you anywhere in the world. There's these little pockets of freedom. Well, relative freedom. Just slip into one of them. That's what I'm trying to do."

It wasn't that he hadn't thought of it. "That's all well and good," he said, "and it's a . . . yeah, some place to go, but it would never . . . Aw, fuck, Jessie, all I ever wanted was to be a girl like my sister."

"Oh, really?" she snapped back at him. "I'm sure Irene must be very happy. Working as a secretary for some asshole and not getting paid a tenth of what he's making. Stuck in dumbass clerical jobs with no future . . . except maybe to marry some man who'll scoop her up and take her away, the old Cinderella myth. And living with her violent alcoholic father. Oh yes, she must be a very very happy girl."

Mason was hurt. She must have seen it on his face. "There's my sharp tongue again," she said. "Sorry. It's just that—"

"No," he said. "I'm not talking about the way things are. I'm talking about the way things ought to be."

"Okay. I understand that."

"Aw, hell, Jessie, I don't even know how to be a boy. All the time I was growing up, I had to listen to all these guys talking about how they want to stick their pricks into somebody . . . into girls . . . and I had to take their word for it . . . that they really want to do that. Because I can't feel it. I've got no desire whatsoever to stick my prick into anybody. I mean it, *I literally can't feel it.* I can't even imagine why anybody would want to do that."

"You don't want to fuck somebody. You want somebody to fuck you."

"That sounds right. Yeah, I'd say you got that exactly right."

She gave him a long sorrowful look. "Ah, Mason. You won't always be stuck in the middle of goddamned Ohio. That cute boy you've been waiting for is bound to show up some day."

11.

The rain had blown through and left the campus cool and sweet like springtime all over again but now the summer heat was starting to come back. Mason was crossing Level Five the way he always did, walking along the balustrade. He got to the end of the stacks, turned, and headed toward Jessie's carrel. Halfway there, he could see that it was empty but he kept on going anyway because it was part of the ritual.

Her desk was bathed in the flat quiet morning light. No sign of her, no papers, no stack of books. It had only been three days but it felt like an eternity. Well, she was probably busy. Yeah, and if you're busy, three days can go by in a flash. But shit. If she wasn't coming into the library, how was he supposed to see her? He couldn't just turn up at her place again, that was something you only do once. "Call me," she'd said. If she'd really wanted him to do that, she could have given him her goddamn phone number.

He stood there not knowing what to do next. He was kind of disgusted with himself, had to find some purpose in life other than Jessie Collier. Probably should go home and work some more on his thesis. Then, all of a sudden, he heard guys talking and laughing. It was a jolt. He'd got used to the library being mostly empty, just a few vague quiet summer scholars drifting through. Loud-mouthed boys should not be turning up. It sounded like they were coming up the stairs to Level Five. He had to go see.

Something told him not to cross back along the balustrade where he'd be visible the whole way so he went through the stacks. He came on them too fast. They looked like frat boys. They were in the 910s, geography, pawing through the books. Well, yeah, that's what you come into a library for, isn't it? Four of them, polo shirts and beige Bermudas, buzzed off hair, dressed so much alike they might as well have been stamped out with a cookie cutter. They were blocking the whole aisle. His whole life Mason had avoided packs of boys and he wanted to avoid this one. They'd already seen him. The easiest thing to do was duck into the men's can.

"Hey, honey, wrong one," one of them yelled after him.

Somebody else laughed. "That's a boy."

"You're kidding me."

Jesus, one of them was following Mason right into the can. "Hey! Nice hair."

The little prick didn't look that far out of high school. "Fuck off," Mason said.

"What did you say to me?" He was staring at Mason, puzzled and scared. Kind of round, yeah, pudgy was the right word, and he'd got a little bit too much sun lately, red faced and sweaty, smelled like a gym with Aqua Velva splashed in it. The three other boys had followed him into the can. "Hey, Jim, come on," one of them was saying to him.

"Hey, faggot. I asked you a question. What did you say to me?"

"Hey, Jim, Jim, come on."

"Oh, for Christ's sake," Mason said in his best shit-kicker voice, "I don't want any trouble with you. Just minding my own damn business—"

"Faggot," Jim said, "I'll mind your business, faggot," and he took a step forward and punched Mason in the mouth.

Mason's head smacked into the wall behind him, the world flashed with sparkler lights, and he must have folded at the knees and slid partway down the wall because that's where he was. The boys were hauling ass out of there. Yelling. Angry. Pissed off at Jim for making trouble.

Eilum's fingers were probing around on the back of Mason's head. "Hurt?"

"Um . . . a little tender."

"*A little tender?* Jesus. Let me see your lip."

Mason was sitting on a kitchen chair holding crushed ice in a washrag on his mouth. He lifted it away. "Yeah, a bit puffy, got to admit. But it's redder from all that fucking ice than it is from the devastating blow you received."

"I never said it was a devastating blow, Jesus, man."

"Listen, buddy, I'm an expert on getting punched in the head. You might even say I've got an advanced degree in it. Yeah, I could lead a graduate seminar or two on that topic. Scalp wounds bleed like an absolute son of a bitch, kee-rist, you think you've been killed! Did you get enough of a wound to bleed? No, you did not. Not one drop. *A little tender*, you say."

"Eilum, for fuck's sake, I was just—"

"I know, I know, Ace, I'm just trying to bring you up to date on reality, just checking out the empirical evidence. Okay, let us consider what he might have been done to you. He could have been punched you out and you could have ended up in the hospital with a concussion. Did that happen? No, it did not. He could have broken your jaw or dislocated it. Did that happen? No, it did not. He could have bashed out a few of your pearly white teeth, split your fucking lip wide open. Did any of *that* happen? No, it did not. I'd say the cocksucker gave you a modest little tap. When you get up tomorrow, it won't even show. So in my highly informed opinion you got off lucky."

"Lucky? Sure. But if I can't even— I just couldn't believe the little son of a bitch *hit me*. If it was a modest little tap, that was probably all he had in him. And I never even saw it coming. I just stood there. Jesus."

"Yeah, going into most social situations it don't hurt to assume the worst. If I'd been there, his head would have gone through that fucking wall, but I wasn't, was I?"

"I never would have thought . . . Never in a million years . . . The little bastard was scared."

"You remember what he looks like?"

"Oh, yeah. I'll never forget what he looks like."

"Okay, so don't sweat it, champ, this campus ain't that big. We're bound to run into that cocksucker sooner or later and when we do, you're gonna see your ole buddy Eilum stomp some rump."

Elilum reached down and flipped Mason's hair. "This is still a free country the last I heard, but some assholes don't think so. Listen, buddy, let me give you some advice. Artsy though it may be, maybe you ought to consider getting an inch or two sheared off this mane."

Unless he could find the next thing to do Mason might remain stuck forever on that kitchen chair holding that washrag on his mouth. Just like a girl, he was worrying about still being pretty, Jesus. And the thing he couldn't understand, he really couldn't, was why that dumbass little boy had hated him so much that he had to hit him. You could tell just looking at the little prick that he wasn't a scrapper, you could tell that he was scared, it showed in his eyes, but he had to do it anyhow. Why? Just because he'd thought for a minute that Mason was a girl?

It was bringing back that sick sense of dread from his senior year in high school. He'd sat for hours in the school library so he'd be sure that Skip and those little pricks had left for the day.

He'd been afraid to even take a walk anywhere. And all he'd been able to think was *I've got to get the fuck out of here* and that's exactly what he'd done. He threw the washrag into the sink and heard the slushy clunk as it hit the porcelain.

Eilum was right, this was getting ridiculous, he was creating his own damn trouble. What would happen if he ran into some asshole who really knew how to throw a punch? Lots of boys now were showing up with Beatles, so if he had a Beatle, he'd at least fit into some category people could understand, and that would be an improvement, so where was he gonna get his hair cut? Campus Barbers? Those two foul-mouthed old birds would rag his ass big time and he'd walk out of there looking like a Marine recruit.

Okay, he'd just found the next thing to do. He got up off the kitchen chair and started flipping through the Merida Yellow Pages. Under what? Beauty? No, under Hair Styling. Here was "Patty's Primping Parlor." Oh Lord, no. How about "Karen's Kute Kuts"? Yeah, maybe. He picked up the phone but kept his finger down on the cradle while he thought about it.

It shouldn't be a major ordeal, it was just a phone call. He was sweating, could feel it in his armpits, ridiculous. He dialed the number and too soon a woman's voice answered, cheery, almost singing it, "Karen's Kuts."

"Excuse me, uh . . ." If he went on much longer not saying anything, she would think it was a prank call and hang up on him. "Would you do a Beatle haircut for a boy?"

"Yes, of course. We'd be happy to cut your little boy's hair. How old is he?"

Very gently Mason hung up.

Of course Irene would want to talk about the old man. "You really hurt him. I've never seen him like this. He's brooding—"

"*Brooding?* Jesus. All he'd have to say is he was sorry. Say he lost his temper—"

"That goes for you too, Eddie. You could start by saying *you* were sorry—"

"*Me?* What am I supposed to be sorry for? He knocked me down and kicked me."

"He says you got excited and fell over something. The foot stool. He says he never touched you."

"Yeah, but he did. You were right there. You saw it."

"I don't know, Eddie. I was in the dining room."

"Oh, for fuck's sake."

"Don't you swear at me. If you swear at me, I'll hang up on you."

Shit, why had he thought that this time was gonna be any different? "Reenie? I don't want to fight with you. I just want to ask you some things. Maybe you don't want to talk to me?"

"I'm wasting my lunch hour standing in a damn phone booth. Does that sound like I don't want to talk to you? Okay, Eddie, so what do you want to talk about?"

"Okay? When we were little, how much did I wear your clothes?"

"I don't know. Maybe once or twice. We just did it for fun sometimes."

"That's not the way I remember it."

"What good does it to . . . ? You shouldn't be dwelling on that stuff. That was years ago. You should just put it all behind you."

"We used to play the boys against the girls and I was always with the girls. I was always with you."

He heard her sharp indrawn breath. What did that mean? Was she gonna start yelling at him or start bawling? Why had everything changed since last summer? He'd thought they were on the same side. "Reenie? I'm sorry I'm bothering you, okay? Maybe you don't want to talk anymore?"

"No, we can talk. Go ahead and talk."

Talk? He listened to the traffic outside her phone booth. What was he hoping to get from her? "Okay, there was this day when I was eleven."

He wanted to describe it clearly, all the details of it, just the way he remembered it, and he started to do that. Alone in the house, the fever, the jumpy wallpaper, the weird hot buzz in his mind, putting on her clothes—

"Wait a minute, Eddie. That can't be right. We never would of left you alone if you were running a fever."

"Yeah, but you did. It was raining like a son of a bitch and I started walking down to the Landing and old Mrs. Krieger picked me up in her straight-eight Buick. All the old ladies down at Mrs. Cochran's store thought I was you."

"Oh, Eddie, nothing like that ever happened. We never would of left you alone. And Lula Krieger? She didn't even have a driver's license. They took it away years ago. She was always getting stuck or running into things, phone poles and . . . She was kind of a legend. I think she ran into a cow once. Don't you remember? Maybe you were too little."

This was absolutely hopeless. God, he remembered it so clear. As soon as he got in Mrs. Krieger's Buick, she asked him how his grandma was doing, so she must have thought he was Irene. When they got to the store, he had to buy something, otherwise what was he walking down there for? All he could think of was a bag of flour and then he didn't have any money. He'd never thought to bring any money. "Don't worry about it, honey," Mrs. Cochran said to him, "I'll just put it on your grandma's bill." So she must have thought he was Irene too.

"Eddie?"

"Yeah?"

"Let me ask you something. Do you still consider yourself a member of this family?"

"Do I *what?*"

"It feels like you disowned us."

"Jesus, Reenie, it feels more like all of you disowned *me*. You never call me any more—"

"Why the hell should we call you? You never answer the phone."

"That's not true! I always answer the phone now." That wasn't strictly speaking true but it was close enough.

"Phone lines run both ways. And you could come home. You got that scholarship and you think you don't need us anymore, is that it? After everything we've sacrificed for you?"

"Oh, for Christ's sake. The old man—"

"He doesn't hold a grudge. You think he does, but he doesn't. Just come home for a few days, say you're sorry, then he'll say he's sorry—"

"Hey! Reenie. Wait a minute. Slow down a minute. Is he working?"

He heard her hesitate. "There's a . . . at Shillito's," she said. "There's a man in the men's department gonna retire. Dad's got a pretty good chance—"

"How about Mom? Is she working?"

"Oh, come on, Eddie. She's got that . . . you know, whatever it is in her foot. It's hard for her to stand for very long."

"Irene! Jesus, you're twenty-four years old! What the fuck are you doing supporting two drunks?"

She hung up on him.

Mason seemed to be walking in circles around the kitchen. He couldn't think straight, lots of things in his mind but he couldn't focus on any of them. He'd always believed that you got some warning before you started to cry, that you felt it in your chest or your eyes stung or some damn thing, and he'd always believed that you could stop yourself from crying, but now all of a sudden he was crying and he couldn't stop. He ran into his bedroom, slammed the door, threw himself down onto the bed, and pressed the pillow over his face. He didn't want anybody to hear him.

It didn't last all that long. After it was over, he laid there and stared up at the fucked-up paint on the ceiling. Maybe Irene was right, they would never would have left him alone in the house with a fever, and there was something else he hadn't thought of before. He and Irene didn't look a thing alike. He favored the Masons and she favored the Macquaries and he'd been a skinny little boy, eleven years old, and she'd been fourteen and already starting to look like a woman. Hell, she must have weighed a good twenty-five pounds more than he did. He could have impersonated a girl his own age easy, but *a fourteen-year-old girl?* No, that was impossible. So most likely he'd made it all up, part fever dream and part imagination. If he'd made that up, how could he tell if he was remembering anything right? Aw shit, what was history if it wasn't memory? What if nobody was remembering anything right? What if it was all just a bunch of stories people made up and nothing meant a fucking thing?

He was still laying there when Eilum knocked on his door. "Hey? Buddy? Get your ass in gear. It's Goldwater night at the Buckeye."

Jesus, fuck. "Come in. What?"

Eilum pushed through the door and grinned down at the phantom lying off to the right side of Mason's bed. "Goldwater night. The fucker's gonna be on the television. They got the Goldwater special, ninety-nine cents."

Mason just snapped. "Oh, for fuck's sake. I can't be blowing money on restaurant meals. I'm not gonna make it till the Freddy T kicks in as it is."

"What? You getting tapped out? Why the fuck didn't you say so?" Eilum pulled his wallet out of his shorts, opened it, reached in, extracted a wad of bills and dumped them onto Mason's bed.

Mason sat up. "Hey? What are you doing? You don't have to do that."

"Forget it, man. I know you're good for it. You can pay me back when the Freddy T kicks in." He turned and walked out. Mason heard the ice box door bang open and Eilum popping something open, an RC Cola or, more likely, a Bud.

Jesus. He counted the money. Eighty-five dollars. If he kept it, his problems were solved. Well, mostly solved. Fuck, he had to keep it, he had no choice. "Hey. Eilum. Thanks a lot."

"Don't worry about it, forget it. Come on, fuckface, get your sorry ass in gear."

When Eilum pulled up in front of the Buckeye, the first thing Mason saw was Jessie's Lark parked there. Just the sight of her car made his heart jump and then the minute they walked inside, he saw her across the room and he didn't know what the fuck to do so he walked over to say hi.

They'd hauled the portable TV out of the bar and set it up on the restaurant side, arranged tables around it. People were already choosing their tables and Jessie was standing next to what must be the history table. The same guys who'd been at Henry's party were sitting there and the girl grad who'd asked if Mason was a boy or a girl was standing right next to Jessie.

The Buckeye was off-campus, but both Jessie and the girl grad were still playing it safe, following the dress code, Jessie in one of her pleated linen skirts and the girl grad in a droopy summer dress, yellow, not a good color for her. Mason should know the girl grad's name but couldn't remember it. She was pretty in a rabbity kind of way, had that earnest female academic look to her, serious eyes and dead straight hair, holding a cashmere sweater in case it got chilly later which it wasn't going to. She might be the only girl in the history MA program so of course she would attach herself to Jessie.

"Hi, Mason, how have you been?"

This time he could read her eyes. "Caesar's wife," they were saying. With the girl grad right next to her, Jessie was talking to him just the way a TA would talk to an ex-student. He shouldn't be hurt, that's just the way it was going to have to be. "Not too bad," he said.

The girl grad was giving him a somber puzzled look like she was still trying to fit him into the general scheme of things. How would Jessie explain him later? Oh, he's from West Virginia?

Jessie was asking him how his thesis was coming. "Almost got a first draft of it." That was overstating it by a long shot but he had got some work done.

"Wow, that's great. If you want me to read it . . ."

"Oh, yeah. After I get it all down and cleaned up . . ." and if you ever give me your goddamn phone number.

If he stood there any longer, it was going to get embarrassing, so he made a stiff little goodbye wave and went to see where Eilum had gone. He'd joined Dave and Mick at a table on the other side of the room. Mason sat down with them.

"Ah, the tricky one," Eilum was saying to Nixon's dumbass face on the television.

"Yeah," Dave said, "you can't lick our Dick." It was an old joke, and not that funny anyway, but the three of them were yucking it up. They hadn't been in the Buckeye ten minutes and already Eilum had knocked back a large draft and was waving for another one. "What's ah . . . ?" Mason pointed at the TV.

"He's introducing him." Mick's hair was getting so long in the front that he had to flip it to one side. Mason looked into Mick's big sympathetic chocolate-brown eyes and thought, would I go to bed with you? If it was an ideal world where boys did that sort of thing on a regular basis, the answer was an unqualified yes, but compared to what he felt for Jessie it didn't even come close.

"All of you having the Goldwater special?" It was that nice middle-aged lady who'd been waitressing at the Buckeye for as long as Mason had been at Merida.

"What *is* the Goldwater special?" Mason asked her.

"The fried chicken dinner with a slice of that good old one-hundred-percent-American apple pie," said with a wink, "à la mode, fifteen cents extra."

"Nope," Mason said. His stomach was feeling better these days but he couldn't imagine gnawing on a fried chicken leg. He was hungry though. He'd been eating normal lately, or trying too, but he wanted something that would go down easy and sit there easy. "You folks do Cincinnati chili?"

"Sure we do. You want it three ways?

Mason was absurdly delighted. "Yeah, that's exactly how I want it," and looking over toward the entrance, he saw that Henry Algren was standing at the door looking in, just standing there staring. Even as far away as he was, Mason could see that there was something not quite right about Henry. What could he be looking for?

Goldwater night had packed them in. There was Walter, sitting not with his usual collection of boys but with his peers, the cheery old guy who owned the Buckeye, the manager of the supermarket on Delaware, the editor of *The Monitor*, the pharmacist from Heike Lewis, a bunch of other old birds, looked like a meeting of the Rotary Club. Mason didn't know whether to give Walter a wave or not, afraid he might blow his cover, but Walter waved at him and Mason grinned and waved back. Good for Walter. He didn't give a shit.

On the television people were cheering, balloons were going up, and the band was blasting out "The Battle Hymn of the Republic," of course they were, it was a Republican convention, wasn't it? Some frenzied but unseen choir was singing, "His truth is marching on!" Whose truth? Goldwater's? Sure as hell not Abraham Lincoln's. And Mason saw Jessie walking over to talk to Henry.

She got there and Henry turned his back on her. The move was so formal and abrupt it looked like a ROTC cadet doing an about face and it left Jessie floored and flat footed, her mouth a big sad open zero. Embarrassed, she turned and hurried back toward her table. Mason decided that he'd better be going somewhere too, maybe to the men's can in the bar, so they could meet, strictly by accident, well away from where anybody could hear them.

"Jesus," Jessie said under her breath, "I just got the cut direct. That's what they called it in the nineteenth century."

"Yeah, I saw that. So what . . . ? That was mean of him. What's with him?"

"He's pissed off at me because he thinks I filled up Lorianne's head with a bunch of nasty feminist ideas . . . and it's true, I did. I think she might make it stick this time. She wants a divorce. Anyhow she says she does."

There was a limit to how long they could stand there before it would stop looking accidental. "Carl's gone back to Canton," she was telling him. "He couldn't take any more. In one of his rare moments of sincerity he told me that Henry was driving him nuts. Henry's kind of . . . I told Lorianne to get a restraining order. Whether she'll do it or not is another matter."

"Jesus."

For anybody who might have been watching, Jessie smiled like a toothpaste ad and made a cheery see-you-later gesture. "Fun and games," she said. At the convention they were drowning in balloons, millions of balloons, so many that Goldwater and his family couldn't walk through them to the podium. People were running madly around kicking balloons away. The crowd was chanting, "We want Barry!"

To keep up appearances Mason had to continue on his way somewhere but Henry was still standing there like a marble monument. The poor bastard, Mason thought, he's lost it. Mason had lost it a few times himself so he knew what it felt like. He hadn't planned to walk straight over to Henry but that's what he was doing. "Hey, buddy, how's it going?"

Mason had been prepared for Henry to be weird but maybe not as weird as he was. He stared into Mason's face, *directly* into Mason's face, and began to puff like a steam engine, jerking his arms up and down like pistons.

The only thing Mason could think to do was pretend that this was perfectly normal. "Come and sit with us, Henry. We got lots of room at our table."

Henry didn't change expression. He kept on going puff, puff, puff. His eyes were bulging and air was blasting out of his nose and mouth.

"Come on, Henry." Mason turned and walked away. To his surprise, Henry followed.

"Sweet Lord Jesus on a flying machine," Eilum said, "Henry, you are looking just so very fine tonight," and he jumped to his feet, whipped out a chair, and hustled Henry into it. Henry, suddenly deflated, sat and stared at the table top.

Goldwater and his lovely wife and lovely family had finally made it to the podium. The band was still blaring, the crowd was still cheering, Tricky Dick Nixon was still hanging around there somewhere. "Hey," Eilum yelled at their waitress, "ole Henry here needs a beer and a special." Goldwater raised his hand to get them to quiet down but they weren't quieting down.

The owner of the Buckeye, Jay or Joel or whatever it was, that happy old man who was always smiling, jumped up, stood next to the TV, and shouted, "Thank you, thank you, thank you all for coming tonight, and thank you to Tony from the kitchen who's lent us his fine hi-fi speakers . . ." and Tony with a wave made some adjustment on the back of the TV, and wham! the folks at the Cow Palace in Daly City, California, were suddenly louder than the folks at the Buckeye in Merida, Ohio. Tony had set up two huge stereo speakers at the far corners of the dining room.

"Anyhoo," the owner was yelling, "and with no further ado, love him or hate him, here he is, one heck of a guy, Barry Goldwater!"

It was perfectly timed. "To my good friend," Goldwater intoned, "and great Republican, Dick Nixon, and your charming wife, Pat . . ."

It was the man himself, white-haired, granite-jawed, weathered face, no-bullshit black-framed glasses, not hard to sound tough when you looked like that. He was thanking everybody there was to thank, and a large draft beer appeared on the table and slid toward Henry. Just like he'd been expecting it, Henry picked it up, tilted it back, and drank about half, his Adam's apple bobbing, making loud glugging noises. Eilum and Dave were laughing at him but Mick leaned toward Mason. "What's the matter with him?"

Damn good question. "Split up with his wife, I guess. I don't really know."

"I accept your nomination," Goldwater told them and of course the folks went wild.

The nice lady waitress brought Mason's plate of chili three ways. She'd even brought him a spoon in case he wanted to twirl the spaghetti. Now that he was temporarily a rich man, he was gonna leave her a decent tip. Goldwater, meanwhile, was talking about what the good Lord had done to raise the Republic, the land of the free. ". . . not to stagnate in *the swampland of collectivism!*" his voice harsh.

"Fuck you," Mason said.

All the specials were hitting the table. Mason was glad he hadn't ordered one, the smell of fried chicken was making him a little bit sick. And he was having trouble with his beer. He loved the taste of it but he was afraid to dump it down on top of the chili. What was the matter with him? He used to drink beer by the gallon. "Hey, a ginger ale," he called after the waitress.

"Every action, every word, every breath, every heartbeat," Goldwater was proclaiming, and all those everys were headed where? *"Freedom!"* Then he was hammering the Democrats for all their military failures, Berlin, Bay of Pigs, Laos, Vietnam. Not only that, but those bastards were permitting violence in our streets.

"Shit," Mason said, "that's for Martin Luther King. Birmingham."

"More than that," Mick said. "They're rioting in Harlem."

"What? When?"

"Started today. Still going on. A white cop killed a black kid."

"No shit?"

That was the first Mason had heard of it. He usually tried to keep up on things but he hadn't read a paper or listened to the radio since the first day of the convention when he'd got so disgusted by what they did to Nelson Rockefeller that he'd thought, fuck the GOP. And then, of course, he'd got lost brooding about Jessie Collier.

"Yeah," Mick was telling him, "he was only fifteen. A sophomore in high school. He wasn't doing much of anything. Just assing around. That white cop shot him dead."

"Jesus fuck," Mason said.

Now Goldwater was talking about the failure of public officials to keep the streets free from bullies and marauders. Mason met Mick's eyes and felt something pass between them, something substantial. He'd thought that all the engineers were raging right-wing assholes, but maybe not. Instead of fantasizing about sleeping with Mick, maybe Mason ought to consider having a conversation with him.

". . . elevate the state and downgrade the citizen," Goldwater was saying.

"It's a consistent philosophical position," Henry said. Well, that was pretty fucking startling. They all turned to stare at him. That was the first thing he'd said since he'd sat down there.

"What's that, Henry?" Eilum asked but Henry had dialed out

again, his eyes fixed on the TV. Mason pushed what was left of his draft across the table. Henry picked it up and drank every drop of it.

". . . false notions of equality," Goldwater was saying.

"*What* false notions of equality?" Mason asked him. "That the poor are equal to the rich? Black folks equal to white folks? Women equal to men? Come on, Barry, explain it to me."

But Barry wasn't about to explain it. He'd moved on. "Only the strong can remain free."

"You can't argue with that," Henry said. "You don't have to agree with him to appreciate how consistent he is."

Henry was using the same calm reasonable voice he did when he was teaching. "'You can't legislate morality.' That's what he said when he voted against the Civil Rights Act. You see, from his point of view, any do-good legislation is by definition a limitation on individual liberty."

Henry looked around the table just as though he expected everyone to start discussing this fascinating matter. But nobody was about to reply, they weren't even looking at him, all just munching away on their chicken.

"Make no bones of this . . . We are at war in Vietnam."

Vietnam! "Holy fucking Christ, he's gonna get us all killed!" That was Dave. So far he hadn't been saying much, like he could give two shits less about Goldwater, but now the boys were all talking at once. The US Army would just love to get its hands on engineers, the minute they graduated they'd get drafted in a flash, what the fuck were they going to do? "I don't know about you," Mason said to Mick. "I guess I'm gonna stay in school for a while."

"Well, you know what?" Mick said, smiling, "I have been considering the advantages of a master's in mechanical engineering."

Goldwater was telling them to be vigilant and strong but they weren't listening. Goldwater was continuing on in his grim inexorable way, telling them about liberation from tyranny, the flowering of an Atlantic civilization, the whole world of Europe unified and free . . . the great ocean highway to the United States . . . a day when all the Americas, North and South, would be linked in a mighty system . . .

"Yeah," Mason yelled back at the TV screen, "it's called *empire*."

More blather, all these stock phrases . . . dead-end streets of collectivism . . . the talent of the individual . . . self-reliance . . . the sanctity of private property . . . and here Goldwater hit it hard, *enforcing law and order*.

"You son of a bitch," Mason said.

But the Republican Party was the party of free men. Goldwater was shouting now, so loud that the speakers crackled with distortion. *"I would remind you that extremism in the defense of liberty is no vice!"*

Eilum was making his fourth pass through the empty streets of downtown Merida. They were out riding around in Eilum's Buick because Mason hadn't been able to take any more of Goldwater's shit. "Got to get out of here," he'd said, planning on walking home, but Eilum had stood right up and joined him. They'd walked out of the Buckeye when half the crowd, appalled, had been firmly glued to their seats and the other half, ecstatic, had been on their feet and cheering like fucking maniacs.

With one hand on the steering wheel, the other draped over the open window, Eilum was not driving with his usual swash-buck-ling nuttiness, he was humming to himself and oozing his Buick along at exactly the town's speed limit. What was he thinking? "What do you say, Mase? You're the history major. Ole Barry make history tonight?"

"Fuck."

Eilum turned at the top of the hill and started drifting down Fraternity Row. Just like the previous three times when he'd done that, there was absolutely nobody to be seen anywhere.

"On the first fucking day . . ." Mason said. He was so pissed off he could hardly speak. "On the first day of the fucking convention Nelson Rockefeller tried . . . Rockefeller tried to inject some sense . . . and those fucking Goldwater boys booed him down. He named names. *The John Birch Society. The KKK.* All he was asking was that Goldwater and the party disavow those fuckers, those *extremists*, right? And those conservative cretins booed him down. And now Barry's just said, 'Fuck you. I'm not gonna disavow anybody.' How about George Wallace? Not gonna disavow him? No, sure as hell not, Wallace support would be good for the GOP, might even help them take the South, right? And while we're at it, are there any more little weirdo extremist groups we can attract? How about the Minutemen? Barry want their support too? They probably love him to pieces."

Eilum had dropped his speed again, was just letting the car drift along on the slight downhill slope leading into the warehouse district. He reached over and flicked off the headlights.

"Victory in Vietnam," Mason was saying. "How's he gonna do that? Nuke the fuckers?"

Eilum pulled over and let the car ooze to a stop.

"What the fuck we doing here?"

"Just gonna take us a little stroll, that's all."

Eilum got out of the car so Mason did too. He followed Eilum through the wrecked doors of the old abandoned Merida Lumber Company building. "Hey? *What are we doing here?*"

"You following this fucking mess in *The Monitor?*" Eilum asked him. "Everybody's saying it's somebody else's problem."

Once inside, they stopped, letting their eyes adjust. It wasn't totally dark in there. The moon was just about half, the right side of it as bright as a search light and it was shining through the door and windows. Mason could make out the crap that the teenagers had left behind from their parties, empty beer bottles, pizza boxes.

"Not sure I got the details right," Eilum was saying. "The legal ramifications are byzantine but the gist of it goes like this. The university says this ain't on university land, so fuck you."

Mason looked up, could see moonlight coming through cracks in the ceiling far above his head.

"The Something-or-other company of Cincinnati, Ltd., says okay when we purchased the sorry remains of the Merida Lumber Company, we only bought the assets, and this piece of shit ain't no asset."

Careful, watching where he was stepping, Mason followed Eilum over to the edge of some big platform. It looked like people had been dumping shit off that thing forever. Packing cases and cartons, scraps of wood, big pieces and little pieces of wood, lots of wood.

"The Municipality of Merida says are you out of your fucking mind? This miserable building and the land it's standing on is *private property* and somebody's got to own it, and more than likely that somebody is you."

God, the whole damn place smelled like old wood.

"So the case is winding its inexorable way through our venerable court system. But you know who's got forgot here? As usual? The humble citizen. Wouldn't you say so, Mase?"

"You got a point."

"Yeah, I thought so. You got a match?"

From where Eilum had parked at the very top of Adams Street they could look straight down to the Merida Lumber building at the bottom. In the distance it looked like a jack-o'-lantern, a dark square box with flames inside, visible through the door and windows. No sirens yet. Jesus, how long was it going to take before somebody called it in? Eilum was still humming to himself.

There was sound like a big thump and suddenly flames were shooting through the roof. "Yeah," Eilum said, "Yeah, come on!"

Another big thump and then holy fucking Christ all of a sudden it was a tower of fire. Yeah, that was no exaggeration, a whole goddamn *tower of fire*, must have been forty feet in the air. Fucking insane. "Yeah!" Eilum yelled.

Cartons, scraps of wood, all kinds of shit were being driven upward in that monstrous blaze and then, burning, went sailing off into the night.

Eilum was laughing hysterically. He was jumping up and down. He was waving his arms in the air. "Let me remind you," he screamed. "Extremism . . . in the defense of liberty . . . *is no vice!*"

12.

At least Mason had stopped waiting for the cops to drop in. After a couple days he'd realized that they were never going to drop in because there was absolutely nothing to connect him and Eilum to that fire. Eilum was not one of those crazy fuckers who did weird shit and bragged about it. No, he was one of those crazy fuckers who did weird shit and forgot about it.

Meanwhile the lumber company who claimed not to own the building said it would be improper of them to comment on a matter before the courts. Merida's venerable Mayor said he wasn't going to comment either except to add that with all the teenage gangs using that abandoned building for their parties it had been only a matter of time. The Merida fire chief said that never in his entire career had he seen a blaze that fierce, all they'd been able to do was hose down the nearby buildings so the fire wouldn't spread. That old lumber building had burned right down to the ground. It was a week later and you could still smell the smoke in the air. Nobody had been hurt. That was the only thing Mason felt good about.

Shortly after that Mason had finally gotten around to doing what he could have done at any point in the last couple years, a little research to find out just who the hell T. Davis Eilum really was. It wasn't hard at all. Mason started with the Cincinnati phonebook and city directory, then checked some of the big fat biographical reference books, and finally moved on to the newspapers. His roommate was the son of James McFadden Eilum, the president of the Davis and Eilum Coal Company of Cincinnati, Ohio. They operated mines in West Virginia and eastern Kentucky.

Originally from Charleston, West Virginia, James McFadden Eilum was the third generation of Eilums to be in the coal business. Mom, Dad, and the two kids, Tyler Davis and Margaret Althea, lived in the quaint village of Indian Hill, just about the damn most wealthy suburb of Cincinnati. Mrs. Eilum and her lovely daughter appeared frequently in the society pages of the *Cincinnati Intelligencer*, attending cotillions and charity dances and other fancy-ass events. Jesus, Mason thought, T. Davis probably gives his family the absolute falling down screaming fits. What was Mason going to do with all this new information? Not a goddamn thing.

Mason heard a car, looked up and saw Jessie's Lark floating to a stop. Well, that was pretty fucking amazing, she'd never dropped in for a visit before. Then with the slam of the car door there she was herself, in motion on the sidewalk, and through the branches of the white oak he caught a brief flicker of her waving at him and *the swing of a skirt?* She bounded up the steps and threw herself onto one of the wicker chairs. Yes, she was wearing a skirt, on a dress, an honest-to-God cocktail dress, cobalt blue, and her handmade leather sandals with it. "Hey," she said.

"Hey," he said back.

"Thought you might like to see me dressed up. It's such a rare occasion . . . occurs slightly less often than Halley's Comet."

Like a lot of her clothes the dress was a little bit out of date but expensive looking. It had a small waist circled by a narrow belt and a full skirt, not super full but definitely that good old '50s A-line. Cobalt blue was a perfect color for her dark skin.

"You look great," he said, both because that's what he was supposed to say and because it was true. He hadn't seen her since Goldwater night at the Buckeye. He hadn't seen much of anybody since then. Don't worry, boys, he thought, I've just been laying low.

"Ev took me to lunch at the faculty club," she told him. "It was a big deal. He went over my thesis, okayed all my latest additions. If I can get a final draft to him by August, he'll take it with him on vacation. I could be Dr. Collier by Thanksgiving."

Lots of times when she smiled, it didn't have much joy to it, was what he'd call ironic or wry, but her smile today wasn't like that. It lit up her whole face. "Congratulations, Jessie. That's just great."

He was doing what he always did when he didn't have a clue, waiting to see which way the wind was blowing. She was sprawled back on the chair, sitting the way she always sat, not changing a thing for the sake of the dress. She'd even put her feet up on the old battered table. She looked to Mason like a beautiful boy with a dress on. Would anybody else see her that way or was it only his weird mind? Looking at her was like doing something painful that you can't stop yourself from doing, like picking at a scab. Aw, fuck, he had to say something. "I can't believe it," he said. "A cocktail dress. Are you wearing a petticoat under it?"

"Of course I am. It wouldn't have the right shape if I didn't." She lifted the edge of her skirt to show him. "Even a fashion klutz like me knows that much."

That set her off onto one of her neat little lectures, this one about Simone de Beauvoir, he should read her book, by the way, the part where she talks about men begging women not to give up all those cute feminine things that mark them as the Other. "Those damned little gloves," she was saying. "The middle of fucking summer, eighty-some degrees, and you're supposed to wear those damned little gloves. I had four or five pairs in different colors."

They were laughing about that, how ridiculous it was, but Mason was thinking that if he was a girl, he'd love wearing those damned little gloves, yeah, he'd be exactly the sort of girl that Simone de Beauvoir would hate on sight, and he thought about telling Jessie that, she'd probably laugh, but no, it didn't feel right. Their easygoing feeling was gone, that sense that they could relax and say anything to each other. It was like they were right back to square one. She was probably feeling it too. She'd stopped talking and was just looking at him. He couldn't read her face. "That night in the Buckeye?" she said. "Goldwater's speech? When did you leave? I just looked over and you were gone."

Mason felt his skin prickle all the way up his back. Oh? Well, Eilum and I were just off burning down the lumber building, ha, ha. "Had to get out of there," he said. "Couldn't take any more."

"Right. Don't blame you. Did you hear anything about what happened? After you left?"

"No."

"Okay. Well, Henry got insanely pissed. He was playing some kind of game. He'd argue for Goldwater and then he'd switch over and argue against him. There was no getting away from him. He was driving everybody nuts."

"Yeah?" Mason said. "That's the way he teaches. He'll take one side of something and argue the hell out of it and just about the time he's got you convinced, he'll walk over to the other side of the room and argue the other side."

"The great debate method, huh? The Buckeye wasn't the best place for . . . He was a mess. Walking into things, falling down, repeating himself, slurring. I've known him for years and I've never seen him like that. It was just jammed with his students. It was *really embarrassing.* The bartender had to ask him to leave."

"Yeah? I think he was half loaded when he first showed up. Or half something."

"So the next day I called Carl. He and I are not exactly . . . We seem to communicate better over long distance than we do face to face. I had to listen to him bad-mouth Lorianne for a while. All her fault, you know, that crazy hillbilly girl. I said, 'Carl, be that as it may, Henry's falling apart. Can you do something about it?' So Carl called Henry and whatever he said must have worked. Henry's back in Canton and let's hope he stays there. That would make things easy for Lorianne. She could go for desertion and non-support."

"So she's really gonna divorce him?"

"Christ, I don't know. If I can get her into a lawyer's office . . . This is split-up number three. Both times before, Henry weaseled his way back in."

What was he supposed to say about that? He didn't have a clue. He didn't want to keep on talking about Henry and Lorianne. He had to search his mind for the next topic. "Hey, Jessie, my hair? You know how we talked about it? I think maybe the time's come. Who does your hair?"

"Oh. A real nice lady. Anna Polacek. She runs a little hair salon out of her kitchen. She and her husband were DPs, he works for Buildings and Grounds. They're really a sweet couple."

"Would she know how to cut a Beatle?"

"Oh, absolutely. She's very good. A lot of the faculty wives go to her. And she's very literal. I told her I wanted a very short pixie, kind of like Audrey Hepburn, I said, and this is what I got. Do you want me to make you an appointment?"

"I don't know. I guess not. I'm not quite ready yet," and then they both got to take a break as the McKinley Tower bonged four times. He was afraid that would be her excuse to get going but she didn't move.

Their eyes met again and he felt how tangled up they were. Of course she was feeling it too. "How's your thesis coming?" she asked him.

"It's kind of . . . okay, I guess. Once I started looking, I found lots of accounts of the Mason brothers slaughtering those Indians. Some folks thought they should have been tried for murder but they never were. In order to do what Dr. Braithwaite told me, all I have to do now is talk to my grandma, transcribe her story. But I don't know . . . it seems too easy, and . . . I got kind of sidetracked. I've been thinking about some other stuff."

"Yes?"

"You know that old idea of the commonwealth? That the society will have inequalities in it, but yeah, if you're a good ruler, you're gonna rule for the benefit of everybody? All the Founding Fathers believed that. And all our political parties believed that . . . up until now. It feels like Goldwater and those extremists made a huge break from that."

"Where are you going with this, Mason?"

"I don't know. Just seems like a big jump to me. Those Goldwater conservatives don't believe in the commonwealth. For them it's pure laissez-faire, pure individualism. Kind of like, I'm gonna get mine and the rest of you can go fuck yourselves. Where did that idea come from? That small government, rugged individualism shit? Edmund Burke?"

"Some of it. Or it would be better to say, from how some people have used Burke. But, look, Mason, just hold off on that big philosophical stuff, okay? Get your damned thesis done, okay?"

"Yes, ma'am."

He'd got a smile from her with that. "Do you want me to read it?" she asked him.

"Well, sure, that'd be . . . If you wouldn't mind."

"Of course I wouldn't mind. Call me."

"Jessie, it's real hard to call you. I haven't got your phone number."

She frowned. "Haven't I given it to you?"

"And you're unlisted . . . or un-something. You're not in the Merida directory and you're not in the faculty directory either."

"That's right, I'm in nobody's directory and that's the way I like it. I was *sure* I'd given it to you. Do you have something to write on?"

He handed her a folded up piece of paper he'd been using for a book mark. "Do you want some tea?" he said to keep her there. "I bought some Earl Grey."

"That's nice. Thanks but no, I've got to get going."

She was gone and her cobalt blue dress with her, leaving Mason to think about it, but he knew that if he didn't stop thinking about it, he was going to sink down into the pit. He had to find something real to do. He wheeled his good old reliable Norman into the basement, took it apart, cleaned it, oiled it, and reassembled it. The tires were worn some but they'd do for now, he pumped them up to a good pressure. He went back upstairs, made himself a peanut butter and jelly sandwich and ate it.

All he did was aim himself west and go. He knew that trying to make the Indiana line was a ridiculous idea. He definitely could ride fifty miles but then what? He'd be fifty miles away from home. He never for once stopped thinking about Jessie. Here was one way to look at it. She'd dropped by to show off her dress to her gay friend.

Somewhere out in the middle of nowhere cornfields he turned around. By the time he was coming back into the Merida city limits twilight was settling in and he liked that, the sky going that fickle color that always made him ache, the street lights coming on, city-night yellow against sad country blue. His legs felt weak as rubber bands and his ass was sore, but he didn't mind. He felt almost peaceful.

He swung by the Buckeye to make sure that Eilum and the engineers were in there, and they were, so he had the apartment to himself. His shirt was soaked with sweat. He stripped it off and began running a bath. When Reenie had shaved her legs, she'd done it in the bathroom with the door shut so he never did know how she did it but he'd watched Grandpa Mason shave lots of times, he shaved in the kitchen. Why he did it there and not in the bathroom Mason had never before stopped to wonder. When Mason had shaved his legs to look like Reenie's, he'd used Grandpa Mason's safety razor.

He lay back in the tub, washed himself good and washed his hair. Then he shaved his legs. He got out of the tub and studied himself in the mirror. He changed the blade and shaved his face. He combed the tangles out of his hair and fluffed it up with his fingers so it'd dry into its natural curls. He brushed his teeth. He ringed his eyes with black liner. He coated his lashes with mascara.

He put on Irene's panties and his white dress shirt and his twenty-eight-inch jeans and his cowgirl boots. He dotted F# onto his neck and wrists. It was full dark by then so he lit the light on his desk, shaped his nails with an emery board and painted them with clear polish, went outside, sat on the girls' porch, and waited for them to dry. The moon was full and it lit up a night that was still and quiet, not much to hear, some cars a few streets over and a dog barking, saying, "Go away, go away, go away."

At Henry's house a great wash of classical music was pouring out of the windows. Mason left his bike right there by the front porch and went up the stairs quick before he had a chance to think about it. It took Lorianne a minute to hear him knocking. When she opened the door, she gave him the same warm smile she always did. "Mason Macquarie. I thought I'd be seeing you one of these nights." She ushered him through the screen door and into the light. "My heavens, you look so pretty and I'm such a mess." She took his hand. "Do you mind if we listen to the rest of this. It's almost over."

"No, I don't mind."

She was dressed the way she'd been the last time he'd seen her, pigtails and shorts and sneakers. The house was immaculate. Without saying another word she settled herself back down in the chair by the stereo where Henry usually sat, motioned for him to sit in Carl's chair. She had the volume up real high. Mason didn't like classical music, couldn't tell one piece from another. While she was listening, Lorianne lay back and closed her eyes.

The music ended, the record hissed in its grooves, the tone arm lifted. "Beautiful," he said to be polite. "What was that?"

"Brahms's Fourth. I started listening to it in high school. They let us borrow records . . . you know, from our little library in Solid . . . and I borrowed it over and over. No matter how sad I got, Brahms was sadder."

She stood up and so he did too. She took both of his hands in hers and held them, looked into his face and then just kept on looking. Her eyes were a very pale blue, almost a gray. He'd tried to do his eye makeup like hers and seeing her right there in front of him told him that he'd come close but he'd used too much eye liner, she went real easy with that, but he'd got the mascara just about right. She'd been out in the sun so much that it was bringing out her freckles, just a light scattering of them. Her mouth was open slightly, he could see her teeth below her upper lip, it gave her a puzzled look, or maybe a better word was entranced. A clear face, he didn't know what else to call it. Way far back along some ancient bloodline they were related and he could feel it. "Honey," she said, "I don't know what's going on between us, I really don't."

"Me neither." He hadn't planned anything. He'd just done one thing after another and here he was. For the first time it occurred to him that he might not be completely in his right mind.

She let his hands drop. "Do you want a drink? Do you want to smoke some tea?"

"No. I'm sorry. But I don't."

"Don't be sorry. I don't want to either. I was just being hospitable. How about some ginger ale?"

To be polite he had to accept something. "Yeah, that'd be nice." He followed her into the kitchen. This was strange, this was strange, this was very strange. Maybe he was back in that world where everything was required to appear perfectly normal even though it wasn't. What would happen if he said fuck it to that? "Lorianne," he said, "do you remember when you kissed me behind the sycamore?"

She didn't answer immediately. "Sure I remember."

"You said something about a woman kissing a woman. If you're kissing her, you're kissing yourself. Do you remember that?"

"Of course I do. It's Djuna. *A woman is yourself caught as you turn in panic. On her mouth you kiss your own.*"

"That's right. That's what you said. Okay . . ." He had to think for a minute to find the best way to put the question. "When you kissed me, did you see me as a woman?"

That one seemed to have thrown her for a loss. She stood there with a bottle of ginger ale in one hand and a glass in the other and looked at him. "Lorianne?" he said.

"Just wait a minute, wait a minute. I don't want to say something just to say something. I want to give you a true answer."

She poured the ginger ale, handed him the glass. She walked away, stood with her back to him. Then, turning back, she said, "Whatever I was, you were the same thing."

He didn't know what to do with that. That might be a true answer but it wasn't enough. He was fascinated by it, though, because he'd felt something like that too. "Okay," he said, "and did you feel like you were kissing yourself?"

"Aw, hell, Mason, I was so stoned." She took the glass out of his hands, set it on the counter, and kissed him.

He wrapped his arms around her, bent his knees so they were the same height. She smelled a little bit sweaty but it was fresh sweat, a nice smell. She must have cleaned her teeth after dinner, there was still mint in her mouth. She stopped first, stepped back to look at him, their faces only inches away. "Did you feel like you were kissing yourself?" she asked him and he knew that there was a certain kind of game he should never try to play with her because she would always win it.

"Whatever perfume you're wearing," she said, "I absolutely adore it."

"F#."

"Like the musical note?"

"Yeah, exactly."

Taking one of his hands, she led him upstairs and into the bedroom. "I'll be right back," she said, "I've got to check on Tammy."

It was Lorianne and *Henry's* bedroom. Mason had been there once before, that night when he'd got high on marijuana. He couldn't remember the room very well but what stuck in his mind was the mess, clothes thrown everywhere, books and magazines piled up on the bed table, that big ashtray full of butts, but now everything was clean and orderly and put away. The bed was made up as neatly as if it was a hotel room. He'd sat on the edge of that bed that night and he'd never thought two things about it. He didn't want to do that now.

Lorianne came back, shut the door behind her, and kicked off her sneakers. "I don't have to check on her as often as I do but . . . She's always perfectly fine. I just . . . I don't know. It doesn't hurt to check." She started unbuttoning her blouse.

"Lorianne!" Her eyes. "What are we doing in here?"

"Isn't this what you came here for?"

"No. No, it's not. It's not what I came here for."

"Don't you want to?"

"No. I don't. Honest to God I don't."

She sighed, let her arm drop. "I don't either. Really—"

He felt bad. He didn't want to embarrass her. He didn't want her to think that he didn't find her beautiful. How could he say that so it would come out right? "I came out here to *see you*, to see how you were doing . . ."

"Did you? I thought because . . . You waited till Tammy was in bed. You knew she'd be asleep."

"I didn't know I was coming out here until I was on my bike and doing it."

"Oh. Gee. Then it's . . . If you'd wanted to, I would have let you."

"Oh, for Christ's sake. Why?"

"Because I like you. Because sex doesn't matter that much to me anymore."

"Jesus, Lorianne, that's really fucking sad."

She looked like he'd thrown a bucket of water over her and then she started to cry. A girl like Lorianne was not mysterious to him when she was crying, he took her into his arms. She pressed her face into his chest and cried harder. "Sorry, sorry, sorry," she said.

"Don't be sorry."

"Oh fuck. Mason . . . Everything's so . . . God . . . damn . . . hard."

What was Mason supposed to do now, go home? He stood, leaning against the wall. He took a drink from the glass of ginger ale that he'd somehow carried into the bedroom with him. The only thing he could figure out was that all bets were off. Lorianne had stopped crying. She was sitting at her vanity table, looking at herself in the mirror. "I should take a bath," she said, "but I don't feel like it. I should take these out," the pigtails, "and wash my hair but I don't feel like it. Oh, I get so goddamn tired." She swung around on her stool to look directly at him. "Stay with me?"

"Okay. Sure."

"Henry's in Canton."

He almost said, "Yeah, I know," but he stopped himself. He didn't know whether he was supposed to know that or not.

She opened the door to the closet, stood there, her back to him, and began to undress. She dropped her bra and shorts and blouse into a basket, took down a folded nightgown and slid it over her head. It was white, plain cotton, decorated with little flowers the same color of pink that she painted her fingernails and toenails.

Coming back to him, she ran her fingers lightly through his hair, looked into his face. "You've done your eyes so pretty. You *are* careful where you go, looking like that, aren't you?"

"Yeah, I'm careful."

"Come on, honey, at least take your jeans off."

Oh. They were going to bed. He pulled off his boots and his socks and then his jeans. He saw her see his shaved legs and his sister's panties. He thought she was going to say something but she didn't, smiled instead. She turned down the covers and got in first. He slid in next to her. "Hold me?" she said.

Amazing, there was a whole full-sized human being in bed with him, a warm live girl. "Oh dear, I made your shirt all wet. Crying all over you."

"It's all right."

She reached over and turned off the light on the bed table. "I'm usually asleep by now. Tammy gets up as soon as the sun comes up."

The blinds were still up and the full moon was radiating through the window. The more his eyes adjusted to the light, the brighter the room got. He didn't have a clue what he should say to her. "The crickets and katydids," he said, "and . . . I don't know what all. It's a lot louder out here than it is in town."

"That's right, you're out in the country now. A whole other world comes to life at night. The nocturnal crowd. Sometimes I hear an owl. I've looked for it but I've never seen it."

"What's that bird that . . . ?"

"Oh. The whip-poor-will. He'll just go on forever."

He didn't have to worry about what he was going to say, she was talking enough for both of them, probably nervous. "When I was a little kid, I used to think he was saying potpourri. Listen. Pourri, pourri, pourri, POH pourri. Oh Jesus, Mason, sometimes I lie in this damn bed with Henry snoring beside me and I think, why, why, why?" She laughed. "I could go on forever like that damn bird."

Maybe she *was* going to go on forever like that damn bird, her voice blending in with the night sounds. "You know, Mason, sometimes I think I never want to have sex again. Not with anybody ever again in my whole damn life. Jessie says, 'Oh, Lori, you'll want to later on. When you've been alone long enough. When you meet the right person.' Maybe she's right but I can't feel it."

What could he say? It was a topic about which he had neither knowledge nor experience. "Maybe she's right."

She was already somewhere else. "You know what? This is like when Nora goes to visit the doctor and asks him to tell her about the night. Have you read it yet?"

She must mean *Nightwood*. He wasn't about to tell her that he'd tried but he couldn't do it. "I got it out of the library but I haven't got around to it."

"Oh, shoot. I was hoping you'd read it so we could talk about it."

"We can still talk about it. What are you thinking?"

"Well okay, so in the middle of the night Nora goes to see Dr. Matthew-Mighty-grain-of-salt-Dante-O'Connor. She just turns up out of nowhere. He's in bed in drag and he says, 'You see that you can ask me anything.' She asks him to tell her everything he knows about the night and he tells her . . . Do you want to hear about the night?"

"Sure."

She switched into her quoting voice. *"The night is not pre-meditated . . . Let a man lay himself down in the Great Bed and his identity is no longer his own . . . His distress is wild and anonymous. He sleeps in a Town of Darkness, member of a secret brotherhood."* She laughed. "How's that for making you feel comfortable?"

"Wow, how do you keep all that in your head? Did you memorize that whole damn book?"

"Parts of it. I don't set out to memorize things but if I read something over enough, it stays in my mind word for word. Sometimes I can shut my eyes and see the page it's on."

The night? Who would want to know about *the night?* Mason had something much more specific on his mind. "Lorianne, when you gave me your answer, you had to stop and think. You wanted it to be *true.* I appreciate that. So if you and I were the same thing, what were we?"

"Oh," she said and left him waiting. "You want another true answer, don't you? I never would have seen any of this without Djuna. When I read her, it was like . . . *impaled,* she says."

She kept hesitating. It was like she was unwrapping something slowly, something that she wasn't sure he would like. "Oh, my goodness, there it was, that feeling . . . *the thin blown edge of reverie,* she says. I'd been out there, on that thin blown edge where there aren't any words and then she gave me the words. *For in the girl it is the prince, and in the boy it is the girl that makes a prince a prince, and not a man."*

"Wait," he said, "wait a minute, I don't get it." But he had got it. He just didn't know what to do with it. Impaled *was* the right word. "That . . . Whatever it is you think we are . . . ?"

"Only once does she use the term *the third sex.* Only once in the whole book."

"I've heard that somewhere. I've read that somewhere. Is that—?"

"All the other times she uses the term *invert.* She got that from the sexologists, Havelock Ellis and those guys. They think that we're just normal people flipped upside down. But we're not. We're completely different."

"It's the *we*, Lorianne, that's what I'm having trouble with. Who are *we*?"

"Djuna used the only words she had available to her but . . . Remember the first night when we met each other? You were here at the party and we ended up talking out behind the sycamore and we told each other about our lives? At first I thought it was because we were both hoopie kids, but then I thought, no, he's like me. Deep inside he's like me. I wonder if he knows it?"

Sleep was one of the night voices now, sounding just a little too low for Mason to be able to make it out. It kept inviting him to join it but he couldn't do that yet. He was telling her about trying to be like Irene, wearing her dresses, reading her books.

The tower bonged once. "Oh, my goodness," Lorianne said, "we've got to go to sleep!" She jumped up and lowered the blinds to get rid of the cold moonlight, transformed the room into Djuna's town of darkness.

"*The girl lost, what is she but the Prince found?*" she said. "*The Prince on the white horse that we have always been seeking.*"

"Is that Djuna?"

"Of course it's Djuna. *And the pretty lad who is a girl, what but the prince-princess in point lace, neither one and half the other.*"

It was all starting to make a crazy kind of sense, though he'd be damned if he could explain it to anybody. The prince-princess? His grandparents' big old farmhouse had lots of rooms in it, he told her. He shared a room with his sister, a screen separated them, old brown wood, kind of like slats, and the wallpaper had small red roses on it, arranged in triangles, running all the way up to the ceiling. That paper had been on the walls so long that the cream background had faded to dirty yellow. When he was shaking with fever, that wallpaper buzzed, jumped up and down. The rain pounded on the windows. His grandmother had left paregoric for him, in water, it tasted like licorice, and he shaved his legs so he could be his sister. He must have imagined walking down to the Landing in her raincoat, yellow as a lemon. It couldn't really have happened.

"Who says it couldn't? Who says you weren't your sister?"

"No, it was a fever dream."

"You're just like Jessie. You historians have such direct minds. You always want to know what really happened."

"No, we want to find the most probable account of what happened. Based on the evidence. I think . . . It was reading all those Nancy Drew books when I was little. I've always wanted to be the one who solved the mystery."

"Yeah, but Mason, some mysteries aren't meant to be solved. Some mysteries should remain mysterious. So if you're the girl, then I'm the boy. I'm the questing knight who sleeps in the perilous chapel where all the previous knights have lost their lives."

"Is that Djuna?

She laughed. "No, that's *me*. Just a little girl sitting in the library in Solid, West Virginia, reading romances. I was always the prince. Always, always, always. We do have to go to sleep. We really do."

He was asleep, well, three-quarters asleep, when she said, "Mason?"

Not deep asleep. He'd been awake enough to hear the McKinley Tower bong three times and to count the bongs. "Yeah," he said.

"I keep drifting off and then . . . I can't get my mind to stop."

"Where's it going?"

"Still thinking about Djuna and how . . . Okay, so the main thing I was interested in was the Romantics but I took Dr. Dyson's upper level course on the Moderns and it had pretty much everybody in it you'd expect but no women. He could have put H.D. on the list, or Gertrude Stein, but he didn't. I'd never heard of Djuna Barnes. Most of the time we spent picking around in *The Waste Land*. That's the main thing he was interested in."

She was talking fast now, like she was trying to tell him everything all at once. "Okay, do you know what studying literature is like? It's like going into a natural history museum. There's all these dead stuffed animals in there and you study them in their glass cases and write notes about them. Maybe when you first met some of them, they were still out in the woods, wild and strange and *alive*, and they made your heart sing, but in order to study them in school, you've got to kill them and stuff them. I was pretty good at that. I'd had a lot of practice. So anyhow, Dr. Dyson liked chatting to me and I knew I was on my way to an A and one day he said, 'You know, Lorianne, you might enjoy reading Djuna Barnes' *Nightwood*.' He must have thought I would like it because I'm a girl and he was right. I read it over and over. It was all full of wild strange live animals and I didn't want to kill them and stuff them.

"I read everything I could on *Nightwood* and I didn't agree with any of it. I'd go into his office and talk to Dr. Dyson about it. 'That's interesting,' he'd say and I knew he was thinking I was this cute little hillbilly girl from way out in the middle of nowhere and it was his job to educate me, lead me out of my abysmal ignorance. So one day I was showing him where Djuna talks about the once and future *doll* and he was looking at me like I was out of my ever loving mind. 'Yes,' I said, 'isn't that a wonderfully funny twist she puts on it? She was playing with King Arthur, *rex quondam, rexque futurus*,' and I quoted Malory to him. He said, 'Oh, have you read Malory?' and I said, 'Yes, and I've read Chrétien de Troyes too.' And I talked about how all the writers in Djuna's generation had been interested in the Matter of Britain and the Grail Quest, it had been in the air, and yes, I knew about the intentional fallacy, I'd read Brooks and Wimsatt and Beardsley and all those people but I didn't have to agree with them, did I?

"He looked at me a long time and then he said, 'You know, Lorianne, where you're going really *is* interesting. Very interesting. Keep on going.'"

"How close are you?" Mason asked her. "To being finished?"

"I did most of my coursework in my first year. I'm just short three credits. I think that's all I'm short, I'd have to talk to Dr. Dyson. And then there's the thesis."

"Jesus, Lorianne, you're so close!"

"Yeah, that's what Jessie says too. But . . . when you've got a kid, that takes over everything. It's real. All this real stuff you've got to do. You haven't got time to be going off to fairyland."

He should say something more, encourage her, give her hope, but sleep was pulling him down.

Jesus, some horrible yowling noise, he didn't want to wake up but he *was* waking up, "Just Orville," Lorianne's voice so close he could feel her breath. "She wants out."

In the murky half light he could see the cat shape like a cartoon, the points of her ears sticking up. Lorianne was already sliding out of bed. "Come on, you irritating thing."

The yowling stopped, the front door opened and shut, Lorianne was back in the bed. "She always goes out this time of the morning, right when it's getting light. If you don't let her out, she'll just stand there and yell forever."

Lorianne pressed herself in tight to him. *"When the dew is dewing and it's murky overhead . . ."*

"Hey, I know that from somewhere," he said.

"Grandma Archer says that all the time. *It's nice to get up in the morning but it's nicer to stay in bed.* The funny thing is, Grandma says it but she always gets up."

He laughed with her, wrapped an arm around her, felt the smooth sleepy warmth of her, and he was just beginning to drift off when the McKinley Tower bonged six times. Yeah, that was exactly the time he'd thought it was.

The next time he woke up, it was a jolt, full daylight. Somebody was banging on the back door, it sounded like the back door. "Lorianne! Let me in. I just want to talk to you." For Christ's sake, it was Henry.

Mason sat partway up, opened his eyes, saw Lorianne's eyes already popped wide and staring at him. What the fuck was Henry doing here? He was supposed to be in Canton.

"Come on, Lorianne. I know you're in there." Henry wasn't shouting. It was more how Mason imagined a town crier would sound, forceful and deliberate.

"I gotta get Tammy," she whispered and was out of the bed like a shot. Mason was up and pulling on his jeans before he had time to consider it.

Lorianne had just come back, carrying Tammy. "Shhh," Lorianne said, a finger raised to her lips.

"Shhh," Tammy said, a finger raised to *her* lips.

"We're playing the shhh game," Lorianne whispered to Mason. He raised his finger to his lips and went shhh too.

"Lorianne!" Henry had changed locations. Now he was somewhere at the side of the house. "Come on, for Christ's sake. All I want to do is talk, okay? Believe me. I know you're in there. I'm not going to hurt you."

With Tammy in between them, Mason and Lorianne sat on the edge of the bed. He couldn't read her expression.

Henry was at the front of the house. "Jesus! Fuck!" A loud

crashing sound, well, not really a crashing sound, a weird metallic sound, and then Henry was hammering on the front door hard. Must be using his fists.

The deliberate voice was gone, now he was yelling. "Lorianne, you fucking bitch, open the door. You slut, you whore, you cunt, you bitch, Jesus Christ, I swear to God, you goddamn fucking bitch."

Mason couldn't remember Lorianne taking his hand but she was squeezing it so hard she was hurting him, her nails digging in. She might have been holding her breath, he was holding his breath, there was time the length of gasp, a silence, and then they heard something like two whip cracks. Christ, it almost sounded like gunshots.

Running footsteps, engine starting up, stalling, cranked up again, catching, tires screaming, digging the hell out of there, blasting away, engine revving, getting fainter and fainter, on down the road, gone.

"Dear Lord Jesus," Lorianne said. "Tammy, honey, you stay here with Mason a minute, okay?"

"May? Son?"

She picked her daughter up and set her onto Mason's lap. "It's okay," he said, "Tammy, Tammy."

Lorianne grabbed her bathrobe from the back of a chair. He heard her unlock and open the front door. She wasn't gone for very long. When she came back, every speck of color had vanished from her face. "Tammy, honey," she said in a sing-song voice, "you wanna help Mommy make breakfast?"

She picked Tammy up, set her on her feet, and with a pat on her behind aimed her out of the bedroom. Bending close to Mason, she whispered, "Please can you . . . *do something*? I don't want her to see it."

Outside on the porch Mason didn't know what he was looking for. Then he saw that Henry had picked up his bike and thrown it into the fence. That's what that loud metallic bang must have been. Mason checked the bike and it was fine. Thank God for good solid English construction. But there had to be something more.

At first glance the cat looked like she was asleep, peacefully stretched out on the glider. As Mason got closer, he saw the ribbon of blood spilling from her open mouth. Then he saw the two small round bullet holes in her side.

13.

It was gonna be a scorcher, the sun well up and blazing over
the vanishing point of that crappy two-lane road that was aimed
toward the far distant mountains of West Virginia where Mason
wished the fuck he was at the moment. A little .22 target pistol,
that's what she'd said it was, and that gun was the main thing on
Mason's mind. "He kept it in the glove compartment?"

"Yeah. Kind of bothered me that he'd . . . My dad owned guns,
rifles and shotguns, but he kept them locked up and he never owned
a handgun. I'd never even *seen* a handgun. Henry didn't tell me
about it till I was rooting around in there for something and there
it was. At first I thought it was a toy but . . . I told him it was just
crazy to keep a gun in there and never tell me about it. I said, 'What
the hell's this for, Henry?' and he told me that he and Carl used to
go out to the city dump and shoot rats."

"Shoot rats," Mason said. He and Lorianne were sitting on
the back steps watching Tammy do her tricycle motor imperson-
ation. It had taken a hell of a lot of work to get her there, she'd
been clingy and whiny, just the way I'd be, he'd thought, if I was
a little kid and heard my father banging on doors and windows,
calling my mom horrible names. But Tammy had been changed,
had her breakfast, and seemed to be back to her usual self. "She's

a naturally happy kid," Lorianne said, "she's a gift, she was born that way."

She leaned closer to him to whisper. "She hasn't missed Orvie yet, but she will. Poor old cat." Tears ran down her cheeks. With a dismissive gesture she wiped them away. "I can't believe it. I really can't. I keep telling myself it's all a bad dream."

Yeah, he wished that's what it was, something you could wake up from. That old sickening dread was pressing down on him. He knew how it could make him clumsy and brainless and the only way to get rid of it was to grab it, pick it up, and set it a ways away. He needed to see things like a Nancy Drew mystery, something to think his way through, step by step. "Lorianne," he said, "how come Henry didn't break a window to get in?"

She turned to look at him. "I don't know . . . Because he's a nice boy from Canton, Ohio, and nice boys don't break windows? Because he thinks it's his house? Or maybe . . . okay, he's been saying all along that all he wants to do is talk to me and breaking a window isn't a very good way to start a conversation, is it?"

"Yeah, but after he saw my bike?"

She made a face, wrinkled up her nose, and shook her head. He dug his squashed pack of Camels out of his shirt and offered her one. She didn't hesitate. He lit hers and then his.

"Okay," he said, "Henry parked at the back of the house. He yelled at you and banged on the back door. Then he came around the side of the house and banged on something—"

"Yeah, the living room window."

"Then he came around to the front. He saw my bike. He got pissed off. Picked it up and chucked it up against the fence. Ran up the steps and banged on the front door. Yelled at you again. Really pissed off. That's when he could have broken a window to get in but he didn't. He shot the cat. Maybe he shot the cat *instead* of breaking a window."

She just looked at him. "How much time was there between when he saw my bike and when he shot the cat?" he asked her.

"Not much time at all. I don't know. Less than a minute."

"Okay, Lorianne, here's what's bothering me. He kept that gun in the glove compartment of his car, right? That's what you said. But he never went back to his car to get it. All the time he was walking around the house he already had that gun on him."

She was staring at Tammy riding back and forth. "Sweet. Jesus. Christ," she said, making three soft little puffs out of the words.

She ground out her cigarette on the step. "Mason," she said, "you watch Tammy for a minute, okay? I'm gonna call my mother."

Lorianne's father could not be consulted because he was at work but the first thing her mother wanted to know was did Lorianne think Henry would come back? Yes, Lorianne said, he was certain to come back but not before nightfall. Henry being there at seven in the morning didn't mean that he'd got up early, it meant that he'd been up all night, so the better part of the day he was probably going to be sleeping it off. Then her mother's opinion was that Lorianne and Tammy should come straight home to Akron on the first bus out of there. Lorianne could see some sense to that but she and Henry had been to Akron to visit so Henry knew exactly where their apartment was, and anybody who would shoot a cat, well, you never could tell what he might do next, especially if he was drunk and walking around with a gun, so Lorianne's mother called Grandma Archer who was of the opinion that the best place for Lorianne was at her place way back up in the hills where nobody would ever find her.

The phone lines started heating up with everybody calling everybody. Aunt Nell, Uncle Arch, and Cousin Wayne got included in the conversation. Everybody agreed that Lorianne should get out of Merida lickety-split. Uncle Arch and Cousin Wayne said they'd be more than happy to drive up and get her. Lorianne said, "No, no, no, that's too much trouble," but she talked to her grandma who had a feeling about it so she called Uncle Arch back and said okay. He said it would take him and Wayne about six hours to get there. Lorianne said she'd be ready and then she called Jessie.

Mason took off his makeup and nail polish, wet his hair and brushed it back out of his face. He was prepared for the worst but all Jessie had to say to him was, "You and Lorianne are more trouble than a world war." She'd stopped by the supermarket to collect empty cartons and she was dressed to get work done on a hot day, in a T-shirt that said Penn State Athletics, a pair of track shorts, and an ancient pair of boy's athletic shoes. "Are you sure you want to go back to West Virginia?" she asked Lorianne.

"I don't know, Jess. I don't think I have a whole hell of a lot of choice, do I?"

They were sitting on the steps again waiting for Tammy to get tired enough to have her nap. Mason had got to know Tammy well enough by then to be able to read her mind a little bit and he knew that she liked having people watch her ride her tricycle, the more people the better, and she wasn't about to get tired any time soon. He also knew that she knew that something was up and the last thing she wanted to do was go to sleep and miss any of it.

"I can't believe that neither one of you thought of calling the cops," Jessie said.

Mason and Lorianne exchanged a look.

"Okay, I know the campus cops are useless but you could call the Sheriff's Department."

"Oh, for Christ's sake." Lorianne said, her voice a hissing whisper. "Jessie, to be so smart about some things you really are dumb about others. Okay, so I call the sheriff and he comes over and says, 'Yeah, somebody shot that cat, all right, got two bullet holes in her plain as day, so I guess we'll have to go have us a chat with Henry about that. And then Henry says, 'What a terrible thing! That poor ole cat! I didn't shoot it. My wife's lying to you. You know how these hillbilly girls are, they lie like rugs.'

"Okay, so Henry's really pissed off at me for calling the cops on him. One night he gets most of a fifth in him and he comes out here and this time he breaks a window and puts a couple of bullets in *me*."

"Henry wouldn't do that."

"Jesus, Jess, just how *the hell* would you know? I've been married to him for a couple years and I thought I knew him really well, all his good points and all his bad. He's got a nasty mean streak to him, I know that, but . . . Oh Lord, right up until he did it, if you'd asked me, could Henry shoot a cat? I would've said, 'Oh, no! That's just sick. How could you even think of something like that?'

"I can't say what Henry would or wouldn't do. Henry loved that cat. It's like, I don't know . . . It's like your whole world's been turned upside down. I don't know what to think anymore. I don't know who he is anymore."

They'd finally got Tammy in bed for her nap and now they were trying to get as much done as they could before she woke up again. Jessie was packing a suitcase, Mason was ready with an empty carton, waiting for somebody to tell him what to put in it, but Lorianne had stopped halfway across her bedroom, was simply standing there, holding a bag full of socks. "Yeah, we lived in Elner when I was little," she said. "Didn't I tell you that? We didn't move to Solid till later. My cousin Wayne still lives in Elner. It's . . . Well, you couldn't call it abandoned because there's a few people still living there. But it's . . . The mine shut down years ago. It's your classic company town. The mine operator named it after his wife."

"*Elner?*" Jessie said.

"Eleanor," Mason translated for her.

223

"It's all still there," Lorianne said, "like a ghost town. The crapped-out mine, the coal tipple, the tracks where the trains don't run any more, lots of little identical houses sitting there in a row, and you're out in the middle of absolutely nowhere. A bunch of hills. It's a twenty minute drive into Solid."

"Lori, come on. We've got to get you and Tammy out of here."

"Oh, I know, I know. I just have to . . . When I was little, you'd drive into Solid on a Saturday, the place was just jammed with people. Dry goods store, hardware store, feed store, drug store, pretty much anything . . . farmer's market. The little library where I spent half my life . . . It's so nice of Wayne and Uncle Arch to drive up here and get me. Wayne's my favorite cousin. Did I ever tell you that?"

"Pack up her shoes," Jessie said to Mason, pointing at the floor of the closet.

"Wayne was in Korea. When he came back, he was never right after that. In and out of the VA hospital for years. He was shot in the hip but that healed up okay, he hasn't even got a limp, but what hadn't healed up was his mind. He was drinking something fierce and kept getting into fights. He'd learned hand-to-hand combat in the service and he was always getting charged with assault. He even did some jail time for it."

"Do you want *all* these shoes?"

"Yeah, pack everything," Lorianne said.

"Hey," Jessie said. "You can't take *everything.*"

"Yes, I can. I'm not coming back here. I'm never gonna set foot in this goddamn house again in my entire life."

"Lori. Listen. You don't have to come back here again. After the dust has settled, Mason and I will come back and pack up all the rest of it."

We will? Mason thought.

"Oh, that's so sweet of you." She handed Jessie the bag of socks.

"Whew, some of Wayne's stories about Korea . . . just scared the bejesus out of me. He said you couldn't believe how cold it got in Korea. When he got shot in the hip, it knocked him clean out and when he came to, he was on the back of a truck with a bunch of other wounded guys. The driver was trying to get them out of there but they were still under fire. Some of them were dead. Some of them were dying. Wayne had a terrible thirst. There was so much blood in the truck that it ran down onto the floor and froze solid. Wayne and some of the other guys started chipping off pieces of that frozen blood and sucking on it. Like a blood popsicle, he said, just like that. He said the doctor told them later that sucking on that frozen blood probably saved their lives."

What were they supposed to do with a story like that? Mason didn't have a clue and looking at Jessie, he saw that she didn't either. He turned his attention back to the closet. God, girls owned a lot of shoes. "Which ones of these . . . ?" He couldn't imagine what use she'd have for high heels on a chicken farm. "Do you want any dress shoes?"

"Oh, I guess not. Oh, maybe. One pair. The blue pair. Yeah, right there on your left. Oh, yeah, and the patents. Anyhow, Wayne's kind of a legend. Everybody talks about how you can turn your life completely around but nobody ever does it. Well, Wayne did it. For a while he was going to one of those crazy churches . . . You probably don't know the kind I mean," she said to Jessie. "They usually meet on Wednesday nights in some empty room up above a store somewhere. They call them Independent Holiness, and when they say independent, they mean *independent*. Those churches aren't in fellowship with anybody but the Lord Himself. So Wayne joined one where they took fits and fell over on the floor or took off screaming through the woods and that had his attention for a while—"

"Lorianne?" Jessie said, a warning rasp in her voice.

Lorianne started to cry. "Well, then he joined AA. For a while he was driving all over the state going to meetings, and he'd fall off the wagon but he always jumped back on, and eventually it took. He hasn't had a drink in years. He told me he doesn't even miss it. And he's calmed down completely. Everybody says Wayne would give you the shirt off his back, and it's true. Now he restores cars. He started out doing that just for fun, you know, to pass the time, but in the last few years he's discovered he can make money at it. With the right car and the right buyer, sometimes he can make big money—"

Lorianne wiped away the tears, turned to her book shelves. "Oh, my beautiful books." She pulled one from the shelf, held it, ran her finger tips over the cover.

"What's that?" Mason asked her.

She showed it to him, *The Collected Poems of Alfred Lord Tennyson*. "All my books have my name written in them. It's the first thing I always do when I buy a book. My name and the date." She turned to Jessie. "So if you and Mason are packing up my books, you'll always know which ones are mine."

"Okay, okay."

"My aunt Myrtle gave me this when we moved to Akron." She held it up, a fountain pen. "It's a good one too, a Parker. I used to keep it full of ink all the time. I always used turquoise blue ink."

"Lori? It's going to be all right."

"Okay, okay, I know. Solid used to be such a *nice* little town. They had a newspaper that came out once a week, a radio station, a movie theater. About a dozen churches. There used to be a number of mines around Solid and they're all shut down now, and the lumber mill's shut down too. Now it's . . . Most of the stores are boarded up. Everybody's on some kind of relief. Uncle Arch has got his social security but it never quite goes far enough."

Lorianne was sobbing. Jessie stepped over to her and wrapped her arms around her. Lorianne pressed her face into Jessie's chest and cried hard. "How could he *do that?* Orville loved him. She spent half her life sleeping on his lap. Oh, Jess, I've lived in Merida *for eight years.* I wouldn't call it home but I'm used to it."

"Listen, Lori. This is temporary. *Temporary.* You're going back to West Virginia for a visit. Just to see how everything sorts out. You're not going to be there forever."

Uncle Arch and cousin Wayne arrived a little after two in an old Ford station wagon, the kind with the wood panels on the side. "Oh my goodness gracious, it's a woodie," Lorianne said.

"Yeah," Cousin Wayne said, "but it ain't as old as the one in the song. It's only a 1950."

"It's beautiful, Wayne. What a beautiful job."

"Yeah, it come out pretty good. There's a fellow up in Charleston might buy it off me. Or if he don't, maybe I'll just keep it. Aw, Lorianne, you're a sight for sore eyes." He hugged her, then picked her bodily off the ground and held her a moment, suspended and giggling. Cousin Wayne was a big man.

Uncle Arch was offering his hand to Mason and Jessie. "Archer Blesdoe. And this here crazy mountain man is my boy Wayne."

Uncle Arch and Cousin Wayne had spruced themselves up for the occasion, both wearing dress shirts and pressed pants, both freshly shaved. Mason could smell the bay rum on them. It was hard to tell how old Arch was. He'd had a rough life and it had left him with a lined pitted face and shrewd narrow eyes. Wayne was another matter. He had a good crop of hair on him, not as long as Mason's but getting there, and he had a smile like the sun coming up in the morning. Lorianne had been right what she'd said, how everybody talks about quitting and nobody ever does it, it made you cynical. But here was a guy who'd actually done it and he looked the picture of health, a man in the prime of his life and enjoying every minute of it.

Jessie was standing back, watching, as they all talked at once. Mason, introduced as a cousin, had immediately got tangled up with Arch in a genealogical puzzle. "Aunt Mandy Venn," Mason said, "that's all that sticks in my mind. She was a McPhee."

"Yes. Mandy McPhee. Who married a Venn. We called her *Aunt* Mandy too. Now whose aunt she is, I couldn't tell you. I'll have to ask my mother when we get back down to the farm."

Lorianne and Wayne seemed to be going through a card sort of every one of their relatives, he was bringing her up to date, Sandy's oldest girl about to graduate from the high school and somebody else getting married. "Work?" Wayne was saying. "Naw, nobody's working much. There's nothing to work at."

"JFK said he was gonna do something for us," Arch said, jumping into their conversation, "but if he did, we sure haven't seen it," and then to Mason, "It'd be interesting to know exactly how you're related to us. Where you from, son?"

"Mason's Landing. If you're ever driving up the River Road from Parkersburg to Raysburg, you'll pass right through it and never notice."

"Yes. I've been up that road many a time. And you're right, I never noticed. Well, some of our people settled on the river. Maybe you're them."

Looking at the Blesdoes, Mason could see that they were related, hell, anybody could see that, but exactly what they had in common was harder to put your finger on. They didn't all have pale blue eyes, Wayne's were darker, nearly hazel. They didn't all have high cheekbones and nicely rounded off chins, Lorianne and Wayne did but Arch didn't. But there was *something* and maybe Mason had it too. He couldn't tell if it was real or if he was only talking himself into it. Maybe he wanted to be related to the Blesdoes just so he could be related to somebody. He looked around for Jessie.

She met his eyes and he could tell that she was amused. Yeah,

228

he said to her in his mind, this is really us, this is what a bunch of hoopies are like when we get together.

Lorianne brought Tammy forward to meet her relatives. The little girl had been overcome by shyness, hung onto the edge of her mama's shorts and stared. "Your uncle and your cousin," Lorianne said.

Wayne hunkered down to make himself the same level as Tammy, turned on his beautiful smile.

"She's usually afraid of men," Lorianne said. "She's not afraid of Mason because she's decided he's a girl. Because of all that hair. But she doesn't know what you are."

Arch laughed. "A lot of people could say that."

"I'm not just some man out of nowhere," Wayne said, "I'm your cousin. *Cousin.*"

"Kuh? Sin?"

"Well, my goodness," he said, "you're smart like your mama."

Mason couldn't imagine why Uncle Arch and Cousin Wayne wanted to see the dead cat, but they did. It was wrapped in a towel and clipped onto the back of Mason's bike. He wheeled the bike around the side of the house well out of view of the girls, unclipped the cat and unwrapped it, laid it out on the ground. Arch and Wayne hunkered down to look at it. ".22," Wayne said.

"Yes," Arch said, shaking his head.

Wayne turned the cat over, ran his fingers over its fur, gave his father a look. Then he looked at Mason. "You said there was blood coming out of her mouth, did you?"

"Yeah. Some. I cleaned it up."

"You see, buddy, no exit wounds. He was using hollow points and that pistol didn't have a hell of a lot of muzzle velocity."

Wayne was looking at Mason closely, making sure he was getting the message. "Them two shots went in there, hit bone, and blew apart inside that poor cat. The first shot did the trick. The second shot was pure meanness."

"Pure." Arch massaged the back of his neck and looked up at the sky. "His baby daughter's pet. A grown man doing that. Lord, I don't know."

"Yeah," Wayne said, "pitiful. Did Lorianne ever tell you how she come to marry that man?" he asked Mason.

"Yes, she did."

"Did she tell you the *whole* story?"

"Yes. I'm pretty sure I heard the *whole* story."

"Yeah? Well. Shit. It's long past time she got rid of that piece of trash."

"I'd say you got that about right," Mason said.

Wayne wrapped up the cat again and handed her to Mason. He clipped her back onto his bike. Now they should go back around the house and join the girls but that's not what they were doing. They were just standing there. "A real shame Lorianne couldn't finish up her second degree," Arch said. "That was a . . . ?"

"A master's," Mason said.

"That's right. A master's. She learned to read before she was ever in school. Do you remember that?" he asked Wayne.

"Sure, I remember that. Everybody remembers that. Not in school yet and she could read the headlines in the newspaper."

"Yes. And do you remember when she found out she could get any book she wanted? You know, from the library there in Solid. She thought it was magic, any book in the world. I can still hear her saying that, *any book in the world!* She went around and told everybody that. She was so happy. She must of been about ten or eleven at the time. Whatever she wanted, they'd order it, you know . . ."

"Interlibrary loan," Mason said.

"That's it. Lorianne decided she was gonna read up on every religion in the world and decide which one she liked best. She used to go talk to her Aunt Myrtle about what was on her mind and Myrtle said to me, 'Arch, I don't know what to do with her. She's way ahead of me. That girl's got to go to the university.'"

"That's right," Wayne said, "she had a real hunger for knowledge. When I got out of the service, she wanted to know everything about Korea. What the people was like, what they believed in, what they ate, what their customs were. I said, 'Are you writing a report for school?' and she said, 'No. I just want to know,' and she wanted to know all about the war too. A *conflict* they called it. Hell yes, it was a *conflict* all right. Not too many of the American people wanted to know about that conflict but Lorianne did."

A weight seemed to have sunk so heavily onto Arch and Wayne that Mason could feel it himself. It made a long pause like a sigh that the three of them were taking together. "Well," Arch said, "her grandma is sure gonna be glad to see her."

When people drive six hours to pick you up, you've got to feed them, as both Lorianne and Mason understood even if Jessie didn't. With the little bit she had in the ice box, iced tea and cheese sandwiches was the best Lorianne was able to offer. The Velveeta and the fixings were on the table, the butter, the lettuce and tomato, diced onions, Miracle Whip, ketchup, hot German mustard, sweet pickles and dills. It was all going down pretty good. Uncle Arch was finishing up his sandwich and Cousin Wayne was constructing a second one. Mason hadn't been able to eat much, his stomach still tightened down with fear, so he was sitting on the floor playing with Tammy, hoping to keep her preoccupied, rolling a ball back and forth with her.

Cousin Wayne leaned toward Lorianne, said in a low conspiratorial voice, "Honey? That gun? You say he carried it around in his glove compartment, did he? You say it was a .22 target pistol?"

"That's what Henry said it was."

Tammy's eyes went up toward the table. Yeah, Mason thought, you know this is some pretty dire shit, don't you?

"Had a real long barrel, did it?" Wayne said.

Lorianne looked puzzled. "No, it had a real short barrel. Hardly any barrel at all."

"Was it a fairly big thing, shiny metal, kind of squared off?"

"No, it wasn't like that at all. It was small, more rounded. Yeah, real small. When I first saw it, I thought it was a toy gun. You know, like kids play cowboys and Indians with."

"Oh!" Cousin Wayne and Uncle Arch exchanged a look. "Cowboys?" Wayne said. "It was a *revolver*, was it?"

"Yes. That's exactly what it was. A revolver."

Wayne sat back in his chair, laughed. "He was lying to you, honey. That weren't no target pistol. It was one of them cheap little self-defense guns."

"Yep," Arch said, "sometimes what they call a lady's gun."

"Right," Wayne said, "easy to conceal. You drop it in your pocket or you give it to your wife to carry around in her purse."

"I don't know why they're still selling them damn things," Arch said. "Useless. Dangerous. Every year more people get hurt with them damn things. With a gun like that you couldn't hit a rat to save your soul."

Tammy looked at Mason, her eyes saying, what, what, what? He smiled back at her, hoping that would help. "We better get on the road," Uncle Arch said. "We ain't gonna be getting to your grandma's much before midnight as it is."

Mason had thought that as soon as the Ford woodie drove away Jessie would take off but she didn't. That left them standing side by side staring down the empty road. Without looking at him, she said, "What's your excuse this time?"

"All we did was talk."

"You two femmes?" she snapped at him. "*Of course* all you did was talk."

After a moment she said, "Sorry. That was bitchy of me. I'm not at my best."

"Are you pissed off at me?"

"No. Not really. I should be but I'm not . . . It's just that . . . I care a lot about her."

"Yeah, I do too."

"I suppose you do. If getting Lorianne to leave that crazy son of a bitch was the goal, you've accomplished more in one night that I have in months. The dead cat clarifies everything, doesn't it? But there's . . . It wasn't supposed to end like this."

Then Jessie did that gesture he'd seen her do only a couple times before, pinched the bridge of her nose and closed her eyes. By now he'd figured out that she only did that when something was bothering her a lot. "Henry's absolutely convinced that Lorianne and I are having an affair. We aren't."

She opened her eyes to look at him. "The patriarchy is protecting her just the way it's supposed to. And it's the patriarchy that will break her heart. She'll never get out of West Virginia now. Never. It's a real shame."

She linked her fingers and pushed her arms upward, stretching, then bent forward, letting her knees bend, and he heard vertebrae snap in her back. It was an eerie moment, like a hole opening up in time so he could look back and see her as the girl she'd been, the Penn State jock.

She straightened up. "Oh God, Mason, I'm so fucking tired. No, I'm not that mad at you . . . a little bit mad at you. I'm just . . . *tired*. It really wasn't supposed to end like this. I've got one week to get my thesis to Ev, exactly one week, and I just lost the better part of a day. Well, it's one foot in front of the other, right? And Mason? You are going to take care of that dead cat, aren't you?"

T. Davis Eilum had picked a pretty spot out in the woods some-where near Mingo Lake. He'd dug a quick grave there, dropped Orville into it, and covered her up. He gave Mason a solemn nod and turned his eyes up to the stripped-out blue of the evening. "Dear Lord," he said, "are you up there? I hope to God you're up there because if you're not, then we're all fucked.

"Okay, if you are up there, Lord, I'd appreciate it if you paid a little bit more attention to me. But that's a whole other matter. We're here, Lord, to lay to rest the mortal remains of this poor ole pussycat. She never hurt nobody. Except for a few mice. Yeah, she probably did that. She did what cats are supposed to do. She lay around and purred and made a little kid happy and she killed a few mice. Yeah, Lord, she was a good ole cat. And then some fuck-face idiot went and put two .22 caliber bullets in her and ended her poor life. We're not talking any great marksman here, Lord, she was just laying there on the glider, if she'd been up and running, he never would've got a shot into her.

"Anyhow, this poor ole cat died without a peep, and she didn't deserve it, and we're asking you to take her into your care and hold her in your ever-loving arms. There's some folks say that cats don't have no soul, but we know better than that, don't we, Lord? Because if cats don't have no soul, then we don't have no soul neither, and then we're really fucked, right? Anyhow, we give the soul of this poor ole pussycat over to you, Lord, and we ask you to give her peace and give her rest. We ask this in the name of the Father, the Son, and the Holy Ghost. Yeah. The Holy Ghost is probably the one who can take care of this matter. Anyhow, Lord, it's over to you. Amen."

"Amen," Mason said.

August

14.

"**Henry says he's gonna kill you.**" Well, Jesus, that was a fairly alarming way to kick things off.

Eilum had just dropped into the wicker chair on the girls' porch. What got to Mason was not only what Eilum had said but how he'd said it, grim and serious, not like himself at all. "What the hell you talking about?"

"He came into the Buckeye around . . . oh, I don't know, ten-thirty, eleven. Pissed out of his gourd. I mean fucking *pissed*. Well, he didn't come *in*, he just stood there in the doorway staring in like he did on Goldwater night."

Eilum offered Mason a smoke. Mason took it. "I'm just sitting there minding my own fucking business. It's dead in there, right? It's the Lord's day so Merida's fine citizenry are off communing with their savior and I'm enjoying the peace and quiet. Oh yeah, here's the paper if you want it." He threw the Sunday *New York Times* down onto the table.

So Eilum had been finishing up some article in the *Times*, drinking the last of his coffee, and he looked up and lo and behold, there was Henry. Being both curious and filled with compassion for the profoundly drunk, Eilum wandered over to see if he could be of some assistance. The first thing he did note was that somebody had beat the holy living shit out of Henry. Split lip, broken nose, swollen eye, the whole works. "What happened to you, buddy? You look like you went a few too many rounds with Joe Lewis."

"None of your fucking business."

Okay, that topic was not gonna get them anywhere so Eilum asked if Henry was looking for anyone in particular, standing in the doorway as he was, and Henry allowed as how he was looking for Mason Macquarie and Mrs. Collier. "That's that lady professor you got the hots for, right? She's a *Mrs.?*"

"She's not a professor," Mason said, "she's a TA. And yeah, she is a Mrs. Divorced. She doesn't like people to know that."

"Yeah? Well, that's the first I heard of it. So I asked him what he wanted with those two particular people and it turns out that wasn't any of my fucking business either. So I said, 'Okay, Henry, let us just start us over. Why don't you join me for a nice quiet cup of coffee and we will discuss only matters of mutual interest."

The waitress took one look at Henry and didn't want to serve him. "Don't worry," Eilum said, "he's gonna be no trouble at all. Henry's facing a few difficulties this morning, I've got to admit, but he just needs some of your fine link sausages and full stack of hots. And some coffee. Yeah, you just bring us a pot and leave it on the table."

From time to time, as the spirit moved him, Eilum was known to have a heavy hand with the tip so the waitress did what she was told. When the food arrived, Henry started chowing down like he hadn't seen a meal recently and that loosened up his tongue and he began to recount the disasters of his life. Turns out that the forces arrayed against Henry were *legion*, just about everybody and their dog was out to get his sorry ass, starting with his frigging rotten parents and gradually working up to the present when it seems his miserable wife left him and took his darling daughter with her. And that brought him around to the two main authors of his afflictions, Mason Macquarie and Mrs. Collier.

"That's how he always referred to you," he told Mason, "your full name like that and he always called her Mrs. Collier. It was like he was writing a business letter. Okay, so it seems like the two of you have been fucking around with his wife and lately he's had a thought or two about that. As he's telling me this, he looks all around to make sure there's nobody anywhere near us and then he leans forward and starts talking real low like, I don't know, maybe he thought there's a hidden microphone somewhere, and he tells me he's been thinking that if he killed the both of you, all his troubles would be over.

"I pointed out to him that murder was still a capital crime in the state of Ohio the last I'd heard, in fact, they'd just fried somebody not so long ago, and most likely they wouldn't mind frying him.

"Henry says, 'Well, I probably wouldn't be around. Or if I was, they probably would be lenient with me after I tell them *the whole damn story.*' And anyhow he says he still isn't absolutely sure he's going to kill Mason Macquarie and Mrs. Collier, maybe what he should do is have *a discussion* with them, but even if he did kill them, it wouldn't matter much what happened to him anyway because his life's pretty well over and I say, 'Henry, how the fuck old are you?' He tells me he's thirty-three, the age of Christ crucified. Well, that kind of stops me for a minute but then I say, 'Okay, let's just say that you don't get your ass crucified, ole buddy, which is more than likely, given that you're not God, just think of all the things you could do with all those years you got left, but he doesn't want to hear it. He's got *no* years left, to hear him tell it, and about half the time he's pretty sure that shooting the two of you is definitely on the agenda.

"Then he tells me he's got this little gun fits right in his pocket. Nobody's gonna even know it's there till he whips it out and starts blazing away so he can walk right up to either one of you and *blammo,* that's it. I express considerable interest in seeing this useful little gun and he tells me he's got it out in the car. I swear to God he's right on the edge of inviting me out to see it. I'm figuring if he shows it to me, I'll just take it away from him, right? Well, soused as he is, something turns over in the back of his head and all of a sudden he gives me this horrified look. It's finally dawned on him that I'm the enemy too and he jumps up, goes lurching out of there, heads straight to his car, locks himself in, and goes screeching away into the afternoon."

"Jesus," Mason said.

"Now what you're gonna do with this information, buddy, is entirely up to you. I'd suggest that you warn that lady professor so she knows what's what. Maybe she can figure out what to do about ole Henry, it ain't my job to do that, but if you want my informed opinion, he did appear to me to be seriously foamed right out of his gourd. I feel kind of sorry for the son of a bitch but he could be dangerous, you know what I mean? In a half-assed kind of way.

"Anyhow, I'd suggest that you keep your eyes peeled. Yeah, you can kill somebody with a .22, you've just got to get the bullet in the right place. Now I don't figure Henry to be much of a marksman, particularly if he's half lit, and that stupid little gun he's carrying around may have many fine virtues but accuracy is not one of them. So there's two things you've got to keep in your mind. Number one is distance. The farther away you are, the less chance he has to get a shot into you. Number two is stay in motion. Don't be like that poor ole cat, just laying there on the glider. The chances of Henry hitting a moving target that's more than twenty feet away from him are fairly remote. Okay? Of course there's always luck and we can't account for that. But even if you're hit in some fairly safe spot, you don't want to go to the doctors having to dig the fragments of a hollow point bullet out of you. Are you getting my message, Mase?"

Shit. The fear had frozen Mason up as solid as a monument. He sat there on the porch staring at nothing. Eilum had gone off to meet the other engineers at the Merida public pool. They'd taken to doing that in the muggy afternoons, trying to pick up townie girls, so far they'd picked up none but seemed determined to keep on trying. Eilum had invited Mason to come along but even if he'd wanted to, Mason couldn't do that with his goddamn shaved legs. He had to find some way out of this brainless funk. He'd ridden all the way out to the ag school and back, ridden pretty hard, and that had helped but hadn't solved anything.

The telephone. Jessie had called him once, to tell him that Lorianne had arrived safely at her grandma's. Now it was his turn to call her and he had a damn good reason, didn't he? Why was he putting it off? The first thing she said was, "Mason! Do you know what day it is?"

"Yeah, it's Sunday."

No, that's not what she'd meant. Ev and Mattie were leaving for the Cape at the crack of dawn tomorrow morning and Jessie had till ten o'clock tonight at the latest to get her thesis to Ev. "Aw, shit," Mason said. "I forgot. Sorry. Maybe we can talk about this tomorrow? It just seemed . . . kind of important. Real important if you want to know the truth of the matter."

"All right. Tell me quick."

Quick? That was like writing an abstract. "Well, Henry is going around telling people that he's gonna kill us." He told her the details he thought she ought to know. For a long time she didn't say anything. Then she said, "Fuck. I don't want to think about any of this."

"From the sound of it, he's probably sleeping it off," Mason said.

"I really don't . . . Oh, Jesus Christ. For my entire life people have been warning me about perfectionism but I can't help it. I penciled up the whole draft last night and now I'm retyping it. It's driving me up the fucking wall. Henry can shoot me tomorrow."

241

"Okay, Jessie."

"*Not* okay. *Of course* it's not okay. I called Carl, did I tell you that? I thought he needed to know about the dead cat and Lorianne going back to West Virginia. But I didn't get him. I tried him two or three times but his phone just rang and rang. I checked the number with the operator and yes, it was in service, and there was another number for the same address in Canton. A *James* Truscott. That must be his dad and Carl has his own phone and he's just not answering it. Or maybe he went away somewhere. Vacation? I could have called his parents but I didn't. It was . . . just too goddamn much trouble. I forgot all about it. Carl's the key. He might be the only one Henry will listen to. Do you want the numbers?"

Mason did not want the numbers but he wrote them down anyway. "Call me tomorrow," Jessie said. "Or no . . . call me tonight after ten. I'll be able to talk then."

Mason called Carl's number, let it ring until the operator came on to say, "I'm sorry but the customer is not answering."

Mason could not bring himself to call Carl's parents. What the fuck would he say to them? He'd have to start out by identifying himself, saying who he was. So who was he? He went back and sat on the girls' porch. He smoked a smoke. He was running out of daytime. Shit.

Now Mason was contemplating Henry's rusted-out gray Dodge. Henry hadn't parked it, he'd abandoned it, looked like he'd been trying to drive it right on into the house but he'd got interrupted by the front steps, must have hit them with a pretty good smack, bent the front bumper on the driver's side. Not too bad though, still drivable. Mason straightened up. He didn't give a shit about Henry's car, just taking a breather before he would have to contemplate Henry himself, and then, on cue, the McKinley Tower bonged five times.

Mason turned away from the blinding glare of the low sun to look at the eastern horizon where a pile of clotted up dirty clouds were drifting in. Yeah, it was gradually coming to an end, the kind of senseless muggy August afternoon that the only relief for would be twilight.

The front door was standing open and the screen door wasn't locked. Mason knocked light, then harder. "Henry?" and felt a squashed stillness in the house even before he walked into it. Henry was laying back on the big chair by the hi-fi, the chair he always sat in. He was catfished right out, his mouth hanging open and a deep rattle coming out of him with every breath. The fucking gun was laying right there on the side table close to Henry's right hand.

Mason sat down directly in front of Henry in the chair Carl always sat in. The last time Mason had been sitting there, Lorianne had been across from him and they'd been listening to Brahms. On the end table along with the gun were a shot glass and a big water tumbler, a pitcher of water, an open fifth of Evil Williams and an unopened second one standing behind it there in reserve. The green glass ashtray was piled so high with butts they were spilling out of it. The gun wasn't as small as Mason had expected but there it was, a revolver with a short stubby barrel. Mason never would have thought it was a toy gun.

What Eilum had said was right, somebody had beat the crap out of Henry. He had a dandy shiner on his left eye, bruises all over his face, his nose and mouth swolled up pretty bad, his lower lip split clean open, it had bled some. His striped polo shirt and khaki chinos were so filthy he looked like he'd been sleeping in a ditch. Must have been a one sided fight, no marks on his knuckles. The poor bastard had taken off his shoes and socks. His veined white feet looked pathetic sticking up there on the hassock.

Was Mason supposed to sit there until Henry woke up or should he wake him? The blinds were pulled down over all the windows, the sides of them edged with liquid light so brilliant it didn't look real. Henry had a crappy old fan going somewhere, probably in the kitchen, it made a chuggy kind of sound, a clicky kind of sound, and even over it Mason could hear flies. Why did Mason want Henry awake? That was the last thing in the world he should want. What he should do now was fairly simple, grab that gun and duck out of there but then he saw that Henry's eyes were open a slit and looking at him. Jesus, he thought, I'm way too slow. Nancy Drew would have been there and gone.

"Hey," Henry said, "it's the Kid." His voice was thick with phlegm.

"Hey," Mason said. "How you doing, Henry?"

"Fairly shitty." He sat up, leaned forward, and clutched the back of his neck. "Holy fucking Jesus shit. Hey, Kid, you want to do something for me?"

"Sure."

"Get me a glass of ginger ale. Yeah, and some aspirin. I think there's some in the downstairs bathroom."

Amazing how quick Henry had turned the kitchen into a fucking pig sty, dirty dishes in the sink and half-eaten deli sandwiches, TV dinner trays, greasy scrunched-up paper laying around on the counter like he'd never heard of a garbage can. Mason found a clean water tumbler, filled it with ginger ale, and yeah, the aspirin was in the medicine cabinet in the downstairs can.

"Thanks, Kid. How many of these are you allowed to take? You got any idea?"

"You're supposed to take two, aren't you?"

"Yeah, but how many *can* you take? Three shouldn't hurt you, should it?"

"I couldn't tell you, Henry"

"You want to do something else for me?"

"Sure."

"Get me a bowl of ice cream? And I think there's some choco-late syrup . . . It's out there somewhere."

It was sitting on the counter, Hershey's in the can with the lid partway open and bent halfway up. Let's give Henry lots of ice cream, Mason thought, lots and lots of ice cream.

"Thanks. I really appreciate it." Henry gobbled about half, set the bowl down and stood up. He took a couple steps before he remembered the gun, went back to get it, took it with him to the can. Mason listened to Henry peeing a gallon. Then he came back, set the gun back down on the end table close to his right hand. Mason hadn't liked the look of any of that. "Henry? Were you in a fight or something?"

"Fight. Shit. I wouldn't call it a fight. You know what, Kid? It's a topic I do not care to discuss."

"Yeah? Well anyhow, maybe you ought to see a doctor about that lip."

"A doctor. Oh ho, yes. All you assholes want poor old Henry to *see a doctor*. I know what you're doing. You can all go fuck your-selves." He poured himself half a shot, added a splash of water to it, and drank it down like medicine. He finished off the ice cream.

Even though they were just sitting there, Mason had a sense of things in motion, of him and Henry sniffing around each other in circles like dogs. Might as well get right to the point. "Heard you wanted to shoot me, Henry. Well, here I am. Do you want to shoot me?"

"I am thinking about it. Why don't we discuss it later?"

"Fine with me. I heard you might want to discuss the matter with me."

"I do, yes. I definitely do want to discuss the matter with you. But I *said* we'll discuss it *later*."

"Okay, okay. Well, um . . . Okay, so what were you listening to, Henry?"

Henry looked over at the motionless turntable. "Fuck, I don't remember." He picked up the record jacket. "Apparently I was listening to Monk."

"Remember that night when I first turned up here? Back in June? You were playing Miles Davis. I wouldn't mind hearing that again."

"Davis? Oh, yeah, I know the one you mean." He flipped through his records, put one on, handed Mason the dust jacket. The last time Mason had seen it, it had been in French and it still was. Then that exquisite golden trumpet was coming out of the speaker, saying that there was something really sad somewhere, that it was a lot more than sad, that it was fucked up and sinister. "Thanks for reminding me," Henry said. "Jesus, he's good. I forget sometimes how good he is."

Henry didn't seem to have much more to say. He took out his pack of Pall Malls and offered Mason one. Mason took it and Henry lit it for him with his big shiny Ronson. Then Henry poured himself a full shot of whiskey and knocked it straight back. They sat and listened. The McKinley tower added its chime to the sad trumpet, telling them that by the grace of God they'd made it to six o'clock. "Henry," Mason said, "you feel like eating something?"

Andrew Johnson was a fucking idiot," Mason said.

"I don't know how you can say that about somebody who was elected to public office as many times as he was."

"He came within one vote of getting his sorry ass booted out of the presidency, that's how I can say that."

Mason was using up the rest of the Wonder Bread, the only bread that Tammy would eat. He smeared a coat of hot German mustard on one slice, slapped some Velveeta on another slice, put them together and fried them in butter. Once he flipped them out of the frying pan, he cut them diagonally to make four triangles, and as long as Henry was eating those triangles dipped in ketchup,

Mason was going to keep frying them. He'd eaten a few himself. "When it came to cessation," he said, "Johnson may have sided with the union but when it came to what to do about the freed slaves, he sided with the Confederacy."

"It was *Lincoln's* plan. All Johnson was doing was continuing Lincoln's generous open-hearted plan for reconstruction. 'With Malice toward none, with charity for all . . .'"

"Bullshit. Nobody knows what Lincoln's plan was. He took it to the grave with him. But one thing for sure, Lincoln was too shrewd a politician to get the whole damn Republican Party pissed off at him. What the hell? The Union won the war, didn't it? Why the hell shouldn't they dictate the peace? That's what Thaddeus Stevens said and he was right."

"Of course you cite the most radical of the Republicans! Braith-waite's got you brainwashed. You can't read history like that, Mason. You've got to put yourself back in the mind of the times, feel the pressures that people felt—"

"They fucked up reconstruction and so we have to do it all over again, do it right this time. Mississippi's a goddamn fascist police state. Those three missing civil rights workers are dead, they were dead the first night they went missing, everybody knows that, and the only reason anybody gives a shit this time is because two of them were white. That's why we've got all these students down there now—"

"Meddling. Yes. They got their Civil Rights Act—"

"The Civil Rights Act? Jesus, Henry, it don't mean shit if nobody's going to enforce it."

"Yeah. Meddling. Mrs. Collier's girlfriend is down there, isn't she? Meddling in shit she doesn't know a thing about. That little Jew girl."

Mason felt a million hot nasty prickles on the back of his neck. That one stopped him. There was nothing he could say to that. Henry looked at him in silence for a long time. "You want some more ice cream, Henry?"

"No." Henry picked up his gun and walked back into the living room.

This was all too fucking familiar, Mason had watched the old man perform this show on many an occasion. Mason used to think, hey, he's a grown man and he's had lots of experience with this, doesn't he know what's gonna happen to him? There had to be something about being a drunk that makes it impossible to learn anything. Yeah, and there had to be something about *trying to take care of a drunk* that makes it impossible to learn anything. Mason had watched his mom and Irene trying to get some food shoved down the old man's gullet, trying to distract him from the goddamn bottle, and it never worked for them and it wasn't working for Mason. For a while he and Henry had been batting ideas back and forth just like they were back in the classroom but now Henry was slowing down some, getting stupid. He was even starting to slur. Well, shit, Mason was going to keep on trying.

"Your man, Rutherford B. Hayes," Mason said, "I really was trying to put myself into his mind, you know, *back in the times.* Yeah, he really was a man of integrity, a man of honor, and he could have said, no, I'm not going to be part of any shady backroom deal, not even to be president. Then we'd remember him as a great man . . . *who served his country best,* right? But the more I read about him, the more I figured that there was a damn good reason he was in that back room with the boys. He was a non-entity and they picked him because he was a non-entity and they knew damn well he'd go along with whatever they told him—"

"Aw, Mason, that's not fair. That's not even—"

"Fair? Shit. Now we remember him as the guy who ended reconstruction, let the south do pretty much what it damn well pleased, yeah, so they could get things back as close as possible the old days of slavery. Oh, and we remember his lovely wife too 'cause she dried out the White House, yep, good old Lemonade Lucy. Jesus, what a mediocre president! Oh yeah, and he used federal troops to break up a strike, let's not forget that, the first president who did that. And it seems really ironic that they could use federal troops to break up a strike but they couldn't use them to defend the rights of black folks in the south, as was pointed out by some astute commentators *at the time.*"

Henry had given up on the shot glass. He'd poured himself a few good inches of straight whiskey into the water tumbler and was taking a sip from it every few minutes. Mason knew exactly what Henry thought he was doing. If he kept sipping away, just took it easy, he thought he was gonna find that beautiful edge of happiness and float along on it forever but no, Henry was gonna get just as pissed as he had the last time, and time before that, and all the fucking times before that. "Oh, for Christ's sake, Mason, radical reconstruction was a total failure. Anarchy. People in the South are still bitter about it—"

"No, it wasn't. Some places it worked better than others, but it was pretty good. The black folks were getting off to a good start."

"The natural leaders were disenfranchised. They feared for their lives—"

"Who? The old planter class? Nobody was gonna kill any of them."

"They were the intelligence of the South. The scalawags didn't have it, the white trash didn't have it, and newly freed slaves certainly didn't have it—"

"Henry! I can't believe you're saying that shit, all that fucking *Gone With the Wind* bullshit. None of it's true."

"Jesus, Mason, there's different points of view on this. I'll let you in on a—" and then they both paused to count the eight bongs.

"Fuck," Henry said, "I'll let you in on a little secret. The sun does *not* rise and set in Everett Braithwaite's asshole. He's a communist, did you know that?"

"The hell he is. He might have been back in the thirties, but . . . He may be a Marxist but those are two different—"

"That arrogant son a bitch is the reason I never got my thesis done. Used to meet with him every couple of weeks and he'd . . . he'd tell me all the ways I was fucking up, all the ways I was wrong. Eventually I just thought, fuck it, just fuck it fuck it."

The evening was wearing on at a leisurely pace, Henry was disintegrating, and with nine bongs the McKinley Tower was keeping score. Amazing, Mason thought, you wouldn't know that Henry was the same person who'd been talking to you a couple hours ago. "Following the fucking army," he was muttering now, his words thick. "Scavenging for shit, any old shit, picking over rotten corpses, servicing the soldiers, doing any sick dick . . . dick sick things . . . disgusting . . . sick disgusting shit they wanted. The absolute dregs, the lowest of the low. Whores and sodomites."

Henry seemed to have arrived at this topic by way of scalawags and white trash but Mason couldn't figure out exactly where it was they'd arrived. "Which particular army are we talking about, Henry?"

"Any army, for fuck's sake! Always been around, always will be. Hiding out in little dark pockets, little godforsaken desolate . . . hollows and bogs . . . generations of incest, every generation one step farther down . . . further down . . . further down on the rung. Cretins, morons, mindless idiots."

Yeah, Mason thought, you're doing pretty well in the mindless idiocy department yourself. "Give me a hint," he said. "What century are we in?"

"Mindless violence. *Mindless! Violence!* Jesus fucking Christ.

In that pack of . . . of of . . . shit . . . idiots, imbeciles, cretins, and morons . . . dull normal looks like fucking Einstein. It's like . . . like *a chimpanzee.* You think it's intelligent, but all it's doing is . . . is, you know . . . *imitating a human being.* And here I am, saddled . . . Jesus, Mason, I've done my best. Like they say, you can take the girl out of the . . . Take a girl, a girl out of the . . ."

"Country?" Mason offered.

"Yeah, but you can't take the hillbilly out of the girl."

You know, Henry, Mason thought, I could take a very strong dislike to you.

Henry picked up the fifth to add a bit more to his glass but the fifth was empty. With a grinning ceremonial show, he punched it over, *bang, another one down.* He cracked open the second fifth, poured out a splash. His eyes rested for a moment on his gun and then, just like he was just discovering it for the first time, he picked it up and studied it. He caressed the grip.

Fuck, Mason thought, I'm a sitting duck. But Henry was pretty slowed down and if he had to, Mason could make a run for it. Instead of doing anything with the gun, Henry simply continued to hold it as he slumped back into the chair and his eyes fell shut.

There they were right back to where they'd started. Mason was sitting in Carl's chair, watching and waiting. Henry was sprawled out in his own chair, holding that fucking gun in his lap. He wasn't drinking any more. Was that a good thing or a bad thing? He kept drifting off. Sometimes his head would bob forward and that would wake him. Other times his head would fall back against the chair and he'd snore. But every time Mason thought, okay, he's gone, now I can make a grab for that gun, Henry's eyes would pop open and he'd give Mason a red-rimmed evil-eyed look. He kept saying things from time to time, like he was still trying to deliver that ancient long-winded lecture he'd started awhile back.

The tower bonged ten times. Sweet Jesus, Mason had been at Henry's place for five fucking hours! Maybe the best thing to do would be give it up and get the hell out of there. He knew he could do that without waking Henry, especially now that Henry did seem to be finally down the well, his mouth hanging open and that steady angular rasp coming out of him. But damn, Mason wanted that gun. He'd invested all that time in trying to get it, maybe if he hung on just a little bit longer.

All of a sudden Henry's whole body jerked like he'd been stung. He sat up, pawed around on his lap, found the gun, clutched it, stared around the room, saw Mason, and then, of all the weird shit, started to cry. "Oh God, oh God, oh God, I thought it was Orvie on my lap! Oh fuck, oh Jesus, it was so real! I could *feel her fur.*"

He hung his head and sobbed, smeared away the tears and snot with his left hand, hung onto the gun with his right. "Jesus, oh Jesus Jesus, I loved that cat. That cat was my *true friend.* She picked me, she chose me, she favored me, she was *my fucking cat.* Oh God, how can I go on without my cat? My dearest friend. Whenever I felt bad, she always knew it, always came straight to me to make me feel better. She *talked* to me. I knew what every one of her fucking meows meant and she knew what *I* meant too. I talked to her *all the fucking time.* We had a bond that . . . Oh Jesus, Jesus, Jesus, Orville *Orville!* She was a part of our family. Just as much as Tammy was. How can I live without my cat? You want to tell me that? How can I live *without her?* My cat, my dear cat, my dear dear cat. How can I go on? I *can't* go on, I just fucking can't. Go. On. Oh fuck fuck fuck."

Mason couldn't believe he was hearing any of this shit. "Henry," he said, "you shot her."

"How the fuck do you think I felt?" Henry shrieked at Mason. "Huh? How? Pretty fucking miserable, wouldn't you say? Pretty goddamn *fucking low,* wouldn't you say? But does anybody give a

fuck how Henry feels? Fuck no, nobody. Not a fucking soul in the world gives a holy flying fuck how Henry feels."

His eyes were burning with accusation. "Does anybody come around here and ask, 'Hey, Henry, how you doing?' Does anybody pat me on the shoulder and say, 'Don't worry, Henry, it's going to be all right.' No, nobody. Don't I deserve to have *a family?* Don't I deserve *to be loved?* No, apparently not. Nobody gives a fuck about me. Not one fucking soul."

He leaned forward in his chair, dropped his voice like there were all these people around him and he didn't want them to hear. "I'm a good teacher. I worked hard for years."

"Yeah, you are," Mason said. "You're a good teacher."

"Did you ever see me show up to class unprepared? Did you ever see me when I did not know the subject matter inside and out?"

"No, Henry, never."

"Well, fuck, don't I deserve some minimal respect? At least that much?"

"Yes, of course you do, Henry."

"Kid? You want to do something for me? Lori keeps a box of Kleenex up on her dressing table."

It was absolutely and utterly ridiculous but Mason went upstairs and got that box of Kleenex. Henry thanked him for it, wiped his face, blew his nose. He leaned way forward in the chair, motioned Mason to come closer. Mason scooted Carl's chair forward a foot or two, sat down in it. When Henry started to talk, he dropped his voice even lower. Yeah, this was definitely a matter that was strictly between the two of them and those nosey phantoms were not gonna hear it. "That fated night," Henry said, "I'd had a bit too much to drink. I woke up around dawn. I had a mystical experience. Yeah, for real. The only one in my life. *A. Mystical. Experience.*"

Henry dropped his voice another notch. Mason had to lean forward some more. "That colored preacher's not the only one who can have a dream. We've all got our dreams, right? And mine was so clear and beautiful, so damned beautiful, like pure white light. I understood lots of things all at once. The first thing I understood was that this stuff," and he picked up the new fifth of whiskey, "was poison pure and simple. It destroys your life. It destroys your soul. So you know what I did? I poured every drop down the drain. And then I took a shower and changed my clothes because *I was a new man*. I knew I would never drink again.

"Do you want to know what I saw then? *My dream.* You know how when you're still a boy? But you're almost a man? You're right on the edge. And you know there's a perfect love out there for you somewhere. Your soul mate, your shining perfect girl, and when you find her, you'll love her with all your heart and she'll love you back with all her heart. Then you get older, you get cynical, you say that was all bullshit, right? Okay, well I saw that it wasn't bullshit, it was true. And I saw that shining perfect girl was real and I was already married to her. What do you think of that?

"Yeah, and I knew that this was *poison*." He shook the fifth. "I knew it could *destroy you*." He unscrewed the cap and winged it across the room. "I knew it could *kill you*." He tilted the bottle back and started chugging it like it was beer, his Adam's apple bobbing up and down. He was going glug, glug, glug. He was chugging down about half that fifth. Mason had never seen anything like it. Holy shit, Mason thought, when that hits him, it's gonna be like a fucking sledgehammer.

Henry stopped finally, yelled out, "Brrrr," wiped his mouth with the back of his hand. He slammed the bottle down hard onto the table. He stared into Mason's eyes. "All I had to do was get Lorianne to share my dream." He was talking fast. "It was early in the morning, I knew she'd just be waking up. Because that's when Tammy wakes up. I tapped at the door. I tapped at the window. I knew we were. Making. A whole new start. With

Lorianne by my side. With Lori *as my wife*. There was nothing I couldn't do. Nothing. *My wife*. The sky was. Was the limit. I was sure I could. I could make her see that. Yes. It was love, Mason, do you get that? *It was all based on love*, do you understand that, you fucking asshole? And then what happened? Well, shit, you know what happened."

Henry leaned forward even farther. His face was maybe only a foot away and Mason knew that Henry was gonna shoot him. After all that time with nothing happening, this was way too fast. Mason had to make a grab for the gun. He just had a few seconds to do it. He had to keep his eyes glued to Henry's, the minute he looked away, Henry would know what he was doing. He took a slow deep breath.

But then, looking into Henry's face, Mason wasn't so sure any more. Henry didn't look like he was going to shoot anybody, he had a weird kind of fucked up smile. Then he broke eye contact, stared off into the dark edges of the room where the phantoms lived. What the fuck? Mason let his breath out, careful and easy. Henry's mouth dropped open, his whole face went slack, he looked surprised. Well, no, more than surprised, he looked bewildered, yeah, like there was something coming at him he just couldn't get.

All of a sudden Henry levered himself up to his feet. He had to use both hands to do it. The gun tumbled out of his lap and fell to the floor with a thud. He lurched forward, started to fall, grabbed Mason's shoulder, used it to steady himself.

Henry was staring at the stairs, willing his body to go there. He let go of Mason's shoulder, then his legs were scissoring forward but they weren't working right, he was going down for the count. Mason jumped up and caught him, wrapped one of Henry's arms around his shoulders. "Hang on there, ole buddy," he said, "you're almost there."

Henry was damned near a dead weight but Mason kept waltz-ing him forward until Henry reached out, grabbed the bannister, and hung onto it. Mason turned Henry loose. Instead of falling onto his face, Henry hung suspended a moment from his one clamped hand, then worked his whole damn body up to get the other hand on the bannister, pulled with both hands, sawed with his feet, hauled himself partway up the stairs. Groaning, he kept on going, repeating that ugly scrabbling motion one step at a time. At the top of the stairs he went down on all fours and crawled. Then Mason heard the creak and rattle of the bed frame, the final crash on the bed springs, that told him that Henry, thank God, had made it home.

Mason was out in the fucking dark night, in the front yard, kicking off the kick stand, shoving his bike forward with his left hand, realized that he was holding that goddamn revolver in his right hand, holding it just like he was gonna shoot somebody with it. Jesus, he couldn't be riding across campus like that, waving a gun.

A waning crescent moon was up, a pretty good sliver of it, but not a whole fuck of a lot of light. He was panting and his heart was beating in his throat. He'd had two years of ROTC because they'd required it, he was qualified on an M-1, but he'd never held a handgun before. It *was* kind of like holding a toy. Like a lot of other things it would clip onto the back of his bike but how should he point it? Not at himself, obviously, so he aimed it backward, slightly off to one side. He clipped it down and rode.

15.

"**Christ, no,** I don't want that fucking gun in here." Jessie was in her vertical striped pajamas. She and Mason were standing outside her open front door and he was coming unglued, that's how he thought of it, he couldn't find any other way to think about it. "Disarm . . . I disarmed him. Fuck, I don't . . . Took me forever."

"Where is it?"

"There." He pointed at his bike. With the street light shining, you could see the gun. Even from that distance you could see it.

"Oh, for Christ's sake. Wait a minute."

She ran into her apartment, came back with a towel. "Wrap this around it so it isn't so obvious. Then put your bike under the back porch. Way back in the back." Yeah, he could do that but then how was he supposed to get home?

She was still waiting for him on the landing. The night was hot and muggy but he was shaking all over, even his teeth were chattering. "You're in shock," she said in a matter of fact voice like she'd say, "You've got a bit of ketchup on your shirt."

He was having a hard time putting words together. "Yeah, I guess. Yeah, that must be what it is."

"Okay. Come in here. Just take it easy."

"Did you get your . . . ? You know, your thesis . . . ?"

"I did. Ev's got it. I'm done. I still can't believe it. Do you want a drink?"

"Oh God no."

She took his hand, led him to a chair, and pointed him at it. "A smoke?" he said. "Maybe I need a smoke?"

"Well, you know where the ashtray is. I'm going to start a bath for you. Is that okay?"

That didn't make any sense but he said, "Yeah, sure," and kept on going, out the back door and onto the porch. He fired up a Camel and dragged. Some cigarettes you smoked out of habit and some you smoked because you fucking well needed them and this was one of the latter category. Was he in shock? It had to be still up in the eighties but he was chilled and shaking, at the same time he was sweating like a pig. It was helping to smoke, maybe just standing there was helping. At night there was nothing to see of Jessie's scraggly back yard except the shape of that stupid bird bath, crooked. The crescent moon had to be up there somewhere but not visible from where he was. Jesus, he thought, back in June I tried to kill myself. It didn't make any sense. He was afraid of dying, terrified of it. He'd spent five hours, getting on to six hours, that whole time at Henry's, terrified of dying.

He went back inside, saw that when she'd said bath, that's exactly what she'd meant, the tub was filled. "Soak in the water," she said, "you'll feel better." Maybe she was right. "You want me to wash your things? There's a machine in the basement."

"Yeah. I guess. No, no, no, wait a minute." What? Wash his clothes? That really didn't make any sense. "I don't know. I gotta go home?"

"No, you don't. You're going to stay here. You can sleep in Sarah's bed."

"But what if . . . ? You know, the university?"

"Nobody pays any attention to those absurd regulations. And it's August. Who's going to see you?"

Once he was in the tub, he felt how tense he was, the muscles in his back knotted up like golf balls. The bathroom was painted an overblown flamingo color and it seemed like a wrong place for him to be, like he'd got there by trickery or some damn thing. Whenever he closed his eyes, he could see Henry. He kept going over things in his mind, remembering some part of it, something he'd said or Henry had said. It was like an old late-night vampire movie constantly playing. Maybe it would stop eventually. Well, shit, he'd got Henry's gun, hadn't he?

Jessie had left a terrycloth bathrobe for him. He dried himself, put the robe on, went out looking for her. She was sitting in one of the big chairs, not reading or anything, just sitting there. As soon as he saw her, he realized how fucked his mind had been before, maybe because, yeah, he had been in shock and he hadn't been able *to see anything right*, but now he could see her sharp and clear again, there she was, absolutely clear, that big tall strong girl, her eyes shining dark in the lamplight. "Okay," she said, "tell me about it."

Well, that was a big order. "Shit, he seemed almost normal when he first woke up. He had the world's worst hangover but he just seemed like himself. Except that somebody had beat the piss out of him. He said he didn't want to talk about that and he never did."

Mason walked her through it the best he could remember, how they listened to Miles Davis, how Henry started drinking again, gradual, the ice cream, the grilled cheese sandwiches. "Yeah, and we were arguing history just the way we used to back in his class. That's how he likes to teach, you're supposed to hold an opinion, get in an argument. Okay, so we had us a pretty good duke-out over Reconstruction and then we went at good old Rutherford B. Hayes and I got the feeling that Henry wasn't arguing just to argue, that he was telling me what he really thought. He called Dr. Braithwaite a communist, said he's got us all brainwashed."

"Oh, for Christ's sake. I didn't know Henry's politics were that far to the right."

"Yeah? Well, I don't know where the fuck his politics are." He told her about how Henry started drinking hard, how he called Lorianne a moronic hillbilly with no more brains than a chimpanzee and then, an hour later, and a lot more booze later, she'd turned out to be Henry's ideal girl, his perfect wife. "I felt like I was looking into the mind of somebody who was . . . I don't know, Jessie, he was just fucking *nuts*. He scared the bejesus out of me."

One thing he had to tell her about, in considerable detail, was Henry crying over the cat. As horrible as it was, Mason told it funny and they both were laughing. "Christ," she said, "that man's capacity for self-delusion must be utterly boundless."

Then there was that last weird look Henry had given him just before he'd passed out. Right when Mason had been convinced that Henry was about to shoot him, he'd given him that look instead. "Kind of a fucked up smile or something. Like he was saying, 'Hey, it's all a joke.'"

"That's right, and it *was* all a joke. Henry and Carl, their sick sense of humor, they're famous for that, exactly the sort of thing they think is funny. Henry's not going to shoot anybody, are you kidding? He put on a big show for you, ran you through the wringer, and that's all he wanted. But boy, am I ever glad you got his stupid gun! At least now he can't hurt anybody."

She stood up and stretched. "Mason, I'm just *so bagged*. Let's get you to bed so I can go to bed."

He followed her into Sarah's room. "Right after she left I made up the bed for her, clean sheets and everything, so she'd have a nice bed to come home to. Well, fuck, she's never going to come home to it, is she? So it's a . . . It's fresh and clean. If you need to smoke, you know where. If you get hungry, eat anything you find. I'm from a noisy family so once I'm asleep, I'm dead to the world and you don't have to be particularly quiet. There's your things."

His cigarettes and pack of matches, his wallet, belt, and keys were on the bed table. Jessie had turned down the sheets on the bed. She'd even left a pair of pajamas for him, vertical striped just like hers. And Sarah's room really was a *girl's* room, one of those fuzzy French art prints on the wall, a vanity table, little lacy pillows, everything done up in blue and cream. "Hey," he said. "Jessie. This is so nice of you."

She shrugged, like it was no big deal. "It's a nice room," she said. "It's pretty in the morning. Sleep as long as you want. This is a ... I'm *finished*, Jesus Christ, I can't believe it, *my fucking thesis*. But I'm so tired, I can't ... I can't even be happy about it. Good night, Mason. I'm glad you're here. I'm glad you got his gun. Really glad. That was courageous of you. Sleep, okay? Sleep."

Eventually Mason did sleep but he kept waking up every couple hours, feeling a kind of stretched out amazement. That seemed an odd way to put it but he couldn't think of a better one. He was in somebody else's bed, Sarah Feingold's to be exact, that phantom girl he'd never met, prissy, Jessie had called her. It was good to sleep in between prissy Sarah's clean blue sheets, he should probably wash his bedding more often than he did.

It was a long skinny room, faced east at the far end, so when the sun came up and started blasting through the frilly sheer curtains, he couldn't sleep anymore. The walls had been recently painted a pale cream, the woodwork and all the furniture a darker cream. The drapes and pillows and covers and the seats of the chairs were in that color they called French blue. Feeling like a thief, he got up to look around.

Sarah was a real girl all right, bottles and jars on the vanity table, cold cream, night cream, hand cream, nail polish, five different colors of lipstick, yeah *five*. Of course he had to look in the closet. Holy fuck, did she have a lot of clothes! Well, if your family's in the business and you're getting them for free, you would have a lot, wouldn't you? And shoes. He'd thought that Lorianne had a lot of shoes but she had nothing on Sarah, wow, look at all those heels. He couldn't help it, picked one up, red as a cherry. How often would you wear red high heels?

Standing there holding Sarah's shoe in his hand, Mason remembered what Henry had called her, *that little Jew girl*. Mason hadn't told Jessie that part, he hadn't wanted to repeat it. Well, Henry could go fuck himself, that miserable piece of trash. Mason was getting a good sense of Sarah, the girl who'd created this peaceful cream and blue bedroom for herself. She was in Mississippi where it was definitely not peaceful, and she was there because it was the right place to be. Good for you, Sarah Feingold, he told her. You've got more guts than I do.

Keeping things quiet, he slipped out of Sarah's room onto the back porch to have a smoke. Nice morning, clear, birds chirping, and his clothes hanging neatly on the line, even his socks hanging by their toes, one clothespin to each sock. He had to smile at how meticulous Jessie was. Back in Sarah's room, he got dressed, made the bed, and left Jessie's pajamas folded on the top. It was after ten and she still wasn't up. Should he go home? Well, maybe not yet. He should at least stick around to say thanks. That would be polite.

Meticulous only went so far with Jessie, old coffee grounds still in her percolator. He cleaned it out, put on a fresh pot to perk, checked the ice box, found a grapefruit that didn't seem too old, cut it in half, segmented it, and sprinkled sugar on the top. He was outside having a cup of coffee and another smoke when he heard her get up. "The smell of the coffee did it," she said.

He came back inside, saw that she was looking at the little

turquoise table. He'd opened the leaves on it, laid down two daisy placemats he'd found in a drawer and put the bowls with the grapefruit halves on them. "My goodness," she said, "aren't you the little homemaker?"

Shit. He probably should have left as soon as he got up. "I told you I was determined to be the girl. How do you like your eggs?"

Sunny side up was how she liked them. After breakfast they sat on the back porch drinking the last of the coffee. Her yard really was dreadful, hard to believe that all that bleached out straw might once have been grass. "Thank you," she said, "that was so nice of you, coffee and everything." He could tell by the tone of her voice that it was an apology.

"Thanks. I'm going to be on my way soon. I just wanted to, you know—"

"You don't have to go. I'm taking the day off."

Was that an invitation to stay? "Okay."

She hadn't washed her face yet, bits of sleep still stuck in the corners of her eyes, her short hair still tousled. "I'm just so happy to get my thesis in."

"No, you're not. You're as prickly as a cactus."

She gave him a startled look and then laughed. "You're right. I am. I keep thinking I *should* be happy . . . Aw fuck it. I was so damned tired last night and then I couldn't go to sleep for hours, lying there stewing about Henry Algren. What a fucking asshole!"

"Yeah," Mason said, "you've got that one right. How's Lorianne doing? Have you talked to her?"

"No. I haven't. Not since she called to tell me that she'd got to her grandmother's safely. I'm terrible. For weeks whenever anything came up, I'd say to myself, don't think about it till you get your thesis done. Okay, so it's done and all the shit I haven't been thinking about is still waiting for me. Yeah, I should call Lorianne.

I should try Carl again too. Jesus. And maybe *I* should go have a little chat with Henry. *Tomorrow*, okay? Today's a day off."

She was staring at the crooked birdbath but he knew that she wasn't seeing it. "Jesus. Goddamn fucking Henry. A married man and still roaming around with Carl, picking up undergrads. Did you see those last two, those sad little girls?"

"Yeah. The red-lipstick girls."

"Do they wear red lipstick? That's something *you'd* notice. I noticed how young they were. Just imagine it. One year you're in high school and the next year you're being chased around a university campus by guys damned near twice your age, trying to get in your pants. Guys who *teach* at the university. There should be regulations against it but of course there never will be. The university's run by *men*.

"It happened to me when I was an undergrad, did I tell you that? I was still an English major. I don't even want to remember his name. I'd had one course with him. He was a good teacher and I'd signed up for another course, upper level. I was in his office and I got *the line*. 'You're not like the other girls, you're special. You're one in a million, a brilliant scholar, you have a first-class mind.' Well, that's pretty flattering for a kid to hear, right? But then he had to keep on going. 'I'm stuck here with a lot of papers to grade. Are you free for dinner tonight?' Well, unfortunately for him I wasn't just another dewy-eyed sophomore, I was Joe Minotti's daughter and Dad had told me all about the dubious shit that some of his colleagues did. I walked out of that miserable prick's office and over to the departmental office, said, 'Is it too late to drop?' It wasn't, thank God. He never spoke to me again after that, we'd pass in the hallway and he'd cut me dead. He was a big part of the reason I switched my major. So I suppose he did me a favor."

She leaned back in her chair to get her face clear of the sun, closed her eyes. He didn't know what to say to her. He knew she had to be thinking about something, she was always thinking about *something*. "Mason? Do you mind if I ask you a personal question?"

"No, I don't mind."

She opened her eyes, sat up, and looked at him. "Do you always shave your legs?"

Well, holy fuck, that came out of nowhere. Well, not completely out of nowhere, he'd been wearing nothing but her bathrobe last night and he'd forgot completely about his legs. The hair had been growing back but it obviously hadn't been growing back fast enough. "If it's none of my business," she said, "just say so."

"No, I don't mind talking about it. Well, anyways, I don't mind talking *to you* about it. I just do it sometimes."

"Do you cross-dress a lot?"

Jesus, where was she going? "No. Just sometimes."

"I do too. Not very often. But sometimes. You want to see?"

Of course he wanted to see. He followed her inside. She opened the door to her closet, kept sliding the hangers over until she got to a man's double-breasted wool suit in a dark brown herringbone. "'30s classic," she said, "got it in a second-hand store. Took it to a nice old Italian tailor and had it altered for me, told him I was going to a costume party. He teased me a little but not too much and he cut it perfectly."

The pants were on a hanger. She lifted them up to show him the pleats in the front. "Nifty, huh?" She pointed out the crisp white dress shirt with the French cuffs, held out for him a broad '30s tie with diagonal stripes in the unlikely colors of navy blue and red, pulled a snap-brim fedora off the shelf, modeled it for him, tossed it back, pointed at the shiny brown brogans on the floor. "Fit me perfectly, fit me a fuck of a lot better than women's shoes."

"Jesus, I bet you look wonderful."

"Oh, I do, I do. I feel like Sam Spade. Sarah loved me in it. I wore it in New York sometimes and back home on rare occasions. Very rare. My dad thought it was a riot but my mother was definitely not amused."

"And there's all your kilts."

"Yeah, my TA outfits. You want to wear one of them? I'll wear my suit and you wear a kilt and we'll go out to dinner?"

What he felt was so sudden and intense it didn't have words attached to it yet. "If we put makeup on you," she said, "nobody would think twice. I'd be the one everybody would be staring at anyway."

He still couldn't say anything. How could she be doing this to him? He'd trusted her.

"You're too easy to tease. You're so fair I can see the blood rising into your face. You're red as a beet."

She was right. He could feel his whole face burning up.

"I'm just kidding you. Mason, come on."

"Okay, okay." He was too angry to say anything more. He walked back into the living room.

"I've upset you. I'm sorry. I'm really really sorry. I won't ever tease you about any of that again."

"It's okay, Jessie."

"Oh fuck. No, it's not. Come on, let's get out of here. Let's go for a walk."

When she said a walk, she meant it, in her ancient-days sandals she was stepping right along. It was turning into a hot muggy day and he was already running with sweat. He could see that she was too. She glanced over at him, at his old threadbare jeans, said, "Oh. You can't wear shorts. That's too bad."

"Yeah, I guess." Jesus, she was still thinking about his shaved legs. "Those are nice," he said, nodding at her khaki green camp shorts. They really showed off *her* legs.

"Thanks," she said, "I'm deliberately flouting the dress code. But . . . Mason, I'm sorry, I really am."

"I know. You've said that. It's just that . . . I can't . . ." He was so pissed off at her he couldn't let go of it. "Look, Jessie, if you went out in public with that suit on, you might offend some people but nobody would . . . If I wore one of your kilts, somebody could fucking well kill me."

"Yes, I know that."

"Do you really? Really know it? I can't tell you what it's like, it's . . . You know, not just a matter of putting on a kilt, or a dress, or any damn thing. *It's not about the fucking clothes.* I spend all this . . . like just too damn much . . . like just an insane amount of time looking in the mirror. I saw a fucking shrink and I told her that and she said, 'Doesn't that strike you as excessive?' Well, fuck *yes*, it's excessive. But I don't know what else . . . No matter how long I look in the mirror, I'll never see a girl."

He was appalled at himself, saying all that shit. Well, she'd wanted personal and she'd got personal. Jesus, it was airless out here with the sun beating down, August and no fucking compromise.

"I'm sorry, Mason. I shouldn't have teased you. But I just wanted . . . I don't know what I wanted. Did I ever tell you about my TA outfits?"

"No. What?

"Kilts with knee socks is not a Jessie Minotti look. I'd never worn anything like that before in my life."

Her first year as a TA she'd bought herself two nice pairs of slacks, a black pair and a gray pair, and that's what she wore when she was teaching. Some anonymous asshole in her class ratted on her, she was pretty sure she knew who, a boy of course, and she was summoned to the office of the Dean of Women, who told her that she was in violation of the university dress code. "I said, 'Oh. Sorry about that. When's the last time you revised the dress code,

1906?' The Dean of Women was extremely unhappy with me. 'We have to set an example for *the girls*, don't we, *Mrs. Collier?*'

"Oh, I thought, so I'm supposed to set an example for *the girls*, am I? I looked around the campus and there were a million girls in kilts and knee socks and I thought, okay, that's what I'll wear. I wanted the girls to look at me and think, hey, she's not that different from me. If she can be a TA, maybe I can too."

"That's cool, Jessie. I love it, how deliberate you are."

"Deliberate?"

"Yeah. How you can just think about something and then plan your life."

"Aw, Jesus. Yes, that's me all right. Planning my whole fucking life. I don't know if— Jesus, this has stopped being fun, hasn't it?" She raised her arms to show him the circles of sweat on her blouse.

"Yeah, it kind of has," he said. "The sun's murderous."

"Mad dogs and Englishmen." But she didn't turn back, kept walking fast, leading them out toward the edge of the campus. "My contract runs out at the end of June next summer and I damned well better have a job by then."

She'd had it with men, she told him. She wanted to teach in an all-girls school, "a *female academy* they called them in the old days." She'd already met some women professors at conferences. Barnard and Mount Holyoke had already expressed interest in her. "Before I'm done, every one of the Seven Sisters is going to be hearing from me. One of them is bound to take me. I've kind of cornered the market on Lucy Stone. And if they don't, there's some really quite good women's colleges."

Despite how hot it was, she was still going at an insane clip. He was a bike rider, not a walker, and he was having trouble keeping up. "When you kissed that boy," she asked him, "is that the sum total of your sexual experience?"

He almost stopped dead. They were out beyond the ag school and she was not looking at him, was staring at the heat waves on the horizon. He was pissed off at her all over again. What the fuck did she want? "Well, no," he said, "I used to make out with Luke Ewing's little sister."

"Did you like it?"

"Yeah, I liked it just fine. But I never got as hot as that one time I kissed Bobby Springer. Is that what you wanted me to say?"

"No, I didn't mean—"

"The hell you didn't. What are you after, Jessie?"

She gave him a quick look that was almost like panic. "I don't know. I don't know what I'm after. If you don't want to talk about it . . . I've told you everything about myself."

He was so angry it was making the sky quiver. "Who'd you like better, Barb or Sarah? You know, in bed?"

She answered him instantly. "Sarah. She was much more adventurous. We acted out all of our sexual fantasies . . . well, except for the German Shepherd. We never got around to that one."

That shut him up just the way it was meant to. "Jesus," she said after a minute, "I shouldn't have said that. I'm sorry."

They stood there motionless in the hot sun sweating like a pair of idiots. "You know, Jessie, I've been out here on my bike lots of times and if we keep on going, there's nothing out here but corn. Yeah. Some tomatoes. But mainly corn. Acres of fucking corn."

They came back on the outer edge of the campus where Mason didn't know the street names. Mingo. Ruggles. Elm. Falley. "Do you own a pair of sunglasses?" she asked him.

"Yeah."

"Where are they?"

"On the top of my dresser. Where are yours?"

"In my book bag." They both laughed.

KEITH MAILLARD

"Look, Mason, you seem to think I have everything figured out but I don't."

"You don't? Well, Jesus, Jessie, that's a real shocker. I'm just astounded to hear that." He'd got what he wanted, she was still laughing.

"I'm not just some fucking pain-in-the-ass busybody prying into your life," she said. "I'm trying to figure something out, trying to find some kind of coherent picture. I thought when . . . The way we were drawn to each other, I thought we were . . . I don't know how to put it. On the same team."

"Why? Because we're both queer?"

"Yes. Exactly."

"Well, I don't know, Jessie. I've always been on the girl's team . . . whether you guys want me there or not."

"You're always welcome on my team . . . although I don't know if *I'm* on the girl's team."

They were walking by old buildings he'd never seen, not so old as to be of any historical interest, just sad and run down, fusty and obsolete. That huge pile of red bricks said MATHEMATICS. He pointed it out to her. He'd never known where it was. "Euclid alone has looked on beauty bare," she said.

"What?"

"Lorianne used to say that all the time, one of her favorite lines. From some poem or other. I really miss her. Damn, I should call her. The funny thing is, I didn't like her when I first met her."

"A little too hoopie for you, was she?"

"God, you guys are so sensitive! But yes, there was . . . She kept saying, Jess, you're such a big city girl and she's right, I suppose I am."

It was last Thanksgiving when Jessie and Lorianne became close friends. Sarah was going home to New York and somehow she hadn't built Jessie into her plans and Jessie *was really pissed off.*

And Tammy had a cold and Lorianne didn't want to travel with her so Henry and Carl were driving back to Canton together. Lorianne called Jessie and said, "Looks like we're both being left behind. Why don't you come out here and we'll have us our own Thanksgiving dinner?"

At that point Jessie wasn't sure she liked Lorianne but she bought a bottle of good wine and a pumpkin pie. Lorianne teased her about drinking wine with dinner, she thought only French people did that. She'd roasted a small turkey. It was delicious. So they had a wonderful dinner and drank the wine and after they got Tammy in bed, they opened a second bottle and started talking and couldn't stop. It was one of those times when you really click with someone and you know you're going to be friends for life. They talked till damn near four in the morning.

"Of course Henry had heard all about *Nightwood*," Jessie said, "about Nora being in love with Robin, so when he came back and heard about the Thanksgiving dinner . . . I gather Lorianne had been singing my praises . . . he was convinced that she and I were having an affair. And Sarah was jealous too! I couldn't believe it. 'What kind of a feminist are you?' I said. 'You're objecting to a friendship between women.' Well, she thought it was more than a friendship. I don't think she ever didn't . . . Wait! There's too many negatives in that sentence. Let me start over. I don't think she was ever convinced that Lorianne and I hadn't jumped into bed. It's funny . . . I suppose it's bitter funny. What neither Henry nor Sarah understand is that Lorianne is a *literary* lesbian."

She was laughing but he couldn't quite get the humor and then something flicked over in his mind. "Hey," he said, "I just had one of those weird thoughts, the kind that just drop into your head out of nowhere. Do you know that thing that Lorianne quoted from *Nightwood?* About how a woman kissing a woman is like kissing yourself?"

271

"Of course I do. That was one of the key lines in the book for her . . . which always struck me as ironic. Lorianne's never kissed another woman in her life. Not the way that *Nightwood* means it, anyway."

"Well, I always sort of got it. I mean I thought I'd got it but I hadn't really. And what just hit me is, if you take that line and make it so it applies to me and Bobby Springer, then all of a sudden I get it. I mean I really really get it. *A boy is yourself caught as you turn in panic. On his mouth you kiss your own.*"

She stopped walking and there they were, once again, standing on the street looking at each other with the sun blazing down on them. What the fuck was going on? "I can even feel the turn in panic," Mason said. "Maybe that's why it was so hot."

"I don't know. For me hot is fairly simple. Hot is getting what you want. It's almost like . . . It feels to me like Djuna Barnes, or her character, is thinking about it too much. Maybe that's the point."

Where they had stopped was at the intersection of Falley and Main. If they walked on down Main, they'd be off campus, in the business section, and Jessie turned to him with an absolutely brilliant smile. "Hey," she said, "do you want to get some ice cream?"

It was a relief to be out of the sun, particularly into a place as cool and shadowy as the soda fountain in Heike Lewis. It had that distinctive pharmacy smell, what that was Mason couldn't say but all pharmacies smelled like that, maybe it was the medicines being compounded in the back. There was usually a boy jerking soda but not in August with zero customers. The pharmacist himself, that old bird named Al, came out to see what they wanted. "Oh hi there, Jess, haven't seen you in a while. How you been?"

Finished her thesis, she was telling him, and then she was making small talk in a chirpy little voice, something Mason hadn't heard her do before, Jeeze, always something new to learn about her. She and Al seemed to be buddies from way back. "We're sort of half closed," he said, "not making sandwiches. I can always give you ice cream."

"Do you want to share a banana split with me?" she asked Mason. "I can't eat a whole one."

"Yeah, sure." He wasn't all that fond of banana splits but what the hell. He took his wallet out and laid a dollar bill on the counter.

"Let me get it," she said.

"Aw, no. It's only fair. How many of your sandwiches did I eat half of?"

"You folks want pineapple syrup or caramel."

"Caramel," Jessie and Mason said simultaneously. "We're soul mates," she said.

She picked up the ice cream, Mason collected his change and followed her to the booth in the farthest corner. "I was afraid he was going to ask me about Sarah. We used to come in here two or three times a week. She has a real sweet tooth. But she'd never share anything with me."

"Yeah? I guess some people don't like to do that." He was contemplating the banana split. The damn thing was enormous. Maybe Al had laid it on with a heavy hand for his good old customer.

"She said sharing was a little too Norman Rockwell for her but I think she was just afraid that somebody would see us."

"What? Eating ice cream together?"

Jessie was already working on the strawberry scoop. When Mason had shared with Irene, they would start off on opposite sides and meet in the middle. It was understood by both of them that it was impolite to race. A banana split bowl didn't lend itself to that approach so he wasn't sure what to do, joined Jessie on the other side of the strawberry. "I was afraid to come in here," she said. "Afraid it would hurt too much, but it doesn't. It only hurts a little. Just a twinge or two."

273

She was jumping around from scoop to scoop. The rule must be that you had to be careful not to eat more than your half. Nobody orders a banana split for the banana and neither of them had attacked it yet so maybe he should eat a bite of it to be polite. Now she was making her move on the caramel topping. "Fun, isn't it? I haven't done this since I was in grade school."

"Me neither, not since I was a little kid. Me and Irene used to share lots of things, even bowls of soup sometimes."

He was remembering the first time he'd been at a soda fountain and he started telling Jessie about that. It was in the drug store in Factor. Mom had given Irene some change, they could spend it any way they wanted, and he'd still been wearing Irene's dresses. The soda jerk said, "What can I get for you girls?" and that made him feel good.

"Pharmacies always seemed mysterious to me. Hell, they still do. I mean just jam-packed with mysteries. Like secret passages to other worlds. Like just what weird magical shit is the pharmacist mixing up in the back?" Mason pointed to the end of the shelf where old pharmacy bottles were displayed. From where they were sitting they could read a few on the end: BISMUTH SUBCARB, KAL II BROMID, AMYGDALAE OLEUM. "The labels are always in some bizarre ancient language nobody understands, that's what I thought when I was a kid. And the astrology magazines. Wow. There was always a rack of them right by the soda fountain. I thought they were so neat. All those strange symbols. I didn't know they stood for planets—"

Then all of a sudden he had such a strong sense of Irene that she might as well have been there with him, and right after that a sense of losing her. Jesus, the one person he'd thought he could count on for the whole rest of his life. Gone. Just like that. Hurt too much? Shit, yeah, the loss of her was like a pain tearing through him and he didn't know what to do with it, he sure as hell wasn't ready to talk about it.

Mason went on eating ice cream like it was automatic. He felt the clink of his spoon hitting Jessie's, both of them going for the caramel, and he looked up, looked straight at her, Jesus, she was close, their faces only inches apart, and he sure as hell was not eating ice cream *with his sister*. He stopped and so did she. He saw in her eyes something he'd never seen before. He couldn't find a word for it.

She sat back in her chair like she needed some space between them. He needed it too, he guessed, and he sat back, and then they were just sitting there holding their spoons and looking at each other across that goddamn banana split. She's gonna tell me to go away, he thought. Jesus, how's she gonna do it?

"Mason?"

"Yeah?"

"Do you want to have dinner with me tonight? I really want to celebrate. Make this an occasion. You want to go out to that fancy restaurant by Mingo Lake?"

He couldn't make any sense of that. "Um. Well, sure. I guess."

"I know it's expensive, but don't worry, it's on me. This is one of those once-in-a-lifetime things. They've got tables on the balcony where we can look out over the lake and watch the sun go down."

Mason was back on his bike, thank God, and halfway home before it hit him. *Hey, did she just ask me out on a date?*

After the banana split they hadn't said much of anything of any import, just hot weather talk and shit like that, but yeah, she really had asked him out on a date, that's exactly what she'd done. He was gonna have to take a shower. Holy fuck, that fancy-ass restaurant at the lake. Was he supposed to wear a suit?

Eilum's Buick was parked where it usually was. Mason wheeled his bike up to the door, left it there, and then to his surprise Eilum himself came popping out into the sunlight. "Hey, buddy, that lady professor just called you," and added with his greasiest grin, "*Mrs. Collier.* She said it was real urgent."

What could she want? Shit, maybe she'd changed her mind about dinner. Yeah, that's what it had to be. He'd memorized her number but he hadn't called it yet. On the phone her voice was more than flat, it was absolutely expressionless. "Sorry to . . . It's probably nothing but . . . I think somebody just shot at me through my window."

"Wait a minute. What? Shot at you through your window?"

"Yes. I can't figure it out. It's really strange. Maybe that's not what happened."

"But I got his fucking gun."

"I know. I'm not sure what really happened. Could you come over?"

"Yeah, I'll be right there."

On the other side of the kitchen Eilum was staring at the tall person to Mason's right. "*Shot at her?* What the fuck you talking about?"

Mason was still holding the phone. He hung it up. "I don't know. She thinks somebody may have shot at her."

"What did you mean, you got his fucking gun?"

"Henry. I went over and . . . Shit. He drank his ass off and passed out and I got his gun. You know, the gun he shot the cat with."

"Where is it?"

"On the back of my bike."

"Show it to me."

Eilum followed Mason back outside. "Why the fuck you got it wrapped up in a towel?"

"I didn't want to . . . You know, anybody seeing me . . . riding around with a gun . . ." Mason felt as stupid as mud. He unclipped the gun from his bike and started to unwrap it.

"Hey. Buddy. Stop. Just stop, okay? Put that fucking thing down on the ground, okay?"

Mason had never seen Eilum like this before. He was acting like a man who gave a shit. Mason laid the gun on the ground. Eilum hunkered down, patted the bundle in the towel, feeling for its shape. Then he unwrapped it, got the gun out, aimed the barrel away from them. He clicked something and the revolver part fell open. He shook the bullets out into the palm of his hand. "Fully loaded, you fuckface idiot. And this ain't the gun he shot the cat with. This here is a snub-nosed .38, what they call a police special."

"I don't get it," Mason said.

"Yeah? Well, buddy, I'll tell you, I don't get it either. If this is the handy little gun that Henry was going to shoot you guys with, that paints a totally different picture. Yeah, it alters the matter considerably. With a gun like this he was definitely intending to kill you."

Jessie was pointing at a hole in the window screen above the kitchen sink. "That's . . . I'm pretty sure it wasn't here before. But is it a bullet hole?"

Mason felt so antsy he wanted to jump out of his skin. It'd taken them forever to get there because Eilum had cruised the neighborhood to make sure that Henry's car was nowhere to be seen. Now Jessie was giving Mason a look that said, clearly, why on earth did you bring this weird asshole?

"Okay, ma'am," Eilum was saying, "tell me what happened the best you remember it." Jesus Christ, Mason thought, who does he think he is, Sergeant Friday?

"Well, I was right here and I'd just washed a few dishes and put them in the rack to dry and I was, um . . . just daydreaming." She wasn't looking at Eilum. She was talking to Mason in that dead flat voice he'd heard on the telephone but he could tell how upset she was by the tense way she carried her body.

"Then I thought, okay, Jess, it's time to get moving. I turned and headed for the bathroom and I felt something . . . It's hard to describe. Afterwards I thought of it like a bee but it wasn't really. It was like a hot hum and then there was a slam on the front door, a thwump sound. I mean it was really fast, the bee and the door, like at the same time? And then *immediately*, like it was attached to the bee, there was a loud crack and I thought, Jesus, that sounded just like a gunshot. It didn't make any sense."

"No, ma'am, it makes perfect sense. The bullet got to you before the sound did."

Jessie's expression said that she still didn't get it. "Then I heard a car start up and drive away. In a real hurry. Tires screaming. "

"Yeah, our boy making his break. Okay, that big building across the yard from you? What is it?"

"It's a men's rooming house."

"Look up there on the second floor. You see the only window that's open?"

Mason joined them and then they were all peering up at the window. "See the drapes flapping in the breeze? That's where he made his shot."

Eilum turned and walked toward the front of the apartment. "There's not a mark on the door," Jessie said. "I went over every inch of it."

"Right," Eilum said. "A lot of people think a bullet travels in a straight line. That's what you thought when you drew a line straight to the door, right? But a bullet don't travel in a straight line, it describes a parabola. Okay, and his shot didn't come in straight, it was coming from high up at an angle."

He pointed at the wall directly to the left of the door. There was a small hole about four feet from the floor. "Let's go see where it went."

They followed Eilum through the door and outside. He pointed down to the wall next to the front door. There was the hole where the bullet had come out. "Jesus," Jessie said, "it went all the way through the wall? I don't believe it."

"Well, hell, ma'am, this is an old wood frame house. Some concrete would stop the bullet, a few bricks would stop it, but nothing much in here but insulation and drywall. Must be fairly high caliber, could be a hunting rifle, could be military, thirty-aught-six maybe, anyhow he's shooting military ammunition, full metal jacket. Of course it went right through the wall. Let's see where."

They followed Eilum across the hot empty street to the house directly opposite. He knelt down and searched the old wooden steps, pointed to the hole in the second step from the bottom. "Yep, it's in there. Down in the dirt somewhere. One of those gentlemen from law enforcement could dig it out if he was so inclined."

Mason had never seen Jessie so completely at a loss. "I'm having trouble believing this," she said. "That bullet went all the way through my apartment, and through the wall of the house, and across the street?"

"Hell, ma'am, a rifle bullet will carry a mile. Let's go see where he shot from."

The front door to the rooming house was not locked. Nobody seemed to be home and the janitor must have been through there recently, the whole miserable place stunk of Pine-Sol. They followed Eilum up the stairs to the second floor. There at the end of the hall was the open window.

"Yep, our boy left in a rush," Eilum said. "He didn't put the screen back, didn't close the window, just hightailed it out of here. Don't touch anything, folks."

Eilum examined the floor. "That's too bad, he had enough sense to grab the casing. See, he probably knelt down on the floor and rested the rifle on the window sill. If he went to a land grant college, he had two years of ROTC the same as me and Mason. If it was Army, he's qualified on an M-1. As you can see, it's not a hard shot to make, although getting it in on the first try would require a bit of luck. What did you do after he shot at you?"

"I turned back and looked at the window."

"Well, ma'am, I hate to tell you this but that was not the world's most intelligent reaction. If he'd stuck around and had another go, he would have got you."

Mason hadn't been saying anything but he was scared shitless. He knew he had to push it away from him, think about it like a math problem, and now that he could do that, he had it clearly in his mind. Growing up with the old man, he'd had plenty of experience dealing with drunks. "Look," he said, "he's kneeling here with the rifle, and he's got it steady, and he's sighting down it, and he's got you in the center of his sights. He's not falling down dead drunk but he's fairly pissed and he's thinking, should I? shouldn't I? should I? shouldn't I? All of a sudden you move and your motion goes straight to him and he jumps. His finger's so tight on the trigger that the rifle goes off and then he thinks, holy fuck, and he takes off."

"Hey," Eilum said, "that's pretty good, buddy. You're reading him pretty good."

"That's right," Jessie said, "and eventually he's going to wake up and be absolutely appalled at what he's done and then maybe he'll realize he needs some help."

"That could be," Eilum said, "or maybe he'll do some more serious drinking and think, shit, I almost got her. Maybe I'll go back and have another try. Ma'am, is there some place you can go tonight? Do you have a lady friend you can stay with?"

"No. I don't."

"Well, I'd strongly suggest that you don't stay in your apartment. He could pump a few rounds through your front door, or your back door, or any of your windows. He could spray your whole damn apartment. There's no place to hide. It's not like the movies. If you got down behind a chair or under a desk or some damn thing, the bullets would just come sailing right on through. There's gotta be some place you can go."

Eilum was driving Jessie's car. She'd stopped protesting awhile back, now she was just going along with whatever he suggested. She seemed dazed and Mason couldn't blame her. Eilum was hiding her Lark in the woods where Henry would never see it. "Lock it," he said. "Watch your step. It's kind of treacherous." He bent a tree branch out of the way so Jessie and Mason could get by.

When Eilum lead them out of the woods, they were not more than a hundred yards from the old Merida Inn. Jessie was carrying her few things in her leather book bag.

"Ma'am," Eilum said, "my personal inclination is to never involve law enforcement. The minute you involve law enforcement, things always get a hell of a lot worse. But they do have their uses upon occasion. Now if you was to call the sheriff's department, I'm sure that they would send one of their fine deputies out here to talk to you. If you was to describe what happened as clear as you described it to me and Mason, then, most likely, they would pay a visit to Henry. If they was to find that rifle, they would have a good reason to arrest him. Sun comes up in the morning, they dig that bullet out of the dirt, gets better and better, right? And the great advantage to you, ma'am, is that Henry is no longer running loose with a rifle thinking about whether he wants to shoot you or not. Are you following me?"

"Yes, I'm following you. But . . . Jesus, I've known Henry for years. It's not like we're talking about some deranged killer. He's going through a bad patch, and he's drinking too much, and he may be a colossal asshole, but it's just Henry, for Christ's sake."

"Okay, ma'am, this is still a free country the last I heard, and far be it from me to deny you the right to your opinion, but I do believe that it is my duty as a concerned citizen to convey my thoughts.

If you don't do anything at all, ma'am, what you're left with is some fool who took a shot at you through your kitchen window. Don't that strike you as a little bit nuts? Call the goddamn sheriff, okay?"

"Yeah," Mason said, "call the sheriff."

She looked from one to the other. "You're double teaming me," she said. "Oh, hell, I'll think about it. I'll seriously think about it."

16.

At first it was only something screaming at him, then he figured out that it was the goddamn fucking phone. Before he could think he was in the kitchen, snatching it off the wall.

"Mason? Mason!" Lorianne's voice, metallic like she was hollering through a tin can. "I'm so glad I got you, I'm so— Tried to get Jessie all morning. Must have been . . . I don't know *seven*, first time I . . . and . . . no, it wasn't even seven yet. I was sure . . . Where *is* she?"

He'd been so goddamn deep asleep, he needed time, needed some time, shit. The Merida Inn was where Jessie was. Should he tell Lorianne that? "No," he said, "you wouldn't get her. You wouldn't get her at home. No."

His mouth was foul, he'd smoked damned near a whole pack of Camels last night pacing up and down on the street in front of their house. He needed water. "Mason? Are you there?"

"I'm here. You want me to tell Jessie you called?"

"Have you seen Henry?"

Shit, shit, shit. "Henry? Yeah. I guess I seen him. Yeah, I did." When was that? The day before yesterday?

"Is he all right?"

It was a terrible phone line. Mason could hear little voices no

283

bigger than match heads, one of them saying, incredulous, "Didn't Mom tell you about Arthur?" He had been leaning hard up against the kitchen wall, now he slid down to sit on the floor. He slept in nothing but a T-shirt so his bare ass was pressing down on the dirty linoleum. It was one of those moments when you don't simply take the world for granted, when you know just how truly bizarre everything is.

"Mason?" Lorianne right in his ear.

"Not awake yet. Sorry. I don't know how Henry is. I couldn't really say . . . Well, no, that's not right. I guess I'd have to say he's not looking too good. Where you calling me from?"

"I'm at my grandma's. Right where I said I'd be. Mason?"

He heard her gulping air. "Was Henry okay? Did he look . . . *injured?*"

"Yeah, he did. He definitely had the look of a man who's sustained some injuries."

"Real bad?"

"I don't know. He was upright." Yeah, Mason thought, upright and talking about killing me. Upright and firing a rifle though Jessie's window. "I guess he won't be feeling too good for a while. Lorianne? Can I call you back?"

"Was he drunk?"

"Drunk? Yeah, I'd say you could apply that word to him. Yeah, I'd have to say that word would definitely apply."

She was crying. Being down at her grandma's must have brought back her hoopie accent full tilt and she was talking so fast he could barely follow her. She didn't want to bother him, or bother Jess, she was saying, it wasn't fair, but she didn't know who else to talk to. Uncle Arch kept telling her to call the sheriff but Wayne kept waltzing her outside to whisper in her ear, "No, no, no, you don't want to call the sheriff. You do *not* want to call the sheriff. Think about it, Lori. What's he going to do?"

If the kitchen clock was right, it was half past ten. Mason had slept in just like he didn't have a care in the world. Well, it had taken him forever to get to sleep, maybe he'd been exhausted. Maybe he'd been running away from everything, thinking fuck it. "Wait a minute. *The sheriff?*"

She was crying hard. Then all of a sudden she took a big breath and stopped herself from crying. When she started talking again, her voice was as flat as a bread board. "I'm sorry, Mason. I'm so sorry you had to be . . . *there.* I just didn't know. The only gun I knew about was the twenty-two he kept in the glove compartment. I'm so ashamed."

"I'm not getting this, Lorianne."

"Carl had been living there before Henry and I got married, I told you that. When Carl moved out, he left some of his stuff behind. Anyhow Henry *said* it was Carl's stuff. He was probably lying to me. A big wooden chest in the basement with a padlock on it and I asked him, 'What's in that big chest?' and he said, 'That's Carl's stuff. Don't worry about it.' Jesus, I feel like Bluebeard's wife."

She started crying again and he heard her fighting to get control of herself, get control of the story. He could hear how bad she needed to get control of the story.

Okay, Henry drove down there looking for her. He drove into Solid and started asking around. Well, you can't really get to grandma's place unless you know exactly where it is. If you don't know, you could just drive around in those hills forever, going around and around in those hills forever, so Henry got directed in to Jimmy Whitaker's garage and Jimmy said, "Well, buddy, maybe I can help you out. Let me call around," and he called Wayne and said, "There's some red-haired son of a bitch down here looking for Lorianne. He's driving an old gray rusted out Dodge with Ohio plates," and Wayne said yep, he knew who that was, and he told Jimmy to direct Henry on out to Hartwig's motorcycle shop. When Henry got there, Wayne and a few of the boys met him and escorted him on into the back, all friendly like, and then they closed the big doors and Wayne said, "Hi, cat killer," and punched him out.

"They got him back on his feet," she said, flat, "and slapped him around some and that's when they found the guns. He was wearing one of those hunting jackets, you know the kind, like a vest? With all the pockets? And in one of those pockets he had a pistol like the police carry. Wayne told me what kind but I forget. He said it was an automatic pistol like the police carry. And on the backseat under a blanket Henry had a military rifle with a scope on it. Wayne said it was a sniper's rifle. Wayne said he could understand how a man might drive down here with a pistol in his pocket. He might be worried about having to defend himself, right? But a sniper's rifle with a scope on it? That's a whole other matter."

"Lorianne? You got to give me a minute here. Don't hang up. I'm coming right back. You just got to give me a minute or two."

Mason had pulled his jeans on, was sitting at the kitchen table drinking one of Eilum's RC Colas and having a smoke. His mind had started to work again, filling up with disaster, but he and Lorianne were discussing this matter like two calm and reasonable adults discussing the weather. "Every time I step out on the porch at night . . . you know, to take in the night . . . I don't want to be wondering if Henry is out there somewhere in the woods watching me."

"No," Mason said, "you absolutely do not." Now the goddamn university was telling Mason what time it was, eleven bongs. Jesus, it was turning out to be a long phone call. He was glad he wasn't paying for it.

"So what was he doing down here with a sniper's rifle? That's the million dollar question, isn't it? Grandma says him shooting the cat was a *sign*."

"She's probably right."

"So who was he going to shoot? Me? *Tammy?*"

"Yeah, if he's gourded right out, it's hard to tell . . . you know, how far gone he is."

"That's right. It's like I don't know him anymore so I can't predict . . . I can't say as I never had any warning at all. He's done a couple things to me— Hell, I don't want to go into that. But he's— No, I don't want to talk about that."

"No. There's no reason you have to."

"But I never thought he'd . . . Mason, it's just such a shock. The cat *was* a sign. It's like my whole world's been flipped upside down."

"That's right."

"Wayne and the boys beat him up. Wayne said they were being careful, didn't want to do him any serious damage, just give him something to remember. Then they put him in the back seat of one of Wayne's cars, in between two of the boys, and Wayne and Charlie in the front seat, and somebody else drove Henry's car, and they headed off into the hills. Just doing a little driving around in the hills, that's what Wayne told me, and they put on a good show for him. Wayne and Charlie got into a serious argument about whether they should shoot him or hang him. Wayne's telling me all this just like it's a big joke but . . . I don't know, Mason, I still have some feelings for Henry."

"I expect you do."

"I'm all mixed up. Henry could be a real sweetheart sometimes and I still remember him like that but . . . I don't know what . . . Wayne thinks Henry's an evil son of a bitch and everything they did to him, well, he had coming, but I don't think he's evil, I just think he's fucked up. Not thinking straight. Confused. You know, just plain *sick*. Even if he was planning on shooting me, I don't want him hurt. Does that make any sense?"

"Yes, it does."

"After they'd been riding around for a while, they had Henry crying and begging for his life. They pulled over and got him out and walked him over to his own car. They had to hold him up he was so scared. Wayne said, 'Listen up, cat killer, you're a lucky man today. You don't have to think. This road will take you straight to Charleston and then you just keep on going till you get your sorry ass home. The word's gone out on you, buddy. If you ever come back down here again, anywhere *around here* again, you're a dead man. Okay, now you get in that piece of shit car and you drive it.' He handed him his keys and Henry just gunned her right the hell on out of there."

"When was that?"

"Let's see. End of last week sometime. Must have been Friday."

That made sense. So Henry drove back to Merida, probably took him all damn night, and then he devoted the rest of the weekend to some serious drinking.

"You know, Mason, when you've got lots of time on your hands, your mind kind of runs away on you."

"Yes, it does tend to do that."

"If somebody owns property, it's got to be registered somewhere. They've got to say who owns it and what the dimensions are, exactly where it is. I don't know how they do that, maybe they use latitude and longitude, but it's all got to be recorded somewhere officially, right? Henry knows my grandparents' name, so it'd be easy for him to find out where I am. It's the kind of research he's good at. He could find out exactly where I am without even leaving the library. Wayne took those guns away from him, but he could get more of them. His red hair's real distinctive but he could buy hair dye in any drug store. He could drive into West Virginia somewhere and rent a car with West Virginia plates. And then some night I step out onto the porch just to look at the stars and *blam*.

"I don't know what to do, Mason, I really don't. Uncle Arch says talk to the sheriff but what's the sheriff going to do? He can't station somebody out here twenty-four hours a day. The key to all this is Henry. He's got serious mental problems, that's the only thing I can think. Nothing else makes any sense. Jesus, he must feel so sad and lonely and scared. He needs medical help. This is a big thing to ask, but maybe you could . . . could you and Jessie try to talk him into committing himself at the University Hospital?"

"Yeah, maybe. I don't know if he'd listen to us, but we could try." Right, Mason thought. He was sure that Dr. Elspeth Fairfield MD could do wonders for Henry.

"I just don't know what to *think*. Where *is* Jess? I need to talk to her."

"Yeah, I expect you do. I'll be seeing her later today. Do you want me to tell her—?"

"Yeah, you tell her . . . and please ask her to call me. Oh Lord, Mason, I don't know. I keep having these little . . . Henry was so sweet sometimes. With his jazz records. He'd get a new one and he'd be like a little boy at Christmas—" She was crying again.

As Mason listened to Lorianne talking about poor old Henry, what a sweet guy he could be sometimes, it was finally all coming together in his mind. It was like when he'd been reading about some particular year, say back in the 1870s, and one thing happened and then the next thing happened, and so on, just a bunch of unrelated events, but sometimes all of a sudden he could see something bigger, how those events were not unrelated at all, how they made a pattern.

That sad dim puzzled look Jessie had given him just before she'd walked into the Merida Inn, he understood it now. No matter what she'd said, she had no intention of calling the sheriff's department. Why? Well, if he was *just Henry, for Christ's sake* you don't sic the sheriff on him and then there was another reason and it was a damn good one too. Let's say the sheriff checked things out and they got Henry dead to rights and charged him with attempted murder. Henry would certainly tell his lawyer exactly why he'd been so pissed off at Mrs. Jessie Collier and she would be right smack in the middle of a big trial that would be splashed all over the papers and it wouldn't matter whether they found Henry guilty or not, no college or university would ever hire her to teach anything.

Yeah, but Jessie hadn't heard the rest of the story and Mason had. Someone who would drive for six hours to downstate West Virginia with a pistol in his pocket and a sniper's rifle on the back seat of his car was absolutely not *just Henry, for Christ's sake*, that was somebody nobody knew, and that unknown Henry was still running around loose with a fucking rifle. Mason felt the chill of it in his stomach. "Lorianne," he said, "I've got to go. I'll call you back, or Jessie will call you back—"

"Mason!"

"Real soon, okay? We'll do the best we can for Henry. I promise we will. But right now I've got to go." He could hear her still talking but he hung up anyways. He was so far out of time it was ridiculous. He jumped to his feet, shot straight out the door, and kicked over some damn thing. It felt like kicking a football.

He picked it up. A good sized package wrapped in brown paper. The mailman had left it right smack in his way. From Sears Roebuck and Company, addressed to *Miss* M. Macquarie. Fuck you, he thought. But wait a minute, maybe it was a sign. Maybe it was telling him not to go off half-cocked.

He made himself slow down. He carried the damn package back inside and stuffed it away in the back of his closet. He sat down on the edge of his bed. Yeah, he absolutely had to calm down. He was so scared it was making him clumsy. Weird how you could feel your heartbeat sometimes, most of the time you couldn't. Yeah, taking a little bit of time now that could save him lots of time later. So where was he going first? He laced up his sneakers tight and tied the laces in double knots, Jessie.

17.

"I'm sorry, sir, the guest is not answering." The owl-eyed townie prick in his gray flannel suit was so fixated on Mason's hair that's all he seemed capable of looking at.

"It's kind of urgent. Can I go up and knock on her door?"

"No, I'm sorry, sir. Visitors are not permitted beyond the lobby unless they are accompanied by a guest."

Mason did not need this shit. "Something's come up. It's really *really* urgent."

"I'm sorry, *sir*," icing the sir, "but the *guest* is not *answering* her *telephone*. Would you care to leave a message?"

Mason just turned and walked away. He was almost back outside before the girl caught up to him. "Mrs. Collier's not here."

She was about Mason's age, in a drab brown dress with a white apron, beat-up waitress shoes. She'd been sweeping the front lobby. "Thanks for telling me," he said. "It's really important . . . a family matter."

Her grin was sharing a joke with him, he wasn't sure what, maybe "us kids against the old pricks," against ole owl eyes, for instance, who was glaring at them from behind the desk.

"I think she's gone for a walk," taking a step closer, dropping her voice. "She got up real early and had breakfast. Then she went back to her room for a while. Then she came down about . . . I don't know, about an hour ago. We had a nice chat. She *said* she was going for a walk."

Mason needed something good right then and she was giving it to him. "Hey, thanks a lot." But then, back on his bike, he felt the fear crawling up from his belly like a snake he had to keep swallowing down.

In the too-bright light of that stupidly ordinary August day he could see now just how clever Eilum had been in the night. He'd picked a narrow dirt road that nobody used. It wound down through a long stretch of woods the developers hadn't got around to yet to arrive at that little crick they called Woods Run and hey, there was a flicker of metallic green through the trees. He dismounted, pushed his bike through the branches, parted some, and yeah, there was her little Studebaker Lark, dejected and still locked up tight. Oh, for Christ's sake, Jessie, where the fuck are you? Going for *a walk?* Why couldn't you stay put like you were supposed to?

Mason was pumping it hard, aimed for Henry's house. If the son of a bitch was still sleeping off his latest end-of-the-world hangover, then it didn't matter where Jessie was, well, not for the moment it didn't, and Mason couldn't shake the feeling that there was something about all of this frantic activity that was utterly ridiculous. A car was coming in his direction and he'd already whipped to a stop, grabbed his bike, jumped off the road and hunkered down behind a bush, thinking yeah, that's exactly the right word, *ridiculous.* It was a Chevy three-quarter-ton pickup, probably from one of the farms, piled up with burlap bags, and it rattled on by him in no hurry at all. Then, in a big fat empty pause in which he wasn't moving a muscle and didn't know why he wasn't, he saw Henry's rusty Dodge headed toward campus at a good clip, yeah, really carrying the mail, whooshing by him and gone. If Mason was reading Henry right, he was headed straight for Jessie's.

Mason couldn't go anywhere near Henry's Dodge, even if he stayed a couple blocks back, he'd still be too goddamn visible, so he didn't approach Jessie's from the front, instead rode straight to the men's rooming house behind her place. He walked his bike into that narrow shadow between the rooming house and the house next door, and then it was way too fast, he wasn't ready for it, there was Henry himself, big as life, headed up the steps to Jessie's back porch.

Mason flung himself down onto the rough pebbles of the alley and crawled up to the hedge that bordered Jessie's wretched little patch of back yard. Henry was standing perfectly still on the porch like he was thinking about something. Then he knocked on the back door. Not loud. Kind of discreet. "Jessie? Jess? Are you in there? It's just me. Henry. I just want to talk to you, okay?"

His voice was low, dull, like his heart wasn't in it and holy Jesus, he seemed to be sober. He must have got there well ahead of Mason, must have already driven around the block looking for Jessie's car, already tried the front door. He stepped back, looked quick behind him like he was afraid there was somebody there, turned to look directly above where Mason was hiding, his eyes aimed high up to the window where he'd fired his shot. All he'd have to do was look down and most likely he'd see Mason pressing himself into the dirt, but he didn't do that. He scanned the back alley like he was making absolutely sure there was nowhere Jessie could have parked her car. Then he stood there a while longer, staring at nothing that Mason could see.

Henry hadn't bothered to change his clothes, still wearing the same polo shirt and grimy wrinkled chinos. His face was looking a little bit better, the shiner faded, the swelling going down, but still lots of Technicolor bruises and his nose would never be as straight as it used to be. Mason almost felt sorry for him. The poor bastard looked too beat up and dilapidated to be dangerous, until you got to his eyes. Turning to look at Jessie's kitchen window where his shot had gone in. Nothing to see there, the drapes were drawn. Turning back with a nervous jerk to look over his shoulder again like, yeah, by God, he knew *somebody* was watching him. Then Mason finally saw what he should have seen right away. Henry was wearing a fisherman's vest with so much weight in it that the pockets were pulled straight down.

Mason didn't move a muscle until he heard Henry's car start up. Okay, so now Henry was gonna drive all over town looking for Jessie's car. In Henry's mind Jessie and Mason were connected so he might start by checking to see if she was at Mason's. He'd take Jefferson to get there because that's what you did in a car but Mason knew a few bike shortcuts that would dump him in the alley right across the street from his place, so he went for it. By the time he got there, his T-shirt was sopping and his heart felt like it was going to burst right out of him. He bent double, panting like a dog, then straightened up, pressed himself flat to the wall of the big gray house on the corner. He edged forward until he could see out into the street. He was diagonally across from the big white oak. But what if he hadn't guessed Henry right? Then it'd all be for nothing.

He had to keep wiping sweat off his face, out of his goddamn hair. He was getting so he could breathe normal when he saw Henry in his Dodge drift by slow and easy. Jesus Christ, I did it, Mason thought, I read his fucking mind. Yeah, I'm a Nancy boy all right, *I'm Nancy Drew.*

Now what? If Henry couldn't find Jessie's Lark, then he might conclude that he'd scared the bejesus out of her and she'd gone home to Chicago, and that was exactly what Mason wanted him to conclude. But if Jessie had *gone for a walk*, then Henry was sure to find her eventually, so that meant that Mason had to find her first. Where the fuck could she be? Maybe at the Buckeye. That felt right, yeah, and if that was the first place Mason thought of, that was probably the first place Henry thought of too.

Delaware ran parallel to Main and he got there in good time, walked his bike up the passage between Pfefferman's hardware and the five and dime. Standing just at the corner of Walter's he could see all the way up Main. Eilum's car was parked in front of the Buckeye but Henry's wasn't.

He kept expecting to see Henry's car go by but he didn't. The longer he stood there waiting for it, the jumpier he got. The clock in the McKinley Tower bonged twelve times, telling him he was running out of time. As long as he'd been riding around, trying to think like Nancy Drew, he'd been okay, like it was somebody else's story, but the fear was getting to him again and that made it pretty fucking personal. He knew how the fear could make him clumsy and brainless. The last thing in the world he wanted was to have another face-off with Henry Algren.

Okay, Nancy Drew, he told himself, think it through. The Mystery of the Crazy Asshole. Henry wasn't there so he must have thought of somewhere else. And where was that? Kind of obvious when you got around to it. Henry didn't know that Jessie had handed in her thesis in to Dr. Braithwaite so he'd expect her to be in the library. But of course she wouldn't be there today, would she? She had no reason to be there. Well, except maybe she'd been sitting around in her room in the Merida Inn all morning, staring out the window and waiting for somebody to call her, just laying low and maybe getting bored out of her goddamn skull. What place could be more inviting, more familiar, more *safe* than her carrel in the Old Main Library?

Yep, Henry's car was right there in the lot behind the building, parked neatly between the lines just like a sane man would do it.

The quickest way to Level Five was to come in right there on Level One and take the staff-only elevator up, but quick was not the main thing on Mason's mind. He zipped around to the front, didn't bother with the bike rack, just kicked out the stand, ran up the front steps and walked right in. The August heat got to him first, along with the bleary rattle of the fans. The old library lady at the check-out wasn't just drowsing, she was deep asleep, her mouth hanging open. Keeping close to the wall, Mason started up the staircase. Quick was less on his mind than quiet.

The noise of the fans was helping him, covering up his footsteps, and he was moving light, on his toes. There was nowhere to hide on the stairs, or on the landings, so he ran straight up to Level Five, arrived winded, pulled a hard left into the stacks, took a moment to get his breath back. Then he crept from stack to stack, looked down each aisle toward Jessie's carrel. On his third try he saw for only a fraction of a second the silhouette of a man. Or he thought he did. Holy Jesus fuck, did he really see that? It had looked exactly like a man carrying a rifle at port arms.

He knew better than to head straight for Jessie's carrel. He darted back to the north wall and crept along it. If he followed the nearest stack all the way to the end, he'd come out looking at the *side* of her carrel, not the front of it, and he'd still be a good ways away. He got there, stepped out into the clear, and froze. He was looking at Henry's back.

Henry was standing in Jessie's carrel. The rifle looked a lot like an M-1. It was hanging from a sling over Henry's left shoulder. He was looking down at Jessie's desk, poking around there with his right hand. Mason was too far away to see what was on the desk, probably some books Jessie had been looking at, maybe some notes she'd been taking, and sitting there big as hell was that beat-up old book bag she used as a purse. Henry looked up, scanned the ends of the stacks, looked across the empty space in the center toward the far side, probably thinking the same thing Mason was thinking, *where the fuck is she?*

An impossible amount of time trickled by as Henry just stood there and Mason just stood there. Nothing to hear but the fans rattling away. Mason was afraid to move, even afraid to breathe. If Henry glanced behind him, he'd see Mason there. Then Mason heard the distant gush of water rushing down the big pipes in the library's ancient plumbing system. If Mason could hear it over the fans, then Henry could hear it too, somebody somewhere had flushed a toilet. The men's washrooms and the lady's washrooms alternated with each other on the levels. Maybe because they'd figured there would be more ladies in the 800s than in the 900s, the lady's was down on Level Four. That meant that Jessie would have to walk across the Level Four landing and up the staircase to Level Five.

Mason could already hear her footsteps. He'd heard that sound before, heard it plenty, more muted than the click of high heels but just as distinct, she was wearing her leather sandals. Her pace over the hardwood floors was what he'd call leisurely. He could hear it when she crossed the landing and started up the stairs.

Henry wrapped the rifle sling around his left arm just the way he'd been taught in ROTC, just the way Mason had been taught, and sank onto his knees, resting his left elbow on Jessie's desk. He raised the rifle into firing position, sighted down it. He took a deep breath, exhaled slowly, and waited. Every move that Henry made told Mason that Henry was sober as a stone.

If Jessie walked back the way most people would, along the open walkway next to the balustrade, she'd turn at the end of the stacks and would be halfway to her carrel before she noticed Henry waiting for her. She'd be about twenty feet away. Startled, she'd probably freeze, making herself a perfect target.

Jesus, Mason thought, what am *I* supposed to do about it? He could hear Jessie's footsteps getting closer. She was walking back just the way he'd thought she would. Maybe Henry wasn't going to shoot her. Maybe all he was going to do was scare the bejesus out of her. Maybe Mason didn't have to do anything.

You're not thinking straight, he told himself, *move it!* He grabbed the biggest book he could see, ran straight for Henry, and swung the book down hard onto the back of his head. Henry made a kind of grunt and the book bounced out of Mason's hands. "Jessie!" Mason yelled. "Run. Get the fuck out of here." Mason dashed back into the stacks and threw himself onto the floor, sliding.

"Mason?" Just from that one word he could tell that she was not getting the picture. Oh Christ, he thought, she's never had to run from anything before. "Where are you?" she called to him. "What's going on?"

"Get out of here," he yelled at her. "Get out of the fucking library."

He heard nothing for a moment. She was probably thinking about it. Then he heard her sandals, rapid and hard. She wasn't running fast enough but she *was* running. He heard the sound of Henry running too.

Henry fired. Holy fuck, that was loud. Jessie was running for all she was worth. To get out of the building she'd have to go back the way she'd come, down the stairs and across the landing, and she'd be exposed the whole way. Henry fired again, and then again. Mason heard Jessie's footsteps stutter and slide, then break back into a run. Henry fired five more times, fairly fast, and it was so loud, echoing off the walls, that if Jessie was still running, Mason couldn't hear it. He heard sounds he remembered from the rifle range, the metallic clink of an empty clip hitting the ground and the click as Henry inserted a new one into his rifle.

The fans were rattling away, that's all the sound there was. Henry was wearing tennis shoes but he was a man heavy on his feet and Mason had always been able to hear him move but he didn't hear him now. Nothing was moving, not a fucking thing. Was Jessie shot? If she'd been hit, she would have screamed, wouldn't she? Was she dead? His old familiar sick dog fear had thrown him to the floor but this new fear was worse. He sprang up and ran, slid to a stop at the end of the stack. Henry was standing by the stairs, holding his rifle at port arms, just standing there. He wasn't looking anywhere near to where Mason was. And what was that? A metallic thunk and a mechanical hum. Jesus, somebody was coming up on the elevator.

It had been down on Level One but now the little brass pointer was rotating as the elevator rose. Probably library staff who'd heard the shots and were coming up to see what the fuck was going on. Henry walked deliberately toward the elevator door. He wrapped his sling around his left arm. A book cart was standing near the elevator. Henry pulled it over so he could use it to support his left elbow.

Jesus, there was something about Henry that Mason couldn't put his finger on, call it weird but that was just a word, so what was it? It was like Henry was acting in a play, that all of this had been planned out ahead of time, that he had all the time in the fucking world, that of course there was no reason to hesitate about any of this, it had all been decided a million years ago and it couldn't be any other way than it was. The moment the elevator doors began to open Henry fired.

The elevator rang like a bell, Henry fired again and Jessie was on him. She was barefoot. In a couple good leaps she'd crossed the distance from where she'd been hiding, had her hands on Henry's rifle, pulling on it. "Stop it," she yelled at him. Jessie had suckered Henry good. She must have snuck out and punched the elevator button. Mason ran toward them.

You can't shoot somebody with a rifle if they're right on top of you. She had both hands on the stock. She was stronger than he was. He wouldn't let go. She was dragging him forward. "Stop it,

Henry. Just stop it." Henry's eyes looked like something you'd see after the taxidermist got done with it.

All of a sudden Henry let go with his right hand. Jessie would have jerked the rifle free except for the sling still attached to Henry's arm. Mason couldn't get a good look at what was going on, still a tug of war, saw Henry going for something in a right hand pocket in his vest. Mason knew what it was before he saw it, started yelling, "Gun! Gun!" Yeah, the little fucking gun that shot the cat. Mason grabbed a book from the stacks and threw it at Henry's head. Heard the crack. Like a whip crack. That little gun. Ran like a son of a bitch. End of the stack, whipped around the corner. Flat against the wood. Bullets hitting, thud plunk. Crack. Jesus.

For a minute Mason thought maybe he'd been hit and hadn't noticed. He'd read about shit like that happening in war. But nothing felt like he'd been hit. "Henry," Jessie yelled. She must have run. Her voice was coming from way back near the eastern wall where her carrel was. "You can still come back from this, Henry. You haven't hurt anybody yet. Put that rifle down on the floor. We'll take you to the hospital. Henry? You need help. We can get you help. You can still have a good life. Henry?"

Henry fired six shots. The sound was hideous, loud, way too loud, echoed off the walls, thunder, Mason's ears ringing with it. He'd heard glass breaking. The windows in the east wall. He heard a clip hitting the floor, heard a new one going into the rifle. He stuck his head around the end of the stack to look, saw Henry at the end of the aisle, pointing the rifle in his direction. Mason ran. Henry fired. Holy fuck.

What did I just see? Mason thought. He was scrambling along on the floor, running, falling down, crawling, trying to get away from that fucking gun. Henry was pumping out bullets like a robot.

He was going to every aisle and firing shots down it. Forget about counting them, he'd gone through four clips, maybe five, that made over thirty fucking shots, the horrible ear-shattering thunder never stopped. What the fuck, nobody else in the library? Maybe not. August. Staff took their vacations in August.

What did I just see? His mind finally caught up and answered him. What he had just seen was a bullet slamming into a shelf of books, coming in at a sharp angle, and *getting stopped*. Then the stack Mason was hiding behind got hit. It quivered with every bullet like it was shaking itself, and a whole bunch of dust blew out, but not a single bullet pierced through it.

Jesus, those bullets could penetrate the wall of a house but they couldn't penetrate the stacks. Not if they were coming in at an angle, not if they were hitting books. The stacks were part of the original architecture, good old solid hardwood, and they were *load bearing*, a stack sat on a stack, sat on a stack, all the way to the ground. Up here, on the top level, they supported the arches that held up the roof. No, the stacks weren't going anywhere. As long as Mason had a stack between him and Henry, he was safe. That was the theory anyway. But was it true?

Henry just kept firing. Either he didn't notice that most of his shots were slamming into books or he didn't care. Maybe he'd fallen in love with pulling the trigger. Maybe he thought he was laying down an artillery barrage that would drive Mason and Jessie back into the far corner by Jessie's carrel. And then what? He was going to keep on coming, keep on firing, until they ran out of any place to hide and then he would shoot them dead.

Yeah, and if that was his plan, it had been working, he *had* driven Mason back, but now Mason thought no. Every instinct in him, every feeling, every fiber in his body was telling him to get away from the man with the gun but his mind was telling him just the opposite. If he went on something he *knew* rather than something he *felt*, maybe he could get right past Henry and flank him. To do that, he had to go *toward* Henry.

The trick was to pick an aisle between stacks where Henry had already shot and hope that Henry wasn't going to revisit it any time soon. Okay, there, the one on the right, and Mason ran down it. Henry's bullets were slamming the stack on Mason's left, making it shake, so when he got to the end, he ran to the left, up another aisle where Henry's bullets had already been. Jesus, that was fast. He'd already passed Henry, he was pretty sure he had, the question was, how far? But Henry wasn't firing any longer. Henry was yelling, "Fuck fuck fuck." Was it some kind of trick?

Whatever it was, Mason had to see it. Ready to jump back if he had to, he popped his head around the end of the stack. Yeah, just the way he'd planned it, he'd come out way behind Henry. He was looking at Henry's back. I've got you, he thought, you son of a bitch.

Henry was pawing through the pockets of his fisherman's vest. It wasn't hanging down heavy with weight the way it had been before. It was flapping loose, not much left in it "Fuck fuck fuck fuck fuck fuck." He threw the rifle onto the floor. Sweet Jesus, the goddamn fool had run out of ammunition.

Henry pulled that little .22 out of his vest, clicked the revolver part open, dumped the casings onto the floor, and then started stuffing new bullets in. What, Mason thought, he thinks he's just gonna walk on back through the stacks and finish us off with that little gun he used on the cat? The hell he is.

Mason ran straight for Henry. Just about the time Henry heard him coming, jerked around to look, Mason was on him. A small jump made him high enough and he whipped his left arm around Henry's throat, grabbed his own elbow with his right hand and pulled hard.

Henry was weaving side to side trying to shake him off but Mason had learned this trick from Skip in Cincinnati. He hadn't wanted to learn it but he'd learned it anyhow. He was a cat on Henry's back and there was no way in hell Henry was ever going to shake him off.

Henry was staggering, stumbling, running out of time. He jerked the revolver back toward himself, aiming it at Mason. But Mason pulled his head way low behind Henry's back. He'd wrapped his legs tight around Henry's thighs, digging in with his heels. There was no part of Mason that Henry could get at without aiming at himself and Mason was ready to die before he'd let go. He only had one job to do. Hang on and pull like a son of a bitch.

The crack of the little gun going off, Jesus. Henry howled like a fucking animal. Whatever was happening, fuck it and pull. Henry was going down. On his knees. Then sprawled on his face.

Stop it, Mason told himself, or you'll kill him. He let go. Henry's arm was laid there on the floor, fingers loose, still attached to that goddamn little revolver. Mason stomped on the back of Henry's hand, hard, kicked the gun away, went after it, grabbed it up and threw it over the balustrade. He heard it land down on Level Two, heard it bounce on a reading desk.

Henry was dying for air. Coughing. Fighting for it. Dragging in air for all he was worth. As soon as he got enough, he was howling again. Screaming and howling. He doubled up on the floor, tried to get up, howled louder, fell. He reached out, grabbed ahold of the stacks with his right hand, and pulled himself up to his feet. His left arm was hanging straight down. Mason saw the bullet hole in Henry's shoulder. It looked just like the bullet holes he'd seen in the cat.

With his right hand Henry ripped his shirt off, stared at the hole in his skin. He was crying like a man who'd just run smack into the deepest grief he'd ever known in his life, wailing and sobbing, tears rolling down his face. His eyes had lost their glassy dead look, Mason could see Henry's terror and his grief. Henry reached over with his right hand, pushed his left arm and let it fall, showing Mason how useless it was. His eyes were accusing Mason, *how could you do this to me?*

Mason was still riding high on fury, he was a flaming piece of debris carried aloft by a tower of fire. "What are you looking at *me* for," he yelled. "You shot yourself, you dumb fuck."

Crying with great huge wracking sobs, Henry turned away, shuffled by in front of Mason, walked over to the elevator, pushed the button. The elevator doors opened, he stepped inside. The elevator doors closed. Mason had just stood there and watched Henry do it. Jesus, the crazy fucker was going down to Level Two to get his gun. Why the fuck had Mason thrown it down there? Why hadn't he just hung onto it?

But the elevator wasn't going down, it was going up. He could still hear Henry yelling and sobbing but the sounds were getting fainter. Mason followed the little brass pointer as it rose through Level Six, on its way to Level Seven. Jesus, where was he going?

Then Mason knew where Henry was going and he knew that he'd have to go after him. He didn't want to but he didn't have any choice in the matter because it was the right thing to do. Could he run up all those the stairs faster than the elevator would get him up there? No, he couldn't. The elevator stopped at Level Seven, then started to come back down again. Hurry the fuck up, Mason told it.

He was too late. The sound went on so long, deep rolling and dark, a fuck of a lot louder than he'd thought it would be, down low and underneath like maybe an earthquake is underneath, but wet, and with that wet was the doom of it so complete that it blotted out any stupid idea that Mason would ever have again about death. Splatters of sound continued after the main event, small pieces airborne that still had to land, and already the shrill voices of the poor bastards who'd seen it were crying it out to the world, and the sirens.

Mason knew that he could never again be as ignorant as he was before. He turned and stumbled back through the stacks that had been shot but had stood up to it, books that had stopped bullets, old book dust everywhere, the air thick with it, making him cough, stepping over all those fucking casings. He thought again maybe he'd been shot and hadn't noticed, hit down low because his pants were sopping, but no, it wasn't blood, sometime or other he'd pissed himself. Please dear God, he prayed to nothing, please dear nothing God, don't let her be shot.

She was crammed up behind the end of the stacks facing her carrel, crammed up tight there, hugging her knees. She'd made herself as small as she could. The desk in her carrel was punched full of holes, if she'd tried to hide behind it, she'd be dead. He could smell the ancient dry wood blown open by the bullets. He slid down next to her. She was drawn up so tight she wasn't even shaking.

Alive, she was white and silent. "Jessie," he said and she didn't react at all, "Jessie," he said, louder, "listen. I know you're not thinking too clear, but you got to listen. They're coming and we've got to decide real quick what we're gonna tell them."

18.

There shouldn't be any cars on their street, not in the dead third week of August, but Mason could hear one coming to a stop. Then through the branches of the good old reliable white oak he saw that it was Jessie's Lark. He felt a hard jolt inside himself, a physical sensation, he couldn't sort it out, couldn't think straight, pushed himself off the glider, stood up solid on his feet. She didn't say hi or wave, came bounding up the steps in her old confident way just like they were back in the past. She stopped when she saw him, surprise splashed across her face.

They'd talked on the phone damn near every day but this was the first time they'd seen each other since the night in the hospital. This wasn't how he'd imagined their first meeting. She'd caught him dressed like a girl in his Sears and Roebuck outfit, everything copied from Lorianne, white blouse and beige camp shorts, white sneakers not too pointed. He'd done his eyes like Lorianne's too, shaved his legs and smoothed them with suntan lotion so they gleamed in the sun.

"Whew," Jessie said, "sorry. But I'm kind of . . . I don't know what to say."

She was planted on her feet just as solidly as he was. All they were doing was looking at each other. She was wearing a plain white blouse that was a lot like the one he was wearing and a full summer skirt with big loose pleats, white with a floral design on it, looked like something she'd had in her closet for ten years, must be nice to wear in the heat, flowy and cool. She made a nervous little laugh. "Mason, you're red as a beet."

Yeah, he could feel it, that burn on his face. "Well, I'm embarrassed."

"Oh, for Christ's sake, don't be embarrassed. Is that how you see yourself as a girl?"

"I guess."

"It's a nice way to be a girl."

"Thanks."

"I'm not being sarcastic, I mean it."

"I know you mean it."

"But what are you doing out here? Isn't it kind of tempting fate?"

"Yeah, I guess. But who's gonna see me? The campus is dead as a post."

"It is, isn't it? The tide came in and went out again."

That sounded about right but he'd have to take her word for it, he'd never seen the ocean. All these people had poured into Merida, university officials, professors, politicians, reporters. They'd all had something to say, and they'd said it, and then they'd all poured out again, going back to what was left of their vacations. "I don't know," he said, "I just . . . I don't know. I wanted to be out here in the sun, not hiding in that fucking gloomy basement. Eilum went home today, and . . . I don't know. I just wanted to be out in the sun."

"Yes, well that's . . . It was kind of theoretical before, but this makes it real. Oh my goodness, you look like a pretty tomboy. It makes me want to do it too but it's too damn hot for my suit."

"Any of your Penn State I-used-to-be-a-jock outfits would do."

She smiled for the first time. "They would, wouldn't they?"

They stepped into each other's arms like they'd planned it. This was what he'd wanted, to feel how substantial her body was, to feel the muscles in her back, the rise and fall of her breath. She never wore perfume but he caught a hint of something besides his own F#, her soap maybe, or her shampoo, not flowery, more like apples, and also that fresh sweet animal smell of a human being alive in the sun. That she was alive was a miracle and always would be. "Mason," she said, "thank you."

He knew what she meant. "Aw, hell, Jessie, for what? We both of us fought back the best we could."

She let go of him, stepped back and took his hands. "How are you? Things any better?"

"I don't know. Yeah, maybe. Some."

"Still the nightmares?"

"Yeah, still some." One thing he couldn't get out of his head was the sound of Henry hitting the concrete. That kept waking him up in the night. He didn't think Jessie needed to hear about that. "Can't sleep much at night."

"I can't either. Did they give you sleeping pills?"

"Yeah, but I don't take them. Except in the hospital when they made me."

"I can't take them either. They leave me too ... bleh. I've been ... I didn't know how much I'd been depending on Ev and Mattie, just to—" She cleared her throat, seemed to be having trouble talking. "Just to have people around. All I wanted was to get to back to my place where I could— They flew back to Boston yesterday. I was— I'm sorry I didn't call you. They've been so sweet, but Jesus, did they ever wear me out. But it's too damned quiet. Too many things going bump in the night. I'm so glad to see you."

"Me too. Glad. Real glad."

"We're going to be okay."

"Are we?"

"Yes, we are. I was going to ask you— I got back to my place and I've been like a zombie." She shook her head, smiled again. "Hell, Mason, I'm still trying to figure out— It's just . . ."

He waited for her to tell him what it was just, but it looked like she wasn't going to. "Mattie dumped this huge amount of food on me," she said. "A ton of it. I thought you could come back to my place and help me eat it."

"Yeah. Sure. Let me go change."

"No. Don't change. I like you like that."

For the first few days Mason had been waiting for the sheriff of Merida County to show up and ask him more questions but the sheriff never showed up so he must have been satisfied with what Mason had told him in the hospital. When you've jumped off the McKinley Tower, the cause of your death is fairly obvious, so the coroner must not have done much of an autopsy because nobody was talking about any .22 bullet in Henry's shoulder. The coroner had released the body in less than forty-eight hours and it had gone home to Canton to be buried with the Algrens.

The cock and bull story that Mason and Jessie had made up in the five minutes before the campus cops arrived was so flimsy, so crazy, so full of holes that they'd been afraid that nobody would believe it. Well, everybody believed it. They'd even made the *New York Times*. Henry Algren, a history student in the PhD Program at Merida University, had become so anxious when he couldn't finish his PhD thesis that he had a psychotic break, went into the university library and shot up the history section. He was so out of touch with reality that he didn't notice the two students who just happened to be working there at the time and he came very close to killing them. When he realized what he'd done, he committed suicide by jumping off the library tower.

This was the biggest story that the *Merida Monitor* had covered in years and they devoted their entire resources to it. T. Davis Eilum, a fourth year engineering student at the university, might have been the last person to speak with Algren before his death and Eilum's account provided some insight into Algren's state of mind. On the morning of Sunday, August 2, Eilum encountered Algren in the Golden Buckeye, a popular campus restaurant. Eilum told the *Monitor* that Algren was highly inebriated and appeared to have been drinking all night. Algren confessed to Eilum that he was profoundly anxious because of his inability to finish his thesis and said that his wife had left him because of it. He felt as though his life was meaningless and said that he had come to hate the study of history.

Algren's colleagues in the department of history corroborated Eilum's account. Many said that Algren had expressed anxiety about his inability to finish his thesis. They described Algren as a conscientious scholar and excellent instructor, although they also noted that in recent weeks Algren had been drinking heavily and behaving oddly. Dr. Everett Braithwaite, the Head of the Department of History, had been vacationing with his wife on Cape Cod when he received the terrible news and immediately returned home. He described Algren's death as "tragic," said that if Algren had requested an extension on his thesis, he certainly would have been granted one. Dr. Braithwaite has since implemented a departmental policy to ensure that all future graduate students will be carefully monitored as they progress toward their degrees.

Speaking on behalf of the Mental Health Unit of the University Hospital, Dr. Elspeth Fairfield also described Algren's death as "tragic" and called it "needless." She told the *Monitor* that with proper modern medical treatment even the most severe of mental illnesses could now be managed. Dr. Fairfield has struck a committee to produce a brochure that will be given to all incoming students to make them aware of the excellent mental health services available at the university.

The two students who had been forced to hide and take cover from Algren's hail of bullets declined to speak to the *Monitor*, saying that they were still recovering from their terrible ordeal and requesting that their privacy be respected. Algren's estranged wife, purported to be staying with relatives in West Virginia, could not be reached for comment.

Mason loved the way his shaved legs gleamed in the patches of sunlight flickering through Jessie's little Lark as it drifted across the empty campus in no particular hurry. "Have you talked to Lorianne again?" he asked her.

"Yes, I did. She was a little bit more coherent this time. Alternating between grief and rage. If Henry wasn't dead already, she'd cheerfully kill him herself. Says it's good to be down on the farm. Plenty to do so she's never just lying around. Tammy likes it. Her grandma has three cats."

"Yeah, three cats should go a long way with Tammy. I got ahold of *my* grandmother. Did I tell you that?"

"No. How was it?"

"Good. We had a good long talk. She was real glad to hear from me. She's an old-time hard-shell Baptist and strong spirits have never crossed her lips so she's not exactly delighted with her daughter. Seems like Mom's been getting loaded and calling her up. Grandma had to tell her, 'Ruth, if you ever call me up drunk again, I'm gonna hang up on you.'

"She told me to stay in touch, told me that the farm would always be my home. That made me feel good. I need some place I can call home. I asked her about the Mason brothers and she told me the story just the way I remembered it. I took good notes. Now all I have to do is type it up and my dumb little thesis is done.

"But here's the best part. That day I remember walking down to the Landing in the rain dressed like my sister? It's been driving me nuts. I was starting to doubt my own memory . . . hell, I was starting to doubt my own *life*. Irene's been telling me it didn't happen and my mom won't talk about anything to do with my childhood and . . . Well, shit, Jessie, my personal history's no different from any other history. Primary sources, primary sources, you always said. So my mother and my sister may have decided to forget all about it but my grandmother hasn't. 'We never would have left you alone,' Irene told me. But it turns out that they did. It was my cousin Cheryl's wedding."

Mason's grandmother remembered it vividly. No, they hadn't wanted to leave him but he'd insisted on it, said that if they didn't go to the wedding, he'd feel terrible. His fever had broke and he seemed fine there in bed with his radio and his books, so off they went. Cheryl was getting married at that Old Regular Baptist church out back of Factor, a pretty little church. About halfway through the service the rain started, a terrible storm, and it knocked out the phone lines. Grandma tried calling the farm but she couldn't get through. Then, like that old saying, the Lord willing and the crick don't rise, well, the crick rose, Colemans Crick, and they couldn't get across the bridge, had to go around the back way to the River Road and it took them forever to get home. Grandma was worried sick, rushed upstairs, "and there I was, safe in bed, just happy as a clam."

"Okay," Jessie said, "so you *did* walk down to the Landing?"

"I'm getting to that."

Jessie parked in the back alley where she always did. Mason got out of the car, took a moment to enjoy the sun. Being dressed like a girl didn't feel much different from the way he usually felt. Maybe he'd feel different if he had on something ultra-feminine, stockings and heels, for instance, but right now he just felt like himself. He looked up toward the big brick rooming house.

The drapes were drawn in all the windows. Nobody would fire a rifle from one of those windows, would they? No, that was impossible. Nothing like that could ever happen in Merida, Ohio, on a nice sunny afternoon in August.

Jessie had walked on ahead of him, turned back to see what was holding him up. "The story keeps getting better," he told her. "Old Mrs. Krieger's still alive, ninety or close to it, living with her daughter in Huntington. Grandma gave me her daughter's number."

"Yes? Did you get her? What did you find out?"

"Well, that's *the story.*"

Jessie had all of her windows open and there was a nice breeze blowing through her apartment. She'd taken her sandals off and thrown herself down into the big overstuffed chair by the window, was lying back in it, her old-fashioned skirt flowing out around her knees and her bare feet on the hassock. Mason was too keyed up to sit still, was pacing back and forth while he talked. "I always thought maybe it was a fever dream."

"You've told me this," she said.

"Yeah, I know but the point . . . Okay, I was gonna impersonate my sister. Just gonna walk down to the river and walk back. It was . . . It looked like it was gonna rain, and I needed it to rain. You see, Irene had a raincoat with a hat that went with it, you know a rain hat with the brim and the tie under the chin. I can't remember what you call it—"

"A sou'wester?"

"Yeah, that's it. And I thought if I pulled the hat down and tied the tie and put up the collar of the raincoat, then it'd look like my long hair was tucked up into the hat. That coat . . . that coat and that hat were yellow as a lemon, it was a very girlish coat, had a belt at the waist and a flare at the bottom so if you're wearing a full skirt, there'd be plenty of room for it. Well, Reenie had just started shaving her legs, so I had to do that too. She'd cut herself the first time, and—"

"Mason? You really *have* told me this. I've heard *all of this* before."

"Yeah, I know but I just want you to . . . you know, really *be there.* Anyhow I wanted to look like Reenie just on an ordinary school day so I put on one of her sweaters and one of her plaid skirts with the kick pleats, and her saddle shoes, you know, with bobby socks. The girls at the Landing wore their bobby socks very neat—"

"Mason?"

"Yes?"

"Can you give me a shot of whiskey? It's in the cupboard right above the stove."

"Okay, sure. I know where it is."

It was J. T. S. Brown. He had to smile at that, Fast Eddie's drink from *The Hustler.* The shot glasses were right next to the bottle. He filled one, not quite to the top, and carried it to her. She met his eyes, took the shot, downed it in one hard toss, and handed him the glass. "Thanks. Do you want a drink?"

"No. I quit. I guess I quit. It was like . . . Well, a lot of times when I decide something, it gets decided down deep inside me somewhere and it don't let me . . . *doesn't* let me know about it until later. I was using my stomach as an excuse but I guess I quit."

"Good for you."

He rinsed out the shot glass, dried it, and put it back on the shelf. "Anyhow," he said, walking back into the living room, "Reenie had just started wearing lipstick. She wore pink because that was okay with Mom, but Mom wouldn't let her wear bright red and that's what all the girls wore, so Reenie hid hers and put it on after she left the house. Okay, so I knew where she hid it and I put some on the way I'd seen her do it, you know, blotted it with a Kleenex—"

"Mason?"

"And she had a pair of fake leather gloves, real bright red, just as red as her lipstick—"

"*Mason!*"

"*What?*"

"Do you still have a terrible crush on me?"

Jessie's bedroom was nothing like Sarah's, nothing feminine or decorative about it, more like an office, all beat-up old stuff, an ancient desk with pigeon holes, a bulletin board behind it, a wooden file cabinet, book cases on the walls, and a bed of course, an old-fashioned metal frame bed, a double that had once been painted white but was chipped pretty bad, showing wrought iron under the paint. They were standing right next to that old wrought iron bed. "We don't have to do anything," she said. "We can go back in the living room and forget this ever happened."

"No, we can't. No, this definitely happened."

He still couldn't understand exactly how they'd made it from the living room into her bedroom. When she'd stood up and walked over to him, he'd thought that all she'd wanted to do was hug him but he could still feel her kiss on his mouth, still taste a hint of that old J. T. S. Brown. "I've always had a bit of a crush on you too," she said.

"Yeah? Have you? For Christ's sake. *For. Christ's. Sake.* And you let me go around the whole damn summer sick in love with you?"

"My job was to teach you some history. I was absolutely *not* going to be like one of those asshole men."

"You said you don't grade your friends. I thought we were friends."

"Yes. I tried that."

Mason felt stopped. He badly needed to know what was going on and he didn't have a clue. "We could go back in the living room and make tea and talk about it," she said. "Or we could stay here and get to know each other better."

316

"Jessie, if you think I'd go back in the living room now and drink tea, you're fucking nuts."

Mason had seen naked girls before, he'd grown up with a sister, but he wasn't ready for Jessie. She was stretched out on her bed as naked as a jay bird. Those loose baggy blouses she wore all the time made her look flat as a boy but she wasn't, she had neat little breasts, and those blouses covered up the shape of her too. Her hips only looked lean and boyish when you had nothing to compare them to. She curved in to a small waist with an indentation across it about an inch above her belly button, a line as neat as if somebody had drawn it across her, and below it her stomach curved out just slightly. A lot of her height came from her legs, and she only shaved what she had to, up to where her shorts stopped. The hair between her legs was darker than the hair on her head, damned near black, and she didn't shave her armpits either. Her shoulders and arms looked just as strong as he'd thought they'd be. "Come on," she said.

He finished undressing because that seemed to be on the agenda, threw his blouse and shorts onto a chair, kicked off his sneakers. He left Irene's stretch panties on. "Jessie," he said, "I've never seen a human being in my whole goddamn life as beautiful as you."

"Oh, for Christ's sake," she said, laughing, "come here."

Very gingerly he lay down next to her.

"You're pretty cute yourself, Mason. What's with the underwear?"

"I don't know."

"Sure you do. Come on, we are who we are and there's nothing we can do about it."

He slid Irene's panties off and threw them across the room. He felt terrified and exposed. She rolled over and kissed him. "Don't worry about your goddamn penis. We both know you've got one. And it's not going in me."

Relief flooded through him and he felt himself starting to get hard. Resting on one elbow, she was looking down at him. She ran her fingers across his chest. "You shaved there too."

"Yeah. Well. There wasn't much to start with. I thought a girl shouldn't have hair on her chest."

"It feels nice. You're so smooth. You want to be a girl, go ahead and be a girl. You'd be amazed at all the wonderful sexy things two girls can do together."

Now he was getting real hard and he saw her see it. She started running her hands over him everywhere. "I love how smooth you are. I love your legs. My goodness, they're like steel. Must be all the bike riding you do."

"Yeah, I guess. Hey, we're both insies." He did what he'd been wanting to do, kissed her stomach. Then he put his tongue in her belly button, felt her inhale. "You've got a beautiful stomach."

"Thanks. But I wish you could have seen me when I played sports. I'm getting soft."

"Soft? Hell, Jessie, you don't look soft to me."

"When I tensed it up, it was like a slab of concrete. Not anymore. Being in grad school is not good for your health."

She kissed him again. She was very aggressive with her tongue. Then, and he could see a bit of a wicked smile, she bit his earlobe, hard enough to hurt but not too hard. She thrust her tongue deep into his ear. Jesus, his prick was sticking up like a hunk of granite. "Here," she said, "let me show you something," and guided his hand down between her legs, parted the hair for him. "There. Yes. That's the right place. Just approach *cau-tious-ly*."

He'd read about it so he knew what it was, her natural lubrication. He used it to moisten her where she'd showed him, that little lump.

She was breathing harder. He wouldn't call it panting but something was happening with her. "Well, you sure get the hang of things fast," she said.

She pressed her crotch against his leg, trapping his hand there. He kept his fingers where he knew she liked them, moving a little, but she was doing all the work, a steady rhythmic thrusting of her hips. Her breathing got deeper and then she started moaning, or something like moaning, it was like she was saying *ah* deep in the back of her throat. She started moving faster, and then made a deep breathy sound that was almost a scream. "Oh," she said. "God."

A breeze kept coming and going, rippling the curtains at the windows. Whenever it did that, her room filled with bright light, then it sunk back into warm twilight. They'd been laying there a long time wrapped around each other. Mason was happy just to lay there with her. He thought she was deep asleep but then she opened her eyes. "Do you want to have sex?" she asked him.

"I thought that's what we were doing."

"Well, *I* was. I'm talking about you. Do you want to?"

"Yes."

All she was doing now was looking at him. They'd crossed an impossible divide awhile back and were in a whole new world. "Okay," she said, "I'm going to tell you everything I know about sex. Don't worry, it's not a big lecture. It'll fit into one measly sentence. If sex doesn't happen in the mind, it doesn't happen."

It took him a minute to get it, then he said, "So what's in your mind?"

"I want to be the cute boy you said yes to years ago."

"Yeah. Okay. Yeah, you can do that."

She opened the drawer to the side table, pulled out a jar of Vaseline and an artificial penis. Jesus, the damn thing looked realistic. She was looking at him to see his reaction. He nodded to tell her yes. It was getting hard to talk.

She got out of bed, stood there, and began strapping that penis onto herself, her motions slow and deliberate. Trying to be just as slow and deliberate, he slid out of bed too, opened the jar, and shoved a good handful of Vaseline up himself. He was nervous as all hell, felt sick, his stomach clenched in knots. He wiped his hands with Kleenex.

"I don't want to hurt you," she said. "We can stop any time you want."

"Jessie? I appreciate how nice you're being and all . . . but maybe you don't have to be *that* nice?"

She had no expression on her face except one he might call concentrated. Then she smiled, just a glint of it.

"Do you know what I mean?" he asked her.

"I know exactly what you mean."

Now they were inside what he could call a long pause, an empty space where the curtains could billow at the windows, making flickers of light. Where they had got to he called zero. That concentration in her eyes, or whatever it was, that focus, had narrowed down to a pure energy directed at him.

She took a bit of Vaseline into her fingers, handed him the jar, and then, with a movement of her hips shoved that artificial penis toward him, showing him what she wanted him to do. He dug his fingers into the jar, got a good wad, and took that penis into his hand.

He'd never felt an erect penis that wasn't his own. The more he rubbed Vaseline onto it, the more realistic it felt, probably getting warm from his hand, and he started to massage it in a twisty motion like he was jerking off, well no, like he'd do if it belonged to a real boy and he was trying to get that boy hotter than hell. Then with a mixture of pleasure and fear, he thought, hey, whoa, *this huge thing is gonna be inside me.*

She had been watching him the whole time. He was getting good and hard. She took his penis into her hand and imitated the slow twisty motion she'd just seen him do. She did it a few times and then stopped. He kept on massaging her prick, that's how he was thinking of it now, that she and that phantom boy were one person and she was all of one piece. It wasn't real but it was real.

She was massaging him just enough to keep him hard. Whenever she got him solid as a rock, she'd stop. He was getting hot in the peculiar way he got hot, his knees getting weak. He wanted to sink to the floor, wanted to melt into a sweet blob of candy at her feet. "Jessie?" he said. "*Jess?* I. Can't. Stand. This."

Then, to his amazement, she picked him up, with one arm swept his legs out from under him, with the other arm caught him when he fell backward, literally picked him up and deposited him back onto the bed.

Mason had been sure that he'd imagined every possible sexual position but he hadn't imagined this one. The cute boys in his fantasies always fucked him doggy style but now he was laying on his back, his legs raised, one on each of Jessie's shoulders, his ass arched upward. She was looking down at him, face to face. You'd think with all the various objects that he'd shoved up there over the years he would have got himself ready for this but no, he was tight with fear.

She tried to get it in again and he winced with pain. "Maybe we should give up for today," she said. "I don't want to hurt you."

"No, no, don't stop. Just give me a minute. I got to relax."

Breathe slow, he told himself, take deep breaths, think of something peaceful. Laying on the grass somewhere with the sun shining down. By the river, maybe. Was he relaxed? "Okay," he said, "Come on, Jess. Come on, do it."

He felt a bright shearing shaft of pain. "Oh, Jesus!"

"Was that a good oh Jesus or a bad oh Jesus?"

"Good. I think. I think it was. Are you in?"

"Oh. Yes. Definitely."

Now that she had penetrated him, the pain was gone, well, most of it anyways. "Okay, okay," he told her, "I think we're okay." He felt her move. "Yeah, that's great, that feels good."

She bent forward, let his legs slip off her shoulders. Not sure what to do next, he wrapped his legs around her waist. She pressed her mouth into his, shoved her tongue into his mouth, and began to move her hips in a steady rhythm. This was what he'd always wanted. Sweet heaven, the reality was better than the fantasy. "Jessie? Jessie, I love you."

"I love you too, sugar. You sure you're okay?"

"Oh, yeah, oh, yeah, I'm fine."

She caught his wrists and pinned him to the bed. Impaled, yeah, that was the right word for it. "You still okay?"

"Yeah, yeah, Jesus."

"Come on, move with me."

Amazing, he could move. He didn't have to lie there like a lump, he could fucking well *move*. When she kissed him again, he wanted to inhale her.

She let his wrists go, drew back a little, pulled his legs back up to her shoulders. He arched up to help her. He could feel the difference. In this position she could get in as deep as she could go.

It was all too goddamn much. He couldn't stand it any longer. He reached for his prick but she stopped him, caught his wrist, pulled his hand away and guided it back to the head of the bed. Okay, so he was supposed to be totally helpless, was he? Okay, that's what he'd always wanted, wasn't it? To give up completely?

He grabbed the bed frame behind him, grabbed it with both hands, and that gave him the leverage he needed to arch himself up, thrusting his whole body up against hers, meeting her. She wrapped a hand around his prick and held it, making that maddening twisting motion just a little, not nearly enough, just enough to make sure he stayed hot and hard.

322

She was dripping sweat on him and he heard himself moaning like somebody in pain but it wasn't pain. Nothing in the entire history of the universe had ever felt this good. He fell into her rhythm, pushed and arched. She was picking up the tempo and he went with her. He was working, felt bent and contracted like a steel spring, but he'd do anything to get more of her. He wanted her to pound him good and that's what she was doing. Come on, come on, come on, he didn't know whether he was saying it or only thinking it.

Up until then Mason had thought that people screaming when they had sex only happened in stories. He came back to see her brilliant smile. She looked as pleased as a kid who's just won her race. "You came all over my stomach, you bad girl."

"Ah. Yeah. Jesus." He ran his hand across her stomach and wiped it clean. She kissed him. "Oh, we're terrible," she said, still smiling, and slowly pulled out of him.

She slipped out of bed, unstrapped herself from her New York gadget. He heard it go clunk on the floor. He was getting his breath back, his mind back. She got into bed with him and pulled the sheet over them. "Are you okay?" she asked him.

"Yeah, I'm great."

They lay there for a while, both of them panting. Then she said, "Was *I* okay? When I'm playing the guy's role, I get . . . It's ridiculous, I know. Just like a guy, I get performance anxiety."

"Aw, Jessie, you were fucking *wonderful*. Literally. That's a joke but it's true. And to tell you some more truth, *I'm* fucking wonderful. The whole goddamn *world's* fucking wonderful."

Later, when he felt her roll over in the bed, it woke him. It was like he could feel her eyes on him. He opened his eyes and looked back at her. "Now we know how we can sleep," she said. The day's heat was fading away, it was nearly twilight, a hint of autumn in the breeze billowing the curtains, and everywhere out in Ohio Country the trees were humming with locusts.

"First things first," Jessie had said, so they'd stripped the bed, dumped the bedding into the wash machine in the basement, and had a shower together. Now they were sitting at the little turquoise table eating Mrs. Braithwaite's wonderful cooking. Mattie was a real Depression kid, Jessie told him. She would never throw anything away, even if it was only half a plateful, so she'd cleaned out her fridge and given all the leftovers to Jessie. It was literally too fucking much. Fried chicken, Swedish meatballs, a stuffed pork chop, baked ham— "She seems to think that I don't know how to feed myself."

"Well, you don't."

"Oh really? You can come over here and feed me any time you want to, sweetheart."

This insane spread of little dabs of food was perfect for a day that was turning out to be perfect. Mason wanted to taste everything. Green bean casserole, succotash, corn on the cob, coleslaw, Spanish rice— Angel food cake, pecan pie, lemon tart—

"How's your ass?" Jessie asked him, grinning. She was in a mood he wouldn't have believed possible for Mrs. Jessie Collier, TA, a kind of screwball giddiness. He'd felt it too, had been drawn right into it. "Well, a little bit sore," he said, "but no, that's not the right word. *Used.* That's how it feels. But in a good way. I'll tell you what's sore, my lower back muscles. My whole damn lower back."

"Oh? Well, like any muscle group, you can strengthen it through exercise."

"So that's what I need, huh? A lot more exercise?'

"Absolutely. We're definitely going to have to work on that." Her eyes had never looked more flashing. "When school starts," she said, "you'll have to be careful. I don't mean obsessively careful because nobody gives a shit, but reasonably careful. Always put your bike under the porch. Use the back door. I'll give you a key if you want."

He couldn't believe it. "Jessie, did you just ask me to be your girlfriend?"

She didn't answer right away. Then she said, "I suppose that's what I did. Yes, that is exactly what I did."

"I'd be *delighted* to be your girlfriend. What did you think I was going to say?"

"That's what I thought you were going to say." She reached across the table, took his hand, squeezed it. It felt like she was sealing the deal.

Mason was washing the dishes and Jessie was drying them and putting them away. She stepped back from the cupboard, turned to him, grabbed a good handful of his hair and pulled on it. "Hey," he said, startled. It was not hard enough to hurt but hard enough to get the job done, she tilted his face up and kissed him. He could taste lemon tart. In that instant he was hot again, hotter than all hell. "Don't cut your hair," she said, murmuring into his ear.

"Okay, I won't."

She let go of him, stepped back. "No, we absolutely can't do it again tonight. You know what's stopping me? I can't face washing another load of goddamned bedding."

Yeah, this was a whole new world all right. He'd never felt like this before, never imagined it. Even though they weren't touching, he could feel a current running between them like they were two halves of a little engine that never stopped humming. "Are you surprised?" he asked her. He was sure that she'd know what he meant.

"Yes, I am. Very surprised. Deliberate, you called me. Well, I suppose I am. Sometimes way too deliberate."

"Jessie? There's only one thing that's bothering me. What are we going to do about Lorianne? We can't just leave her down there on a chicken farm, can we?"

She started to answer and then stopped. Maybe she was pissed off, but no, that wasn't it. He'd thrown her for a loss.

"Look," he said, "when you've had a huge tragedy in your life, the best thing to do is get back to work. Everybody tells you that. She ought to come back here and finish her degree."

"Oh, she'd never do that."

"You've got your thesis done and I'm only carrying fifteen credits. We could take turns looking after Tammy. Lorianne could have her degree done by the time your contract runs out in the summer."

"Jesus, Mason, that's not fair. Now you're the one who's being deliberate. She couldn't take a course this fall. She's missed registration."

"Oh, I'll bet they'd bend a few rules for her. You know, the grieving widow."

He watched her thinking about it. "You're right. They probably would. But Lori and Tammy . . . they'd never fit . . . This place is too small. With a kid. But . . . I could rent a bigger place, couldn't I? A whole little house somewhere. But she's an absolute mess, poor thing. She'd never come back here."

"She would if we went down and got her."

She started to say something but then stopped, shaking her head. What did that mean? No?

"We really do have to do it," he said. "If it wasn't for Lorianne, we wouldn't be here together, would we?"

She gave him her blazing smile. "Mason, you are incredible. You are. Just. Fucking. Incredible. Okay, we've got a week. We'll do it!"

Now that they weren't using it to have sex on, Mason could appreciate Jessie's bed. It had matching tables and reading lamps on both sides. They were each on their own side, sitting up with pillows behind them. Because he'd asked for it, he was holding her thesis on his lap. Dr. Braithwaite had written on the title page: *Splendid work, Jessie. Congratulations. One of the best I've seen.* Could Mason ever write something that good? It was a scary thought. It would take fucking years.

This was strange, so very strange, but there was nowhere he'd rather be. They'd remade the bed so it felt brand clean and fresh. The sheets must have been hung to dry, they smelled of the sun. And here he was with Jessie. Maybe he could get used to this new world but it still felt too good to be true, a dream as fragile as a soap bubble. But it wasn't a soap bubble, it was as solid as could be. "What are you reading?" he asked her.

She showed him the cover. Baldwin. *The Fire Next Time.*

"Is it good?"

"Excellent. Required reading. I've read these essays before. It's good to see them published together like this."

She laid the book aside, closed her eyes, and massaged her forehead. He'd never seen her do that before. "Are you okay?" he asked her.

"Bit of a headache. The goddamn optometrist thinks I need reading glasses."

"Maybe you do?"

"Fuck. I'm not even thirty. My vision's always been perfect."

Mason was not getting it. "Okay. So why did you see him?"

"Who?"

"The goddamn optometrist."

"I was afraid I needed reading glasses." They both laughed.

She went back to reading Baldwin. The curtains were drawn but the windows were open and the locusts were making that ancient throbbing sound that always told Mason that summer was almost over and school was about to start. "Hey, Jess," he said, "I never told you the rest of the story."

She laid her book down again. "So tell me."

"Okay, so I got old Mrs. Krieger's daughter on the phone. Down in Huntington. 'Sure you can talk to her,' she said. 'Mom loves to talk on the phone. She won't know who you are even if you tell her a hundred times. But that's okay. If you get her way back in the past, she remembers quite a bit.'

"So I got Mrs. Krieger. I told her who I was but she never did get it. I asked if she remembered a terrible rain storm, remembered picking up a kid in her straight-eight Buick. Well, *rain storm* got her going, and by God, did she ever remember that rain storm! Washed out the bridge over Colemans Crick. Mama and Papa couldn't get the horses across, it was terrible, they couldn't get home. Well, okay, that was the right crick but the wrong year. We're back in the 1880s.

"Okay, so I thought I'd go at it from another angle. Did she remember Ruth Mason? Well, of course she remembered Ruth Mason. She was the youngest of that bunch of Willie Mason's kids. Ruth married some drummer, didn't she? Sold door to door. What was his name. McArthur? McDonald?'

"'Macquarie,' I told her.

"'Oh, that's right,' she said, 'I knew that. He was that boy from up the river. Selling encyclopedias. Not much good. Come home from the war and took to the bottle.'

"'Yes,' I told her, 'you've got that one exactly right,' and I kept trying to keep her on track with Ruth Mason and her husband but I couldn't do it. We're back in the old days again. We're waiting for the packet boat to come in. It would blow its whistle and all the kids would come running down to the Landing.

"I was getting nowhere so I decided that once again I would go straight at it. 'Mrs. Krieger,' I said, 'there was a day back in the spring of 1954. You were still driving your old black Buick. There was a terrible rain storm. One of the Macquarie kids was walking down to the Landing. The girl. She had on a raincoat as yellow as a lemon. And you picked her up. Do you remember that?'

"Bingo! Of course she remembers that. She'll never forget it if she lives to be a hundred. That rain just come up all of a sudden, come up from the river, and it was worse than Noah's flood. 'Oh, no no no,' she says, 'it wasn't the Macquarie girl I picked up, it was the boy. You know the one, that little boy that went around all the time telling people he was a girl. Poor child, he was going to catch his death. All he wanted was to buy a sack of flour.'"

ACKNOWLEDGMENTS
AND AFTERWORD

If you were to follow the instructions implied in this book – drive north halfway up the highway between Cincinnati and Detroit and then turn west – you will not find Merida, Ohio, or Merida University, because I made them up. *In the Defense of Liberty* is a work of fiction. Public figures, ranging from George Washington to Barry Goldwater, are just as real as they always are, but the other characters in this book are fictitious, and any resemblance they might have to real people is purely coincidental.

American history is one of the main themes of this book, and many of the ideas in the minds of the characters – particularly in Dr. Braithwaite's mind – originated with the great revisionist historian, William Appleman Williams. Please see his *The Contours of American History* (1961).

I have tried to give my characters attitudes and ideas that would have been current among American university students in the early 1960s. My friends and I thoroughly loathed Barry Goldwater. Since then, I have learned a great deal more about him, and even though I still disagree with everything he believed in, I have come to respect him as a man of impeccable personal integrity. He hated liars. Even though he created a path for him, he would have despised Donald Trump.

I believe that Djuna Barnes' brilliant and difficult novel *Night-wood* (1936) is just as important as Lorianne does. Yes, those are real jazz records that Henry is playing. Follow the clues, and you can find them.

I want to say what I have often said in the past: writing is a social act. Thanks again to Kelsey Attard and the whole Freehand crew; your continuing support of my work means more to me than I can say. My wife Mary is still my best critic. I'm sure that my agent, John Pearce, is tired of being called "tireless," but that's what he is. Once again Lee Shedden joined me as my editor, to the enormous benefit of both me and this book.

I cannot close without thanking Wesley M. Bagby (1922 – 2002), historian and, for many years, a beloved professor at West Virginia University. The first time I heard the term "revisionist historian," it was from him. Listening to him lecture, I gradually came to the conclusion that damned near everything I had learned in high school about American history was wrong. "The worst thing we can do," he said frequently, "is waste the time of young people." He didn't waste mine.

I wrote this book while I was an uninvited but grateful guest on the unceded territory of the Squamish and Tsleil-Waututh Nations.

Keith Maillard

DECEMBER 17, 2022

Keith Maillard is the author of fifteen novels, one book of poetry, and two memoirs. Twelve of his titles have been shortlisted for or won literary prizes. *Light in the Company of Women* was a runner-up for the Ethel Wilson Fiction Prize; *Motet* won that prize. *Hazard Zones* was shortlisted for the Commonwealth Literary Prize, and *Gloria* was a finalist for the Governor General's Award. *Dementia Americana* won the Gerald Lampert Award for best first book of poetry in Canada. *The Clarinet Polka* was awarded the Creative Arts Prize by the Polish American Historical Association. Of his quartet, *Difficulty at the Beginning*, the first three volumes – *Running, Morgantown,* and *Lyndon Johnson and the Majorettes* – were shortlisted for the Weatherford Award while the quartet's final book, *Looking Good*, was longlisted for the Relit Award. His novel *Twin Studies* was awarded the 2019 Alberta Book of the Year Award in the fiction category.

Throughout his long career Maillard has published nonfiction essays and articles in newspapers, journals, and anthologies. In 2018 he contributed to *Refuse: Canlit in Ruins,* edited by Julie Rak, Hannah McGregor, and Erin Wunker.

Maillard has taught in the Creative Writing Program at the University of British Columbia for over thirty years. He lives in Vancouver with his wife, author and editor Mary Maillard. For further information on Keith, including a complete publication list, please visit his website: keithmaillard.com